Praise for Eric Van Lustbader

"Lustbader is an automatic buy-today-read-tonight author for me—and should be for you."

—Lee Child,
New York Times bestselling author of
the Jack Reacher series

"Like Robert Ludlum, Lustbader is at his best when he is creating a twisted web of intrigue, violence, double cross, and his own brand of oriental esotericism. . . . A master storyteller."

—*Publishers Weekly*

"One of the great thriller authors."

—Joseph Finder,
New York Times bestselling author of
Vanished

"A master who knows how to manipulate the reader in fiendishly exciting ways."

—Steve Berry,
New York Times bestselling author of
The Venetian Betrayal

BLOOD TRUST

Eric Van Lustbader

A TOM DOHERTY ASSOCIATES BOOK
NEW YORK

This is a work of fiction. All of the characters, organizations, and events portrayed in this novel are either products of the author's imagination or are used fictitiously.

BLOOD TRUST

Copyright © 2011 by Eric Van Lustbader

All rights reserved.

A Forge Book
Published by Tom Doherty Associates, LLC
175 Fifth Avenue
New York, NY 10010

www.tor-forge.com

Forge® is a registered trademark of Tom Doherty Associates, LLC.

ISBN 978-0-7653-6777-8

First Edition: May 2011
First Mass Market Edition: July 2012

Printed in the United States of America

0 9 8 7 6 5 4 3 2 1

For Victoria

BLOOD TRUST

Prologue

Vlorë, Albania

TWO YOUNG women running. They look like girls, little slips of girls as they fly down ancient cobbled streets, past the blind facades of stone houses, darkened by another of the frequent blackouts. Pale candlelight flickers against windowpanes, medieval and mean, a city within a city. The younger is a girl, barely thirteen, though taller and more filled out than her companion, yet far short of womanly.

Cathedral spires, still silvered in moonlight, ignore the thin thread of red dawnlight tingeing the eastern sky. Stars glimmer defiantly like blue-white diamonds. There is no wind at all; the stillness of the trees is absolute, the shadows they cast impenetrable.

An old man, thin and brittle as the branches above his head, is roused from his drunken stupor by the anxious click-clack of shoes as the women cross his small square. He stirs, regarding them from the stone bench that serves as his home. His arms are crossed over his bony chest as if in reproof. Noticing him, one of the women stops abruptly, slips off her shoes. Now both barefoot, they silently flee the square like shadows before the rising of the sun.

They enter an evil-smelling alley. Garbage over-spills dented cans. A creature lifts its head, growls, baring its yellow teeth. Its ears are triangular, and very large, making it look more like a jackal than a dog. The women swerve out of its way, race to the far end of the alley. The street beyond is nearly as dark. It is littered with ripped signs, shoes, and caps rioters left in their haste to retreat from the truncheons and guns of the advancing militia.

They turn a corner, the taller woman now in the lead. The smell of roasted corn and the sharp odor of urine assail them. Halfway along the street, the taller woman stops in front of a door. About to knock, she hesitates, turning to look into her companion's eyes. Emboldened by the nod of encouragement she receives, she raps sharply on the door with her scabbed knuckles. No sound, and reaching past her, her companion slaps the flat of her hand insistently against the wood.

At last there comes a stirring from inside the house, a scraping followed by a hacking cough. The door opens a crack and a woman with gray-streaked hair and sunken cheeks opens her ashen eyes wide. She is gripped by the look of a hare who sees in the fox's presence its imminent death.

"Liridona!"

"Hello, Mother," the taller woman says.

Her mother gasps. "What have you done? Are you insane? How—?"

"I escaped." Liridona gestures. "With the help of my friend, Alli."

For just an instant, the expression on Liridona's

mother's face softens. Then the abject terror returns and she says to Alli, "You stupid, stupid girl."

"Listen, your daughter was a prisoner," Alli says.

Liridona's mother says nothing.

"Did you hear me? Do you understand what I'm saying?"

Her eyes are fixed on a spot above her daughter's head, as if she is willing herself to be far away.

Alli turns Liridona around and pushes up her shirt to reveal a constellation of weals made by cigarette burns.

"What's the matter with you?" she says. "We need your help. We're both in terrible danger."

The older woman has averted her gaze. "I know that better than you."

Alli can tell that beneath the mother's mechanical tones lie glimmers of pain, fury, and, worst of all, resignation.

"Will you help us get to the ferry for Brindisi? In Italy we'll be safe."

"You'll never be safe."

Alli is undeterred. "Please. We have nowhere else to turn."

Another cough explodes from behind Liridona's mother. All at once, the door is almost wrenched off its hinges and Liridona's mother is shoved out of the way to make room for a huge, hulking man dressed in a sleeveless undershirt and pajama pants. His darkly bristled cheeks and close-set eyes give him the appearance of a wild boar.

He spits heavily, then, stepping out into the street, he peers beyond them, looking both ways. "Foolish girl!" His hand lashes out, striking Liridona across the face. "Go back to where you belong. You'll get us all killed!"

As Liridona cowers, Alli shoulders past her. "This is your daughter."

The boar-man glares at her.

Liridona flinches, then bursts into tears. "I tried to tell you," she sobs.

Alli says, "She's your child, your flesh and blood."

He takes one more look around. "Christ!"

He hurriedly steps back into the shadows of the doorway and slams the door in their faces.

Alli pounds on the door with her fist, but to no avail. She is about to try to find another way in when her gaze is drawn to the eastern end of the filthy street. The sun, rising, spills its light along the cobbles like liquid fire. Out of that dazzle emerge two men armed with handguns. The instant they realize they've been seen they sprint toward the two women.

Alli grabs Liridona by the back of her shirt, whirls her around, and pulls her along. Liridona stumbles after her as they run in the opposite direction. But they are already winded from their long run, and the two men gain on them at an alarmingly rapid clip.

Up ahead, Alli hears the chiming shouts of sounds like a demonstration. Changing direction, Alli heads them toward the boiling knot of students occupying a nearby plaza ringed with rugged hawthorns and lindens. Like the trees, banners rise ahead of them, calling for bread and clean water, decent sanitation, heat and light. Power! Power Now!

Young people are everywhere, piling into the plaza, fiercely determined expressions on their faces as they begin to chant in unison. The raw, seething power of youth shakes the lindens like a sudden storm, and it seems as if hope is rising as inexorably as the flowers of spring.

Grabbing Liridona by the hand, Alli plunges into the maelstrom of bodies. All around them, the air shudders with the angry shouts of the demonstrators. Fires are being lit, fueled by the garbage piled in the gutters. Acrid smoke swirls, mingling with a fog that seems to have risen from the sewer grates, overrunning the streets and the plaza like an army of vermin.

A great shout erupts as a group of about ten young men rock a car back and forth, harder and harder, until, with their combined strength, they upend it. The massed shout gains hurricane force. There the car sits like a turtle on its back. Someone opens the gas tank.

At almost the same moment, the morning trembles to the high-low wail of police sirens. Everything starts to happen in double-time. A length of rag is inserted in the car's gas tank, its visible end lit; the mass of humanity seems to hold its breath.

The car explodes just as the militia appears, pouring out of fog-bound streets into the plaza. Harsh orders, magnified through a portable amplifier, are fired like flares over the heads of the protesters. Then guns are fired, and the melee commences.

Among it all, Alli and Liridona dodge and sidestep their antagonists, sweeping aside fluttering banners, leaping over the fallen, trying to keep themselves from being trampled by the mob, which flows first one way, then another. A clear line of sight is all but impossible, eyes tear from the smoke and debris.

It is then that the two men appear out of the blur

of bodies and faces. They grab Liridona and, as Alli tries to attack them, one of them slams the side of her head. She staggers, loses her grip on her companion, and, slammed by rushing bodies, goes down facefirst. Sprawled on the ground, she is kicked and struck by fleeing feet and tramping boots. She almost loses consciousness, but, gathering herself, manages to regain her feet just in time to see the two men dragging Liridona away.

Wading deeper into the growing madness, she fights her way after them. The car fire has spread, and one of the hawthorn trees becomes a column of flame, its widening plume of smoke a dark banner rippling ominously over all their heads. Alli coughs, her lungs burning. A young woman hits her in the face, a boy drives his elbow into her side in his panic to get away from the militia. The armed men wield metal truncheons, which rise and fall in concert like a thresher in a field of wheat. She gasps and continues on, reeling and in pain, but she will not allow Liridona out of her sight. But the fog, a metallic brown from gunpowder, garbage, and the grit of the streets, thrusts itself against her like a living thing. She is buffeted by the currents of running people. Screams find her as insistent as the tolling of bells from the cathedral, which seems to watch indifferently with its elongated El Greco face.

Alli loses sight of Liridona altogether, and her heart beats even faster in her chest as she plows her way through the mob, nearer now to the mass of truncheons lifting and falling, to the sprays of blood and bone, to the tilted bodies, to the cries of pain and terror.

Then she spots one of the men, his tall frame sinister as a bat, rising for a moment above the heads of the students. Her way lies directly in the path of the militia. There's no time to circle around, so she plunges ahead until she is close to the line of truncheons, advancing en masse like a phalanx of Roman soldiers. On hands and knees, she makes herself inconspicuous, crawling through the melee, squirming through the legs of the militia until she eels her way through to the other side.

Regaining her feet, she looks around, sees the men pushing Liridona around a corner. They are no longer in the plaza. She is on the fringe of the mob, running as fast as she can toward the corner. Running with her heart in her mouth, running toward the sudden roar of gunshots that spurts at her like sleet from around the corner.

"No!" she cries. "No!"

Hurtling around the corner, she is jerked off her feet. She stares into monstrous eyes. One is blue, the other green. They regard her as if each has a separate intelligence, both cold as permafrost.

For a moment, she is paralyzed by those eyes, or, more accurately, the twin intelligence behind them. And she thinks, *Not him, anyone but him.* Then, from somewhere out of her sight, she hears Liridona weeping, and, like glass shattering against stone, the spell breaks. But the instant she tries to struggle free, the barrel of a gun is shoved into her mouth.

"Once again, quiet," a voice like a constricting iron band says. "Before the end."

The air shivers.

PART ONE

BLOOD SPORT

One Month Ago

You can't have a pact with God and with the devil at the same time.

—*The Skating Rink*, ROBERTO BOLAÑO

ONE

Washington, D.C.

"S HE'S DEAD."

These words, spoken by his daughter, jerk Jack McClure out of sleep.

Covered in sweat, he turns in the darkness of his bedroom. "Emma?"

The faintest cool breeze stirs the hair on his head.

"She passed by me a minute ago, Dad. Or is it an hour?"

Hard to tell, Jack thought, *when you're dead.*

"Emma?"

But the ghostly voice was gone, and he felt the sudden lack of her. Again. A great abyss on whose edge he teetered like a drunk reeling out of a bar. He drew a breath, gave a great shudder, and lunged for his cell phone. Punched in the number of Walter Reed Medical Center and heard the familiar voice of the night nurse.

"Mr. McClure, how odd you should call at this moment. I was just about to dial your number." She cleared her throat and when she began again her voice had taken on a formal, almost martial tenor. "At two fifty-three this morning, the former First Lady, Lyn Carson, expired."

"She's dead." The echo of Emma's voice caused another shiver to run down his spine.

"I'm very sorry for your loss," the night nurse said.

"Have you notified Alli?"

"I haven't yet, but as instructed I've called Mrs. Carson's sister and her brother-in-law." She meant Henry Holt Carson, Alli's uncle. "As well as Secretary Paull, of course."

"Okay." Jack thumbed the sleep from his eyes as he swung his legs off the bed. "I'll take care of informing Alli." He padded toward the bathroom.

"Sir, is there anything—?"

"At the end . . . did she regain consciousness?"

"No, sir, she never did."

"Stay with Mrs. Carson." He squinted as he turned on the light. "I'll be right over."

"IT'S THE end of an era," Dennis Paull said as he and Jack stood by Lyn Carson's bedside.

No one knew that better than Jack. Ten months ago, he had been in the vehicle following the president's limousine in Moscow when the limo had skidded on a patch of ice. Almost everyone in that car, including President Edward Harrison Carson, had died. All except Lyn Carson, who had slipped into a coma. Despite two surgeries, the first on board Air Force One, the second here at Walter Reed, she had failed to regain consciousness. Both procedures had succeeded only in prolonging her twilight life.

"Did you call Alli?"

Jack nodded. "Several times, and they said they'd get the message to her."

"What about her cell?"

"Fearington has a strict policy about cell-phone use." Fearington was the FBI Special Ops school in Virginia.

"Even for this?" Paull shook his head. He was now Jack's boss. He had hired Jack after President Carson's fatal accident. Jack, who had worked for ATF, had been tapped by Carson as a strategic advisor immediately following his old friend's inauguration. That all ended as abruptly as it had begun, and Paull, seeing his opportunity, had scooped Jack up. Now Jack tackled the antiterrorism assignments that daunted Paull's other agents, using his dyslexic mind to unravel puzzles no one else could handle.

"Rules are rules."

Paull took out his phone. "We'll see about that." While he was waiting, he said, "You must've moved heaven and earth to get her in there." Then he held up a finger. "No answer." He closed the connection.

"Fearington periodically goes into lockdown as a drill."

Paull nodded and put his phone into his pocket.

"But the truth is Alli did her own heavy lifting," Jack went on. "She passed the entrance exams with the highest marks they'd seen in more than a decade."

"Smart little thing."

Jack snorted. "It takes more than smarts to get into Fearington. After her father was killed, she wouldn't talk to anyone, even me. She curled up into an emotional ball. But there was so much anger inside her that when I took her to my gym, she slid on a pair of boxing gloves and started pounding the heavy bag."

Paull laughed. "I'd like to have been a fly on the wall."

"Yeah, she almost broke her right hand. Then I began to teach her how to box and, damn, if she didn't pick up all the fundamentals right away. At first, she didn't have a lot of power, as you can imagine, but then, I don't know, something clicked inside her. She was like a ghost—it seemed as if she could anticipate my punches. She has this ability. By reading a person's face she knows whether they're lying or telling the truth. Now she's extended this ability to knowing what they're about to do."

"So she put the boys down?"

"Did she ever!" Jack said. "But admiration wasn't what she got from a lot of her classmates."

Paull nodded. "I can only imagine. Fearington's a men's club. Didn't you warn her?"

"Well, I *reminded* her." Jack sighed. "Not that it did any good. She was determined. No one and nothing was going to get in her way."

ALLI CARSON was pulled from sleep, roughly and without warning.

"Get up, Ms. Carson. Please be good enough to rouse yourself."

Alli turned over, opened her eyes, and was almost blinded by the fierce glare from the overhead light. Who had turned it on, who was barking orders at her? Her mind, still fuzzed with the dream of Emma's face glowing in the light of—what?—a streetlamp, a full moon, an unearthly luminescence?

"What is this? I don't under—"

"Please do as I say, Ms. Carson, quickly, quickly!"

"Commander Fellows?"

"Yes," Brice Fellows said. "Come, come, there's no time to lose!"

She sat up. The oversized T-shirt she slept in was black, covered in white silk-screened skulls. Though twenty-three, she looked more like sixteen or seventeen. Graves' disease had interfered with her growing, so that she was slight, almost pixieish, just over five feet in height, her tomboy figure more suited to an adolescent than an adult.

"Can you please tell me—?"

"Hurry, Ms. Carson. The police are outside."

Fellows glanced around the dorm room, pointed to a chair on which she had casually tossed the clothes she had been wearing during dinner. Beyond was an empty bed with the covers pushed back.

"Where—where is Vera?" Alli asked.

"You don't know what happened to her?"

"No, I don't." Beneath her anger at this treatment, she felt a wave of fear rising inside her. "She fell asleep before I did. She was there when I turned off the light."

A catch in the commander's voice. "Well, that, at least, is a relief.

"Now, please, Ms. Carson, get dressed."

"Where is Vera?"

"She's in the infirmary."

A clutch in the pit of Alli's stomach. "Is she okay?"

"At the moment I can't say."

"Commander, you're scaring me."

"Please, Ms. Carson, just do as I ask."

Crossing to the chair, she drew on a pair of black jeans and a thick turtleneck sweater of the same color. She always dressed in black. Sitting on Vera's bed, she placed her palms against the bottom sheet as if to make certain that Vera wasn't there. Then, drawing her shoes over, she stepped into them.

"Here, you'll need this."

He passed her her leather jacket. She swung it around and zipped up.

"Come with me."

She stood up, silently, with a fiercely beating heart.

Beyond her door, the hallway was only dimly lit, so as not to awaken the other recruits on the floor, she assumed. She saw two police detectives, a three-man forensics team, and a pair of Secret Service agents, one of whom, Naomi Wilde, had been the head of her mother's detail. Cops *and* the Secret Service? What in the world had happened?

All at once, her heart skipped a beat. "Naomi, is Vera all right?"

"Keep your voice down."

She turned to see three forensics techs snapping on latex gloves before they stepped into her room. Turning on the lights, they began to methodically go through it.

"What are they looking for?" Then Alli turned back to Naomi. "Please," she begged. "Just tell me if Vera is okay." But Naomi's face was as blank as a field of snow.

"Ms. Bard is in the infirmary," Naomi said.

"I already know that," Alli said. Something in her voice had spoken of a forced detachment, which caused Alli's stomach to clench in anxiety. If Naomi wasn't in control of the situation . . .

"She's been drugged. She was disoriented, sick to her stomach. She went out into the hallway without, apparently, knowing where she was, and collapsed. A security guard found her."

"What?" A chill ran through Alli. "My God, how . . . who would do such a thing? I want to see her—!"

"Ms. Carson—"

"Hey, Vera's the only one here who gives a damn about me."

A member of the forensics team emerged from Alli's room holding a plastic evidence bag with something in it. Approaching one of the Metro detectives, he handed over the bag and whispered in the detective's ear, before disappearing back inside the room.

The Metro detective cocked his head. "Interesting you should say that now."

Alli turned on him, her cheeks aflame. "What the hell does that mean?"

He held up the bag. "This bottle contains traces of Rohypnol. Roofies in common street parlance, the date-rape drug. It was found under your bed."

"What?"

"You deny it's yours?"

"Of course I deny it."

"So it's your claim that you didn't drug your roommate?"

"What the what? Why on earth would I?"

"Please keep your voices down," Commander Fellows interrupted.

"Ms. Carson," the detective said in a steely voice, "I must insist you come with us now."

She looked around. "Just let me find my cell phone."

"The academy is in lockdown. You know the rules." The commander gestured to the doorway. "This way, Ms. Carson."

She knew better than to argue further with Fellows. He ran Fearington like an Army boot camp, and talking back would only get her into deeper trouble. Fearington was one of only a couple of elite academies that fed the government secret services. Like its brethren in other regions of the country, Fearington was a closely guarded secret. Its cadets were the cream of the crop, exhaustively vetted and tested before being chosen to fill its ranks. The courses were rigorous, both physically and intellectually. It had taken all of Jack's skills to get Alli accepted into the examination phase; following Jack's intensive tutelage, she had done the rest. But from the very first day, she had been acutely aware of the fact that she didn't fit the traditional Fearington mold.

As she was marched down the hallway and out onto the grounds, she wondered dazedly why she was in trouble. Her legs were shaking and the core of her felt cold. Nevertheless, she had no choice but to take her first step into the nightmare.

"GENTLEMEN, WHAT a surprise finding you here."

This was how Henry Holt Carson, oldest brother of the late president, announced himself as he walked through the door into his sister-in-law's room. Immensely wealthy and influential, he wore a silk-and-cashmere made-to-measure suit that Jack estimated must have cost at least five thousand dollars. On his feet were John Lobb shoes, mirror-shined, but not, Jack was certain, by Carson himself. His cold blue eyes, huge as an owl's, studied them both, but failed, Jack noted, to even glance at Lyn's corpse. But then, she was dead, Jack thought, and of no use to him.

"Interlopers to the end, I see." His lopsided smile failed to blunt the barb of his remark.

He was in every way his brother's polar opposite. A hard-nosed businessman, he distrusted and detested politicians, especially the ones he couldn't buy off. He owned mining interests in the Midwest, for which he was forever buying pollution credits so he could continue pulling ore out of the ground and refining it. More recently, he had bought up a number of regional banks at bargain basement prices, merging them into one, InterPublic Bancorp. He had been married and divorced four times that Jack knew of. He had children, but, according to Edward, could neither remember their names nor what they looked like. He was an empire builder through and through. But, somehow, possibly because of his affection for all things familial, Edward had forgiven his brother his peccadillos and loved him as one ought to love a brother. It was anyone's guess how the elder Carson felt about Edward. A rock might reveal more of its personal nature.

He moved into the apex of the triangle with them; he was the kind of man who was continually conscious of his power vis-à-vis those around him, perhaps out of a deep-seated sense of inferiority. After being expelled from high school for defecating on the principal's chair, retaliation for some slight, imagined or real, he had toiled fifteen-hour days in an iron smelter's, working his way up to foreman, then day manager, from which position he had obtained a bank loan in order to buy the company. From that moment on, the path of his life was set.

"We all had a deep and abiding fondness for Lyn," Jack said.

"My brother's wife has passed to her final reward, McClure." Henry Holt Carson's head, as round as a medicine ball and almost as large, swiveled in his direction. "She doesn't give a good goddamn whether you're here or not. If she ever did." This unnatural head, with its great eyes and turnip nose, sat atop sloping shoulders seemingly without the benefit of a neck. He had the overlarge, rough, slabbed hands of a hod carrier, and his face was deeply scored by wind, sun, and backbreaking work. Though he was now an owner, he made it an ironclad rule never to sit behind a desk. He was vocal in his contempt for those who, as he put it, were that disgusting modern mythological beast, half man, half chair. As a consequence, he never sat when he could stand, never walked when he could run. And he never spoke when he could order or accuse.

Now he looked around. "Why isn't my niece here?" Dark clouds gathered along his brow. "Has she been informed?"

"We tried." Paull's voice was mild and even. "It seems that Fearington is in lockdown."

The clouds were fulminating. "At this ungodly hour?"

"Rehearsal lockdowns are designed to come at inconvenient times," Jack said. "As in real life."

"Indeed." Which was what Henry Holt Carson said when he didn't know how to respond and didn't want to lose momentum. He abhorred silence the way nature abhors a vacuum. "This is unacceptable. The girl needs to know the altered state of her mother."

"Is that what you call it?" Jack said.

"Listen, you"—Carson's stubby forefinger stabbed the air like a dagger—"you've already done enough to that girl. As far as this family is concerned, you're a fucking menace."

"Oh, I see. This isn't about Alli at all, is it?"

Carson took a step toward him. "The fuck it isn't."

Paull put his hands up. "Rancor isn't appropriate, especially at this moment."

The two men ignored him, glaring fixedly at each other.

"The. Fuck. It. Isn't," Carson repeated, emphasizing each word with a degree of menace. "And then you go and let my brother get killed."

"Now it comes out. No one could have—"

"*You* should have." Carson squared his shoulders like a linebacker ready to make an open field tackle. "I mean, that's what Eddie was always saying about you—Jack can do this, Jack can do that. According to him you were a fucking wizard."

"He had a squad of Secret Service agents whose job it was—"

"They weren't *you*, McClure." He was up on the balls of his feet now, his hands curled into fists. "They. Weren't. You."

At that moment, Paull's phone burred. Something

about the moment, the phone ringing in the dead of night, or the portentousness of the sound, stopped the escalating argument in its tracks.

The two men stared at Paull as he drew out the phone, checked the number on the readout, then took the call. For what seemed the longest time he said not a word. But his gray eyes slid across the room and met Jack's. His expression was not encouraging.

"All right," he said at length. "Make certain nothing gets out of control." He sighed. "Yes, I know it's already out of control. I meant—for God's sake use your head, man!—don't let it go any further. I'll be right there."

He closed the phone and stood staring into space for some time.

"Well," Jack prompted, "what is it?"

Paull, seeking to pull himself together, turned to Jack. He rubbed a hand across his forehead and said, "That was Naomi Wilde."

Jack's adrenaline started to flow. "The Secret Service agent?"

Paull nodded. "She's at Fearington. The lockdown isn't a drill, Jack."

FEARINGTON'S GROUNDS were as dark as an abandoned coal mine. Not a light shone, not a figure could be seen in the blackness where trees, training courses, and firing ranges loomed. It was as if she and her detail were the only ones on the academy campus as they crunched through a thin layer of frost. Her breath appeared before her like an apparition. Then, from behind her, lights popped on in the dorm rooms, first one, then others, like eyes opening. Heads in silhouette told her that some of her fellow classmates had been roused, despite the stealth of her detail.

She was led across the campus. Not a word was spoken. She could hear the soft crunch of their shoes in the icy grass, the brief slither of material against material. Just last week there were patches of snow, like the last tufts on a balding man's scalp. Still, the cops' shoulders were hunched against the chill. Out past the obstacle course, they turned left into a dense copse of towering beech trees, and she felt even more surrounded, hemmed in, and helpless.

All at once, the lead detective murmured into his wireless mike and three huge generator-driven floodlights snapped on, one after the other. They were trained on a space between the trunks of two trees. Alli gasped and, staggering, almost fell. Only the hand of Naomi Wilde, cupped around her elbow, kept her from pitching headlong onto the bed of fallen leaves.

There, in the midst of the Fearington campus, was the naked body of a young male. He was upside down, his ankles and wrists bound and tied to the tree trunks. His skin was a sickening blue-white.

Alli, staring at Billy's body, felt the familiar steel wall spontaneously spring up, shielding her from trauma. Her unconscious had manufactured this mental wall during her weeklong captivity; it was a defense mechanism over which she had no control. She felt the disassociation, the sense of watching a movie instead of living life. This was happening to another girl, the protagonist of the film. She remained perfectly impassive, watching the film as, frame by frame, it unspooled toward its unknown climax and denouement.

After some time, she became aware that the others had come to a halt and now stood in a semicircle with her roughly in its center. They were all staring at her with the stern demeanor of tribunal judges. Her mind was filled with the ominous rat-tat-tat of military drums, and with a determined effort she put this, too, beyond the barrier of her inner wall.

One of the detectives, a beefy man with the splayed stance of a flatfoot, was directly behind her, and she heard his voice now.

"Well?"

Alli, spellbound in horror, felt her tongue cleaving to the roof of her mouth. She could not utter a word.

"What, no shock, no hysteria, not a tear shed?" Flatfoot said with a voice like an ice floe. "Christ, you're a cold bitch." He pressed his fingertips against her shoulder blades, propelling her forward. "Here is William Warren." He came after her, like a hunter with the fox in his sights. "You knew him, oh, yeah, you did." His laugh was like the braying of a mule. "You and he did what together behind that big old tree?"

Two

COMMANDER FELLOWS took a deep breath, let it out slowly. "It's a beautiful night." He cocked his head. "That's a nightingale singing, very peaceful, very romantic." He turned to her. "This is the spot, isn't it?"

"What spot?"

The detective's voice grew quills. "You know what spot, Ms. Carson. This is the trysting spot where you and the victim—"

"William," Alli said. "He has a name."

Commander Fellows appeared to have difficulty pulling himself together. He cleared his throat, but said nothing.

Alli was studying the ground at her feet. "Won't someone have the decency to at least cover him up?"

"This is a crime scene," one of the Metro detectives said in a weary voice. "Premeditated murder. A *capital* offense."

"The ME isn't here yet," said Flatfoot. "Nothing gets touched until he's done his thing."

Alli could see the lie on his bulldog face as surely as if it were a new scar livid on his cheek. More likely the ME had been ordered to hold off until they could get her here to see the atrocity in all its grisly panoply. Why? Ordered by whom? She racked her brains for answers, but the buzzing inside her head, caused by the pulsing of adrenaline, kept her from thinking clearly.

In the end, she turned to Naomi. "You know me, tell them I couldn't have committed such a horrible crime."

Naomi's partner, a square man with a mole on his chin, said, "We aren't authorized to get involved."

"Then why are you here?"

"I was assigned to the FLOTUS and to Alli," Naomi said. "I have a personal stake in the matter."

Fellows cleared his throat. "Ms. Carson, I want you to know that I think highly of you—very highly, despite your . . . despite the traumatic experiences of your . . . your recent past."

Fellows was gripping his hands in a link-fingered ball, flexing the fingers back and forth in a rhythm that reminded Alli of crazy Captain Queeq and his stainless steel balls.

"We've had a hotly contested internal debate regarding your, er, psychological break. A number of prominent board members feel strongly that the pressures you have been subjected to are a cause for concern and, I must admit, review."

"What?" Alli said. "I'm acing all my courses. Ask any instructor."

"And then there's the matter of your, uhm, diminutive size."

"And yet these Metro yardbirds seem to think this

little slip of a thing could kill a big, strong, healthy man and string him up upside down between two trees."

The first detective, clearly of higher rank than Flatfoot, stepped into the circle. He had prematurely white hair, stooped shoulders, and a bad case of razor burn. His name was Willowicz and his partner was O'Banion. He beckoned her to follow him as he went around the body to the back. There, he switched on a flashlight, illuminating a kind of scaffold, roughly made of tree branches lashed together with twine, onto which Billy's body had been strung. A rope, invisible from the front, was tied to the top of the scaffold. It rose straight up into the tree, where it had been looped around a thick branch. The other end hung down.

Willowicz took hold of the free end of the rope with a hand encased in a latex glove, and tugged. "You see how this works, Ms. Carson. The victim was attacked, his body was affixed to the scaffold as it lay on the ground. Clearly, the killer had prepared ahead of time. Looping the rope over the branch created a fulcrum which made it possible to hoist the corpse into the vertical position it's in now." He paused, a small smile creeping into his face. "Anyone could do it, I assure you, even you."

"But then you already knew that," O'Banion said.

"You're grotesque," Alli said, "you know that?"

His laugh was as grating as nails on a chalkboard. Willowicz led her back around to the front. "As you can see, the victim has been stabbed, not once or twice, or even a half-dozen times, but repeatedly, beyond . . ." He turned back to her. "A preliminary count has taken us past fifty. I'm quite certain there are more."

"That's why he bled to death?"

"No." Willowicz pointed. "The vast majority of the cuts are superficial, barely scoring the subcutaneous layers. But they were all near nerve ganglia."

After a moment's hesitation, Alli said, "You're saying that Billy was tortured."

She did not miss the sharp glance exchanged by the detective and Commander Fellows.

"Do you think he was tortured, Ms. Carson?" Willowicz said.

"Well, the evidence points to it, doesn't it." She paused, her terror, horror, and grief once again threatening to overwhelm her. At once, she was cast back into the nightmare of her weeklong imprisonment. Then she took a mental step back, as Jack had taught her to do, disengaging herself from the intimacy of emotions. It was imperative now for her to think clearly and reason the situation out, which she was unable to do when overcome with emotion. Billy was dead, she had to accept that. All death is terrible, but this was beyond comprehension. Why would anyone torture Billy, and then attempt to frame her? "However, that theory leaves one question unanswered."

Willowicz put his hands behind his back. "And what might that be?"

"I don't know," Peter McKinsey, Naomi Wilde's partner, said. "You seem awfully cool for someone whose lover of five months has been brutalized and killed."

"If you've got nothing constructive to contribute,

fuck off," Alli said. Addressing Willowicz, she said, "You said he bled to death. None of these subcutaneous cuts, even en masse, would have done the trick."

Again, that sharp look was exchanged by Willowicz and Fellows.

"So how did poor Billy die?" Alli said.

Willowicz beckoned with a crooked forefinger. Something about his demeanor reminded Alli of a Grimm's fairy tale witch or ogre, anyway someone delighted to be up to no good. "Come closer."

She walked over the uneven ground. The crunch of even her light weight pierced the paper-thin layer of ice, and with each step she seemed to sink farther into the boggy ground beneath.

A sickly smell enveloped Billy, of rotten meat, ice cream, and fecal matter. She gagged once, and then, because everyone's attention was on her, caught hold of herself and fought down her rising gorge. Billy's eyes were so swollen and bruised she had first thought they were covered in flies. Deep contusions showed around the spiderweb of cuts like dark clouds gathering around the heart of a storm. His face was so distorted that, close up, she scarcely recognized him. There could be only one reason why he had been slowly and systematically taken apart.

"What did he know?"

"Well, that's certainly one way to look at it," O'Banion said. "The other is that there was a single killer. A crime of passion."

"You're still at this angle," Alli said.

"We go by the odds," said Willowicz. "In these cases, the person closest to the vic is the perpetrator."

"Not this time."

Both detectives regarded her stonily.

Naomi Wilde, never far from her since she had stumbled, said, "We thought you might be able to shed some light on what happened here."

Alli said nothing, but delivered an Et tu, Brutus glower. Then, she turned to the corpse and looked into Billy's face, trying to stare past the terrible beating he had sustained, into the mind of the boy she had known, briefly but wildly. Even before she had been traumatized by her kidnapping and brainwashing two years ago, she had had difficulty with intimacy. She was embarrassed and ashamed of her body, which was small and immature. Now, through first Jack's and then the academy's help with physical training, her arms and legs were toned. But to her they still looked like a girl's limbs, totally lacking the womanly curves of her contemporaries.

Naomi wrapped an arm around Alli's shoulders. "Whatever you know, you have to tell us."

"All I know is that I had nothing to do with this monstrous . . . this atrocity." She shook her head. "It's beyond me how anyone could do this to another human being." If Jack were here he'd know that for a lie. During her time with him and Annika in Russia and the Ukraine she had witnessed examples of the hatred and contempt for human life some people harbor deep in their hearts or just beneath their skin. And with the Russian agent Annika, at least, she had discovered depths of human betrayal she had not even been able to imagine, even growing up in the snake pit of American politics.

"Ms. Carson," Willowicz said, "no one believes you don't know what happened here."

Alli felt her heart constrict. "How can you say that?"

"You and the victim were having an affair—illicitly, as it happens, on the grounds of the academy. But two days ago something happened. The two of you were seen in an argument—rather violent, from all reports—in a bar in town. Harsh words were exchanged. As a result, he stalked out."

"So, what, you think I tortured him and strung him up like an attic ham in revenge?"

"The theory tracks," O'Banion said. "It hits closest to home."

Alli shook her head. She had fallen down the rabbit hole, and now was sinking deeper and deeper into Nightmareland.

"Maybe he had another girl on the side and you found out. Maybe he was fed up with you." O'Banion shrugged, as if whichever motive it turned out to be made no difference to him.

Alli stared at him. "You're an idiot."

When he took a step toward her, Naomi intervened. O'Banion's eyes were yellow and feral as he squinted over the agent's shoulder. "You think because you're the president's daughter you can talk to us like that? Fuck you!"

"Now, hold on," Naomi said.

"And, by the way," he said to Alli, "your old man was a dickhead."

McKinsey became a shield between the detective and Alli. "Calm down."

"And fuck you, too, sonny! You better tell her to watch her mouth."

"Back off, Bluto," Naomi said.

"Screw you, nanny dearest."

When the detective remained rooted as a tree, she lowered her voice. "I said back the fuck off, or I *will* take you in for disobeying an order from a federal agent."

A pulse beat furiously in O'Banion's temple, then he turned his head and spat onto the ground. "Remember what I said." He pointed to Alli as he returned to his previous position.

Willowicz, who had observed the escalating emotions through skeptical eyes, now stepped up. "This is a homicide—a *civilian* homicide. As I see it, you and the woman are here to ensure the safety of the late president's daughter. My partner and I appreciate your role in this matter, really we do. But the fact remains that this crime is in our jurisdiction and is under our purview. I control the crime scene, I control the interrogations." He flipped open an old-fashioned notebook. "Now here's how I see matters falling out. We have a murder of both premeditation and deep emotion, but we have no witnesses. Commander Fellows here has assured us that no outsider has breached the academy's perimeter tonight."

"Billy had no trouble—"

"We have filled that breach, Ms. Carson," Fellows said icily. "I can assure you that there are no others."

Willowicz looked from Alli to Fellows, as if they were combatants, before he continued. "So, no interlopers. But your roommate, Ms. Carson, was drugged . . . at about midnight, Fearington's doctor estimates."

"I was asleep," Alli said.

"Well, the problem there is the only person who could corroborate your claim can't." Licking his fingertip, he turned a page in his notebook. "Which means that at any time after lights out you could've stolen out of your room and, if you were careful enough—well, pretty much gone anywhere on the grounds unobserved, am I correct?"

He was looking directly at Alli, but she said nothing, principally because an idea was dawning on her, and the horror of why these people were so insistent on pinning Billy's murder on her literally took her breath away.

"So you had opportunity. Tell us a little about the victim."

She took a couple of deep breaths in an attempt to regain her composure. "Billy worked at Middle Bay Bancorp. He was a loan analyst."

"Sounds like a snoozer." O'Banion looked her up and down. "Still waters, yeah."

Willowicz pursed his lips. "How'd you hook up with him?"

Alli tried to ignore the insinuation, but found herself rising to the bait anyway. "We *met* at a bar."

"Uh-huh. Which one?"

"Twilight. In Georgetown."

Willowicz made a notation. "Yeah, been there for twenty years."

"The bar for vampires." O'Banion guffawed.

Willowicz ignored him. "What did he do when you approached him?"

Alli's cheeks flamed. "He came up to me. I was dancing and—"

"What?" O'Banion interjected. "Like pole dancing?"

Alli's cheeks continued to flush. "He came up to me, like I said."

"Was he drunk?"

"Maybe. A little. I don't know."

Willowicz nodded. "Then what?"

"We danced . . . together."

"And things progressed from there."

"Oh so very fast." O'Banion leered.

"And this first meeting was how long ago?"

"About five months."

"And you've been seeing the victim ever since."

"Yes."

"When did you see him last?"

A slight hesitation, for which she could have bitten her tongue. "This evening—well, yesterday, now."

Willowicz's head came up like a pointer scenting game. "When, exactly?"

"After dinner. About eight."

"Did you have permission to leave Fearington?"

Alli shifted from one foot to another. "No."

"So you sneaked out."

Alli stared at him, unflinching. She had no wish to look at Commander Fellows. "Billy begged me. He said it was urgent."

"Uh-huh." Willowicz was scribbling some more. "And?"

"And that's it. I never found out what he wanted to talk to me about."

Willowicz's eyebrow arched. "Why was that?"

"I was supposed to meet him at Twilight. Just as I

came around the corner, I saw him walk off with someone."

"Who?"

"I have no idea."

"Man or woman?"

"The person's back was to me."

"Tall, short, thin, fat?"

"The figure was in shadow."

"So it could have been a woman."

Silence.

"Your contention is that you never spoke to the victim at any time yesterday?"

"No, as I said, he and I had a brief phone conversation."

"You never spoke face-to-face."

"No."

In typical interrogator's style, Willowicz now switched subjects without warning. "And so you had motive."

"Motive," Alli said, taken aback. "What motive?"

Again, Willowicz turned a page. "As it happens, the victim had met someone—a week ago. Her name is . . . let's see, Kraja. Arjeta Kraja."

"Fucking foreign names." O'Banion snickered. No one else moved or said a word.

Willowicz looked up from his notes. "You know this Arjeta Kraja, Ms. Carson? Ever met her?"

"No," Alli said. "No, I haven't."

"Interesting." Willowicz held out his hand and O'Banion placed something in it.

When Alli saw that it was a photo, her heart sank. Reluctantly, she took it when Willowicz handed it over, a surveillance photo of three people talking casually outside a local bar.

"Man, she's smokin' hot," O'Banion said.

"Ms. Carson," Willowicz said, "would you be good enough to identify the young woman with you and William Warren."

Of course it was Arjeta Kraja.

ON THEIR way out of the hospital, Henry Holt Carson said, "Mr. Secretary, I believe your phone's about to ring," just as Paull's phone buzzed.

Paull gave him a sharp glance.

"I think you'd better answer it," Carson said with a perfectly straight face. The gloating was all in his voice.

Paull thumbed on the cell phone and put it to his ear. He listened for close to ten seconds before he said, "Yes, sir," and closed the connection. "Jack, go on ahead. I've got an appointment at the White House."

"At this hour?" Jack said.

"This president never sleeps," Carson said. Then, turning to Jack, he said, "Why don't I give you a lift?"

"I have my own car—"

Carson waved a hand. "I'll have someone come and fetch it."

Jack recognized a summons when he heard one. He watched his boss cross the parking lot and approach his car. Stars were blurred by the city's artificial dome of light and the slow creep of dawn. A chilly wind blew off the Potomac with a dampness that pierced his thick coat like a spear.

Jack turned back to Carson. "What's going on?"

Carson shrugged his meaty shoulders. "Why ask me?"

"Because," Jack said, "you seem to have orchestrated this entire scene."

Carson appeared unperturbed.

Jack hurried to Carson's Navigator and they climbed into the backseat. Carson's driver turned the SUV around and drove away from the hospital.

Jack turned to Carson. "Now what the hell was that all about?"

Carson held up a finger. "Excuse me." He punched in a number on his PDA. After a moment, he said, "Harrison, it's Henry. . . . Yes, damnit, I'm well aware of the time. Get dressed and haul your ass over to Fearington Academy. . . . Nothing, I hope, but on the other hand my niece seems to be in trouble. . . . What sort? I've no damn idea."

After he closed the connection, he sat brooding and silent.

Jack said, "Who are you bringing on board?"

"My lawyer, Harrison Jenkins."

"Is that really necessary?"

"I hope not, but the world doesn't run on hope."

They drove on in a fulminating silence. Sitting next to Henry Holt Carson was akin to living near a blast furnace going full bore.

"You never answered my question about orchestrating that scene back there with Dennis."

"Persistent little fucker, aren't you?"

"That's no answer."

"I've been around politicians all my life." Carson stared straight ahead, his arms folded across his chest. "Say, I don't have to be worried, do I?"

"About what?"

"You being able to read the street signs, that's what." He glanced in Jack's direction, though not directly at him. "Dyslexia's a bitch, isn't it?"

"Especially," Jack said, "if you know nothing about it."

Carson laughed with his teeth bared. "You're a fuckup, Jack. I'll never forgive you for my brother's death."

"That's your choice," Jack said. "But in the same way you're ignorant about dyslexia, you know nothing about Edward's death or the circumstances leading up to it."

"I'm uninterested in your litany of excuses, McClure."

"We're like oil and water," Jack said, "destined never to inhabit the same space."

Carson grunted. "What the hell my brother saw in you is beyond me, McClure. And the fact he allowed you unlimited access to Alli was a grave mistake."

"Alli is an adult. She can make her own decisions."

"She's a psychological train wreck and you know it. Kidnapped, brainwashed, traumatized further by her father's sudden death and her mother lingering on in a vegetative state." He shook his head. "No, what she needs is the firm guidance of an adult who cares about her."

"She has me."

"And how's that going?"

They had drawn up to the front gates of Fearington Academy, which was ablaze with the blinding dazzle of cop cars and unmarked vehicles. After showing their credentials to three different police in ascending order of rank, they were directed and waved through. The car crunched the gravel as Jack headed toward the obstacle course to the left of the main building.

Henry Holt Carson leaned over slightly. "My brother allowed you too much control over Alli, McClure. That's a mistake I aim to correct tonight."

THREE

"WELL, HERE'S something you don't see every day."

The ME, a tall, rangy man in his midfifties with skin like a lizard and eyes like burnt-out pits, was crouched just to the right of Billy Warren's corpse. His name was Bit Saunderson; he viewed corpses the way a philatelist views stamps. His forensic people had snapped photos from every conceivable angle, taken shoe prints from the crime scene area, and had departed as silently as clouds drift across the sky.

"Look here."

He was speaking to Willowicz, but no one stopped Alli from having a look herself. Saunderson's knees creaked like masts at sea as he moved to give them a view of the side of the corpse's neck.

"Yeah, we noticed," Willowicz said, "but what the fuck is it?"

"It's a bit of a plastic straw. See, it's pink-and-white striped." Saunderson touched the protruding end with the tip of his gloved finger. "Neatly punctured the carotid, too. This is how your victim exsanguinated."

Willowicz scratched his razor-burned jaw. "That speaks to a working knowledge of the human body."

"Anatomy is a first-semester class at Fearington." Commander Fellows had begun to look green around the gills.

"Aced her courses, she said," O'Banion growled as he took up position directly behind Alli.

Naomi Wilde frowned as she bent over for a look. "But why a straw, of all things?"

O'Banion was virtually breathing fumes from his sour stomach down Alli's neck. "Why don't you ask her?"

Saunderson turned his half-dead face up to Wilde. "Like sucking an ice-cream soda, you can control the volume of flow."

A deep and horrific silence ensued, which ended abruptly with O'Banion's bray. "Doc, please, you're telling us that Ms. Carson might be a vampire?"

"You've been seeing too many horror films, O'Banion." The ME shook his head. "No, this is something far worse. Your perp is a deeply disturbed individual—a psychopath, though there's nothing textbook about him. He—"

"Or she." O'Banion stared at the back of Alli's head with newfound venom.

Saunderson took a breath. "Your killer is both a sadist and, I would venture to guess, insane, or at least has become unhinged."

"Traumatized," Willowicz said. He, too, was watching Alli as if she were already in a cage. "As from a terrible ordeal."

Saunderson, clueless as to his true meaning, nodded. "Something in the past, yes, that's a distinct probability with psychosis." He tapped the straw. "Who else would think of varying the flow of blood in order to prolong a victim's agony?"

HARRISON JENKINS, Carson's attorney, drove up minutes after Jack had exited the car. Carson was walking back and forth over the frosty ground like a caged animal impatient to be fed. Jenkins was one of those sleek men you see giving sound bites on CNN or Fox News. His gray hair was thick, and long enough to cover the tops of his ears, his cheeks were a healthy pink, and, Jack noted, he had perfectly manicured nails that shone like ten tiny mirrors. He gave the impression of being tall, but up close he was less than median height, maybe five six. He was carrying a battered leather briefcase. His expensive overcoat was open, revealing a steel-gray suit, white shirt, and a striped red tie. There was an enamel pin of the American flag on the lapel of his overcoat. All he needed, Jack thought, was a bald eagle perched on his shoulder. He walked like a lawyer should, as if he owned the ground over which he strode. Jack supposed he should be grateful for Jenkins's appearance, but something about the man chilled him.

Carson whirled around when he saw his attorney approach.

"Anything more you can tell me?" Jenkins asked as he pumped Carson's hand.

Carson shook his head. When he introduced Jack, a small, secret smile played briefly across Jenkins's face. Then he asked Jack to brief him on Alli's recent history.

When he had finished, the attorney said, "In your opinion, as of today, is she of sound mind?"

"Absolutely," Jack said.

"I strongly disagree," Carson responded.

Jenkins blew air through his nostrils like a race-horse at the starting gate. Then, putting his PDA to his ear, he walked several paces away from them and spoke into it for several moments. When he returned, he said, "Right, let's get this show on the road."

Following the directions they'd been given, they skirted the obstacle course, where shapes reared up out of the gloom of a false dawn like pieces of a wrecked ship, then they descended a shallow embankment via a set of narrow stairs, and almost immediately turned left, threading their way through a copse of old trees that smelled of leaf mold and loam. Up ahead was a fierce pool of light, as concentrated as a key spot illuminating an actor on stage. In this case, however, the actor wasn't moving.

Jack felt as if he were in an elevator whose cable had been cut.

"Jesus Christ," Carson muttered, "what the hell is this?"

Then Jack saw Alli walking toward them out of the blinding light. She was between two suits who looked to him like Metro police detectives. Behind them came Naomi, McKinsey, and Commander Fellows, but Jack's attention was riveted on Alli. She was in handcuffs. He began to make a move, but Jenkins, anticipating him, grabbed his arm to restrain him.

"In these matters I've found that methodology is

better than instinct," he said softly, so only Jack could hear.

"For God's sake, she's been arrested."

"Mr. McClure, let me handle it."

Jack, after a moment's thought, allowed Jenkins, whatever his reaction to the horror of the crime scene, to take point. The lawyer strode toward the semicircle of people, with Jack and Carson flanking him, as if they were a raiding party. The moment she spied Jack, Alli's eyes lit up, but despite how well she seemed to be holding up Jack could tell that she was badly shaken.

"Do you think that's a wise move, Detective O'Banion?" Jenkins said.

O'Banion looked blankly at Jenkins. "Who the hell're you and how d'you know my name?"

"I'm Ms. Carson's attorney, Harrison Jenkins."

O'Banion sneered. "An ambulance chaser."

"Watch yourself, Officer," Jenkins said.

"I'm a detective."

"Then act like one."

When O'Banion continued to glower at him, Willowicz stepped up. "Alli Carson is under arrest for the murder of William Penn Warren."

"I assume, Detective Willowicz, that you're referring to the victim strung up behind you," the lawyer said as he picked his way among the trees.

"D'you know what's in my service jacket, as well?" Willowicz said in a mild tone of voice.

Jenkins nodded. "Everything I need to know. Wounded twice in the line of duty, a medal of honor."

All this from the one phone call Jenkins had made. Jack was impressed, despite himself. He despised lawyers almost as much as O'Banion, because they had a knack of knitting a skein of gray areas and half-truths into a story a jury could believe in.

"Jack, this is a crazy mistake," Alli said. "Please listen to me." She recounted what had happened and how she had come to be a suspect in William Penn Warren's torture and murder.

"All of this is circumstantial," Jenkins said, unperturbed.

Willowicz nodded. "True enough." He held up a plastic evidence bag. "On the other hand, our forensic team found a vial with traces of Rohypnol under Ms. Carson's bed and this bloody knife in a trash bin behind her dorm room."

"Please hand them over, and whatever other evidence you have," Jenkins said.

"What?" O'Banion stood with his feet planted in a clearly combative stance. "Back off, windbag, this is our jurisdiction."

The small, secret smile Jack had noticed earlier had returned to Jenkins's face. "Tell me, Detectives, just how did you wind up at the scene of the crime?"

"We caught Commander Fellows's call," Willowicz said.

"So, what you're telling me is that the commander invited you here to Fearington."

"That's right," O'Banion said.

Jack could already see the changed situation dawning on Willowicz's face.

"Fearington is federal property," Jenkins said.

"What?" both detectives said at once.

"The federal government bought this parcel three years ago."

Jack knew a cue when he heard it. Stepping forward, he presented his ID. "Jack McClure, Department of Homeland Security. You have no jurisdiction here. I'll be taking over this case, Detectives."

"Oh, you've fucking got to be kidding," O'Banion said.

Willowicz said nothing because he knew which way the wind was blowing. He handed over the bags with the vial and the bloody knife.

"What's this?" The ME appeared out of the trees. "Those are my evidence bags."

Jack showed his ID. "Not anymore."

"How is this homicide a matter of national security?" Saunderson looked put out.

"That's a matter of national security," Jack said.

"But the body—"

"I'll take care of the body."

The ME looked alarmed. "This is highly irregular."

Ignoring him, Jack turned to Alli. "Uncuff her," he said.

O'Banion took out the manacle key. "We won't be forgetting this."

Keeping his eyes on Alli, Jack beckoned to her the instant she was free. But before she could get to him, Jenkins intervened and, taking her by the elbow, steered her away from Jack, toward her uncle.

"What the hell are you doing?" Jack said.

"Taking my niece to a place of safety," Carson said.

"You have no—"

"Leave it this way, Mr. McClure," Jenkins said in a low voice. "If you take Ms. Carson into custody it will look bad for her when I go before a federal judge tomorrow."

"But—"

"Henry is family. He's got power and influence, which is what she needs right now." Jenkins caught Jack's eye. "You can see this is the best course for Ms. Carson." He cast a glance at the departing cops and ME. "In any event, you're needed here. If you're taking over the case, you need to examine the crime scene as well as interview Detectives Tweedle-Dum and Tweedle-Dee before they can get together and cook up a story." Seeing Jack's gaze wandering to Alli, he added, "Besides, you heard what O'Banion said: 'We won't be forgetting this.' I need you to ride herd on him, make sure he doesn't make good on that threat." He smiled. "That's what you folks do best, isn't it, deflect threats. So do it."

DENNIS PAULL passed through the six layers of security to reach the West Wing, then was vetted one more time, though in a totally different way, by Alix, the president's press secretary. Paull liked her far more than he did the president. Arlen Crawford, a big, rangy, sun-scarred Texan, had been Edward's vice president, a marriage of political convenience that had pleased neither man. Each was strong where the other was weak, but their political ideas, and, worse, ideals, had worked at cross-purposes.

"Morning, Dennis," Alix said cheerfully, "I see we're all up early today."

"Duty calls."

She nodded. "So I heard."

They began to walk together toward the Oval Office.

"How are things with your daughter and grandson?"

"Claire and Aaron are settling down nicely, thanks."

"It was fun meeting them."

"Aaron hasn't stopped talking about you." He laughed. "I don't know what you did to impress him—"

"I let him wear Teddy Roosevelt's Rough Rider hat."

Paull nodded. "That would do it, all right."

They were now nearing the door to the Oval Office and Alix stopped, her face suddenly grave. "Dennis, you know I'm a loyal person. I work for the Old Man, but . . ."

He paused, waiting and suddenly on edge.

"I just . . . well, I just wanted to say watch your back."

Before he could formulate an answer, she had stepped forward, planted a kiss on his cheek, and was heading back down the red-carpeted hallway. He turned. It was deathly still. Even the faint whisper of air from the hidden vents seemed ominous.

Nestling Alix's nugget of intel in the forefront of his mind, he rapped sharply on the thick double doors, turned the knob, and entered.

Dawn had come, seeping through the thick-curtained windows. The president was alone, which surprised Paull. He was sitting on one of the matching sofas that faced each other in the area in front of his desk. On the low glass-topped table was a chased silver tray and an antique silver service from which

Crawford was pouring himself a cup of coffee. Significantly, beside the tray lay a black dossier with the yellow EYES ONLY stripe across its cover.

"Dennis, come on in." He gestured. "Good of you to join me."

In his soft, West Texas accent he made it seem as if Paull had had a choice.

"Help yourself," the president said, stirring in a tablespoonful of sugar. "The tarts and hot cross buns are just out of the oven."

Seating himself across from the president, Paull poured a cup of coffee and took a hot cross bun on a small china plate. Fully concentrated on Crawford, he neither drank nor ate. Crawford had proved himself the kind of man who takes to the presidency the way a chef takes to the cutting board. In the space of the ten months since he had ascended to the highest office, he had quietly but methodically dismantled all of his predecessor's initiatives, replacing them with others that conformed to his conservative agenda.

"Sorry to get you out of bed at this hour."

"I was already up," Paull said. "Your call caught me at Walter Reed."

"You're not ill, are you, Dennis?"

"No, sir. Lyn Carson died."

"Ah." The president put down his cup and stared up at the ceiling, as if watching out for Lyn in heaven. "Sad business, Dennis. My condolences. I know how close you were with the family."

Paull couldn't help but ponder the question of a double meaning. When he was with Crawford he was always aware that he had been one of Edward Carson's closest friends and advisors, even though in his first meeting with Crawford after he'd been sworn in as president, he said to Paull, "I just want you to know, Dennis, that I value loyalty above all other traits."

Leaning forward, Crawford refilled his cup. As he sat back, he gestured at the dossier. "We have one helluva problem."

Paull took the file onto his lap and opened it. On top of a significant pile of papers was a black-and-white photo, a head shot of a man who Paull judged to be somewhere between forty and forty-five. It was impossible to see the face clearly or even to make out particular features, other than a full beard. It could be anyone.

"Who the hell is this?" he said.

"It's not so much who," the president said, "as what." He cleared his throat, watching as Paull began to leaf through the intel that lay below the image. "His name, as you can see, is Arian Xhafa." He pronounced the last word "Shafa."

"He's Albanian," Paull said. "Why should we care about him?"

"That's what I thought," Crawford said. "Read on."

Paull did, rustling pages as he scanned them. Xhafa was the kingpin of the Albanian Mafia, of which there were at least twenty competing clans. That is, before Xhafa's rise to power. Like Mao or Ieyasu Tokugawa, the first shogun of feudal Japan, Xhafa had vision— more than that he had the muscle to cajole, bully, extort, murder, and maim his way to the top of the heap by uniting all the clans.

"He calls his men freedom fighters," the president said, "and I suppose in some respects they are—

fighting for Albanian freedom in Macedonia. But their true business is smuggling, though by the evidence in your hands, they're not averse to a bit of murder-for-hire. There." He pointed. "Read the particulars on that page."

Paull ran his finger down the sheet. Three hundred Macedonian soldiers slaughtered in Bitola, almost the same number in a pitched battle on the outskirts of Resen. The text was punctuated by highly graphic photos of mass graves, gaping pits filled with bodies, exposed to the photographer's lens like raw wounds. Firefights in the mountain villages around Struga, resulting in ruins, cindered, smoking as if just leveled. Scattered around were charred bodies, warped and curled, barely recognizable as being human. The next page held more horrors, a series of photos showing the victims of assassinations, both inside Macedonia and in more far-flung places, such as Greece, southern Italy, even Turkey and Russia, that Xhafa or his people were suspected of carrying out. These areas were so remote, the countries involved of so little interest to Americans, that the atrocities barely made any of the papers and certainly were not rating fodder for CNN or FOX, let alone the three legacy networks.

"This fucker's a real live monster," the president said with obvious distaste. "No one's going to give a crap how we take him out, guaranteed."

But that would be far from easy. Xhafa's base was the impregnable city of Tetovo, in western Macedonia—coordinates 42° 0' 38" North, 20° 58' 17" East—an area as wild and lawless as Afghanistan or western Pakistan. Xhafa, clever fellow that he was, had played on the theme of Albanian freedom, making the rational case that freedom for Albanians was unattainable unless they were united in their efforts against the Macedonian government.

However, in the three years since he had come to power, the main thrust of his activities had been to increase the efficiency of the clans' smuggling operations. This included expanding the white slave trade, exporting Eastern European girls from ten to eighteen from their native countries to Italy, England, and the United States. Most often, these girls were sold to Xhafa's representatives by their own parents, desperate and poor beyond measure, who could see no monetary upside to female offspring.

Paull, pausing in his reading, glanced up. "Surely this is a job for Interpol, not Homeland Security."

"The Pentagon disagrees. They believe Xhafa to be extremely dangerous and so do I. Listen, after the last decade of wars in Iraq, Afghanistan, and now Yemen, America's image abroad is in desperate need of rehabilitation. Edward was on the right track with the arms deal he signed with Russia just before his death. And I'm fully aware of President Yukin's attempts at double-dealing. Without you and Jack McClure, the deal would never have gotten done."

He looked around the room, as if suddenly self-conscious or overwhelmed by his surroundings. "In tonight's TV address I'm making human rights one of the ribs of my agenda. We can't have young girls—hell, girls of any age—being shipped into the United States and sold into prostitution rings. The traffic in human beings is enormous. Every six minutes another girl is sold or snatched off the streets. The trade is epidemic; it has become a worldwide scandal. Think how the image of the United States will profit when we bring Xhafa to justice."

"Have the DoD send in a team of Special Forces—"

The president sighed. "Look at page ten."

Paull pulled it out. It was an "Eyes Only" field SITREP from General Braedenton, the head of DoD, to the president himself. In brief, a Special Forces SKOPES unit of six highly trained black ops agents had been dispatched to Macedonia two weeks ago with orders to take out Arian Xhafa with all due speed. DoD monitoring lost contact with the unit thirty-one hours into the mission.

"The SKOPES unit never returned and was never heard from again," Crawford said.

"How in the hell did Xhafa manage that?"

The president looked like he'd just seen a dog run over by a car. "That's one of the mysteries. This man is not like other crime lords; there's something different about him."

"He's smarter?"

"Among other things," the president nodded, "such as sophisticated weaponry to take out an entire SKOPES unit."

"Sophisticated weaponry takes big bucks."

The president's expression became even more pained. "Simply put, we aren't authorized to send military into Albania. Besides which, the military can't cut it in that region—the mountainous terrain works against them. No, this is strictly black ops. A small guerrilla unit is what's needed. And don't talk to me about Interpol. Those monkeys can't find their own assholes."

"Nevertheless, with all due respect, sir—"

"Loyalty, Dennis." Crawford's voice was soft but with a backbone of steel. "I want you to find Xhafa and shut him down . . . permanently."

Paull sighed in resignation. "All right. I'll get a task force to work up a plan ASAP."

"That's just what you *won't* do." The president set down his cup. "I want you to handle this job personally."

Paull felt as if he were a whiplash victim of a car crash. "Sir, I don't understand. A secretary of HS doesn't—"

"It seems to me, Dennis—and I say this as a compliment, though I fear you'll take it otherwise—that secretary of HS was never the best use of your talents." He turned and took a thick Eyes Only dossier off his desk. "For ten years, during your assignments in the field, you never once failed to complete a mission. Plus, you never lost a man."

"Once," Paull said. "I lost a man once."

"No." The president paged through the dossier until he reached the page he was looking for. Running his forefinger down the page, dense with typescript, he said, "The agent, Russell Evans, was wounded by friendly fire. You carried him on your back for twenty-five miles until you crossed over from hostile territory."

"By then he was dead."

"Through no fault of your own, Dennis." The president closed the dossier with a decisive slap. "You received a medal for that mission."

Paull, chilled to his marrow, sat very still. He was hyperaware of his heartbeat and his breath, as if he were a scientific observer monitoring this unreal scene. "What is this," he said in a voice he did not fully recognize, "a sacking?"

"What makes you say that?"

"A demotion, then."

"Dennis, as I feared, you've completely misinterpreted what I've just said."

"Do you want me to step down as secretary of HS?"

"Yes."

"Then I haven't misinterpreted anything."

Crawford hitched himself to the edge of the sofa. "Listen to me, Dennis. I know you don't trust me. I know your loyalty was to Edward, and since we never saw eye to eye on most matters . . ." He allowed his voice to trail off, as if he was thinking ahead three or four steps. Or, anyway, that was Paull's interpretation of the small silence.

Then the president's eyes reengaged with Paull's. "I value you, Dennis, perhaps—and I know this will be difficult for you to believe—perhaps more than Edward did. This job he put you in—it's not . . . You're not a politician. Your expertise is in the field—it always has been. That's where you shine; that's where you'll be of the most use to me—and your country."

"So the decision has been made."

Crawford looked at Paull for a moment. "Dennis, answer me this: Have you been happy the last year or so? Happy in your job, I mean."

Paull said nothing. He sat thinking of a future that now seemed as treacherous as quicksand. "Since the deed is done, it doesn't matter what I say."

The president steepled his hands together, elbows on his knees. "The reason I scuttled Edward's initiatives is simple: They were doomed. The health care bill—he had to get into bed with big pharma in order to even get it cobbled together. It had more pork in it than a pig farm. The attack on the merchant banks—too punitive and difficult to get through Congress. Edward would have expended all his remaining political capital on this agenda, and he would have failed. His presidency would have foundered. I've been given a chance to right the ship, and I'm taking it."

"Right is right," Paull said sourly.

Crawford laughed and shook his head. "Dennis, I'm going to take a chance. I've decided to trust you enough to tell you a secret."

He paused as if needing another minute to make up his mind. Despite himself, Paull edged forward, the better to hear what the president had to say, because Crawford was speaking now in a hushed tone.

"I'm a conservative by design, not by conviction. Not many people know this; Edward certainly didn't. But I have to deal from strength with certain powerful elements in this country. In any event, I want to do what's right for the country, and as of this moment what we need more than anything else is fiscal responsibility. I'm going to see we get it."

"That involves appointing someone else as HS secretary. Is that what you're going to say in your address?"

Crawford waved away Paull's words. "I'm doing away with the position. Your man Dickinson, who's director, is more than capable of handling the department. Hell, he already is. He's an organizational wizard, isn't he?"

"That he is," Paull admitted.

The president spread his hands wide. "Well, then, there you have it."

"What's to be my new title?"

Crawford's smile spread across his face like jam. "Officially, you'll be ambassador at large. Unofficially, you'll be in charge of a SITSPEC, reporting directly to me."

This might have some potential after all, Paull thought. SITSPEC was gov-speak for a situation-specific black ops group that, in theory at least, could comprise two people or two thousand.

"If this is the way it will be, I want some terms."

"Name them, Denny."

"I don't want oversight."

"Define oversight."

"The group is at Black ICE level. We're dark to Congress, the CIA, and DoD. I report to you, and act on your mandates or ones I deem appropriate and necessary, period."

The POTUS stroked his chin. "Well, now, Denny, I don't rightly know whether I can do that."

"Okay." Paull stood up. "Then I'm out, sir."

For a moment, Crawford looked up at him, then he gestured with one hand. "Aw, sit down, would you?" When Paull did, he added, "Give the group a name, Denny."

Paull thought a moment. "Chimera."

"The monster that changes its shape. An apt creature to destroy Arian Xhafa." The president nodded, pleased.

"The fewer people around you who know, the better."

"Agreed, but you'll have to stick Chimera somewhere," he continued. "Let's start with the department you know best, Homeland."

"I want Jack McClure," Paull said without hesitation.

"That's it? One person?"

"For now."

"Take him, then." The president began to talk about the details. "This crime spree is spreading like a virus. You pull the plug and America's image starts to shine again. As of this moment, you have Alpha Authorization to procure anything you require for this mission. I want you to bring me Arian Xhafa's head."

Paull was leafing through the file. "I'll need a better photo of Xhafa."

The president looked pained again. He produced three more photos, placing them side by side with the first one—grainy, slightly blurred surveillance photos obviously taken with a long lens. He pointed to each one, in turn.

"Xhafa could be this man, or this one, or this one. More likely he's none of these three. We just don't know."

"A bio?"

"Ditto. We don't know his parentage or where he came from."

"You're kidding, right?"

"This is a very special person we're talking about, Denny. A dark prodigy, a creature of pure evil."

"Like Kurtz in his jungle temple."

"No, Denny. Kurtz came from civilization. Xhafa was born in a dark place and there he resides, with the power of a mythical monster."

Paull scraped a hand across his chin. "How could he have amassed so much power and influence?"

"McClure likes solving real-life puzzles, doesn't he?"

Paull rose. As he reached the door, the president's voice caused him to turn back.

"There's something else that isn't in the dossier. Arian Xhafa has more money than an Albanian crime lord ought to have."

"The sophisticated weaponry," Paull said.

The president nodded again. "What's the source of his capital, and, just as troubling, how was he able to obtain the weaponry? You need the highest-level contacts for that. Two more mysteries you're tasked with solving."

"You're not asking for much, are you, sir?"

The president produced a thin smile. "Has to be done, Denny, and now. Along with the sudden influx of capital came the ambition to expand his organization outside the borders of Macedonia and Albania—starting with Italy because it's so close, just across the Adriatic, as well as Spain, France, and Germany.

"The Albanians moved in on the Italian Mafia's territory when the Italian police successfully splintered the mob. Power abhors a vacuum. Xhafa saw his opportunity and jumped in with both feet. Now he has to be stopped before he turns his people into a full-fledged international criminal operation."

"So this isn't a strictly humanitarian mission."

President Crawford smiled an ironic smile. "Jesus, Denny, when is it ever?"

Four

THE MOMENT the shrink left, Alli broke down and cried. She wept as she hadn't wept in nearly a year. Her sobs were deep and heartfelt, all the more so because she had forced herself to keep them in abeyance for the hundred minutes or so that the shrink was questioning her. He was a small, dark man with a scraggly beard and a sharp nose. He smelled faintly of tobacco and loss.

Now that she was alone, she desperately wanted to hear Jack's reassuring voice. But the lawyer had taken away her cell as evidence and there was no phone in her uncle's study where she sat on a voluminous, high-backed chair, so familiar to her from the days when her father took her here and she hung out while he and Uncle Hank went downstairs into the cellar to talk. As a young girl, it had never occurred to her to question why they chose the cellar. Later, however, it became clear that they had ensured that the cellar was the most secure place in the house. Security was the last thing on her mind as she thought about the current nightmare in which she was enmeshed.

The study was exactly as she remembered it, filled

with Old World–carved, hand-turned wood, a coffered ceiling, bookcases from floor to ceiling, and an
immense stone fireplace over which a stuffed buck's
head with impressive antlers gazed down on her with,
she was sure, steady compassion.

Forty-five or so minutes later, her uncle and his
lawyer appeared.

Alli was struggling to blot out the sight of Billy
Warren, drained of blood, cut all over, his carotid
breached as if by a vampire's fang, but the image refused to be banished. It hung in her mind like a guest
who, overstaying his welcome, now threatens to take
over your home.

"Alli," Henry Holt Carson said, as he sat down on
the sofa facing her. "How are you feeling?" Behind
him stood Harrison Jenkins, as immobile as a cigar
store Indian.

"How d'you think I'm feeling," she said dully.

"I'm afraid I have no idea."

"That's just the problem!" She honed the accusa-
tory note to a fine point. "Why are you keeping me
here? Why can't I even call Jack?"

"McClure is busy, trying to clear your name, one
hopes," Carson said. "Besides, by court order you
cannot leave here."

"Then I want to speak with him."

"In time, perhaps."

"What the hell does that mean?"

"Alli, I wish you'd learn to curb your tongue."
He shifted, obviously uncomfortable. Then he set
two prescription vials onto the low table between
them. "The psychopharmacologist who interviewed
you . . ."

At the word she stared at the vials. "You want to give me drugs?" She leapt up and, with a backhand swipe, sent the vials flying across the room. "I'm not taking any fucking drugs!" She was white and trembling.

"Alli, I don't think you understand the true nature of your situation."

"Henry, allow me." Jenkins came around and gestured for Alli to sit back down. When she did, he sat on a chair next to her. "The detectives were anxious to take you into custody. I used a technicality to forestall them. Nevertheless, I had to go before a federal judge this morning and defend you with the district attorney breathing down my neck. This much you know. A horrific crime has been committed and there is a tremendous amount of pressure from all sides to find the murderer and bring him or her to justice."

"I didn't kill Billy!" Alli cried. "Why won't anyone listen?"

"I didn't say you killed him. Frankly, I believe you're innocent, but there are two pieces of incriminating evidence that say otherwise"—he held up a hand to stop her protest—"or lead to the conclusion that someone very clever has, for whatever reason, set you up." He took a breath. "Can you think of anyone who would have cause to implicate you in a capital crime?"

She glanced at her uncle before shaking her head. Her eyes drifted away. "No."

Jenkins studied Alli for a moment, then turned to Carson. "Henry, please give me a few moments."

Carson frowned. "Are you sure?"

"Henry, I imagine there is a backlog of calls impatiently awaiting your attention."

Carson grunted, rose, and, crossing the carpet, went out the door, closing it softly behind him.

Jenkins took a deep breath, then turned to Alli. "Now, my dear, what is it you wish to say?" Seeing her quick glance at the closed door, he added, "Anything you tell me is privileged information . . . even from your uncle."

Alli worried her lower lip before she put her elbows on her knees. "Someone is framing me. I mean there's no way I dosed my roommate or killed Billy. God!"

He nodded sagely.

"You don't believe me."

"What makes you say that?"

Alli ran a hand through her hair. "This is a nightmare." She cleared her throat. "Everyone thinks I'm suffering from post-traumatic stress syndrome."

Jenkins waited a moment. "That's it?"

"Yes."

"So it's your contention that you're fine."

"I didn't poison anyone, I didn't kill anyone."

He slid back in his chair and pursed his lips. "I'll take that into consideration."

"I'd like to speak to Jack."

"Would you now?" Jenkins had a way of saying no without actually saying the word. "It is your uncle's opinion that you have formed a . . . how shall I put it? . . . an unnatural attachment to Jack McClure."

She stared at him, wide-eyed. "And you believe that?"

"It doesn't matter what I believe. I work for your uncle."

She stared out the one window at the snaking gravel driveway. All of a sudden, she took up a poker from the fireplace and slammed it against the window. It bounced off, as if the pane was made of rubber. Alli swung again and again, grunting with each swing, without even a single crack to show for her effort.

She whirled on Jenkins just as the door burst open and a man with the massive sloping shoulders and raw, red face of a weightlifter rushed in.

Jenkins raised a placating hand. "It's all right, Rudy. No harm done."

As if to prove his words, he crossed to where Alli stood and took the poker from her. Rudy relieved him of it, and, with a last look at Alli, went out of the study, closing the door behind him.

"The windows are both bulletproof and alarmed," Jenkins said.

Alli turned to the attorney. "I used to come here when I was a kid. I broke that window once. When did that happen?"

"Five years ago," Jenkins said. "Maybe six."

"So I'm a prisoner in my uncle's house."

"I'm afraid so."

His words hung in the room for some time. A phone rang distantly and then stopped. A dog began to bark somewhere outside, its excitement rising.

"You're both mental as anything." Her voice was thin and ragged with despair. She felt herself crawl back into the shell she had created for herself when she had been kidnapped.

Jenkins appeared to be aware of this, because he

said in his most soothing voice, "The most absurd aspect of the accusation is, of course, the torture. Scientific study tells us that the female of the species, though she can be as cold-blooded and capable of murder as a male, rarely has the stomach for torture. On the other hand, it is the torture of William Warren, so disturbing by its very nature, that is dictating this rush to judgment, at least in my estimation. It's also the largest question mark. What did his killer or killers want from him? What information did he possess that they needed to go to such extreme lengths to get from him?"

He regarded her steadily. Clearly, he was looking for an answer from her. She shook her head. "I can't say. I really didn't know him that well."

"Come on, Alli, you two were carrying on a love affair for five months."

"That's just it," Alli said, "it wasn't a love affair."

"No, what was it then?"

"I was . . ." Her eyes darted away for a moment. "I was trying to regain a sense of myself, to, I don't know, feel my body again, to be in control of it again."

Jenkins sat studying her for a while, or perhaps he was pondering her words. At last, he said, "Did you care about Mr. Warren?"

"Of course I did." She hesitated, but it was clear she had more to say. "But not . . . just not in the way you think."

"What do you think I meant?"

"We weren't lovers in the classical sense—like Romeo and Juliet."

"If memory serves, Romeo dies."

She snorted in derision.

"About the psychopharmacologist," Jenkins went on. "One of the things he said about you in his report is that, in his opinion, you're lacking in affect."

"I think *he's* lacking in affect."

Jenkins gave her a tight smile. "What his diagnosis means is that, basically, you have difficulty locating your emotions. Sometimes you can't find them at all. In other words, there are times when you just don't care about anything . . . or anyone."

She looked away again.

"His evaluation will hold a great deal of weight in the course of the investigation. Typically, people who can't feel—"

"I told you," she flared. "No fucking drugs!"

"You're not listening to me," he continued doggedly. "Your reaction to your boyfriend's death—or rather your lack of one—was duly noted by everyone at the crime scene, including those sympathetic to you."

"You can't possibly understand."

He spread his hands. "Now is your chance to enlighten me."

She stared at him, stone-faced.

Jenkins sighed heavily. "In return for you being held in your uncle's recognizance instead of in a federal holding cell, the judge ordered a psychiatric evaluation." He took another breath and let it out slowly, as if anticipating the coming storm. "You must comply with the psychopharmacologist's diagnosis, which, of course, includes your taking whatever psychotropic medications he prescribes."

Alli leapt up again and retreated behind the chair

back, as if he were a lion from which she needed saving. "I can't! I fucking won't!"

"I'm sorry." Jenkins regarded her with what seemed to be genuine pity. "I'm afraid you have no choice."

DAYLIGHT SEEPED into the grove of trees with the blue-white flicker of a television screen. Jack, exhausted and frightened for Alli, had been scrutinizing the crime scene for hours. The detectives had made their reluctant exit, but Naomi Wilde and Peter McKinsey remained, along with Fearington's commander, Brice Fellows, who had had sandwiches and thermoses of strong black coffee brought out from the academy's commissary. Fellows, to his credit, stood back, sipping coffee, silently observing him as he worked. Jack was unfamiliar with McKinsey, but he had gotten to know Naomi well enough when she was guarding the FLOTUS. Carson had plucked Naomi out of her daily assignments specifically to guard his wife. That was how Edward Carson did things—by instinct. In thinking of Lyn Carson, Jack realized that no one had informed Alli that her mother was dead. On reflection, Jack supposed such news was better left undelivered for the time being.

Jack had spent his time wisely. As soon as there was sufficient natural light he switched off the spots and got to work. He had learned to distrust spotlights, which tended to distort perspective and played havoc with the impressions received by his brain. Circling the body in ever closing circles, his dyslexic brain literally took pictures of the corpse—not only the ashen color and unnatural granular quality of the skin, the grotesque disfigurement of body and face, but aspects other people could not see or perhaps accurately interpret. His brain, however, worked more than three hundred times faster than other people's, and so it could recognize tiny anomalies and dislocations, and, in the time it took a human being to inhale and exhale, analyze them.

This was how he discovered the fracture below the left eye. It was precise, like a break a surgeon would make in the process of resetting a bone. There was, also, a deliberateness about it that intrigued him. He said nothing of either his find or his musings to the people in the grove with him.

He stood up and said to Fellows, "Commander, do you really believe Alli capable of this crime?"

Fellows's meaty shoulders lifted and fell. "To be honest, Mr. McClure, I found myself a failure at human psychology the moment my wife of twenty years walked out on me without a word of explanation."

He turned. "Naomi?"

She shook her head. "I can't imagine it." Her brow furrowed. "On the other hand, she's like a closed book to everyone except you, so I'd ask you the same question: Is she capable of this kind of protracted violence?"

"Absolutely not," Jack said.

"But we have the vial with traces of roofies under her bed," McKinsey pointed out, "and a bloody knife in the trash behind her dorm."

Jack nodded. "We've yet to determine whether it's Billy's blood on the blade, or if her prints are on the haft."

"And if they are her prints?" Naomi asked.

He waved away her concern. "Someone has gone to a lot of trouble setting her up. This has been meticulously thought out."

"What about the bizarre nature of the murder?" McKinsey said. "The knife wounds, draining the victim of blood?"

"Red herrings," Jack said, "designed to get us going around in circles."

McKinsey made a noise in the back of his throat.

"What," Jack said, "you think there's a vampire infesting Fearington?"

"Of course not, but don't you think it's possible that when Alli found out about this other girl . . ." He snapped his fingers.

"Arjeta Kraja," Naomi cut in helpfully.

"Right. Isn't it possible that when Alli found out Billy was boffing Arjeta Kraja she flipped out?"

"And the sky could be falling," Jack said acidly. "Let's deal with reality."

McKinsey shrugged, as if to say, I tried.

"Something stinks in this setup." Jack peered again at the corpse. "It's weird, gothic, over the top. We need to find out where the stink is coming from."

"We need to talk to this Arjeta Kraja," Naomi said. "ASAP."

Jack nodded, only partly engaged. There was another thing he was reluctant to share with Naomi and McKinsey. He had the nagging suspicion that Alli knew more about this girl than she had let on. Why she would keep that secret was anyone's guess, but Jack knew Alli well enough to know that she must have a damn good reason. She better have.

No one would tell him where she was taken. Jack

had called Henry Carson's townhome in Georgetown without luck.

Jack, his mind made up, turned to Fellows. "I want
to interview Alli's roommate."

VERA BARD lay on a bed in the academy infirmary.
The pinkish light of dawn streamed in through windows and a small skylight high up in the ceiling. The
walls were painted a cheerful yellow, but the floor
was institutional gray linoleum, a veteran from another era.

The nurse led Jack over to Vera's bed. Alli's roommate was a dark-haired girl with large, slightly upswept chocolate eyes, an assertive nose, and a wide,
expressive mouth.

"Please, just for a few minutes," the nurse cautioned. "She is still very weak."

Fluids dripped into Vera's arm and her eyes were
hooded, as if she was having trouble staying awake,
but this only made her seem sultry. She looked vaguely
Eurasian. Her long hair had lost its sheen to sweat; it
lay lankly on the pillow in thick, Medusan coils. Still
and all, Jack observed, she was an exceptionally beautiful young woman.

He sat on a painted metal chair and introduced
himself. "Vera, would you tell me what happened last
night?"

"I . . . I don't know." Her voice was soft and husky.
"I went to bed as usual, read for a bit, took my pill,
as usual, and went to sleep." She licked her dry lips.
"The next thing I knew I woke up here."

"Alli was in the room when you went to sleep?"

"Yes."

"And while you were reading?"

"Yes."

"Did you two talk at all?"

"Before I went to the bathroom we were talking about . . ." Her brow crinkled. "I can't remember about what. Boys, maybe."

"About Billy?"

"I don't know. Maybe."

"And after you came back from the bathroom?"

Vera shook her head and a lock of hair fell across her cheek.

Jack sat for a moment more. He smiled at her. "I'm sorry for what happened."

Vera seemed not to have heard him. She licked her lips again. "I want to see Alli."

"I'll speak to Commander Fellows." Jack rose. "By the way, what medication are you taking?"

"Crestor. I have high cholesterol."

Jack nodded and smiled. "Thank you, Vera."

On the way out of the infirmary, Jack encountered Naomi.

"DNA is going to take at least a week," she said, "but the forensic team found Alli's fingerprints on the water glass beside Vera's bed."

"Anyone else's?"

"Just Alli's."

Jack's cell phone buzzed, and then Dennis Paull was speaking rapidly and tensely in his ear. He strode down the hall, away from Naomi and McKinsey, who had appeared.

"A new position?" Jack said after a moment. "Is Crawford kicking you out?"

"Not exactly." Paull further explained the changes. "You're coming with me, Jack. I'm pulling all the details together. At midnight you and I are going to fly to Macedonia, then trek west into the mountains to a shithole called Tetovo, where we will terminate this sonuvabitch Arian Xhafa."

Jack bit back a protest. Though Paull had made it clear that he was sympathetic to Alli's plight, Jack suspected he'd simply argue that there were other people—Naomi Wilde chief among them—who were perfectly adequate to being Alli's advocate. Besides, in Harrison Jenkins she had one of the most savvy criminal attorneys on the planet. Jack could hear him now: *Forget it, Alli's in good hands.* The trouble was, that was only half true. No one knew Alli the way he did, and she wasn't about to open up to anyone else, Naomi included. And keeping silent wouldn't help her cause one iota.

Instead, he said, "Just like that? From what you've told me he's exceptionally well defended and well armed. He won't be easy to kill."

Paull laughed. "I may have spent the last several years behind a desk, Jack, but believe me when I tell you that I still have a trick or two up my sleeve."

FIVE

ALLI, WALKING slowly around her uncle's study, spent the slowly ticking seconds dragging her fingertips across the tops of books, the contours of artifacts and souvenirs, the outlines of framed photos of her uncle with presidents past and present. She paused at a photo of the two brothers and stared at her father. He was smiling into the camera, his hand on his older brother's shoulder. Judging by the hazy mountains in the background, they were out west somewhere, doubtless at one of her uncle's ranches. He clutched a ten-gallon hat in one fist.

She was certain she ought to feel something at the sight of her father's face—a sense of remorse, of pain, of a space inside her into which he had once warmly nestled—but she felt nothing. It was as if her heart had been turned to wood, burned to ashes in a fire, and was now a heart in name only, a hollow vessel, useless as a desert in which nothing could live.

She tried to think of incidents in the past—her time with Emma, Jack's daughter, and more recently, her adventures with Jack himself in Moscow and the Ukraine. All of it felt like a dream, or a film she was watching without becoming fully engaged. Briefly she tried to fight her way out of the disassociation, but it was too difficult for her to defeat. There was a good reason for that, too. Without being aware of it, she had developed a mechanism for keeping her distance from the week of terror when she had been imprisoned in the small, lightless room and subjected to . . .

She was still in a prison, one of her own making.

A barrier came up, like a wall of lead stopping Superman's X-ray vision. Her own X-ray vision— her habit of peering backward into that one section of her past, examining that week, picking at it as if it were a scab that wouldn't heal—had to be thwarted at all costs, even to the loss of feeling in the present.

She made a little inchoate sound in the back of her throat, as a fox will when caught in a spring-loaded trap, when it is about to gnaw off its paw to regain its freedom. The truth was she longed to talk with Annika, though this was the one thing she must always keep from Jack. It was Annika who had convinced Jack to let her go see the mistress Milla Tamirova, who had taken Alli into her BDSM dungeon and made her confront her terror at being tied into a chair. Why had Annika done this? Because she, too, had been held hostage. She knew the hell into which Alli had descended because she had inhabited that very same hell. Unlike Alli, however, she had managed to escape. If only she could meet with her again, but neither she nor Jack knew where she was.

Despair took her up and shook her as a terrier will shake a rat it has caught. She wanted to cry, but her eyes remained dry. She took up a Frederic Remington bronze sculpture of a cowboy on a horse rearing up at the sight of a rattlesnake, and raised it over her head. She felt a burning desire to smash it into a glass vase, but lowered it back onto the shelf.

She knew the noise would bring Rudy, who might decide to stay in order to ensure she didn't commit more acts of vandalism. Being imprisoned again, even in her uncle's study, was making her nuts. An icy ball of panic had sprung up in her gut, and with each rotation was increasing in size. She had to get out of here, and soon. She needed to find Jack, but she had no way of contacting him. *There must be some kind of way out, said the joker to the priest.* She laughed silently and grimly. Jack had told her there was always a way.

She looked around the study, inhaled the familiar scents of leather, her uncle's cologne, the remnants of cigar smoke floating like dust motes in the air. Closing her eyes, she tried to recall afternoons when she was a little girl, curled up in this very chair, inhaling the same scents. She had often been left alone while the grown-ups had conversed as only grown-ups can. She couldn't remember how that had occupied her time. Despite the changes in seasons and times of day, all the afternoons blended one into the other.

Abruptly, her eyes popped open. She had spent her alone hours exploring the nooks and crannies, drawers and shelves of Uncle Hank's domain. Unfurling her legs, she rose from the chair and, taking small, silent steps, she approached the huge burl walnut desk. As a child, it had seemed as enormous as a battleship or a castle, and filled with as many secrets.

But what had seemed like treasures to a little

girl—a box of matches, a handsome humidor, a photo of a little girl—didn't now. She no longer played with the brief and tiny flames, the odors of cigars repulsed her, and the little girl in the photo was Caroline, Uncle Hank's daughter from his first marriage, who was now either dead or alive, but was, in any event, as lost to him as if she had fallen off the edge of the world. She had known Caroline, if only briefly. Playing with her, she had seen a darkness in her eyes. Only much later, long after Caro had vanished, after she herself had gone through a period of fear and suffering, had she recognized the nature of that darkness. Caro had been consumed with an inarticulate pain and rage. She had hit her breaking point and was gone. After the disappearance, Uncle Hank had questioned her, apparently believing she might know what happened to Caro. After that day, Alli had never heard him mention her again.

With her fingertips caressing the desktop, she wondered what secrets lay within the depths of her uncle's burlwood castle. She started from the bottom up, figuring that secrets were safest in the depths. The left lowest drawer held a strip of hanging files, all pertaining to InterPublic Bancorp—memos, letters, quarterly P&Ls, and the like. She pawed through them with little interest, the bottom of the file holders scraping against the bottom of the drawer. The drawer just above was not as deep. It contained the usual stacks of pads of various sizes, packs of yellow pencils, a red plastic child's sharpener, gum erasers, and various sorts of tape. How very neo-Luddite of Uncle Hank, she thought. Save for some spent pencil shavings and a broken bit of pencil lead, the top drawer was entirely empty. The wide middle drawer directly above the kneehole was filled with the sort of accumulated odds and ends—paper clips, staples, rubber bands, and Hi-Liters in several colors—endemic to all offices. The three drawers on the right held, variously, stacks of political magazines like *The Atlantic*; a half-filled bottle of single-barrel bourbon, along with a pair of shot glasses in a holder; a paper packet of cough drops; a metal flask, dry as a bone inside; and a grease-stained take-out menu from First Won Ton, in Chinatown. She scanned it quickly. One item, a Chef's Special, spicy fragrant duck with cherries, was circled in pencil. Beneath the menu was a photo of Caroline and her mother. Caro was young, ten or eleven maybe, but already you could see that she strongly resembled her mother, Heidi, who was tall, slim in an athletic way, blond—pale as a ghost, really—with a high, intelligent forehead and light eyes; it was impossible to tell what color from the photo and Alli didn't remember her well enough to recall whether they were blue or green or hazel. Mother and daughter looked like two equestrians, models out of a Ralph Lauren ad. Sad now to think of Heidi somewhere on the West Coast and Caro in the particular level of limbo reserved for the disappeared. Alli put the photo and the take-out menu back, and closed the drawer.

Perhaps there was nothing.

She sat back on her heels, rocking back and forth thoughtfully, as she stared at the desk. On an impulse, she pulled open the drawer with the hanging files. She pushed them back and forth on their metal tracks, listening to the scraping, dry as an insect's chirrup. All at once, a frown creased her face and, pushing the files as far as she could to the rear, she peered down at the bottom of the drawer. Looking again at the outside, it appeared as if there was a two- or three-inch differential. Rapping a knuckle against the bottom of the drawer, she heard a hollow echo, but feeling around there was no way in. Pulling the files toward her, she drew the drawer out to its fullest extent. A tiny half-moon indentation in the wood presented itself.

Hooking her fingernail into it, she pulled and was rewarded with a meticulously milled rectangular piece of the drawer's bottom detaching itself. Inside the hidden cubbyhole she found a cell phone, and that was all. She double-checked the space before fitting the cover back on, pushing the files back into place, and closing the drawer.

She walked to the study door, pressed her ear against the carved and polished wood, and heard the murmuring of her uncle's voice as he talked with other men, then the muffled slam of the front door. Crossing to the window, she was just in time to see her uncle and Jenkins climb into the backseat of a gleaming black Lincoln Town Car, which immediately drove off in a spray of gravel.

Returning to the wing chair, she curled up and examined the cell. Though it was a brand she recognized, the model was one she had never seen before. She wondered whether it was an old model. Most people threw away their old cell when they got a new one; they did not hide it away in a secret compartment of their desk. She pressed the On button. The phone lit up immediately, connecting to a network. So it wasn't an old phone, or, if it was, its SIM card was still active. Plus, the battery was fully charged.

She waited for the network to give her a signal, but nothing showed except a tiny red SOS.

"Shit on a fucking stick," she muttered. She'd heard stories of certain hotel chains using wireless dampers to keep their clients from using cell phones in their rooms, forcing them to use the hotel's more expensive wired system, but why would Uncle Hank employ one in his house, except as a security measure.

She stuffed the phone in her pocket and tried to get a grip on her rising panic.

INTERVIEWING ARJETA Kraja was proving frustrating, principally because she seemed to have vanished.

"It's as if she never existed at all," Pete McKinsey said when he, Naomi, and Jack rendezvoused in the small suburb closest to Fearington.

"Her name doesn't come up in any government database," Naomi said, consulting her PDA. "Nor does she possess a driver's license, health insurance, or even a Social Security number."

"Family?" Jack asked.

"Negative." McKinsey shuffled from one foot to the other as if he were itching to go someplace.

"Friends?"

"Not anyone we could find when we canvassed the area."

"So either she's a ghost," McKinsey said.

Jack nodded. "Or she's an illegal immigrant."

"Either way," Naomi said, "she's gonna be a bitch to find."

"Which is going to take time," McKinsey said.

They were talking like partners now, or an old married couple.

"Time is the one thing we don't have," Jack told them, and because he didn't want to tell them about his leaving with Paull, he gave them a song and dance about Alli's legal status, as if Jenkins had given him an update. "So we need to find the girl now."

McKinsey was clearly unhappy with being given what was, in his estimation, an impossible task. "How do you propose we do that?"

TWILIGHT, THE bar both Billy Warren and the elusive Arjeta Kraja had supposedly frequented, was on a seedy section of M Street, about as far from the tony shops and town houses as you could get and still be in Georgetown. A sign on the door said that it was closed, but when Jack hit the brass plate the door opened. When they walked into the dimly lit interior, they were greeted by air that smelled burned.

Detective Willowicz, smoking idly, sat on a tipped-back chair, his ankles crossed on a table. Detective O'Banion was behind the bar, drinking what appeared to be whiskey from a shot glass. No one else appeared to be around.

Williowicz exhaled a cloud of smoke. "Well, what do we have here?"

"Place is closed," O'Banion said. "Wassamatter, can't read?"

"I could ask the same of you," Jack said, then to

Willowicz: "I thought I told you the case had been turned over to my department."

Willowicz contemplated the glowing end of his cigarette. "I think I might have heard something of that nature. What's your memory of it, O'Banion?"

O'Banion pulled at his earlobe and shrugged. "In this town, anything's possible." He poured himself another shot. His fingernails were filthy.

"So what are you doing here?" Naomi said.

"Satisfying an itch." Willowicz watched them with a jaundiced eye.

"Checking the liquor license." O'Banion swallowed his whiskey. "Shit like that."

"The Metro police need detectives for that?" McKinsey was shuckling back and forth like an engine revving up. "You guys must really have screwed the pooch."

O'Banion laughed nastily and slammed the shot glass down on the bartop. "Shut it, Nancy."

"Where is everyone?" Naomi said. "The day manager, the bartender?"

"We just got here," Willowicz said.

"How the fuck should we know?" O'Banion added.

"That's enough," Jack said. "You two can clear out." He took out his cell. "Your captain is waiting."

Willowicz dragged his feet off the table and stood up. "The thing of it is, my partner and I don't like being treated like second-class citizens."

"Then stick to your own turf."

"We see this situation and it reeks," Willowicz said. "Where you see a former president's daughter, we see a perp."

"No," Jack said, "you see an easy way to wrap up this case. It doesn't matter to you if she's guilty or not."

"Oh, she's guilty." O'Banion came around from behind the bar. "Guilty as fuck."

"It's just a matter of time before we prove it." Willowicz brushed by them and out the door, O'Banion hard on his heels.

"Metro has a hard-on for Feds." McKinsey relaxed visibly. "We're always treading all over their cases, so all they can do is shit on us."

"The hell with them."

"Seriously." Jack turned and walked toward the short corridor that led to the restrooms and the rear. "Where the hell is everyone?"

Then he paused. What had he sensed or smelled?

"Blood," Jack said, sprinting down the corridor. He heard Naomi and McKinsey just behind him.

"McKinsey," he called. "Restrooms."

He heard McKinsey banging open the doors, then his raised voice: "Clear!"

Two men sat in side-by-side chairs facing the far wall of the small, cramped kitchen. Jack came around to face them. It was not a pretty sight. Both their faces looked like sides of raw meat. Blood had spilled down the front of their shirts, buttons ripped off, the flaps spread open. More blood oozed down their necks onto their chests. Based on their clothes, one seemed to be the bartender, the other the day manager.

Naomi knelt in front of the bartender. "Dead."

Jack pressed two fingers against the manager's carotid. "So's this one."

Both McKinsey and Naomi drew their firearms simultaneously.

"What the hell is going on?" Naomi said.

"It answers the question," Jack said, already on the move, "why there were Metro detectives where there should have been no Metro detectives."

Six

"**W**ELL?"

"Everything has gone according to plan."

Henry Holt Carson nodded. His shoulders were hunched against the brittle wind. The sky looked like porcelain and it seemed to him as if the sun would never shine again. Like the residents of Seattle, he was getting used to the gloom.

"Paull is gone?" he asked.

President Crawford nodded. "And, as you predicted, he's taken Jack McClure with him."

"Good."

Carson looked around him. This time of year the Rose Garden was a rectangle of mush and fertilizer, the sturdy rose stems prickly and dangerous as a porcupine's back.

"I still don't quite understand," the president said.

Carson closed his eyes for a moment. A pulse beat in his forehead and he was certain a migraine was coming on. As was his wont, he fought against it. "They were too close to my brother."

Crawford's brow furrowed deeply and he snorted like a horse. "Do you think they suspect?"

"I don't know." Carson put a hand to his head. Yes, a migraine, definitely. "I hope to God they don't."

"But McClure—"

"My brother told me all about McClure's monstrous brain."

"Then you know it's only a matter of time before he figures it out. That can only lead to more blood being spilled."

"Yes," Carson said through gritted teeth. He did not nod or move his head in any untoward way. "That's why I want him gone. By the time he does figure it out, it'll be too late. The only way to him that wouldn't cause suspicion was through Dennis Paull." He clamped down on the migraine but, as always, it was getting the better of him.

"Still, I worry."

"The American people pay you to worry."

Carson turned, fumbled in his trousers pocket, opened the silver-and-gold pill case, shook two pills into his mouth, and swallowed them with the little saliva he had left. The migraines seemed to suck him dry, until his tongue felt as if it were as big and unwieldy as a zeppelin.

The president eyed his Secret Service detail, circling the garden like a murder of crows. He took a hesitant step toward his friend. "Hank, I think you'd best sit down."

Carson waved him off. "I'm fine."

"Of course you are. But, you know, I find I'm a little peaked." He sat on a stone bench. "Here, sit down beside me so we can continue our private talk uninterrupted. I haven't much time before the budget meeting."

Carson came and sat, holding his body as delicately as if it had turned to glass, which, in a way, it had.

Crawford looked away for a moment, out over the grounds to Washington itself. The White House was like a pearl sitting in the middle of an oyster, peacefully protected. However, today the president felt anything but peaceful.

"I knew this job was going to be difficult," he said after a time, "and I prepared myself for it." He stared down at his hands, folded priestlike in his lap. "But as for the complications . . ." He allowed his voice to drift off like mist off the Potomac.

"Life *is* complications, Arlen. The higher you climb the more they pile up, until you have one cluster-fuck after another."

"Well, then, this must be the mother of all cluster-fucks." Crawford took a breath. "Then again, maybe we're not speaking of complications at all, maybe it's *compromises*."

Carson said nothing; he was too busy trying to keep his thoughts from being shredded by the cyclone of his migraine.

"Maybe it's selling the house down the river without even a wave good-bye."

Suddenly, the president's words flooded into his brain, and he turned his head ever so gently. "For the love of God, do not tell me that you have cold feet, not at this late date. Fuck, Arlen, I moved heaven and earth with both the party caucuses and Eddy to get you the vice president's position. We had a plan, from the very beginning we had a plan."

"No, Hank, *you* had a plan."

"Have it your way." Carson massaged his temples, slowly and methodically. "What mattered then is the same thing that matters now. You hitched your name to my star. You rose as I rose."

"You need me, Hank."

The laugh caused Carson some pain. "Are you trying to convince me, or yourself? The truth you keep avoiding is this: You need me far more than I need you. If you bail on me now there will be dire consequences. You knew from the very beginning, when you're in, you're in for life. Your decision is irrevocable."

The president shook his head. "That was then. From where I'm sitting now—"

"You're sitting in the perfect place for what needs to be done. Fate had a hand in this, the same fate that took Eddy from me. Scales of justice."

Now it was Crawford's turn to laugh. "What a hypocrite you are, Hank. There is no justice in this world. It's men like you who see to that."

OUT ON the street, there was no sign of O'Banion or Willowicz. Jack called in to the Metro detectives' unit. Willowicz and O'Banion existed, Carson's lawyer had been read their jackets, but the real Willowicz and O'Banion were on temporary leave. So who were these two masquerading as the Metro detectives, and who were they working for? The only way to find out was to ask them, so Jack sent McKinsey and Naomi out to search the surrounding blocks. Maybe the bogus detectives got careless and left some trace behind, though he doubted it. Those two were hardened professionals who left nothing to chance.

He stayed behind, preferring to check the crime scene without distractions. While he studied the two new victims, his mind was feverishly at work. First Billy Warren gets himself tortured and killed, but not before the perp goes to the trouble of setting Alli up as the killer. Then Arjeta Kraja goes missing. Billy, Alli, and Arjeta were all seen here at Twilight, and now the manager and bartender, the two people who might have had some information about the trio, wind up murdered by two goons pretending to be O'Banion and Willowicz.

He bent down to check that his finding here with the bartender was the same as the one he'd noticed on the manager. Yes, it was true: In both cases the bone just below the left eye socket had been fractured, just as it had been on Billy's face.

He recalled the fracture beneath Billy's left eye. Ever since then he'd been going under the dubious hypothesis that Arjeta Kraja had killed Billy. After all, excluding Alli, she was the prime suspect in the triangle, and, further, if she were in love with Billy, she'd have reason to want to pin the murder on Alli. It was a shaky premise because the fracture was precise. It couldn't have been made by someone in a rage. Further, the theory didn't explain Billy's torture. If she loved him, she might, in a rage, kill him. But torture him? No way.

And now, with these two murders, the hypothesis was evaporating altogether. Arjeta Kraja killing these two in league with O'Banion and Willowicz? It didn't track for him. Of course, O'Banion and Willowicz could be behind all three murders, but how to explain the deliberateness of the fracture?

The bogus O'Banion and Willowicz were obvious muscle; working stiffs. Someone far more clever than they had mapped out this scenario. Something was horribly wrong, but even with racking his brain, he couldn't figure out what. He didn't have enough pieces of the puzzle yet.

One thing was for certain, however: The link between these murders and Billy's completely exonerated Alli. So he called in to his office to get the crime scene covered. He directed them to have the three corpses sent to his old friend Egon Schiltz, an ME he trusted absolutely. He was about to head out onto the street in search of McKinsey and Naomi when an image flashed through his mind, and he turned back.

The manager's left hand was on the table, the palm open as if offering something when he was killed. His right arm hung down at his side, partially obscured by the table. Jack went around and took a longer look at what his brain had glimpsed the first time. The manager's left hand was a fist, so tight the nails had scored bloody half-moons in the skin of his palm.

Crouching down, Jack pried open the fingers one by one. Something bright and shiny dropped to the floor. He picked it up and, rising to his feet, took it over to the light streaming in through one of the windows flanking the front door. It was a small metal badge, such as one would pin to a lapel or a collar. It was octagonal and had some writing on it, but all Jack's brain saw was the shape. The writing itself was a tiny whirlpool of moving units. He tried to concentrate, as Reverend Myron Taske had taught him to do, by creating the entirely quiet spot in the air just to the right of his head. He tried looking at the badge from that viewpoint, which allowed him to calm the whirlpool of mysterious symbols, painstakingly turn them into the three-dimensional letters he had learned to identify, so he could read. All he could discern was that the badge contained no words in English. As to what language the words might be, he had not a clue. He had learned to speak many languages, perhaps in compensation for his difficulty in reading, but it was moments like this, when he was confronted by the wall of his dyslexia, that still vexed him.

Fighting the intense frustration and helplessness that threatened to overwhelm him, he picked his way to the plate-glass window, as if daylight and the passing traffic could calm him. He wondered why the club manager had been so desperate to hold on to the badge, to keep it hidden from his killers. At the same time, he was calculating who to take the badge to—a linguistics professor, an expert in local criminal gangs, or an underground slacker. The possibilities were virtually endless and made his head hurt.

He stared out the window. It had begun to rain, rather a soft gray mist that muted colors and softened edges so that everything seemed the same, like time-abraded soapstone, the present already faded into a past that could never be retrieved.

All at once, he felt a cool breeze stroke his cheek.

"Emma?"

"*I'm here, Dad. It seems easier to be near you when . . .*"

Jack, hearing his dead daughter's voice in his head, stared at the corpses.

—When I'm near someone dead, I understand.

"*Not dead. Newly dead. Before the body has*

cooled. While the spirit is still undecided about whether to go into Darkness or into the Light."

—But, you, Emma, you've chosen neither. How is that possible?

"*How is life possible? How is any of this possible?*"

—I have no answers, Emma.

"*Neither do I.*"

—Nevertheless, I'm happy you're here.

OUT ON the street, McKinsey and Naomi split up. McKinsey went east, Naomi west. McKinsey had been seconded into the Secret Service after a stellar six years as a Marine in first the Horn of Africa and then Fallujah. Again and again, he had engaged the enemy at whites-of-their-eyes range and lived to not tell the tales. Those grisly tales were locked away in his brain, under lock and key demanded by the various security acts his government imposed on him. He was proud of those secrets, proud of the kills he'd made in the service of his country, for he fervently believed in protecting America, whatever it took. He would have willingly given his life for that belief, but, when it came to war—and specifically guerilla warfare—he was too smart, too wily. The Marines were sorry when he was rotated out for the second time. Then the DoD decided it had a more important task for him.

McKinsey walked easily and loosely, without a trace of military bearing, blending perfectly into the foot traffic on the streets. At the same time, his well-honed radar—an ability to sense anything out of place on the field of battle or in enemy territory—combined with his keen sight to vet each person he glimpsed, even if it was only for a second. He quartered his immediate environment with military precision while appearing to window shop. It was important, he knew, to check the interior of shops, cafés, and restaurants, because contrary to how movies and television shot these things, foot chases were more often slow and plodding, more a question of thinking like your prey than being faster with foot and gun.

He paused in front of a café, thinking he'd spotted Willowicz, but a waitress moved out of the way and he saw that he was mistaken. Nevertheless, he entered the shop, checking the L-shaped space in nooks and crannies not visible from the street. Then he went into the men's room, checked all the stalls, before finding his way back out onto the street. He was now a number of blocks from Twilight, having moved in an expanding spiral from the locus of the nightclub. He went into a public garage and looked around.

Clear.

NAOMI'S TREK west soon took her past several boutiques and a medium-sized restaurant, which she entered, ignoring the manager, picking her way around the tables and banquettes, searching for any sign of O'Banion and Willowicz. She checked the kitchen, where workers looked at her curiously, sullenly, then she backtracked to the men's room. She was neither shy nor squeamish. Taking out her ID, she held it in front of her as she kicked open the door and strode in. One man, at a urinal, jerked around, wetting his polished brogues. A younger man, at the sink, looked her up and down in the mirror and gave her a wolf whistle. She grinned at him, then turned her attention to the stalls.

Naomi had come to the Secret Service because her older brother had expected such a career path for her. She adored him; he had brought her up after their parents had died in a plane crash over the Himalayas. She had been six, a vulnerable age. She had missed her parents terribly, particularly her mother. Her brother hadn't been able to do anything about that. Instead, he had instilled in her a sense of self-worth and of purpose before he had shipped off to Afghanistan. Eight months later, he had been returned home in a body bag.

She had chosen the Secret Service, partly because she could not bear to leave D.C., which was her hometown. An orphan had to feel close to something from her past, and, for her, the District was it. Still, she missed her brother, who was still her best friend. She was closed and she knew it; after her brother had moved to New York, she had isolated herself. She had some acquaintances, a couple of drinking buddies, both male and female, and an employee of DoD whom she counted on from time to time for a booty call. That was it. Except for Jack McClure, for whom she had been carrying a torch ever since they had first met when he was in ATF and still married to that bitch, Sharon. Now that he was officially on his own, though, she found that she lacked the skills, or tools, to let him know how she felt. The fact was, she was as terrified as she was attracted—a cul-de-sac from which she had yet to extricate herself.

Finding neither of the false detectives inhabiting the dank stalls, she retraced her steps to the kitchen, passing through it, and out the back door into a grim alley lined with garbage cans. A Dumpster hulked not far away and, because she was nothing if not thorough, she lifted up the green top and peered in. Using a metal rod she found in the alley, she held her nose and stirred the garbage, jamming the rod into several spots. Garbage and more garbage. She dropped the rod, closed the top, and visually checked either end of the alley.

Choosing one end at random, she moved off.

WALKING UP the garage's ramp, McKinsey thought about the Horn of Africa. That dungheap was never far from his thoughts. Fallujah had been blindingly bright with danger, and any number of his buddies had perished there, most in terrible ways he'd rather forget, but in Fallujah he knew the enemy, even when it was a hurt teenager packed with explosives. He could smell death in the air, and he knew how to deal with it.

The Horn of Africa was an entirely different story—a morass of terror and betrayal. Death lurked not only in every shadow and around every corner, but in the brilliance of sunlight, an extended hand, a warm smile, a whisper of friendship and support. Nothing was as it appeared to be. It was all dark theater, complete with masks, trapdoors, and unknown ringmasters out to skin you alive and string you up for the vermin to feed on. In all his travels around the world, McKinsey had never felt the sting of such implacable, bitter hatred as he had in the Horn of Africa. He liked it there; it was like living on Mars.

Soon enough he reached the topmost level, and walking to the gray late-model Ford, he pulled the passenger's side door open and got in.

"What the fuck?" Willowicz said. "This McClure bastard is going to screw everything up."

SEVEN

JACK EXPERIENCED Emma's laugh as another breath of cool air on his cheek. He no longer bothered to wonder whether he was losing his mind, whether the ghostly visitations or whispered voice were real or figments of his guilt-ridden brain. The truth was she knew things he didn't, things he couldn't know.

—Emma, where are you?

"Who knows? I'm in twilight, neither light nor darkness."

—Shades of gray.

"Not even that. Everything is just gray . . . unchanging gray."

—I'm so—

"Don't say it, Dad. Don't say you're sorry. We're both in a different place now."

—I wish that were so.

"There is peace here, total and absolute, but it's just out of my reach."

—I don't understand.

"I don't either. But it's why I'm here, in this place,

close to you, unable to reach you. I feel like Sisy-phus."

—Cursed to eternally roll the stone up the hill, only to lose control of it, seeing it roll down to the bottom and trudging back to try again.

"Yes. But that doesn't mean I'm not learning."

Jack was surprised.

—Learning. In what way?

"I can see things now—see them clearly, in a way that was impossible to do when I was alive."

—Your perspective has changed.

That odd breath of a laugh. *"There is no perspective here, Dad, just as there is no time. Everything just is. You're so involved in criminality it became an obsession of mine. I studied every text I could find on human criminality, but it wasn't until now—to put it in life's terms—"*

—Terms I'll understand.

"If you like. Anyway, I can see now that the criminal personality—Dad, you'll really like this—is formed from two sides of a coin, both terribly dark. On one side, criminality is born of misdirected re-sentment, a logic, if you want to call it that, of self-destruction. Remember how you and I were drawn to the paintings of Paul Gauguin? At one point, his beautiful, mysterious work was the only thing we could agree on. You know why, Dad? Because of his philosophy. He wrote, 'Life being what it is, one dreams of revenge.' An Impressionist painter wrote that! Can you believe it?

"Anyway, the other side stems from being totally self-absorbed, like the Roman Emperor Nero. What

the hell, the little prick inherited virtually limitless power before he had a chance to grow up. To him, no one outside of himself was real—what happened to them didn't matter in the slightest, so murder, rape, torture, and mayhem were beneath his notice."

Good God, Jack thought. *This can't be happening.* And yet, he couldn't help himself . . .

—Where is she, Emma?

"Where's who?"

—You know. Annika. Where is she?

"You swore you never wanted to see her again."

—That was almost a year ago. A lifetime.

"Even if I did know, Dad, I couldn't tell you. I'm not your guide through this darkness."

Did she know? Jack wondered. And then realized he had said it out loud.

"Jack?"

He almost cracked his neck, turning around so fast. Naomi and McKinsey had reentered Twilight.

"We lost them," she said.

McKinsey, looking around, said, "Does who know?" He couldn't keep a smirk off his face. "Who were you talking to?"

Ignoring his comment, Jack told them about the fractured left eye socket that linked the murders here with Billy Warren's.

"That exonerates Alli," Naomi said with clear relief.

McKinsey shook his head. "Or it could signal that she's not in it alone."

"Don't be absurd," Naomi said. "You don't know her."

"In my experience," he told her, "nobody knows anyone. Not really."

Jack wanted to move in a more fruitful direction. "Look what I found." He showed them the badge. "The manager was clutching it in his fist, as if he wanted to protect it from O'Banion and Willowicz." As they examined it in turn, he said, "Either of you make any sense of the writing?"

As they were shaking their heads sirens sounded, rapidly approaching.

Naomi took the badge, fingering it as if the writing were in braille. "I think I know someone who can help us."

"I bet my wife knows plenty of linguists," McKinsey said. "She's a professor at Georgetown."

"The person I'm thinking of isn't a linguist." Naomi was turning the badge over and over, as if trying to coax a sense memory from it. "I think I've seen something like this before." She glanced up at Jack with a penetrating look. "If I'm right, we're headed into a very dark place."

ALLI SLEPT because of exhaustion, but also to escape the horror of the present, the gruesome image of Billy bound to the tree, blue-white as the moon, and just as distant.

Curled in her uncle's wing chair, she was dreaming about the last snow of winter. It drifted down upon the vast, terrifying expanse of Moscow's Red Square like glittering confetti. Lights that illuminated the onion domes of Saint Basil's seemed to enlarge each flake to a monstrous size. Alli breathed in the frozen, knifing wind as she ran through the clusters of tourists, Red Army soldiers, and cassocked Russian Orthodox priests—robins, hawks, and ravens picking over the ground for sustenance.

She ran in frantic circles, as if lost, rudderless, without any thought save to find Annika. A strange form of hysteria gripped her, as if she were dying, and only Annika could save her. She pushed past people, who whirled like the snowflakes, their eyebrows and lashes powdered white, their eyes staring past her as if she didn't exist, or was already dead. Her dread increased exponentially, tightening her chest, making her heart pound as if she were running a long and terrible race.

And, against all odds, she saw Annika, light hair and deep mineral eyes, outlined against the stark, massive edifice of the Kremlin. She was staring at Alli, but made no move toward her as Alli struggled against the tide of people that tried to pull her away toward the dark, shadowed fringes of Red Square where certain death lurked like a staircase at night. Still, she kept struggling forward, only to find that she was in a different section of Red Square altogether, seeing Annika from a different angle, now closer, now farther away. Grimly, she pressed on, determined.

Then, all at once, breathless and on the verge of tears, she stood before Annika, who was dressed in an ankle-length coat embedded with the bones of what might be small animals. Alli wanted nothing more than for Annika to take her in her arms and rock her like a child.

But Annika said, "Why have you come all this way to see me? Life is a doomed enterprise."

"I need to talk to you."

"Talk is a hopeless activity, like looking at a blank page."

"Please don't say that!"

"Would you rather I lie to you?"

"You lied to Jack."

"But not to you, never to you."

"You lied to him, don't you see it's the same thing."

"I lied to protect him, I lied because I loved him."

"Do you love him still?"

Annika looked at her pitilessly. "How can I help you?"

"Please answer me."

"Why? Would you understand? What do you know of love, how it can shape a heart, how it can twist it, shatter it. Have you experienced irretrievable loss?"

"Yes, yes! We both have. We're the same, you and I—"

"No, Alli. I am darkness, I am death." She stepped away into the spiraling snow, and called back, her voice echoing off the walls of the monolithic Kremlin and Saint Basil's, "Don't come after me. . . ."

Alli awoke with an unpleasant start. Her heart was pounding so hard it hurt. She looked around, disoriented, surprised to find herself still in her uncle's study. Her vision was blurry. When she put her hand up to her face her fingers came away wet with tears. She had been crying in her sleep.

She leapt off the chair as if she had received an electric shock, and turned when she heard the door open. Rudy, the guard who looked like an ex-professional wrestler, came into the study. He closed the door behind him and picked his way across the polished wooden floorboards toward her. He had an odd, almost delicate way of walking that was entirely silent, as if he were barefoot. She watched him, fascinated, as he put his right foot in the precise location his left foot had just vacated.

It was only when he was very close, and about to swing it, that she saw the iron poker in his hand.

Eight

Dime-store slim had one hand. Seemingly, he was proud of it, or rather the stump, which had ingenious metal pincers affixed to it, as if he was in the process of turning into a crab-man or the creature from *Predator*.

He certainly had a personality to match, Jack thought, as Naomi Wilde introduced him and Mc-Kinsey. Dime-Store Slim was very tall, very narrow, and very dark-skinned. He had kinky hair, which he wore in a 70s-style Afro, like an outrageous hat on a runway model. On him, though, it looked ominous rather than incongruous or theatrical, as if that pitch-black cloud of unknowing could reach out and swallow you alive.

Dime-Store Slim liked to shake hands with his pincers, which he proffered in an unavoidable gesture. In fact, he thought it was hilarious to witness other people's consternation and embarrassment. In contradiction to his slight frame, he exuded a powerful menace that was impossible to ignore or to deflect. You simply had to deal with it, Jack realized, long before McKinsey did. He was amused to see how uncomfortable Slim made the Secret Service agent.

"Why'd you think I'd know what this is?" asked Slim, slouched on a chair with his long legs up on a crate of Mallomars, fingering the badge Jack had handed him. They had found him in the rear of his Smoke Shop in a section of Northeast Washington so burned out it seemed an irredeemable slum. Slim seemed to like it that way. Even if this ant hill was grubby, he was king of it. Plus, the area was among the city's most dangerous neighborhoods. That, too, was quite all right with him. The more dangerous the better. Piratically, he wore a large .45 semiautomatic stuck in the waistband of his jeans.

McKinsey's expression darkened as soon as he noticed the handgun. "D'you have a permit for that weapon, son?"

Slim was off the chair in a flash, his Doc Martens banging loudly against the floor. "Who you calling 'son,' fool?"

Compounding his error, McKinsey flashed his ID. "The United States government, that's who."

Slim had the .45 out, the muzzle stuck in McKinsey's face, before the agent knew what was happening. "Ain't no United States government in *this* part of the world, motherfucker."

"Easy." Naomi held up her hands placatingly. "Let's all stand down."

"Tell *him* that," McKinsey said in a voice that was thin and strained to the point of breaking.

"She ain't gonna tell me, nuthin, motherfucker." Slim cocked his head toward Naomi. "Why you bring these fools into my house, anyways?"

"We all need someone to laugh at," Jack said, before she could answer.

There ensued a kind of stunned silence, during which McKinsey's face turned red and Naomi's mouth formed a tiny O. Then Slim started to laugh. He laughed so hard he could no longer keep up the pretense of being pissed off. He stepped back, slid the .45 back into his jeans, and returned to his beat-up old lounge chair.

"Fuck!" His forefinger jabbed out at Jack. "I know whys you brought *this* motherfucker, um-hum."

He nodded, and then brought out a pack of rolling paper and a plastic bag of pot, deliberately, to Jack's way of thinking, antagonizing McKinsey further. The agent stiffened and Jack saw Naomi's hand grip his arm.

"Why don't you go back outside and make sure we aren't disturbed," she said in a soft voice.

After hesitating enough to regain a modicum of self-respect, McKinsey said, "Fuck this shit," and, shaking her off, stalked out of the shop with a gunshot bang of the front door.

"Nice fucking sonuvabitch," Jack said, which returned Slim to a state of helpless laughter.

At length, he wiped his eyes, rolled his joint, lit up, and offered to share. They both declined.

"Straight'n'narrows, the two of you." But it wasn't said unkindly.

"The badge," Jack prompted.

"The what?"

Jack pointed to the small metal object he was holding.

"Oh, you mean this? What the fuck, do I look like

Sherlock-motherfucking-Holmes?" He lifted his head and hollered, "Grasi! Get your ass over here!"

A moment later, a dark-headed kid, who could not have been more than eighteen or nineteen, sauntered into the back room. His starkly corded body marked him as a gym rat. So far as Jack could see, there wasn't an ounce of fat on him. He wasn't muscle-bound like a lot of gym rats; rather, he'd sculpted his body to become a lean, mean, fighting machine. The normally laughable description that reminded Jack of a scene in the comedy *Stripes* was never more apt.

"We call him Grasi," Slim said, "because he's got some fuckin' unpronounceable foreign name, don't you, Grasi?"

Grasi grinned. He wore black jeans, custom high-tops, and an anachronistic leather vest over a white T-shirt that showed plenty of his chest. He had a ton of bling around his neck, and tattoos, most of them amateurish-looking. "Can't buy a fucking vowel to save my life."

Slim tossed him the octagonal badge. "You got a name for this?"

Grasi deftly caught it with his fingertips and held it up in front of his face. In almost the same motion, he tossed it back to Slim. His eyes slid sideways. "Never seen anything like it before."

Slim sighed. "And there you have it, sports fans." He shrugged as he handed the badge back to Jack, and said to Naomi, "I always try to be of service, but . . ." Again his shoulders lifted and fell.

"Thanks, anyway," Naomi said. "It was worth a shot."

Grasi turned to go.

"Hold on a minute," Jack said. "Can you show me where the bathroom is?"

Grasi nodded disinterestedly, and Jack followed him out into the shop proper.

PETER MCKINSEY stood with shoulders hunched, hands thrust deep into pockets containing any number of concealed folding weapons whose honed steel both energized and soothed him. He was oblivious to the light rain or the passing vehicles. With chin jutting and lips pursed, he was sunk deep inside his thoughts.

He had met Willowicz six months into his tour of duty in the Horn of Africa. Willowicz's name was different then, but the man was the same. McKinsey and Willowicz felt an immediate kinship, possibly because they held the same worldview. Their intense and uncompromising gung-ho attitude was nothing more than a facade beneath which existed a rich layer of nihilism. The interesting thing was that neither was conscious of this Nietzschean tendency; they would have vociferously denied it, even if confronted with the truth.

They were fearless, which meant that they were reckless in everything they did, skating along the edge of the black ice of death without ever succumbing to its embrace. They killed, maimed, tortured, and slaughtered the intractable enemy with the righteous zeal of Crusaders or priests of the Spanish Inquisition. They liked to invoke God's name while they laughed, splashing in blood and gore, grinding guts and organs to the consistency of motor oil. Spurred on by the seemingly limitless enmity they encountered every minute of every day and night, there was nothing they wouldn't do to their enemy to make him give up secrets out of the agony they inflicted, never thinking for a moment that these secrets might be concocted in order to end the pain. But no matter how many of the enemy they destroyed, the full measure of the satisfaction they craved never materialized. No matter how hard they tried, no matter how much pain they inflicted, they could never engender in their prey the terror they longed to see. These people were different, inhabiting an entirely different plane of existence than the Americans.

"They're not human," they would tell each other, over the stink of their high-minded work or, later, during bouts of heavy drinking. "If they can't feel terror, they can't feel any emotion. They're for sure not human." If it wasn't satisfaction, it was impossible, during those sessions, to know what emotions McKinsey and Willowicz felt.

That was then. Today they were back home, in different jobs, but with precisely the same mind-set. The trouble was, neither of them could leave behind their time in the Horn of Africa. Like a malarial fever, their exploits rose into their consciousness, regular as an ocean tide, dragging with it a swath of man-made sludge: cracked skulls, congealed blood, fractured bones, and bits of gray matter. It was not enough; nothing was enough. And so the two of them existed like creatures of the dark, bloodthirsty, vampiric, unwilling or unable to readjust to a civilization hamstrung by laws that entangled the forward thrust of their urgent missions.

He didn't like being left out of whatever was happening back inside Slim's crap-joint, but he recognized he only had himself to blame. Seeing these people lounging around with .45s in their belts infuriated him. If he had his way, he'd fire-bomb every one of them. Fuck civil rights. People like Slim didn't deserve to hide behind the laws that were meant to put them in the slammer. He belonged facedown in the gutter. Not for the first time, McKinsey wished he were back in the Horn of Africa.

"I dream about that place," he'd said to Willowicz as they'd sat in the gray late-model Ford. There was no need to be more specific, they spoke in the shorthand of war when they were together.

"Every night," Willowicz said. "But sometimes I think it's a place I made up."

McKinsey stared out the window at the grayness. "What are we doing here?"

"Our jobs," Willowicz said. "Like always."

McKinsey nodded, but with the air of a person staring at something he could see with no real clarity.

"Everything was clear-cut over there," Willowicz said, as if reading his friend's mood. "Here, nothing makes sense."

"We did what we wanted, what was needed. Now what? We put one foot in front of the other. Like old men whose lives are behind them."

"We're in a goddamn fog of unknowing."

McKinsey let out a long breath. "McClure changed ME's on us. The new one, Egon Schiltz, isn't on our payroll."

"Then we'll put him on it."

"Sadly, no." McKinsey sounded disgusted. "Schiltz is a personal friend of McClure's. He won't bite and, what's worse, he's sure to inform his pal of the approach."

Willowicz shifted in his seat. "Then I'll kill the fucker."

"Good idea. That for sure won't alert McClure."

Willowicz drew his neck in like a turtle. "Or we can do nothing. Like toothless old men."

A short, poisonous silence ensued.

"Fuck it!" McKinsey kicked open the door and launched himself out.

Leaning over, Willowicz said, "Be careful of that dirtbag McClure."

McKinsey made a gun with his thumb and forefinger and started down the ramp.

Now, with the rain in his face, he shook out a cigarette and lit up. Smoke drifted past his eyes, obscuring a world he despised, a world in which he did not belong.

GRASI POINTED out the grubby door of the toilet and started off toward the front of the shop.

"Hey," Jack said, "what's your real name?"

The teenager turned back. "Everyone calls me Grasi."

"Even at home? Even your mother?"

"I have no mother." Grasi said this matter-of-factly, without a hint of remorse or self-pity.

Jack came toward him. "'Grasi' is a Romanian word. It means fat. You aren't fat."

"It's a fucking joke, man."

"You Romanian, Grasi?"

The youth stuck out his jaw. "What the fuck of it?"

Jack shrugged, even as he lunged forward, grabbed hold of the bling around Grasi's neck, and yanked it off.

"Little fuck-nuts!" With a soft *snik!* a switchblade appeared in Grasi's fist.

As he advanced, Jack threw the bling back to him. All except one piece: a gold pendant in the shape of an octagon. Jack had noticed it when Grasi was supposedly studying the badge. When he spoke, Jack knew he was lying.

Jack held the pendant and the badge side by side. "They're identical," he said.

Grasi flicked the tip of the wicked-looking blade.

"You're smarter than that," Jack said. "I'm not your enemy."

Grasi laughed. "Fuck you, you're not my friend."

"That depends." Jack kept his eye on the tip of the blade. "I'm the only one who can keep you out of jail now."

"I ain't done nothing, fuck-nuts."

Jack held up the pendant and the badge. "These say you're lying. We're investigating three very nasty homicides. This badge is our only clue. D'you get it? You know something I need to know. If you hold out on me, I'm going to throw your ass in jail for suspicion of murder and obstructing a federal homicide investigation. Believe me, you won't like it in federal lockup. The inmates there eat your kind for breakfast."

For a moment, Grasi looked around, his eyes rolling madly. Then he licked his lips and flicked the switchblade closed. "Thatë. My name is Thatë."

WITH THE iron poker's fall, Alli felt a scream bubbling up into her throat. She forced it aside, converting it into a shout of defiance, as she ducked behind the wingback chair. The poker slammed into the padded top, splitting the fabric, flaying off stuffing, as it would have Alli's skin and flesh.

Rudy, expecting her to make for the door, backed up to stand squarely in her path. But Alli had no intention of heading for the door, at least not yet. She lunged toward the fireplace and grabbed the ash shovel, which was unwieldy but with its wide head approached the defensive-offensive combination of a medieval mace.

Rudy, seeing her struggle with the shovel, laughed.

Good deal, Alli thought. In situations like this her diminutive size was a tremendous advantage. Because she still carried the appearance of a young girl, she was treated as such. She waited, showing Rudy how difficult it must be for her to hold the shovel for any length of time, let alone swing it as a weapon.

"You're dead, you know that," Rudy said as he came at her, poker held high.

Alli didn't bother to answer. Instead, she watched the weapon, its increasing arc, as Rudy, massive shoulder bunched, drew it back and swung it at her.

The poker made a whistling sound, like a bird in flight, or an arrow. She waited for the last minute, as Jack had always instructed her, then brought the broad shovel head into the path of the arc. A hard ringing, like a struck bell, and sparks flew. She staggered beneath the power of Rudy's blow, more than was necessary to steady herself.

Rudy, a fierce grin plastered across his face, moved in, cutting off her line of retreat, backing her up against the fireplace.

"There's a fine spot for them to find you." His rising excitement turned his voice guttural. "Curled in the fireplace with the soot and the ash."

"When people talk, their attention wavers," Jack had told her, and, as usual, he was right. Even as Rudy was mocking her, she lowered the shovel as if it had become too heavy for her, and swung it hard into the side of his left knee.

He groaned as the joint crumpled and he lost his footing. The poker fell to the floor as he grabbed his knee in agony. Alli tossed aside the shovel and ran. As she passed him, she kicked him in the side of the head. Then she leapt over him and, sprinting across the study, threw open the door, and raced out into the hallway.

Behind her, she could hear Rudy cursing, climbing noisily to his feet, then shouting to his fellow guards, alerting them to her escape. One of them appeared in the hallway ahead of her. He drew his sidearm and she backed up, turned, and heading back, raced around a corner, taking the first branching that presented itself.

She knew the layout of her uncle's house well, though she hadn't been in it for years. Now she headed for the kitchen, which had both a back door and a large larder with a trapdoor down to the root cellar, which Uncle Hank had converted into a temperature-controlled wine cellar.

She could hear the heavy tramp of thick brogues pounding behind her, and Rudy's voice bellowing like that of a maddened bull. By her count, there were three guards. She knew, more or less, where two of them were, but where was the third?

She got her answer a moment later, as he stepped out of a shadow and slammed her in the back just before she reached the kitchen. He drove her into the bathroom from which he had just exited. Arms pinwheeling, her lungs gasping to pull in air, her foot skidded on the floor mat and she slid into the gleaming porcelain wall of the bathtub. Her left arm broke the plane of the plastic shower curtain, and she pulled it down around the guard as he reached over to grab her. Driving her body upward, she sought to entangle him in the stiff folds. She smacked away his grasping fingers. She could see his features twisted and distorted with effort through the translucent curtain, and when she slammed the heel of her hand into his nose a bright red rose of blood bloomed on the plastic, obscuring his expression. But she could feel the growing dismay and, possibly, panic in the frenzied movement of his limbs, the uncoordinated shaking of his head like a wolf in a trap. She popped him one more time on the bridge of his nose and he lay still.

She turned, pushed the body off her, and stood, slamming the door shut. There was a pounding in her head and she felt her gorge rising. The taste of stomach acid burned her throat. She shivered as she put her ear to the door, waiting for the sound of brogues to resume, but instead she heard whispers and recognized Rudy's voice. Intuition told her what they were talking about. She could not use the little-girl act on Rudy again, and now was certain she couldn't use it on the other guard, either. Bending down, she drew the unconscious guard's .38 from its holster.

"Conlon!" Rudy called. "Conlon, are you okay?"

The cool heft of the handgun in her fist felt good, her forefinger lying beside the trigger like a cobra ready to spit its poison. There was an intoxication that came from holding a loaded gun, a sense of power that seemed to flow from the weapon into her hand, racing up her arm and into her brain. And it was this disorienting, larger-than-life feeling that caused her to remember what Jack had told her. *"I'd rather face an adversary with a gun than one with a knife,"* he'd cautioned her. *"Guns make you overconfident, they make you feel as if you can overpower any adversary, and that's where the real danger to you raises its head."*

The problem was simple enough: She was in a cul-de-sac with no other egress but the one door; there was no window in this interior bathroom. This was why Rudy and his partner hadn't stormed in. They didn't know the situation in here, other than the fact that Conlon had been neutralized. But that also meant she was now armed, so they were waiting for her to emerge, at which time they would grab her and disarm her before she had a chance to shoot either one of them.

A shootout would only get her killed or wounded, so she couldn't risk even poking her head out the door to assess the situation. She had to make do with whatever was available in the bathroom.

Her hands were shaking, her heartbeat elevated, her breathing erratic. Turning to the medicine cabinet over the sink, she scanned the shelves. She'd heard about spray cans, any of which she could have put into service now, but nowadays only pump sprays were available, and were of no use. But, scrounging around in the cabinet under the sink, she found a bottle of drain cleaner. Judging by its weight, it was at least half full. Her fear was palpable, a bitter, metallic taste in her mouth. She sought to tame it, because eradicating it was a waste of time.

Several deep breaths later, she jammed the bottle into the waistband of her jeans at the small of her back, and turned her attention back to Conlon. He was still unconscious. Watching him softly breathe, an idea occurred to her. It might be crazy, but for the life of her she couldn't think of a better alternative.

Temporarily sticking the .38 into her left front pocket, she bent and, grunting, lifted Conlon in his sticky cocoon onto his feet. It seemed a long, laborious project, but at last she had him on his feet, propped against the wall beside the door. She took a moment only to regain her breath, then, yanking open the door, she pushed him into the hall.

A moment later all hell broke loose.

Someone grabbed for Conlon as he fell into the hallway. In a blur of motion, she tossed the contents of the bottle of drain cleaner all over the front of the suit's shirt. He immediately recoiled, shouting in shock and pain, Conlon's insensate body toppled to the floor, and that was all the time she got. She tore herself away from other hands clawing at her from behind.

Vaulting over the fallen men, she ran toward the open doorway to the kitchen, but as soon as she got there she was forced to jump over the body of the cook or the gardener—one of Uncle Hank's staff, anyway—which lay crumpled just beyond the doorway. With no time to find out if the man was dead or alive, Alli made for the back door. After being trapped in the bathroom, she had no desire to trap herself again down in the wine cellar.

She reached the glass-and-wood door more or less at the same time as her pursuer. She felt his powerful hand on her shoulder, pulling her backward, and, drawing the acquired .38, she whipped the barrel at his face. She heard a satisfying crunch of bone fracturing, and, released, she whipped the door open and fled outside.

It was raining, and she skidded badly on the slick flagstone surface leading to the gardens that comprised the inner circle of property at the rear of the house. She heard his breath first, then felt him on top of her as she struggled to regain her footing.

"Got you now, you little bitch," Rudy said.

NINE

JACK MOVED the young man deeper into the rear of the shop to make certain no one overheard them.

"Go on," he urged.

"Underground," Thatë said.

"How far underground?" Jack asked.

"Not far enough . . . now." Thatë made a disgusted sound at the back of his throat.

Jack saw that McKinsey had turned around and, staring through the front window, was watching him and Thatë talk. He wondered if McKinsey could lip-read. Turning his head away, he said to Thatë, "I want you to move into a section of the store where we can't be seen from the street."

Thatë did as Jack asked, and Jack soon followed him.

"I don't like those two," Thatë said, clearly referring to McKinsey and Naomi.

"You don't like me, either."

"Yeah, but them I'd knife—for real."

"You really are a badass."

Thatë didn't know how to take that, so he did not respond.

"About the octagon symbol," Jack prompted.

"A club."

"I know all about clubs."

"Not this kind of club." Thatë's eyes cut away, as if he'd rather be anywhere but here.

"And that would be?"

"Shit, don't make me say it."

"If I don't," Jack said, "someone else with a uniform and a much different attitude will."

Thatë put his head down. Maybe this kind of life was getting too much for him, maybe he wasn't cut out for it.

"Nothing legal about it."

Jack took a step toward him. "You'd better have more for me than that."

"Hold on. Don't lose your shit all over everything." The boy worried his lower lip, which was growing redder by the moment. "The club has a name. The Stem."

Jack was going to say that he never heard of a club named the Stem, but instead he held his tongue. Something here didn't feel right, the way it hadn't felt right at the Billy Warren crime scene. He studied Thatë's face, which held an expression of anticipation. In this situation it was the wrong emotion, as if he was waiting to see if "the Stem" held a special meaning for Jack.

Jack looked at the octagons—the badge and the pendant. He could focus on the one word that was identical to both of them. After a short struggle, he said to Thatë, "Pronounce this word for me."

"What?"

"This word." Jack tapped the octagons.

Thatë's eyes slid away again for a moment, and Jack could read him now. He might as well take advantage of the teen's nervousness.

"Speak it!" he ordered sharply.

"*Rrjedhin.*" The word almost caught in Thatë's throat, but he managed to splutter it out.

That was a word in a language with which Jack was familiar. Without missing a beat, he said, "*Sa jveç jeni?*"

RUDY SMELLED unpleasantly of blood and sweat. He was as heavy as a Brahma bull and, lucky for Alli, as ungainly. His wounds had both maddened and impaired him. Blood streamed down his face, forcing him to blink continually to clear his vision, and it seemed as if his left knee, where Alli had struck him with the ash shovel, was shattered, because he dragged the leg behind him like a wrecked ship. But as she tried to get up, he used it like a club, the massive limb slamming against her hip so that they both cried out in pain at the same time.

But Rudy's fist was already in her face, the heel of his hand pushing the underside of her jaw back, back, exposing the soft, vulnerable flesh of her throat. She heard a deep, guttural growl that threatened to turn her insides to water. She fought the desire to close her eyes, to let go, to release herself utterly into the undertow of his fury-fueled power and strength. There was a terrible, enervating moment when she experienced the female's sense of acquiescing in the face of the male's overwhelming brute physicality, both of body and personality. But then, remembering who she was, how close to both death and madness she had been, she shook herself awake, shook herself alive, and drove her forefinger straight up Rudy's left nostril, pushing farther even as his head whipped back and forth like a bronco trying to unseat its rider. The soft, moist flesh of his sinus yielded to her fingertip, the arc of her nail slicing through tissue. Up farther into the bone of his skull, searching for the cavity that would end the threat to her life.

With a herculean effort, he threw her off him, clear over a hedge of azalea bushes. She rolled into a thick stand of pitch pines just beyond, the needles sweeping across her face like bony fingers. She could hear him snorting and moaning, flailing to regain his feet.

"I know where you are, little bitch! You're beginning to believe you'll get away, but fuck if you will!"

Rolling through the bed of fallen needles, she reached behind her for the .38, but it was gone. She must have lost it when Rudy had tossed her. Rudy began to crash through the azaleas, dragging his left leg behind him. Then she remembered the cell phone.

Pulling it out of the pocket of her jeans, she saw to her immense relief that there was a signal, now that she was outside the house. Her heart hammered wildly as she punched in Jack's cell number.

She groaned as it rang and rang. She prayed for him to answer. Instead, she got his voice mail. "I'm at my Uncle's Hank's hunting retreat in Virginia. The guards he hired are after me." She recited the address. "I'm out back with a fucking ginormous dirtbag on my ass. Please, please, please get me the fuck out of here."

How old are you? That was what Jack had asked.

"*Shtatëmbëdhjetë,*" Thatë said. Seventeen.

"*Ju jeni shqiptar.*" You're Albanian.

"*Si nuk ju flas shqip?*" How do you speak my language?

Jack smiled and tapped the side of his head. "You're going to take me to the Stem."

All the color drained from Thatë's face. "No."

"Yes," Jack insisted.

"*Ju lutem, mos bëni mua.*" Thatë began to shiver. "*Ata do të vrasin mua.*"

"Who'll kill you?" Jack asked. "Who are you so afraid of?"

But the teenager was in a panic, shaking his head back and forth, and Jack suspected he'd gotten everything out of him he could.

"All right." Jack handed him a pad and pen. "Don't say another word, just give me the Stem's address."

Thatë's hand shook as he wrote a line on the pad. Jack took the writing implements back, then he asked for the teen's cell. He took note of the number, then added his own cell number to the other's phone book. "Now we know how to get in touch with each other. *Mirë?*"

"*Mirë.*" Thatë nodded weakly.

The vibration of Jack's cell had become too insistent for him to ignore any longer. He hadn't wanted to be disturbed, especially by Dennis Paull, who he was concerned might be calling him to move up tomorrow's departure time. Jack needed every hour he could get in D.C.

But it wasn't Paull; it was Alli. Shit, he should have picked up the call right away. Even as he was listening to her desperate message on his voice mail, he was heading out of Dime-Store Slim's. He heard Naomi's voice asking a question behind him, but there was no time to answer. He slammed open the door and sprinted out into the rain-slick street.

ALLI, SHIVERING with the chill rain and the tsunami of adrenaline racing through her, lay in the shelter of the copse of pitch pines, to give Rudy less of a target. There was no use running. He had a gun and she didn't. The minute she turned tail he would spot her and bring her down. Better to wait here and think of how to avoid being found.

And then, as she heard him rooting around in the fringes of the evergreens, she realized her error. She was thinking like a rat or a mouse—like the prey. She forced herself to forget that Rudy was armed. How would she deal with him? It was up to her, she knew. Even if Jack picked up the voice mail right away, who knew where he was and how fast he could get here? No, she couldn't—she *shouldn't!*—count on him. It was up to her to stop Rudy.

The obtrusion of a root caused her to shift her position. Rolling over, she found herself momentarily looking up into the webbed branches of the pitch pines. That's when the idea came to her. Rudy was drawing ever nearer. Scrambling to her feet, she grabbed hold of the lowest solid-looking branch and swung up. Though their wood was soft, pitch pines were easy climbs, with plenty of long, spreading branches. Carefully, she moved upward until she sat on a thick, nearly horizontal branch perhaps fifteen feet above the carpet of needles. A quick glance above her head convinced her that there was no point in climbing higher.

Staring at the roughly circular area below her, she waited for Rudy. Not the prey now—the hunter.

Soon enough, she heard him picking his way through the underbrush. He certainly was making no effort to be quiet, and when he came into view she realized why. In his left hand he held the .38 she had lost. His own .38 was in his right. He knew she was unarmed; he had no need to be discreet.

She knew she had to time this right; she wouldn't have a second chance. She bolstered her courage with the belief that her small size would work in her favor. As he came under her perch, she slid off and fell with legs spread. Landing on his shoulder, she clamped her thighs tight around either side of his head.

He staggered with the shock and the unexpected weight, but instinct took over instantaneously. He raised both weapons, firing them blindly. Alli knocked them sideways, then reached down to his face. The best wound is a new wound, she thought, as she attacked his nostril again, inflicting such pain that he roared and tried to use the .38s as cudgels, battering them blindly against her thighs and hips.

But she had got her grip and wasn't going to let go. His head raised up in order to lessen the pain, but all this did was give her finger easier access. As she plunged it in all the way, his eyes rolled up, his left knee gave out, and he toppled over. He swung out wildly as he fell, the side of the gun barrel in his right hand slamming into her ribs, knocking the breath out of her. She tumbled off him, lost her hold on his nostril, and fell heavily to the ground.

On hands and knees, bleeding profusely from his nose, Rudy crabbed his way after her. He was almost upon her when she grabbed a broken branch. It was old and rotten, but it would have to do. She swung it in a shallow arc into his left knee. Rudy screamed, grabbing for the agonized joint. Alli snatched up the .38 he had let go of and, reversing it, brought the heavy butt down on his temple once, twice, three times.

It was some moments before she realized that Rudy had stopped moving. She stared down at his ugly face. Blood still oozed from his nose, and a thick dribble of it stained one corner of his mouth. Without thinking, she took his own .38 and lay it beside Conlon's. The two weapons looked incongruous on their bed of rough, brown needles, as if they were now without will, without a reason to exist. She wished they would dissolve into the earth.

Staring into Rudy's bloated face, she was never more repulsed. His aggression was enough to put her off men forever. She was reminded of a story Emma had told her of Attila the Hun's death, which, Emma had said, with a grim laugh, had served him right. He had died when a major artery burst in mid-thrust, as he was deflowering one of his beautiful virgins. She wished the same fate for Rudy, a true Vandal in the historical sense, who had delighted in terrorizing her.

Alli found she was weeping. All around her the rain dripped and slithered. She tasted it on her lips, felt it sliding down the back of her neck. Both the rain and her tears tasted of blood. She knew she should move, but she could not. Like the guns, she lay on the bed of needles, without will or volition, resting, heart pounding in her chest, waiting. . . .

That was how Jack found her.

She looked at him as he knelt down to scoop her up. "My hero," she whispered. And, then, in a louder voice, "You look like crap."

Jack laughed, and at that moment cop cars, sirens blaring, started to converge on Henry Holt Carson's house from both east and west.

TEN

DENNIS PAULL was at Claire's apartment in
Foggy Bottom when he heard about the debacle
at Carson's country residence. The news came via a
text message. He stared at it a moment in disbelief,
long enough for his daughter to ask what was wrong.

"Nothing," he said, sliding his PDA back into a
breast pocket.

"Business, Dad. Always business." Her voice was
mocking rather than admonitory.

"The government never sleeps."

She laughed. "No, Dad. It's *you* who never sleeps."

She put a delicate-fingered hand over his. They
were sitting on a sofa in her living room, companion-
ably, even lovingly, side by side, in a manner he'd
never have believed possible up until about a year
ago. That's when he and Claire had reconciled, when
he had met his grandson, Aaron, for the first time.
For him, it was love at first sight; he was certain
Aaron felt the same way. At seven, he'd been in desperate need of a father figure, and Paull had striven to
be just that, rather than the indulgent grandfather

that might be the norm. Claire's strong suit wasn't discipline, something every child required, in his opinion. Clearly, Claire agreed, because she allowed him his head with Aaron. On the other hand, he was careful not to criticize her parenting skills, which were exemplary in all other aspects.

In some respects, he still felt as if he were walking on eggshells around her. He was dismayed that he no longer knew her. When she came back to him, she was, to all practical purposes, a stranger. She didn't even look the way he remembered her. She had left him when she was still a girl. Seven years later, she had returned a woman. While a certain disconnect should not have come as a surprise to him, it nevertheless did. She was his flesh and blood. He and his wife had raised her, and now it seemed to him as if she were someone else's daughter. His heart fractured at the thought, though he never for a moment allowed her to see his pain. Besides, the break was essentially his fault. Recognizing that was his first giant step toward reconciliation, both with Claire and inside himself.

"How long will you be gone, Dad?" Claire stirred half-and-half into her coffee. She liked it light, no sugar, but strong, he had learned. When she had left, she hadn't been drinking coffee at all. So many differences!

He sighed. "I wish I could say."

"Even if you knew, you wouldn't tell me, would you?" She smiled to show him there was no need to answer.

He glanced around the room. It astonished him how quickly and easily a woman could make a home cozy, warm, and bright, right down to the photos and little knickknacks and souvenirs. All he required was a laptop, a comfortable lounge chair, and a well-stocked bar. Oh, and his stack of history books—the history of warfare, the fall of the Roman Empire, the history of medicine, of philosophy, of the struggle between Catholics and Protestants, between Christianity and Islam. The depressing fact was that they all came down to one thing: war, killing, death.

"What will you tell Aaron?"

"The truth, so far as I know it." She took a sip of coffee, then put her cup down. "One thing I've learned out of all this pain, Dad, is the importance of the truth. I strive to raise Aaron with that in mind."

Paull studied his daughter. He didn't know whether to pity or admire her. Perhaps it was both. That's how life was, anyway, he thought, always a series of choices, always a series of contradictions, some of which could be untangled, others not. It was learning to distinguish one from the other that proved to be a bitch.

But, he thought now, just the fact that he felt pity toward her was a prime example of how long he had lived in the shadows, because one couldn't survive there without learning to lie. Where he toiled, lies were a necessity. And very soon—so soon, in fact, it was disorienting—lies became the norm. That was where he was at when he began manipulating the man Claire wanted to marry. The result? She had told him to go fuck himself when she found out, married the man without Paull knowing, and then divorced him. In the meantime, his wife got old and sick, and he just lost interest in everything.

That's what had happened to him, he reflected, and to so many of his compatriots. The ones who it hadn't happened to were dead. So, too, his wife, but he had been given a second chance with Claire and with Aaron, and he meant to make the most of it.

He couldn't take his eyes off Claire. She was so beautiful he had difficulty believing that he'd had a hand in creating her. She didn't look like either him or Louise. Maybe like one of Louise's aunts, or possibly a little like his own grandmother, his father's mother, who was definitely a looker. Despite her looks, she had no one. She'd left her idiot husband and now wanted nothing to do with him. Aaron despised him, so happily there was nothing more to say on the subject.

"Are you seeing anyone new?" he said.

"Oh, Dad . . ."

"Just asking."

She considered for a moment, turning her cup around in its saucer. "Okay, there is someone." She held up a hand. "Before you start the inquisition, I'm putting the subject off-limits. We just started dating and . . . Well, there's nothing more to tell."

"Okay."

She cocked her head, her deep gray eyes inquisitive. "Really?"

He nodded, smiling. "You're a grown woman, Claire. You can make your own choices."

She put a hand over his again. "Thank you, Dad."

Sad commentary on their past relationship, he thought, that she felt she had to thank him for considering her an individual. He sighed internally.

More muddy water under the bridge, one more sin to atone for.

He rose. She looked as if she were about to say, Leaving already? but instead she bit her lip and, rising as well, produced a bittersweet smile and kissed him on the cheek.

"Be safe," she whispered.

He headed for the door. "Tell Aaron I love him." He turned back to her. "You, too."

That bittersweet smile was still in place as he walked out the door.

"WHAT THE fuck happened here?"

McKinsey said it, but Naomi felt it. They had arrived at almost the same time as the first state police responders, having done their best to follow Jack's reckless driving. On their obligatory tour around Henry Holt Carson's country estate, Naomi was gripped by trepidation. The place was crawling with state police investigators and forensic personnel. A veritable armada of official vehicles, including SWAT armored trucks, filled the driveway, overflowing onto the immaculate lawns. Surely an overreaction, she thought, until she saw the havoc wreaked: the cook and gardener recovering from being knocked out cold by person or persons unknown, one guard's chest burned to a crisp and a second one with a broken nose, and the third . . .

"I have a bad feeling about all of this," she said as she stared down at the corpse of Rudy Laine.

"Join the club." McKinsey, glancing up, got rainwater in his eye. "Once again in the fucking trees."

"The fun never stops." Naomi knelt down beside the body. "As advertised, dead as a doorpost."

"And twice as ugly."

She sighed, rising. "Does anyone know what the hell went on here?"

"Not the cops, but a million bucks says McClure does."

She checked her phone, frowning. "He's not answering his cell. No one knows where he is."

"Ditto the First Daughter." McKinsey put his hands on his hips. "Odds are they're together."

Naomi said nothing, but she knew that he was probably right. Jack had a habit of going off the reservation, but this was a particularly bad time for it. The Virginia State Police were howling to question Alli—at the very least. She was the prime suspect in Laine's death.

"The two guards said Alli Carson attacked Laine in the library, ran out, struck Conlon down as he was about to exit a bathroom, then she and Laine got into it for real. The fight spilled out to the rear of the house, he heard gunshots being fired. One guard was busy in the shower washing off the drain cleaner he said Alli threw at him, but by the time Conlon got here the other one was dead and the First Daughter was gone."

"What if the guards are lying?"

McKinsey shot her a skeptical look. "I know you've got a soft spot for the girl, kiddo, but come on. First off, the guards' stories corroborated one another."

"They had time to concoct it before the police arrived," Naomi pointed out.

"Secondly, they work for Fortress, one of the most highly regarded security firms in the country. The First Daughter's uncle hired them to keep her safe and out of lockup." He spread his hands. "Face it, everything's against her." He cast a glance back over his shoulder to where Henry Holt Carson and Harrison Jenkins stood conferring heatedly with a chief of the state police. "Murder, battery, violating a federal judge's order of recognizance, I don't know if even her uncle's contacts or his famous lawyer's legal tricks can save her from being locked up and indicted."

Naomi was busy using her phone to go online.

McKinsey stared down at Rudy Laine's corpse. "Man, for a little girl she packs some wallop."

We can thank Jack for that, Naomi thought distractedly. "You forget, she's not a little girl."

"Well, right now what she looks like is a murderer." He squinted. "And if McClure has spirited her away, that makes him an accessory after the fact."

PAULL'S NEXT stop was the VIR section of DARPA, the Defense Advanced Research Projects Agency. The VIR section was where new weapons ready for the field but not yet in the distribution pipeline were available to Alpha-level personnel.

He tried to keep thoughts of what complications the death of one of the men guarding Alli Carson might cause him—meaning, very specifically, how badly the incident would distract Jack from their mission to track down and kill Arian Xhafa. He'd punched in Jack's cell number several times, always canceling the call before it could be made. There was nothing he could do for either Jack or Alli at this point, and he preferred not to hear whatever lies Jack would tell him regarding his involvement.

Paull needed Jack, of that he had no doubt. Given what the president had told him about Xhafa's capabilities, there was no point in going to Macedonia without Jack's brilliant tactical sense and his uncanny ability to figure out how the enemy thinks and, therefore, what traps, disinformation, and the like he would toss into your path. No matter what, Paull needed Jack on that plane with him at midnight.

Meanwhile, he had to pick out the weaponry that was both portable enough for a difficult mountain trek in hostile territory and powerful enough to both counter Xhafa's firepower and assure his annihilation.

Slowly and methodically, he walked up and down the aisles while his assigned DARPA sorcerer, as the engineers were called familiarly, explained the uses of each strange-looking item.

After a time, Paull began to hum "Somewhere Over the Rainbow." The president had been right—he wasn't meant to be a desk jockey no matter how high up in the hierarchy that desk might be. He was back in his element, as happy as a pig in mud.

McKinsey and Naomi were about to leave the crime scene when Henry Holt Carson waved them over. His face was grave, by which Naomi deduced that his conversation with the state police chief hadn't gone well.

"The police have issued a warrant for my niece's

arrest in connection with this disaster," he said without preamble.

Jenkins looked like he'd just lost his beloved pet dog. "Hank—"

Carson held up a hand. "I want you two to find Alli before the police do."

"Hank, this is inadvisable," the attorney said. "Inserting yourself into a second—"

Carson glared at him. "What did I tell you?"

"You pay me to protect you."

"I'm thinking of Alli now," Carson snapped.

"When we find her," Naomi said, "then what?"

"Call me," Carson said. "I'll tell you where to bring her."

"Hank, I'm an officer of the court," Jenkins protested. "I can't be a part of what is most certainly a felony crime, and I can't allow you to be part of it, either."

"I can't hear you, Counselor. You're not here." Carson cocked his head. "In fact, I'm quite certain I just heard you drive away." He addressed the two Secret Service agents. "Harrison Jenkins isn't here, is he?"

"No, sir," Naomi said.

McKinsey shook his head.

"Christ on a crutch." Shaking his head, Jenkins took his leave, picking his way back to where his car was parked.

"Now then," Carson said, taking a deep breath.

"Sir, with all due respect," McKinsey interjected, "we're Secret Service."

"My niece is still Edward Carson's daughter, all

that's left of the former First Family," Carson said shortly. Then he waved a hand dismissively. "Besides, I cleared it with your boss. For the time being, you report to me and to me alone. Is that clear?"

"Yessir," they said more or less simultaneously.

"Then what are you still doing here? Get to it."

ALLI, COCOONED in a blanket Jack kept in the trunk of his car, smiled up at him, then fell back to sleep. Jack bent over her, kissed her lightly on the forehead, adjusted the blanket slighty, then tiptoed out of the room.

He found Thatë down the hall, listening to Kid Cudi on his iPod, a pair of cheap earbuds cutting him off from the rest of the world. Jack pulled the cord and as the buds popped out of the teenager's ear, said, "Everything's going to sound like crap with those."

Thatë shrugged. "It's supposed to sound like crap. That's the point."

Jack wanted to tell him how ignorant he sounded, but instead, sat down in a chair opposite the kid and said, "Take a listen with these." He handed him the Monster Copper earbuds he had bought to listen to the music on Emma's iPod, an essential part of her he was never without.

Thatë shrugged, supremely indifferent, as he plugged in the earbuds and fit them into his ears. Three seconds after he pressed Play, his eyes opened wide, and he turned to Jack and mouthed, "Fuck me!"

Jack watched him listening to music he'd never really heard before. They were in a kitchen-cum–living room, tattered and gloomy in an all too authentic way that would make most young Goths cream in their tight black trousers.

Thatë lived in a bombed-out building in a section of Southeast Washington that could have been Beirut. The neighborhood was as desolate as a creaking old tree in winter. Out on the pocked and pitted street, trash held a special position of reverence. It was used as clothing, housing, shelter from a storm. The endless inventiveness of the destitute was forever on display. Inside, bare bulbs hung from lengths of wire, though at any given moment the electricity might or might not work. In one corner, the ceiling plaster was distended like a pregnant woman's nine-month belly, sopping with moisture, as if she had just broken her water. In the tiny, airless bathroom, there was a plastic bucket of water beside the toilet to ensure flushing. The apartment smelled of old pizza and pot. Forget dust; soot was everywhere, greasily ingrained on every horizontal surface. Occasionally, small sounds came from inside the walls, as if creatures were scuttling through the tenement's arteries and veins.

As for Thatë, he seemed perfectly at home in a place that had the impermanence of an army tent or an Alaskan house. He was one of those people who wore grime like a tattoo or a piercing, a rebel yell that very deliberately gave the finger to society.

Jack got him to listen to Howlin' Wolf from a playlist on Emma's iPod. His eyes lost their focus as he sank deeper and deeper into the music. Thatë might be a teenager, but he had the eyes of an adult who had already been witness to too many despicable acts. It was likely he had committed some of those acts himself.

At length, the playlist came to an end and Thatë pulled off the earbuds. His face seemed transformed.

"Shit," he said.

"Yeah." Jack gestured to the refrigerator. "Beer?"

The kid nodded, still half in a trance.

Jack rose and opened the refrigerator, which wheezed like an asthmatic. Beer, Coke, a couple of half-eaten slices of congealed pizza, and not much else. At least the beer was imported.

"That girl's too young for you," Thatë observed.

Jack handed him a bottle, then twisted off the cap of his own bottle and took a slug. "She's my daughter."

Thatë looked away and picked at a scab on the point of his elbow.

"Where are your parents?"

Thatë took a swig of beer. "Don't have parents."

"You mean you don't talk to them."

"I mean I never met 'em." The kid rolled the bottle around on the table, making a pattern of wet circles. "Good thing, too. I'd probably kill them."

"Maybe they're already dead."

"Christ, I hope so."

"No school for you, I see."

"I'm in school. I don't want trouble with the law."

"So who's subbing for you?"

"Fuck if I know," Thatë said with a sly grin. "Twenty bucks a day does it."

"I doubt that," Jack said.

"Okay, an eighth a week."

There was an upside-down cross and a skull with an arrow through it on the kid's right biceps.

"Where'd you get the tats?" Jack said.

Thatë shrugged. "Here and there."

"Not in this country." When Thatë made no reply, Jack added: "Albania."

"Shit, no," the kid said rather defensively. "Russia."

That told Jack a lot. "Which family?"

The kid was still picking at his scab. "What?" His fingertip was bright red.

"Which family of the *grupperovka*?"

Thatë jumped as if Jack had jabbed him with a burning needle.

"I know about the Russian mob," Jack said. "I've had dealings with them."

"No shit?"

The kid stared down at the Monster earbuds. He handed them back with no little reluctance. His body shifted subtly. By the alert way he sat, Jack could tell that his disinterest was feigned.

Jack leaned over to take a closer look. "Initiation, right? So which family became your parents?" He had seen these same tattoos on Ivan Gurov in Moscow last year. "No, wait, let me guess."

The kid laughed, but he shifted again and Jack knew he was uneasy. "Izmaylovskaya. Am I right?"

"Jesus Christ!" Thatë stared at Jack as if he were a demon from hell. "Who the fuck are you?"

Jack finished off his beer and set the bottle down. He had nowhere to go until after dark. "I'll tell my story," he said, "if you'll tell me yours."

"I THINK we should split up," Naomi said.

McKinsey regarded her with no little skepticism. "Are we really gonna do this?"

"I am."

"What the fuck's in it for us?"

She contemplated him in the same way someone would a slice of moldy meat. "What the hell's the matter with you?"

"I just don't like taking orders from some entitled prick." He shrugged. "I'm just a working stiff."

"Yeah, in a Giorgio Armani suit."

"What? I like to look good on the job. You think I'd be caught dead in one of those Simm's specials the other guys wear?"

Naomi shook her head as they headed toward their car. "No matter. I think you should follow up with the state police chief who's taken over this case."

McKinsey raised an eyebrow. "And you?"

"I'm going to check out the guards' background."

"A complete waste of time, if you ask me."

Naomi hauled open the car's door and got behind the wheel. "Then it's a good thing I didn't ask."

AFTER DROPPING McKinsey off at his own car, Naomi drove to G Street NW, where Fortress Securities had their offices in one of those gigantic stone-faced buildings, fraught with dentils and Doric columns that dwarf any human who walks up the glittery white steps.

Fortress was on the seventh floor. Walking into its lobby, you could imagine yourself in the waiting room of a medium-sized advertising firm. The space was formed almost completely from horizontal planes of veined white marble, cut glass, bronze tubing, and glittering black granite. The only clue as to Fortress's actual purpose was the bas-relief of an ancient Greek helmet, sculpted out of bronze, that rode over the receptionist's head like the cloud of combat.

When Naomi produced her ID and asked to see Fortress's president, she was politely but firmly told to wait while the receptionist—a young man in a sleek dark suit—spoke quietly into the mike of the headpiece encircling his head like a halo.

A short time later, another young man in a sleek dark suit escorted Naomi down a softly lit, carpeted hallway, lined with paintings of famous battles throughout history. Naomi recognized Alexander the Great, the great Spartan stand against Xerxes's Persian army, Ajax and Achilles outside the walls of Troy, Napoleon at Waterloo, George Patton rolling over Europe, and so on and on, a seemingly endless display of man's propensity for bloodlust and warfare. It was no surprise to Naomi that not one woman appeared in any of the paintings.

Andrew Gunn, the president of Fortress, rose from behind his desk as she was ushered into the room. Her guide immediately withdrew, closing the door behind him. Gunn seemed to unfold like a praying mantis. He was tall and thin with prematurely white hair and a nose like the prow of a ship. His steel blue eyes regarded her out of a rugged face, as scarred and pitted as the curve of the moon.

He came around, extended his hand, and smiled. His teeth seemed to shine in the muted afternoon light. Naomi had dealt with the top echelons of the private security firms. They all seemed to fall into two groups. Either they were ex-Marines, hard, angry, and bloodthirsty, or they were ex-CIA assets, anonymous, slippery, and bloodthirsty. She found it interesting that Gunn fell into neither of these camps. Rather, he seemed like a good old American cowboy, the way he had been played by Gary Cooper or depicted in the iconic Marlboro Man ads. He smelled good, as well, like the woods at night.

Instead of returning behind his desk, he led her to the far more informal seating area, which was comprised of an ultramodern sofa, two matching chairs, and a low coffee table made of a thick slab of white granite.

As they settled themselves, he said, "I assume, Ms. Wilde, that your visit concerns the death of one of my men, and the attack on two others."

She nodded. "That's right."

He shook his head. "Well, then, I'm at a loss to understand the involvement of the Secret Service."

"The prime suspect is the First Daughter."

"Ah, Henry Holt Carson's niece."

"That's right."

His serious expression deepened. The frown made him look like a caricature of himself, as if he wasn't used to frowning. "With all due respect, I find the notion that this young girl could have overpowered three of my men inconceivable."

"Nevertheless, Mr. Gunn, that is very well what might have happened."

He spread his hands. "Surely there must be another explanation."

"That's why I'm here."

"I'm afraid I don't understand."

"Neither do I, but perhaps together we can find out." She took out a small memo pad. "Mr. Carson came to you directly?"

"Yes, that's right." The phone rang, but Gunn ignored it. "Hank and I are old friends."

"So you and Mr. Carson have done business before."

"I said we're friends."

Naomi glanced up, trying to discern whether Gunn's mood had changed. "Has he had occasion to avail himself of your services before?"

"Once."

Only Naomi's training allowed her to pick up on the minuscule hesitation. "And when was that?"

Gunn unfolded his lanky frame again and walked over to his desk. "Can I get you anything to drink?"

"Thanks, no."

"We have our own barista."

She laughed. "A double macchiato, then."

"That's the spirit!" Using the intercom, he ordered a double macchiato and triple espresso, then returned to the sitting area.

"You didn't answer my question," Naomi said.

"I'd rather not, Ms. Wilde."

"And I'd rather not get a federal order, but I will," she said. "I take this investigation very seriously."

Gunn nodded in that grave way presidents of corporations sometimes do. Naomi often wondered whether they taught that at Wharton. The young man who had escorted her opened the door and, crossing the room, set down a tray with two small cups, and bowls of two different sugars and packets of Splenda.

"I appreciate your grit, Ms. Wilde." Leaning over, he handed her a cup and saucer, then took a sip of his espresso.

Suddenly impatient, Naomi said, "Your friend Mr. Carson has pulled one of his many strings. I now report to him."

"Ah. Well then." Gunn sighed and, leaning back, stared up at the ceiling. "Hank called me about six years ago, maybe seven. He was unhappy with his then wife's behavior."

"She was cheating on him."

"Sadly for her, as it turned out."

Naomi put aside her macchiato and scribbled on her pad. "I didn't think Fortress did PI work."

"We don't," Gunn said. "Normally."

"But Mr. Carson wanted a level of discretion only you could provide."

He clapped his hands. "I couldn't have said it better myself."

"And nothing after that incident until he hired you to guard Alli Carson."

He took another sip, a deeper one this time, savoring the espresso in his mouth before swallowing. "That's right."

Naomi glanced up again. "Did Mr. Carson request specific personnel?"

Gunn lowered his cup and stared fixedly at her. "Hank doesn't know my personnel."

"Correct me if I'm wrong, Mr. Gunn, but I hardly think Mr. Carson would allow men to guard his niece without personally signing off on their dossiers."

"Hank trusts me."

The phone rang again, more insistently this time. Then the intercom buzzed.

"Excuse me a moment," Gunn said.

He rose, went behind his desk, and picked up the phone. He spoke for several minutes in a tone so low Naomi could not hear a word. While he was occupied, she took a look around the office. It was spacious, but not the vast, palatial room she had been expecting. But then nothing about Andrew Gunn was what she had expected. He didn't have the typical chip-on-the-shoulder attitude of his compatriots, the burning desire to bilk the federal government out of every possible dollar. Why not? After all, the Mint just printed up more greenbacks to pay the security firms' exorbitant fees. No, Gunn was erudite, urbane, and charming, even while being secretive as hell. Though she had been expecting to dislike him, she found it impossible to do so. Still, while she had a moment she continued the deep drilling on the Web investigation she had begun while at the crime scene behind Henry Carson's house.

When Gunn returned, sitting in precisely the same spot he had vacated, he smiled at her benignly. "Where were we?"

"I wonder," Naomi said, putting aside her phone and taking up her cup, "whether Mr. Carson's trust in you stems from the fact that you're a major investor in his primary company, InterPublic Bancorp?"

McKINSEY FOLLOWED Naomi all the way into the building housing Fortress Securities. He watched her step into the elevator, watched the numbers flicker until they stopped at Fortress's floor. Then he entered the next car and took it up to the fourth floor. Turning left, he walked down the hallway, knocked on the fifth door on his right, even though there was a clearly marked button. Then he walked to the next door down, arriving just as a buzzer opened the door.

He entered a small, grubby anteroom stacked with cartons, some opened, some not. A cheap desk stood to the left. On it was a multiline corded telephone, a Rolodex, and a cup full of pencils. No one sat in the chair behind the desk, and, McKinsey knew, no one ever had.

Passing the desk, he went down a bare, narrow corridor that stank of wet shoes, burnt coffee, and stale sweat. There were all of three rooms, including a windowless kitchenette, where the burnt coffee stink was so palpable it became an entity unto itself. Crossing the threshold of the cubicle opposite, he came upon Willowicz sitting behind a green metal desk that looked like a castoff, and probably was. He was leaning back in an adjustable office chair, his brogue-shod feet, crossed at the ankles, up on the desk. Both shoes were severely run-down at the heel. Willowicz was talking on his cell phone.

"I don't care what it takes," he said. "Get it done and get it done now."

He grinned at McKinsey, beckoning him in. "Laws? What laws?" he said into the phone. "I don't give a shit about laws. If you do, you're in the wrong business. If you like, I'll bring in . . . No, I thought not."

He severed the connection, said, "It's the same all over, good help is scarcer than a toad with balls." His grin widened. "How goes it on the inside?"

"Fine and dandy," McKinsey said.

There was nothing at all on the dented metal of the desktop, save a small plaque in the center of which was a bronze bas-relief of a Greek warrior's helmet.

Eleven

Gunn regarded Naomi with a vaguely ironic smile. "It's public knowledge that I'm an investor in InterPublic."

Naomi didn't like that smile. "A major investor."

"What can I say? I have a facility for making money."

"Uh-huh. And what other things have you and Mr. Carson cooked up?"

"What's that supposed to mean?"

Naomi shrugged. "Maybe InterPublic isn't the extent of your dealings together. Maybe there are deals that aren't public knowledge."

Gunn sat looking at her for a moment. "I do believe you're trying to piss me off."

"Not at all."

"For what reason I cannot imagine."

Now that they were talking at cross-purposes, it was time for Naomi to go. But before she did, there was one item left remaining on her agenda. She rose and headed for the door, before turning back.

"I'd appreciate the dossiers on the three men who were assigned to guard Alli Carter."

Gunn appeared unfazed. "Bennett will hand them to you on the way out."

She smiled. "A pleasure, Mr. Gunn." Her smile widened. "That macchiato was so good I promise I'll be back."

"The Izmaylovskaya recruit," Thatë said when Jack had finished explaining his storied past. "Their representatives go far afield—Albania, Romania, all of Eastern Europe, so I'm told." He looked down at his hands, their long fingers laced together. "That's how they found me." He looked up. "Why should I say no? They offered me a home, training, a steady job, security—none of the things I had. It was everything I wanted—and needed."

"I thought the *grupperovka* were all Russian nationals."

"Once, maybe." Thatë rose, got them two more beers, and sat back down. "But these days the families are under a shitload of pressure from the Kremlin. They gotta expand beyond Russia in order to survive." He shrugged as he snapped off the bottle cap. "They don't like it, but what the fuck else can they do. The fucking writing's on the wall."

The day had wasted itself in gray rain and intermittent spurts of sleet that rattled on the concrete sidewalks. Now, exhausted, day had given way to night, a darkness muffled in low clouds and swirls of icy rain. Far above, the sky was dully phosphorescent with the lights of the far-off prosperous sections of the city, but the glow did little here. Streetlights worked only intermittently; illumination was at a premium, which was just how the roving gangs liked it.

Jack checked his watch. "It's almost showtime."

"Time to go, no?" Thatë glanced over his shoulder. "The girl's awake."

Jack turned. Alli was standing in the doorway, dried blood all over her. She looked even smaller than usual, almost like a child.

"Jack . . ." All at once, tears rolled down her cheeks.

He rose and went to her, held her while she shook and sobbed. "It's always worst the first time."

He felt her freeze, almost as if her breathing had come to a halt. "He's dead?"

"Yes."

"I . . . I didn't mean to, but he wouldn't stop coming after me."

"What happened?" Jack said gently.

After a shuddering breath, Alli described everything that had happened in her uncle's study. How Rudy had waited until Uncle Hank and Harrison Jenkins had driven away before coming in and threatening her with the fire poker, how she had managed to get away and what had happened when she encountered the other two guards, how in her flight she had come across the cook lying on the floor of the kitchen, and how Rudy had followed her out of the house.

"There's no doubt in your mind that his intent was to kill you?"

She shook her head. "When he came for me, he said, 'There's a fine spot for them to find you, curled in the fireplace with the soot and the ash.' "

"Was it just him, do you think, or were they all in on it?"

Alli, thinking back to how Conlon and the third guard had acted, said, "They were all in it together. I just think Rudy was the crew chief."

The tears had dried on her cheeks, making tracks in the dirt. He could see that she had regained a good deal of her self-control. Just the fact that she could make these observations about her attackers was proof that she was heading for the right line of work at Fearington.

"It's okay. You've done remarkably well." He hugged her and gave her a gentle shove in the direction of the bathroom. "Now go wash up."

He turned to see Thatë staring intently at him. "What?"

The kid lowered his head, stared at the floor between his feet. "Nothing."

Jack sat down across from him and took a swig of his beer, which was now close to room temperature. "Spill it."

Thatë gave a little laugh. He sounded like a hyena nervously cackling in the bush.

"How d'you get her to listen to you?" the kid asked. "You threaten her, or what?"

Jack considered the source of these questions. "I didn't get her to do anything. Alli takes my advice."

"So how you make her respectful?"

Jack tried not to show the alarm that sprang up inside him. "Thatë, she trusts me."

"She trusts you?"

Behind the closed bathroom door, the water had begun to run in the shower.

Thatë frowned. "I don't get it."

"Why don't you ask her?"

As the kid jumped up, Jack, laughing, reached over and pulled him back down.

"Not now."

"Why not now?"

"Because she'd find a way to obliterate your nuts."

Thatë looked at him askance. "You're fucking with me, right?"

Jack shook his head. "She killed a man today—a professional bodyguard—and maimed two others." He let the kid go. "You still want to try?"

Thatë shook his head. "Man, I still don't know about you."

At that moment, the bathroom door opened a crack, and, through a small cloud of steam, Alli said, "I need clean clothes."

Jack looked at the kid, who inadvertently gave a classic double-take before making for the bedroom. Jack heard some drawers being pulled out. He and Alli exchanged looks, but he was uncertain of either her mood or what she was thinking until she breathed: "Emma . . ."

"What is it?" he whispered back.

Alli gave a tiny, violent shiver. "I feel her."

Thatë reappeared with a stack of clothes: a pair of black stovepipe jeans, a black-and-white T-shirt with WIG-OUT emblazoned across the chest, a hoodie, and a pair of sweat socks.

Alli sniffed at them.

"They're just washed," the kid said. "I know how to take care of myself." He led with his chin. "Couldn't do anything 'bout underwear."

"No problem," Alli said, taking the pile from him. "I'll go commando."

NAOMI STOOD just to one side of the entrance to the Fortress Securities building, between two columns, hidden from anyone who came and went. She was scanning the dossiers of the three guards, hoping to find some link, some anomaly that might make something click. It was chilly, the evening clanking onto the city streets like a spent shell. Lights sent smears of illumination across the sidewalk. Headlights rolled toward her, then away slowly in the mounting rush hour traffic.

She had done her best to rattle Gunn's cage. If there was something to what she had intimated she wanted to know about it. She'd made a shot in the dark, to be sure, but she was waiting for Gunn to emerge. If he had become alarmed by what she had said he would go see Henry Holt Carson in person; he was too good at his job to risk a phone conversation.

But it had been over an hour since she had left the Fortress offices and still no sign of him. She went back to the dossiers, her eyes anxiously scanning the text while part of her attention was secured in the periphery of her vision, waiting for Gunn. There was nothing, nothing, nothing, so she returned to the beginning and started all over again.

Halfway through she caught herself wondering how Pete was faring. Digging out her phone, she punched in his speed-dial number. He answered at once. Nothing to report.

"I got the Fortress dossiers," she said. "If you're free, we ought to go over them together."

"Right. Two pairs of eyes are better than one," he said. "Meet you in twenty at the office."

She severed the connection, read a little more, continuing to spin her wheels, and sighed. Still no sign of Gunn. She checked her watch. Shit, maybe she had been wrong about him. All at once, her attention shifted. She looked forward to meeting with Pete, hopeful he'd spot something she had missed. Besides, she hadn't eaten a thing all day.

She was about to pack up the dossiers in preparation for heading back to the office when a familiar figure pushed through the doors of the building and came briskly down the stairs.

Pete McKinsey passed not ten feet from where she stood, frozen in dismay.

THATË POINTED with his chin. "What else is on your iPod?"

He held the iPod out and the kid took it, plugged Jack's Monster earbuds in, and scrolled down.

"Don't know any of this shit," he said a little too loudly, as people will when they're listening to music in their ears. Then, apparently finding a song he liked, he turned up the volume. His head began to nod rhythmically.

Jack watched him for a moment. He had to remind himself that the kid was only seventeen. He spoke American street slang almost perfectly; a first-rate mimic. He turned from this thought as Alli came out of the bathroom. She looked fairly comical with the bottoms of Thatë's jeans turned up in oversized cuffs. The hoodie came down almost to her knees.

"Don't laugh," she warned.

"I wouldn't dream of it," Jack said.

She came and brought a chair over to sit beside

him. Thatë's eyes tracked her but he was too deep in the music to pay much attention.

"What's with the Lost Boy?" she said.

"We're in trouble, Alli. The Virginia State Police have a warrant out for your arrest and I have no doubt your uncle wants to get his hands on us as well. Thatë provided a safe haven where no one would think to look for us."

"Any port in a storm."

"This is more than a storm," Jack said seriously.

Alli hitched her chair closer to him and lowered her voice even though it was impossible for Thatë to overhear them. "I don't understand. Uncle Hank hired those men to guard me. Instead, they tried to kill me. I mean, what the fuck?"

"My thought exactly. That's why I spirited you away, that's why I don't want you to turn yourself in. Nothing about this situation rings true and until I can understand what's happening I don't trust anyone, and that includes your Uncle Hank."

"You don't think he would—"

"At this point, I don't know what to think. But the fact is I trust this young criminal-in-waiting more than I do anyone else."

"Then we really are in trouble."

Jack nodded.

"On the other hand, we can't stay here forever."

"I don't plan to," Jack said. He brought her up to date. He told her about the killings at Twilight, how he'd found physical evidence linking them to Billy Warren's death. He showed her the octagonal badge and Thatë's identical pendant.

"The writing on them is Albanian, the icon of an

underground club whose business makes even Thatë nervous," he concluded. "That's where I'm hoping we'll find some answers about who really killed Billy, and why."

Thatë chose that moment to come out of his music-induced trance. "Very cool shit," he said as he pulled out the earbuds. "Old-school roots, man. People put 'em down, but not me. The blues is where hip-hop came from, you know?" Then he grinned at Alli. "So, *vajzë e bukur,* how you doin'?"

Alli glanced at Jack, who said, "He thinks you're beautiful."

She bared her teeth at the kid.

ACCORDING TO Thatë, the Stem was located in Chinatown.

"Best cover in the city," he said when he saw the look on his companions' faces. "Tons of tourists, no one looks out of place, hey?"

The moment they turned onto H Street NW, Alli felt an odd thrill of déjà vu. As they passed Fifth Street, heading toward Fourth, she saw the big square sign of the restaurant toward which Thatë was leading them, and she gasped.

"What is it?" Jack said, bringing the three of them up short.

Alli shook her head. "I saw a take-out menu from this restaurant, First Won Ton, in Uncle Hank's study."

"His house is a long way from Chinatown," Jack said.

Alli nodded. "I thought it curious myself."

Jack turned to the kid. "The Stem?"

"In the basement, below the restaurant."

Turning back to Alli, Jack said, "How well do you remember the menu? Was there anything written on it, anything circled, the way people do when they order?"

Alli concentrated. One of the things she'd been training toward at Fearington was full-memory recall of conversations and crime scenes. Clearly, her uncle's study fit into neither category, but the item was so odd, so out of place that she had spent a moment staring at it. In fact, there was something that was circled.

"Spicy fragrant duck with cherries."

Jack looked at the kid. "Mean anything to you?"

Thatë shook his head.

"Okay," Jack said, "let's move in."

The restaurant, like many in Chinatown, was below street level. A flight of crumbling concrete stairs, dark with grease and city grime, led down to a glass door. A window to the right was filled with roasted ducks hanging by their necks on a series of metal hooks, mahogany-colored and glistening with fat. Below, metal trays held slabs of red-skinned spare ribs, ready for the fire.

Jack had thought about this foray long and hard; mainly whether or not he should take Alli. However, several factors were at play, all of them limiting his options. For one thing, he was reluctant to leave her behind in a strange house in a very bad neighborhood. Thatë was dealing in drugs. People like that were always targets of rivals or enemies. For another, he didn't believe that Alli would allow him to leave her behind. Besides, she had proved herself in combat. He had to stop thinking of her as the introverted little girl he'd first met, incapable of taking care of herself. In the last year alone, she had grown by leaps and bounds. She needed to be taken seriously.

None of this, whether fact or rationalization, or some combination of the two, caused him to be any less concerned about her safety, but, for better or for worse, this was how it had to play out.

Inside, the restaurant was long and narrow, its Formica tables filled with Chinese families and a smattering of tourists busily consulting their travel guides for tips on what to order. No one paid them any attention, including the slim Chinese woman behind the cash register, who was drinking tea and sucking at her teeth. Waiters, exuding a cold frenzy, came and went between tables, laden with huge trays mounded with enormous dishes or piled high with platters of the dregs of murky, gelatinous substances.

"This way." Thaté led them through the restaurant, into a narrow corridor that ended at the door to the toilet. Just before it, on the right, was a steep stairway that descended into the dank gloom of a subbasement.

The kid held out his hand and Jack gave him back his octagonal pendant, which he hung around his neck.

"You have the pin?" he said when Jack reached the head of the stairs.

Jack opened his hand. The pin he'd taken from Mathis, Twilight's dead manager, gleamed dully in the center of his palm.

Thaté nodded. "You'll have to show it." As he began to descend, Jack reached forward and spun him around. "Don't fuck with me, you understand?"

Thaté stared unblinkingly at him for a long, tense

moment. Then he nodded curtly and continued his descent. His voice floated up from the semidarkness. "Keep the girl close to you at all times."

"What the hell does he mean by that?" Alli said in a stage whisper.

They went down the stairs. Thatë was already at the bottom. He knocked on the door and, when it creaked open a crack, a gruff male voice said, "Hey, Flyboy."

The kid had to show his pendant before the door opened wide enough to let him inside. The door had begun to close when Jack put his foot in the gap.

"Yeah? Whatta you want?" the voice said. It belonged to someone with a suspicious eye that looked him up and down.

Jack held up the pin with one hand, while with the other he held tight to Alli.

"I don't know you."

"Mathis sent me. He's down with the flu," Jack said.

"Fuckin' flu." He stared hard at Jack, then looked him up and down. "Mathis was going to bring Mbreti's money. You got it?"

Mbreti meant "king" in Albanian. Jack tapped his breast pocket to indicate this was where he kept the cash.

"Then get your ass in here." As with Thatë, the door opened just enough for Jack to slip in, Alli right on his heels.

The guard was a massive, dark-skinned man, Albanian or Macedonian, Jack suspected. His eyes opened wide the moment he saw Alli, and a huge smile played across his face.

"I approve of the form Mbreti's money is in." He waved them through with a hairy paw. His arms seemed as long as an ape's. His low brow looked like an anvil.

Behind him, there was nothing and no one. Jack had been expecting a large ballroom teeming with people, but the space they traversed was as small and ill-lit as a dungeon. One bare bulb dangling from the end of a length of wire descended from the ceiling like a dripping stalactite. They passed beneath it, then came upon a shabby-looking door to what might be a broom closet. Instead, it opened onto a cavernous space that looked hewn out of the bedrock beneath the city. Gritty concrete steps led down to this space, which was loud with the shouting of male voices, blue-tinted with cigarette and cigar smoke, thick with the musk of human bodies. But gone were the crowds of people, the monster sound system blaring techno and trance. There were no outrageously dressed bodies slithering together. For that matter, where was the dance floor, the bar, the drugs?

Thatë had already gone down the short flight of steps, but Jack and Alli stood transfixed. In the center of the room, surrounded by perhaps a dozen men in shiny silk suits, a boxing ring had been erected. In the center of this, a mike descended from the ceiling. It was held by a young man, slim, well dressed, with slicked-back hair and the air of an entrepreneur. There were no boxers in the ring, no corner men handling their styptic pencils, buckets of ice water, and low stools.

Instead the atmosphere in the ring was woozy with sex, or, more accurately, bare female flesh. Lined up in front of the emcee were six girls—slim-hipped, small-breasted, blonde and brunette. All were naked. At least half of them, Jack estimated, were underage. They had their heads down, staring at the canvas between their feet. The slim young man started to speak in the rapid-fire jargon of all auctioneers, and that was when the actual business of the Stem sank in to Jack's mind.

"Now, for our first cherry, we have a tender morsel indeed, fresh from the shores of Odessa." The auctioneer stepped closer to the first girl on his right. "Only twelve years of age and guaranteed a virgin, good gentlemen, so with that premium in mind we'll start the bidding at fifty thousand dollars." He cupped the girl's chin, lifting her head. "Just look at this cherry! Look into those blue eyes, regard that golden hair, the creamy skin. And, gentlemen, this cherry is guaranteed completely free of lice!" He continued on in this abominable and dehumanizing vein, as if he were selling Texas steers or Arabian horses.

In a trance, Jack descended the stairs, holding tight to Alli's hand. Part of him wanted to get her out of here now, but another part knew that that choice was long past. Turning around now would only call unwanted attention to themselves. He reminded himself that they were here as part of a triple homicide investigation in which Alli was the prime suspect. They had to go forward.

At that moment, Alli whispered in his ear. Now that they were nearer to the action, he could see what had drawn her attention. All the girls had burns or welts marring their flesh. Some were clearly old, but others appeared quite new. The sight was almost too much to take in and, in fact, it was Alli's presence that calmed him down.

"Now we're getting somewhere," she said.

At that moment, the auctioneer yelled, "The bid is against you, Sergei. No? One hundred twenty, then, going once, twice. Sold!" and pointed to a man in sunglasses lounging in one corner, arms folded across his chest.

A man appeared, climbed into the ring, and led the girl out. The auctioneer was about to move to the next girl, when his eyes caught sight of Alli.

"And what have we here?"

Heads turned as he pointed. "Mathis's sub is here with something fresh, and by the look of her, what a load of fresh she is." He beckoned to Jack and raised his voice to fever pitch. "Come on, bring that next cherry up here! I have no doubt she'll fetch a pretty penny, sir, a pretty penny, indeed!" He moved to the front of the ring, taking his mike with him.

Alli clung to Jack, but the man who had escorted the first cherry out of the ring now reappeared and gripped Alli's free arm so hard she cried out. At once, Jack whirled and slammed an elbow into the man's nose. Blood gushed as he went down. The auctioneer made a hand signal and two large men detached themselves from the shadows. One had drawn a Glock, the other was content with displaying his fists.

"She's not going into the ring," Jack said.

"The fuck she isn't," the gunman said.

Jack backed into him, trod on his instep with his heel, and, at the same time, brought the edge of his hand down on the gunman's wrist. The Glock fell to the floor as the gunman grunted in pain, but almost immediately, the second man wrapped his arm around Jack's throat.

"Make a move and I'll snap your neck."

Alli bent down, but the gunman stopped her from reaching the Glock by grabbing the back of her hoodie and dragging her back to her feet. While Jack watched helplessly, the gunman pushed and shoved her toward the ring. The girls stared down at her, shivering and glassy-eyed. But as the gunman began to manhandle Alli up the wooden steps, she tripped. As he reached down to pull her up, she delivered a backward kick to the pit of his stomach. He fell toward her and she twisted, taking the brunt of his weight on her right shoulder, which she twisted away and down, so that he fell against the metal rim of the canvas floor. She took his head and slammed the side of it down, then reached for his gun.

Turning, she aimed the Glock. The man tightened his arm around Jack's throat.

"Let him go," Alli said, "or so help me I'll put a bullet into your brain."

"By the time you do," the man said, jerking Jack's head around, "he'll be dead."

A deathly silence stole over the room. Even the glib auctioneer seemed struck dumb. Alli and the man continued to glare at one another. No one else so much as breathed. Jack had cause to wonder where Thatë was. The shock of being in the middle of a white slave trade ring had driven thoughts of the kid right out of his head. He could use him now.

Then, abruptly, a door in the rear of the room swung open and a voice said, "A Mexican standoff is to no one's benefit." A shadow filled the doorway.

"Put up your gun and we'll talk. No one's going to get hurt, right, Evan?"

The big man nodded. "Whatever you say."

"Ease off, Evan, and the girl will put down the gun, are we clear?"

"I'm not putting down anything," Alli said.

The shadow in the doorway sighed. "Thatë."

The kid stepped to Alli's side. "You don't want to shoot anyone," he said. "That'll just get both of you dead."

"Tell him to let Jack go and step away more than an arm's length."

Thatë turned to the shadow in the doorway.

"Do as she asks," the shadow said.

Evan slid his arm away and Jack took a long, gasping breath, then began to cough.

"Go on," Alli said, waggling the barrel of the Glock. She tracked Evan with the gun as he backed up. When he was a sufficient distance from Jack, she turned the Glock on the shadow in the doorway. "Now we—"

The word froze in her throat as Thatë pressed the muzzle of a .25 to her temple. "Put it down." When she didn't move, he said, "It may be a little gun but it's loaded with Tokarev brass-cased bullets, corrosive, Berdan-primed, 87-grain lead core. In other words, full metal jacket ammo that, at point-blank range, will blow half your head off."

Alli sighed and, at the same time, glared at Jack, as if to say, Another betrayal. I told you so. She lowered the Glock until it was pointing at the floor. The kid took it from her.

"Thatë," the voice said, "now bring them to me."

"I MUST say I'm intrigued by you, yes, I am."

The man who was now their host in the small, closeted room off the auction site was speaking directly to Alli in heavily accented English. He ignored Jack entirely, even though Jack and Alli were standing side by side. Thatë, the .25 handgun still in his hand, stood with his back pressed against the closed door.

The room, which seemed claustrophobic, held a heavy antique desk, a single chair, a task lamp. No telephone, nothing so much as a paper clip on the surface of the desk. On one wall hung a horizontal painting, far too large for the space, titled *Korab*, depicting in exacting detail the spine of ice- and snow-capped mountains beneath a piercing blue sky.

The man tapped an exceedingly long forefinger against his lips. "You're a tiny slip of a thing, but you burn oh so brightly."

He was tall, with square shoulders and the slim hips of a dancer. He leaned back against his desk, hands in the pockets of his striped trousers, but his torso was bent forward, his head at the end of its stalklike neck thrust forward. His eyes were huge, slow, and cunning, in the particular way of evil. Like a reptile's eyes, they seemed to drink in everything with a single glance. He had a nose that looked as if it had been broken more than once, and ruddy skin like badly tanned leather. His priestly fringe of prematurely white hair was so out of place it was difficult to reconcile with the rest of his face.

"What's your name?" he said.

"Alli."

"Ah, well, I know that name."

Alli shook her head. "How could you possibly?"

"A reasonable question." He considered for a moment. "I believe you've earned the right to know. My name is Dardan."

Alli gave a small, involuntary gasp.

"That's right." A smile like a scimitar curved his lips. "You've heard my name, as well."

He walked to the wall with the painting and, taking it off its hooks, set it onto the floor. There was, incongruously, a window, which the painting had hidden. Dardan flipped a switch and hard light flooded the room on the other side of the window.

Alli cried out and put her hands against the glass. "Oh, my God!"

Through the window, Jack saw a young girl, blond and exquisite, her porcelain skin perfect and bloodless, laid out on a black bier. Her skin was pearl white, her bloodless lips bluish in the harsh illumination. Flecks of blood were strewn through her hair.

"Alli, you know this girl?" Jack said.

"Arjeta!" Alli cried.

"Arjeta Kraja?" The mystery girl who had been with Billy Warren at Twilight, the one everyone was searching for.

"I see you know her," Dardan said. "She had been my plaything for some months, but then . . ." His voice trailed off and he shrugged.

Jack rounded on him. "Then what?"

At last, Dardan looked at Jack. "It was a bad idea to bring her."

"Bad particularly for your men outside," Jack said. He produced his ID. "This doesn't look good for you."

Dardan shrugged. "Thatë will not hesitate to shoot you in the back." He craned his neck. "Isn't that right, Thatë?"

"It certainly is," the kid said, brandishing both the Glock and the .25.

Alli turned away from the window, and again her eyes cut to Jack to show her displeasure. They were red-rimmed, but she had not shed a tear.

"You wouldn't harm a federal agent," Jack said. "The glare of that spotlight would wrap up your dirty trade and put you permanently out of business."

"But, no, I think not." Dardan wagged his forefinger. "Because, you see, I'm protected, Mr. McClure. Even the death of a federal agent cannot harm me. The resulting investigation will be deflected . . . elsewhere." He shrugged. "So you see, I can do with you whatever I wish. However"—he pushed off the edge of the desk—"it's this little hellion—that's the right word isn't it?—that interests me."

As he approached Alli, his hands came out of his pockets. He ran a finger down her cheek, tracing the jawline, then plunging the tip between her lips. She made a sound in the back of her throat and pulled away.

"Don't." Dardan held a switchblade, which now swung open, its long blade gleaming. The edge approached Alli's throat. "I propose to entertain myself with her, Mr. McClure, while you watch. Sounds like fun, no?"

Jack touched Alli on the right hip and she swung away from Dardan. Jack launched himself forward. Instinctively, Dardan swung the knife, aiming for Jack's face. Jack came in under the blade, struck

Dardan a powerful blow that rocked him back against the desk.

At once, Jack was on him, pinioning the wrist of his knife hand, bringing his knee up into Dardan's groin.

Alli whirled around to confront Thatë, but to her astonishment, he hadn't pulled the .25.

Still, she was compelled to say, "Don't."

Thatë held his empty hands up. He grinned at her.

Behind her, Dardan had managed to free the knife, which slashed through Jack's jacket and shirt, questing to slide between his ribs. Jack felt the blood running hot down his side as he struck the inside of Dardan's left knee. The knife blade missed its mark, but Dardan slammed his fist into Jack's solar plexus, doubling him over.

Dardan slammed him against the edge of the desk and Jack, dazed, slid to his knees. Dardan reached down and began to draw the blade across Jack's throat. The pain cut through Jack's wooziness and he jammed the heel of his right hand against Dardan's wrist as he tilted his head back. The knife passed directly in front of his face. Jack, struggling for purchase, slipped and, in desperation, and grabbed the base of the blade. As the edge sliced into the meat of his palm, he shoved the point back and up. It passed just above Dardan's cheek and punctured his eye. He screamed. Jack pushed the blade deeper, burying it in his head. Then he slumped down, his heart hammering in his throat, the adrenaline surging so strongly he thought he would retch.

Then Alli was prying the body off him, pulling him to his feet, drawing him away.

"Fuck me." Thatë was staring at Dardan's corpse.

"We've got to get out of here," Alli said without knowing who she was addressing.

A sudden hammering at the door brought the kid out of his trancelike state. "I know a way." He came away from the door. "But you must promise to take me with you."

His eyes were big around. Jack, regaining a semblance of composure, could tell that he was terrified. "What is it?" he said, as the hammering continued on the other side of the door.

They could hear shouts now—curses, imprecations.

"What's happened?"

"There's no time." The hammering was louder. "Without me you're trapped. Will you take me with you?"

A gunshot splintered through the door. The angry shouts grew louder, more frenzied. The pounding increased in intensity until the door shuddered.

"Yes," Jack said. "All right."

Thatë nodded and, putting his shoulder to the desk, shoved it all the way to the door. In the area of the floor that was under where it had been was a trapdoor. Bending, he pulled an iron ring and the trapdoor swung up.

"Quickly," he said. "Quickly, or we'll die here!"

There was an iron ladder leading down into absolute blackness. Alli went first, then Jack. Thatë came last, pausing to lock the trapdoor from underneath. There was no light at all.

"Keep going." Thatë's voice floated through the void.

They were enmeshed in damp, in sharp mineral smells, and in the stench of dying things.

"Thatë," Jack said when he reached the ground, "what happened back there?"

He could hear Thatë breathing. At last, the kid said, "Have you heard of a man by the name of Arian Xhafa?"

Jack felt a chill go through him.

Thatë took a breath. Jack could feel it on his cheek.

"Dardan, the man you killed? He was Arian Xhafa's brother."

PART TWO

BLOOD TIES

Five Days Ago

The worst thing about dying alone, he used to say, is not being able to say good-bye.

—*The Skating Rink*, Roberto Bolaño

TWELVE

"YOU'RE A dead man, Jack, you know that." Dennis Paull shook his head. "All of you. You and Alli and this kid."

Jack tried to find a comfortable position, keeping the pain in his side to a minimum. He'd gone to a surgeon. The slash was superficial. His hand needed a number of stitches, and he was on antibiotics.

"Why state the obvious?"

"Because now it's a race against time," Paull said. "We've got to terminate Arian Xhafa before one of his people puts a couple of sniper's rounds into the three of you."

Thirty thousand feet above the Atlantic, Jack and Paull sat side by side in the front section of the 757's luxuriously reconfigured interior. In the cargo hold below them, packed and ready, was the arsenal of DARPA weaponry Paull had handpicked for Chimera's first assignment.

Alli and Thatë sat in the lounge area near the rear, eating pizza and drinking Cokes. The sight was incongruous and, for Jack, slightly eerie. They were just like two kids at a '50s malt shop. Looking at them, the terrible events of the last twenty-four hours might never have happened.

Paull glanced at Thatë. "This fucking kid. I don't like that you dragged him along."

"I promised him. I had no choice."

"Sure you had a choice." Paull's voice was like granite. "You could've ditched him the first chance you got."

"And leave him to be picked off by Dardan's men?"

"He carried that Stem pendant."

"He didn't lift a hand to protect Dardan." Jack shook his head. "No, he's straight, so far as that goes."

"Still."

"One day that cynicism will kill you," Jack said.

Paull grunted. "In our business, there is no sharper blade than trust."

Jack gave him an ironic smile. "I'll try to remember that in the days ahead."

"Still." There was an insistence in Paull's voice. "Why do you keep putting Alli in such danger?"

"I don't do anything," Jack said. "She does it herself."

"How big is her death wish?"

"She was a holy terror in the Ukraine."

Paull shifted, returning to the topic on his mind. "If I'd been kidnapped and held captive for a week, my death wish might be the size of New Jersey."

So that was it. "She's fine now, Dennis."

"So you've got enough evidence to clear her on Billy Warren. What about her uncle's security team?"

"Trust me."

"Remember what I said about trust, Jack. But of

all the people I know, you're the one I do trust, so I got the fugitive warrant on her frozen—until we get back. I burned significant political capital with the president."

"I appreciate it, Dennis."

"Bullshit. You had me over a barrel. Tell me, would you really have refused to come?"

"I said it," Jack nodded, "and I meant it."

"You must love that girl more than life." Paull shook his head. "You really are a fucking piece of work."

"I appreciate the compliment."

Paull still had a sour look on his face. "Did it ever occur to you that this kid might have killed Warren and strung him up?"

"It crossed my mind," Jack said.

"Then why are you letting her sit with him?"

"She can take care of herself. Besides—" He sensed Alli coming toward them.

"Am I interrupting?" she said, plopping down in one of the empty seats facing them.

"We were just talking about you," Jack said. "What's the verdict?"

Alli shot Paull a wicked look before she addressed Jack's question. "The jury's still out."

"Meaning?"

"He hasn't lied to my face, but there's something he's holding back. He's clearly frightened. Dardan's death has unhinged him in some way I can't fathom."

"Do you think he killed Billy?"

"Too soon to tell."

Jack, responding to the expression on her face, said, "What's the matter?"

"He doesn't trust us—not really, anyway."

"Smart boy. He has no reason to keep trusting us."

Alli risked a quick glance over her shoulder. "I'm doing my best to change that."

"Go slow," Jack said. "The kid's skittish."

Alli nodded and stood up. Jack reached out and took hold of her hand.

"I'm okay." She touched his bandaged hand, and Jack nodded.

She smiled, and went back to rejoin Thatë.

Paull appeared stunned. "What are you two, a team?"

Jack smiled. "Let's say we have an understanding."

"Jesus, I wish my daughter and I understood each other like that."

"Every relationship has its own difficulties."

"Nevertheless." Paull glanced after Alli. "What's the secret?"

The secret, Jack thought, *is Emma, reaching out to both of us from her unquiet existence beyond the grave.* But that explanation would mean nothing to Paull.

"There is no secret."

"Sure. It's personal. I get it." Paull nodded absently and took a swallow of single malt from a glass that sat by his right elbow. "Do you know why the Warren boy was murdered?"

"I now know that Dardan gave the order."

"Why?"

"Billy Warren had something going with Arjeta Kraja, even though Arjeta belonged to Dardan. That's more than enough cause for a man like him."

"So Dardan had him whacked."

"Wouldn't that tie everything up in a nice, neat package."

Paull stared at him. "You think not?"

"You bet I think not. Dardan had Billy Warren tortured. Why? To teach him a lesson before he died? I doubt it. No, Billy was tortured for the usual reason: information. Either he had discovered something about Dardan or he was in possession of something Dardan wanted. I think Arjeta knew it, too, because Billy told her the night he was murdered. Remember that Alli got a panicky call from Billy, but when she went to Twilight, she saw them disappearing together into the shadows."

Paull flexed his shoulders. "So what's the information?"

"That," Jack said, "is the ten-billion-dollar question."

NAOMI AND McKinsey stayed late at the office, fact-checking the backgrounds of the three Fortress employees, plus pulling together a timeline of the murders from whatever other notes and intel they had gathered so far.

"There's nothing from the forensic report on Alli's room at Fearington," McKinsey said.

Naomi picked up a plastic evidence bag. "Except this damn vial the roofies were in."

"With her fingerprints on it."

"And no one else's." Naomi shook the bag and hard light glinted off the yellowish plastic. "Jack thought that was odd and so do I."

"Setup?"

Naomi nodded. "But who? And why?"

McKinsey looked at the whiteboard, where various possible motives were written out, and shook his head.

"How's your look-see into our friends, the bogus O'Banion and Willowicz, coming?" she asked.

"It isn't. The Metro police who interviewed us today took me off that. They say since the real Willowicz and O'Banion are on leave it's an internal matter."

"Do you believe them?"

"Metro police does not harbor spooks, Naomi." He shrugged. "They're two men without names."

She glanced up. "Meaning?"

He shrugged. "For all intents and purposes they don't exist."

She looked vexed. "They must exist, just not under the names Willowicz and O'Banion."

"Not our job now," he said.

"It pisses me off," she said, "those two running around, doing whatever the hell they please."

"Leave it, Naomi. We have bigger rats to run down."

Neither of them said anything for a while. The air system rattled and hummed, a cleaning cart rumbled down a hallway outside their office. A tuneless whistle approached, then was gone. The place stank of hamburgers, stale sweat, and anxiety. Silently, they got back to work. The hands of the wall clock ground slowly forward.

Around midnight, McKinsey said, "We're never going to find Arjeta Kraja." He threw a cup of cold coffee in the trash. "You know that, don't you?"

She sighed, suspecting that he was right. "She's probably buried deep."

"More likely chopped into pieces."

Naomi sat back, surveying the mess of papers, reports, and crime-scene photos, which now seemed to whirl before her eyes like a pinwheel at a carnival. "One person killed Billy Warren and both the guys at Twilight. The MO Jack found proves that, and yet we have not one solid lead."

"We don't have even a ghost of one. We don't even have a motive. I mean why were these people murdered? What did they know? Carson's going to be asking us questions and we're not going to have any answers."

"Fuck him."

"You say that now." McKinsey stretched. "Fuck this, I gotta get outta here."

Naomi realized that she was fried, too. Besides, she had another agenda to tend to. "I'm starved. Let's go get something to eat."

"Really? You want to hang out?"

"I want to eat." She rose, grabbing her coat. "You coming or not?"

He got to his feet. "Sure thing. I wouldn't miss a date with you for all the porn on the Internet."

She smiled inwardly. She couldn't wait to get him hammered.

They went to Marco's, a red-sauce Italian joint straight out of *The Godfather*, except the food was indifferent. It did, however, have the advantage of being close to the office, not to mention cheap. Plus, it had a first-class bar.

The kitchen could have used a lesson or two from Pete Clemenza, Naomi thought sourly as they took their seats around a table with a red-and-white-checked cloth. She was something of a foodie, a frustrating trait for someone on her salary. How many restaurants had she been forced to pass by because she knew she couldn't afford even a Caesar salad or a crudo appetizer?

They started out with whiskey shots. Then, typical of him, McKinsey opted for a cheap wine, which Naomi immediately countermanded, choosing a bottle of Chianti, which at least would not take off the roof of her mouth. When it came, McKinsey attacked it like a roast turkey, downing a third of the bottle before she had finished her second glass. They discussed the case, the fact that all three Fortress employees seemed to check out. Naomi asked him what he thought of the information in the dossiers and he shrugged, as if to say, You've seen one dossier, you've seen them all.

"I must say you're taking this case very personally," he said.

"And that surprises you?"

He shrugged again. "A bit. On the Ranch, you're known as the Ice Doll." The Ranch was the Secret Service "clubhouse," a male-chosen name that set her teeth on edge. It only proved her male compatriots' arrested adolescence.

"What the hell's that supposed to mean?"

"Let's face it, Naomi, you don't get involved—in anything."

"Shit, Pete, I know code words when I hear them. What your young boys' club means is that I won't go down on any of them."

He stared at her for a moment, then burst into laughter. "You know, you're probably right. They ride me about that all the time, which I guess is a compliment."

"A shit-handed compliment if I ever heard one."

He shook his head. "I can't figure out why you ignore the fact that you're beautiful—and smokin' hot."

"That's because you're not a woman," she said tartly. "You go through life thinking you're hot, and that's exactly how men treat you. Boobs, butt, legs, beyond that they won't see an inch. Do you have any idea how hard I have to work to get men to take me seriously?"

"Not really," he said dryly. "All I see when I look at you are boobs, butt, and legs."

"Bastard," she said, and they both laughed.

New glasses and a second bottle of wine appeared, a Lambrusco this time. The waiter poured a little into her glass to taste. She swirled it around, smelled it, then took a sip. It was fine, and she nodded her approval.

McKinsey made a face. "But, see, this is what I mean. You can be such a fucking snob." He swigged down some of the wine. His eyes had a semiglazed look and his hair seemed unkempt. "Honestly, I don't know why I put up with you."

"I was just thinking the same thing."

He began to scan the menu. "Well, I could request a new partner, but no one else would have you."

Naomi buried her face in the menu and decided not to show how deeply he had stung her.

He set aside the menu. "Besides, no one else would come up to your standards."

She raised her eyes to see his tight grin. Everything

about Pete was tight. He was one of those people who worked out at the gym three nights a week. If he wasn't in the Secret Service he'd have been a professional gym rat without any socially redeeming value whatsoever.

They gave their orders to the waiter, who gathered up their menus and departed. That left the two of them staring at each other. The bustle all around them seemed not to exist, or to be muted out of all proportion. Though it was far too late for a normal dinner crowd, this crew was anything but normal. They all worked for the federal government; three-quarters of them—maybe more—were spooks of one sort or another. They were a clannish lot: the field agents over there, the intel parsers over here, the code breakers huddled in back like a bunch of old ladies. A table of four bosses—who knew their real ranks?— was in the center of the crowd, anxiously being observed by everyone out of the corner of their eyes.

"The Bishops are in the process of rearranging the board," McKinsey said. Bishop was the internal name for the bosses, from departmental chairs to ministry honchos to the secretaries in their lofty nests high above the fray at the president's side.

"They're always rearranging something," Naomi said. "It gives them something to do."

McKinsey nodded. "Stratagems within stratagems."

Speaking of which, Naomi thought, *what stratagem are you involved with?* She put a smile on her face. "Pete, we've been partners for a couple of years. What do we know about each other?"

He shrugged. "We always have each other's back. What else do we need to know?"

The food came and she sat back until the waiter had left. She glanced down at her food and knew that she'd made a mistake. The red sauce looked too much like blood and the meatballs—well, she'd rather not even go there.

McKinsey was already forking up his veal parm. "What's the matter?"

Naomi sighed and put her fork down. "I just lost my appetite."

He paused with his fork halfway to his mouth. "This isn't like you, Naomi. What's gotten under your skin?"

"Just about everything," she said, "from what was done to Billy Warren, to four dead bodies in the space of twelve hours, to Alli being the prime suspect in Billy's torture-death."

He looked at her steadily. "You have a soft spot for that girl, don't you?"

She returned his gaze, part of her looking inside herself. "I was with her when she lost her father, when they brought her mother aboard Air Force One. Losing both parents in the space of a year. I feel for that girl. Her world's been turned inside out. And now this mess."

"We've all been through shitty times, Naomi." He popped a wedge of veal into his mouth. "She's no different than the rest of us poor fools."

Naomi clamped down on the urge to say, There's nothing the same between us and Alli, but, instead, sticking to her agenda, she said, "You've been through tough times, Pete?"

"Sure." He rolled his shoulders, the way all gym rats did. "One time, when I was eight, or maybe nine,

I got lost. I mean *really* lost. My parents had rented a cabin in the Smoky Mountains. This was before the blood and guts of the divorce started flying, but already they weren't getting along. I guess they thought the vacation would do their relationship good. Instead, the isolation just brought home to them how unhappy they were. They fought—every night they fought, worse and worse. I couldn't stand it, so I left."

He speared another chunk of veal and cheese. "It's not like I was running away from home or anything, but I had to get out of there. I was so upset, I didn't think, didn't take a flashlight or even a jacket. I ran into the forest the way you run in a nightmare, without sound, with your heart pounding so heavily you're sure it's going to explode and rip you wide open.

"I remember the moon, that cold light breaking through the pine branches, making little pools of light that winked out too fast. Otherwise, Jesus, it was as dark as a pit. After a while, I ran out of breath, so I stopped, bent over, hands on my knees, panting like a sonuvabitch.

"Sometime later, I stood up and looked around. I had no idea where I was. Worse, I had no idea from which direction I had come. I had no one, nothing to guide me home. Hell, right then, I didn't have a home."

He held the forkful of food but it hung in the air, suspended, not going anywhere. McKinsey was lost again.

"What to do? Naomi, I tell you, I've never been so scared in my life. I was flooded with adrenaline. I heard all these strange sounds, amplified to an almost unbearable level, I saw leaves tremble as unseen animals moved through."

He put down his fork and looked at her. "Have you ever seen a bear in the wild?"

"No, I haven't."

"It's a pretty fucking amazing thing. That's what came out of the underbrush, Naomi, a bear. A black bear. A man-eater."

"What happened?"

McKinsey put his elbows on the table, clasped his hands together. "Here's the thing: you never know what a bear is going to do next. There are no signals you can read. Its behavior is totally unpredictable. And that pretty much sums up life in general: It's so fucking unpredictable you've got to do everything in your power to protect yourself from being eaten alive."

Naomi stared at him, and it was some time before she realized that he had given her his motivation for having some kind of arrangement with Fortress Securities. *You've got to do everything in your power to protect yourself from being eaten alive.* This told her why, but not what. What was Pete doing with Fortress, and was it a coincidence that this was the company whose head was in bed with Henry Holt Carson? Naomi didn't believe in coincidences. In her world, a belief in coincidence got you killed.

"How did it end?"

McKinsey finished off the bottle. "It didn't end, but I see what you mean." He laughed, showing her his teeth, ivory-colored and even. "The moment it saw me the bear reared up on its hind legs. He and I, perfectly still, stood looking at each other. I was aware of something breathing just below me. Later, I realized it was my body. Abject terror had taken my mind away from the danger. How long we stayed like that I can't even guess. Eventually, though, the bear went down on all fours, turned, and crashed back through the thick undergrowth."

McKinsey licked his lips. Naomi was pleased to see that he'd had more than enough.

"Go on, Pete."

"That fucking bear." He shook his head. "I never saw the bear again." His voice had lowered, causing Naomi to lean across the table. "But, late at night or early in the morning or just as the sun is going down, I can hear it breathing close beside me, I can smell its foul breath, feel its huge presence, like an eclipse, like death." He looked at her bleakly, his eyes red-rimmed. "There's no way to escape it, you know. None at all."

JACK AND Alli sat together talking softly. All around them was the stillness of movement found only in an airplane.

"Tell me about Billy Warren," Jack said.

Alli shrugged.

"What attracted you to him?"

"He was nice—honest. He wasn't grabby, like the other guys around me. And there was something old-fashioned about him."

"What do you mean?"

"Well, for instance, he liked ice-cream sodas, not Jell-O shots. And, despite what he did for a living, he was a kind of neo-Luddite. He hated computers, hated how easily data could be hijacked, substituted, even faked. Give me a pen and a sheet of paper any day, he used to say." Her expression turned pensive.

"It was horrible what happened to him. I mean, he was a good guy, Jack. He just wasn't for me."

"There are lots more guys out there, Alli. And you have plenty of time."

She looked away, abruptly uncomfortable.

EMMA CAME to Jack in the darkness of the plane, while everyone around him slept and he was staring out the Perspex window at the unending darkness. Far below him, great ships plowed through the waves with their cargos of oil, electronics, washer/dryers, and cars. Men smoked and ate, slept and joked and played cards, or watched porn on their portable DVD players. That was another world, one he'd never been a part of, even when he was younger. He'd been born an outsider and an outsider he remained.

He felt his daughter first as a waft of chill air, then as a stirring of the hairs on his forearms, and then she was beside him, while, three rows back, Paull sucked in deep drafts of sleep.

"You were there, weren't you," Jack whispered, "in that underground house of death?"

"*Yes.*"

—Why?

"*I have no choice in these matters. I'm tied to death, recent death, when it involves you or Alli.*"

Jack ran a hand across his face, as if he could scrub away this hallucination or manifestation of his mind, or whatever it was.

—I don't want this. I want you safe.

Emma laughed.

"*If there's a safer place than this, I don't know about it.*"

I want to hold her, Jack thought. *I want her back.* He spoke to her instead.

—These murders are linked. I can see a pattern forming, Emma, but there aren't enough pieces yet to put in place. Like who tortured and killed Billy Warren. Like who killed those two men at Twilight. I'm sure Dardan could have answered those questions.

"Dad, I thought you'd have gotten it by now. I'm not a seer."

—You can see certain things. You knew about your mother and me.

"I'm connected to both of you. How could I not know you were splitting up?"

Jack didn't understand a thing about this arrangement. How could he; it was beyond human ken.

"You don't miss her, Dad, do you?"

—I don't, no.

"But you do miss Annika."

—You're wrong, Emma.

"I'd like to say I don't mind that you can't admit it to me, but the fact is I do."

—She's evil.

"You know that's not true."

—She murdered Senator Berns.

"How many people has your friend Dennis Paull murdered, I wonder?"

—Self-defense or mission-specific. All understandable, all within protocol.

"Oh, Dad, protocol? Really? Okay, if you want to go that route. Annika's murder was protocol: mission-specific—for her grandfather."

—Now that man—Dyadya Gourdjiev—*is* the devil.

"As opposed to her father?"

Jack sighed. The late, unlamented Oriel Jovovich Batchuk, who had stolen her away from her mother and kept Annika locked up, committing unspeakable acts of sexual violence on her body.

—It's all in the past, so what's the point?

"From where I stand, there is no past, no future, no present. It's all the same. Time is just something human beings made up to keep themselves from going crazy."

He smiled.

—Were you always like this? So damn philosophical?

She laughed.

—Yet another aspect of you I missed, Emma.

"Everybody missed it, Dad, except for Alli."

He was suddenly very tired.

—I want to sleep, but I don't know whether I'll be able to.

His daughter smiled her translucent smile.

"That I can help you with."

She spread her arms. His eyes closed.

"Rest now, Dad."

THIRTEEN

MARTIAL DRUMMING sounded in Andrew Gunn's dream. A long gray line of skeletal people with fire-bombed faces was marching toward him along the banks of a snaking river. The river was on fire, bright flames and crackling sparks shooting upward. The clouds of heat were palpable. Blackhawks whirred and banked precipitously, bristling with weaponry in the brassy sunlight, but not a single helmet was visible. The trees overhanging the river were full of flame, the skin of the skeletal people curled and blackened and fell off. Oblivious, the long gray line advanced to the beat of the invisible drum, which became more and more insistent, until . . .

Gunn started awake to the pounding on his front door. For a moment, still enmeshed in the dream, he sat still in a rumple of bedclothes. The pounding became more than insistent—it seemed frantic.

Rolling out of bed, he pulled on a pair of paint-smeared jeans and a cotton shirt, not bothering to button it as he passed through the living room, into the short entryway, where he pulled open the door.

"Jesus Christ," he said, "didn't I tell you never to come here?"

"Fuck you, too."

Vera Bard pushed past him. She wore a wide-belted iridescent black trench coat that came down so far the hem almost concealed her black high-heel shoes. She didn't look like any FBI recruit he'd ever seen.

Sighing, he closed the door and walked after her into the living room where early morning sunlight poured in through the south-facing windows. Far below, Washington and the Potomac glimmered in a flat, hazy light patterned in grays and faded browns.

"What are you doing here, Vera? How did you get out of Fearington?"

Alli's roommate looked a good deal better than she had when Jack had visited her in the Fearington infirmary yesterday. Her long, dark hair had regained its extraordinary luster and her upswept chocolate eyes were again bright with a fierce intelligence.

"I'm on a week's medical furlough." Her nostrils flared. "I got a visit from a guy named Jack McClure. You know him?"

"By reputation only." Gunn shrugged. "What of it?"

"I think he suspects something."

Gunn laughed. "How could he suspect anything?"

"How the fuck should I know? You're the brainiac of this little venture." Vera Bard's cherry mouth turned sullen. "I don't like him. I don't want him anywhere near me. It feels like he's crawling around inside my head."

"That must be painful."

"Joke all you want," she said hotly. "Just make sure he stays the hell away from me."

Gunn sighed. "You could've told me this using the encrypted cell phone I gave you."

"True enough." Her hands were at the trench coat's belt. "But then I wouldn't be able to show you this."

The belt fell away, the trench coat gaped wide open, and Vera Bard's gleaming naked body stood revealed it all its peach-skinned glory.

"Well, now," Gunn said as he came toward her, "there's an offer I can't refuse."

"YOU'RE NOT getting cold feet, are you?" Gunn said to her some time later.

"I'm not capable of getting cold feet. You know that."

She lay on top of him, tangled in the sheets, perfumed by the musky scents of sex and sweat. Her nipples were still hard; the feel of them against his skin sent quivers through the muscles of his thighs.

"McClure sure spooked you," he said quietly.

"One man, one spook, under God."

Vera laughed in that way of hers that sent his pulse racing. Actually, almost everything about her set his pulse racing, especially her smell, which drew him as if he was magnetized. The moment he had first set eyes on her, he knew he had to have her. He knew he'd move heaven and earth to make it happen.

As it turned out, nothing so drastic was required of him. They had met some years ago—three, four, in the heat haze after sex he couldn't recall—at a fancy D.C. ball given by the ambassador of Kenya. He had been invited because he had done important work there; she had been someone's date—a fairly ordinary-looking DoD functionary. What she had been doing with him, he never discovered. Frankly, he hadn't cared. Nor had he cared when he'd cut the functionary out of his own territory. Suffice it to say, hours later, he had taken her back to his place. Long before that, the DoD dud had faded into the scenery, the swirl of people, the babble of multi-culti voices, the endless layers of stiff Washingtonian protocol that was the hallmark of such affairs. She had been twenty-two, then, and twelve years his junior, a rose on the cusp of opening. He saw the potential in her and, to her credit, she saw it, too. They needed each other, like flowers need the rain.

Gunn threaded her thick, lustrous hair through his fingers. The weight of it thrilled him, and the vulnerable heat at the nape of her neck set his groin to throbbing. "It's absolutely essential to know I can trust you."

Vera snaked her arm down, her fingers reaching between his thighs. "When have I ever let you down?" She smiled. "When have *you* ever let *me* down?"

He grabbed her wrist before her fingers brought him past the edge of coherent thought. "No joke now, Vera. Don't fuck with me."

"I would be insane to jeopardize what you've taught me, what we have." Her chocolate eyes probed his like searchlights. "I'll never find anyone like you." It was she, now, who guided his hand between her legs. "No one else has ever done this to me, no one else ever will."

Feeling her wetness set Gunn's heart to raging in his chest. He felt like he was on fire, like he couldn't catch his breath.

"I'll keep Jack McClure away from you." His tongue was thick in his mouth. He rolled over on top of her. "But remember the most difficult part is just beginning."

"How could I forget?" Vera said. "Your instructions are drilled into my brain."

"Now all that remains is for both of us to do our jobs."

Their lips met, tongues probing just as the doorbell rang. Gunn wasn't thinking straight and he ignored it, until the bell became one long, uninterrupted burr in his side.

"Godammit to hell!"

Pushing off her moist heat, he rolled out of bed, jammed on his jeans, and padded out through the living room and into the foyer.

"I'm coming!" he yelled, so at least the noise would cease reverberating through the apartment. Putting his eye to the view hole, he immediately drew back. *Is it that time already?* he asked himself. Well, it must be.

He unlatched the door, pulled it open, and let Henry Holt Carson into his residence. Carson looked around, taking everything in. Then he sniffed twice and said, "Go wash that stink off you, Andrew."

Gunn nodded mutely, padded into the bathroom, and shut the door. As soon as he heard the shower start to run, Carson stole silently across the living room. At the threshold to the master bedroom he paused, peering in.

"I thought it might be you." He stepped into the

darkened room, heading for the figure in the rumpled bed. "Jack McClure threw the fear of God into you, didn't he?"

Vera raised her sullen, sex-swollen face. "How did you know?"

"He has that effect on people." His eyes never left her face. "For God's sake, put some clothes on."

"I didn't bring any clothes." She sat on the edge of the bed, legs dangling, toes playing with the cuffs of his trousers. She made no attempt to hide the dark patch between her thighs.

Carson studiously kept his eyes on her face.

Vera laughed. "Look at you." She stood up, brushing against him, and watched him take a staggering step back.

By now, Carson was red-faced and shaking. Each time he saw her he promised himself that he wouldn't allow her to get under his skin, and yet somehow she always did.

She parted her thighs. "Don't you want a better glimpse of the honey pot?"

"You have a foul mouth and a vulgar mind."

She swung her hair away from her face. "Don't we all."

He looked away. "Not all."

"Don't play the hypocrite with me. I know you too well."

Carson took an involuntary step toward her. "Where is she, Vera? Where's my daughter?"

"I have no idea."

"Someone has to know."

"Yes, but who? It wasn't Alli Carson."

"Maybe you fucked up with her."

"Impossible." Her eyes locked onto his and wouldn't let go. "I had the best teachers."

His gaze broke away from hers. "You mistake me."

She searched through the rumpled sheets for her thong, then remembered she hadn't worn one. "The cruelest people are the deniers, HH. Delusion is a major component of cruelty: You convince yourself that the situation calls for certain measures. And self-delusion, well, the cruelty becomes extreme because you're certain you're doing what's best."

"And you think that applies to me?"

"No, HH. I *know* it applies to you. Our history is just chock-full of examples."

He wanted to turn away, to dismiss every word she said, but he couldn't. She had for him the dreadful fascination a serpent holds for a rodent. There was a strange strength inside her that made him want to weep.

"Keep your mouth shut," he said with the dangerous feeling, a shortness of breath he knew too well.

"Hit me." She leaned toward him, thrusting out her chin. "That's what you want to do, isn't it?" Her smile was knife-sharp and shadowed. "All that power, HH, and you can't do anything with it. How does it feel to be hog-tied and helpless?"

Carson's eyes looked wounded. "Why do you need to taunt me so?"

Vera's laugh was deliberately cruel. "Who knows better than you?"

Carson gave a quick look over his shoulder. Gunn was nowhere in sight. "What have you found out?"

She contemplated him for a moment. "You're a man who's never satisfied with what he's given—you have to take it all. You always want to know more, and more, and more. It never ends." Her smile grew tiny white teeth.

"Answer me, please."

Her bantering tone evaporated. "There's someone, I'm certain of it."

"I was right, then."

"You're always right, you know that."

He frowned. "You're referring to something, but I don't know what."

"Yes, I know. With your powers of perception you've blotted it all out. It's like it never happened."

He stared at her until she said, "Andy's very secretive."

"His life, it seems, is one huge secret."

"As you said."

"Who is running him?"

"To be determined."

"Still."

She turned to him. "So you want to do this yourself? No? I thought not." She shook her head. "People are complicated, an affair is complicated."

"We don't have time for this, Vera. I need to know—"

"You always need to know. Where is Caroline? Who is Gunn working for behind your back? Where will it stop?"

"It can't stop, Vera. This is my life."

"Sadly." She walked past him into the living room.

"We're not finished. Come back here."

When she ignored him, he strode after her.

"Be careful, Vera," he said.

She seemed incredulous. "You're worried about my safety? Now?"

His eyes searched hers. He seemed to want to say something, then changed his mind. "You'll never hear it coming."

"Who ever does?"

"Who ever does what?" Gunn said. He had a bath sheet wrapped around his middle and was rubbing his hair dry with a matching towel. He looked from Vera's expression to Carson's half-shadowed face, and nodded. "You two are at it again."

"He can't help himself." Vera moved aside as Gunn went into the bedroom to dress. She plucked at the puddle of her trench coat. While she was at it, she gave Carson a good view of everything. Hearing him expel a breath, she smiled to herself.

"I've showered you with gifts and favors."

"And what do I have to show for it?"

"What is it you want?"

"A family," she snapped as she whirled on him. "But all I have is you and Andy."

"Poor you."

She bared her teeth as she slid on the trench coat and belted it up.

"Aren't you going to shower?" Carson said.

"Why should I?" She stepped into her shoes. "I love the smell of sex in the morning."

She left without turning around or saying another word. It was as if the world she had just inhabited had vanished in a puff of smoke.

By this time, Gunn had dressed himself in midnight blue trousers and a crisp pin-striped shirt. A pair of shiny, expensive loafers were on his feet.

"Jesus, Andrew, she's young enough to be—"

"Not quite." Gunn guided an alligator-skin belt through the loops of his trousers and buckled up.

"You're taking quite a risk."

"Ah, now we come to the crux of your displeasure." Gunn went through the living room, into the kitchen, and took a bag of coffee beans out of the freezer.

Carson followed him into the bright lights of the kitchen. "She didn't even stay long enough to make coffee."

"And you wonder why she hates your guts." For the next few minutes he busied himself with grinding the beans, heating the water, then combining them in a Pyrex presspot. He took out a pair of cups from an overhead cabinet.

"I want to kill her."

Gunn arranged a container of half-and-half and a canister of raw sugar. "No, you don't. You want what she won't give you."

Carson reached out and swung Gunn around. "Listen, you, it's fucking dangerous to go exploring in here." He tapped the end of a forefinger against his temple. "More dangerous than you can imagine."

For a long moment, the two men stared at each other. Then, without a word, Gunn turned back to the coffee and depressed the plunger all the way to the bottom.

"Cream and sugar," Carson said.

Gunn stared down at the two empty cups. "You don't have to tell me a second time."

———

"THERE'S NOTHING here," McKinsey said.

Naomi wrinkled her nose. "Nothing but the ammonia stink of an industrial-strength cleaner."

"The manager of First Won Ton upstairs said they had a vermin problem."

Naomi, playing the beam of her flashlight over the bare concrete floor and walls, said, "I heard him, Pete."

"But you don't believe him."

"No," she said. "I don't."

His own beam swung back and forth. "Maybe McClure was mistaken."

Naomi glanced at him. "Are you kidding me? Mistaken about a white slave trade clearinghouse, mistaken about the body of Arjeta Kraja?"

"Do you see any evidence of those things?" McKinsey squinted. "He said he was calling from where?"

"He didn't say." Naomi walked into the back room, which was no bigger than a good-sized closet. "He was with Dennis Paull and Alli."

"GPS?"

"He disabled it on his cell and his signal is being bounced, so he can't be traced. But he must have been on the move because the signal kept cutting out." She was staring at the painting of blue and gray mountains, whose ragged tops seemed to shred the blue sky. "What the hell is this doing here?" She glanced around. "No other paintings, wall hangings, calendars, zippo. But Jack said there was another room with Arjeta Kraja laid out in it, dead as a doorpost."

"I don't see anything of the sort," McKinsey said. "Ever occur to you he was full of shit?"

When she gave him a dirty look, he added, "Between the two of you, Alli Carson could be a serial killer and she'd never get arrested."

"Don't be a dick." She went over to the painting and felt behind it. "There's something here."

McKinsey came over and unhooked the painting, setting it down. They both stared at the one-way glass, then, cupping their hands, tried to peer into the other side.

"What the fuck?" McKinsey said.

Naomi flipped the wall switch, but nothing happened. "Go get the manager," she said.

While he was gone, she checked around the tiny room, trying to find a way into the space beyond the one-way glass. She found nothing, which puzzled her so much that it was the first question to put to the restaurant manager.

He was a slender Chinese man in his midfifties, with a flat face and eyes that darted about like a pair of frightened mice. He licked his lips continually and his clasped hands made washing motions.

"I don't know," he said nervously. He frowned, clearly puzzled. "I didn't even know the room existed."

"But you own this space," she said.

He nodded. "But it's not used by the restaurant. I rent it out." He looked around. "At least I did."

"Who rented it?" McKinsey said.

"A company. Qershi Holdings."

"Who the hell're they?"

The manager spread his hands. "I have no idea."

"Who is Qershi Holdings' representative?"

"I only dealt with a voice over the phone."

"And that was enough for you?" Naomi said skeptically.

"He sent cash over as a binder. Two months' worth." The manager shrugged his negligible shoulders. "Before that, this space just gathered dust. Though I advertised heavily, I couldn't give it away. In my business when cash speaks, I listen."

McKinsey looked around the space. "So what was going on down here?"

The manager shrugged.

McKinsey stared at him. "You're a real font of knowledge, aren't you?"

"You never got curious?" Naomi said.

"I was paid a lot of money not to be curious. A stipulation from my tenant."

Naomi tapped a pen against the side of her smartphone. "So, basically, they could have been auctioning off little girls down here and you wouldn't know about it."

The manager gave no indication that he knew anything.

"We came down here through the restaurant," McKinsey said.

"There's a back entrance," the manager replied. "I was told to keep the lights off in that area."

"So where is everyone?" Naomi said.

"They must have moved out late last night. I was here until closing—around midnight—and I didn't see anything."

"Of course you didn't," McKinsey muttered.

The manager leaned forward. "Pardon?"

"How do we get into this space behind the glass?" Naomi said.

"Like I said—"

A little yelp exploded from the manager's mouth

when McKinsey smashed the glass with his elbow, then began to pick out the remaining shards from the frame. Naomi trained her flashlight on the interior. It was a perfect square, small, airless. A faint but unmistakable sickly sweet scent came to her.

"It smells like death in there," she said.

The manager whimpered. He held up his hands. "I don't want any trouble."

"Too late for that," McKinsey said as he watched Naomi carefully climb through the shattered window. "What have we got?" he asked her.

"A whole lot of nothing." The beam of her flashlight lit up the corners of the space. "Odd, though, the floor in here is wooden planks."

"An older part of the subbasement," McKinsey offered.

"Right." Then the beam came to rest. "Hold on a minute." Crouched down, she snapped on a pair of latex gloves.

McKinsey leaned in. "Whatcha got?"

"One of these boards has something on it." She played the beam directly on it. "I think it's blood, Pete."

Lifting an adjacent board, she played the beam of light into the space beneath. She bent her head down for a better look, and coughed heavily. "Fresh blood."

FOURTEEN

THE SWORD hung in the sky, glittering, remote. It revealed itself through a rent in the thick cloud cover, a sword full of blue-white stars. Jack took a deep breath of the humid air. It was filled with strange scents, just as the night was filled with strange sounds.

Behind him, the jet crouched, having landed on a runway Jack had no doubt was not on any map or near any inhabited area. It was silent, dark. Just beyond was the verge of a thick evergreen forest, its canopy, like groping fingers, mimicking the rough-hewn tors of the Korab mountain range that rose ahead of them. Somewhere up there was Tetovo, impregnable, teeming with Xhafa's men, bristling with high-tech weaponry.

They were in western Macedonia, behind enemy lines. Their world had contracted into a red zone, a potential killing field. It was essential, Paull had told them just before landing, that they keep this in mind every minute of the day and night until such time as they made it back here and the plane took off.

While Paull broke out their weaponry and outerwear for the trek, Jack took Alli aside.

"I really need you to keep an eye on the kid."

She looked at him with her clear eyes. "You don't think I killed Billy, do you?"

"Don't be absurd." He took a breath. "But what I can't figure out is why you lied about Arjeta Kraja. You obviously did know her."

"Billy introduced her to me."

"Did you think you were protecting her?"

"After they showed me what had happened to Billy I knew her life was in danger. I thought if no one knew about her involvement then maybe she had a chance to stay alive, but if all of a sudden cops and Feds came after her I knew she wouldn't survive the next twenty-four hours."

"So you knew about Dardan."

She shook her head. "Neither Billy nor Arjeta mentioned him or the sex slave auction. I had no idea about that place."

"Why would your uncle have a take-out menu from First Won Ton? And why was spicy fragrant duck with cherries circled in pencil? Cherries. It's possible he knew about the Stem."

"Honestly, I don't know what to think."

"You know him better than I do, better than almost anyone."

"Actually, no." Alli looked pained. "My parents would take me to his house, but he rarely spoke to me. I got the impression he didn't like kids, including his own daughter."

"He had a daughter?"

"Caroline." Alli's eyes lost focus as she allowed memories to surface. "Caro was a strange girl."

"Strange how?"

For a moment, Alli seemed lost in thought. "For one thing, she wasn't interested in normal sorts of things—you know, music, movies, talking on the phone, clothes shopping, boys."

"So what was she into?"

Alli shrugged. "Who knows. Secrets?"

"Secrets?"

"Yeah, she was always disappearing—no one knew where she went, not Uncle Hank or her mom, Heidi. It would drive them crazy, especially Uncle Hank, who likes everything done his way. I'm guessing that's why Heidi left."

Jack considered for a moment. "Do you have any idea what happened to Caroline?"

"No. It was like she disappeared off the face of the earth. One night she walked out of the house and never came back."

"How old was she?"

Alli bit her lip. "Thirteen, maybe. That was nine, ten years ago."

"So she'd be twenty-two, twenty-three now. And nothing since then?"

Alli shook her head. "She could be alive or dead, no one knows."

"Someone must know," Jack said.

"Do you think her disappearance is relevant to Billy's murder?"

"I don't know," Jack said. "But I keep coming back to that take-out menu you found in your uncle's study."

"It seems both irrelevant and somehow important. I mean, he wouldn't be caught dead eating Chinese take-out."

"Which is why it's sticking in my mind," Jack said. "Anomalies are always important."

Alli stared at him for a minute. "What are you thinking?"

"I'm wondering if there's a link between the Stem, that take-out menu, and Caroline."

"You think Caro was kidnapped and auctioned off?"

"I'm wondering if that's the direction your uncle is going in."

"But if he knows about what was going on at the Stem, why didn't he have it shut down?"

"That's an interesting question," Jack said.

Alli dug in her pocket. "Maybe this will be of some help." She handed over the cell phone. "I also found this in Uncle Hank's study."

Jack was about to open it when Paull came up to them.

"Okay, we're all set. You need to get into your mountain gear."

Jack pocketed the cell as he took a look at the forbidding mountains. "How are we getting up to Tetovo?"

Paull drew out a map covered in clear waterproof plastic and opened it. He clicked a pen flash and pointed. "This is the best route, according to our geo-tech boys."

Jack nodded. He didn't bother studying the map because he wouldn't be able to make sense of it. "What about the kid?"

Paull's eyes were dark and hooded. "We can't trust him to go any farther."

"You can't just cut him loose out here in the middle of nowhere."

"He stays with the plane until we get back," Paull said curtly.

"That would be a mistake."

They all turned to see Thatë standing behind Paull.

"Get back," Paull flared.

Alli held up a hand. "Hold on a minute, you two."

Paull's head swiveled around and he glared at her. "Listen, missy, Jack may cut you an unreasonable amount of slack, but as far as decisions here are concerned—"

"Thatë's been here before," she said. "He knows the mountains, he knows this area of Macedonia."

Jack turned to the kid. "Is that true?"

Thatë nodded. "I lived in the mountains for eighteen months before I came to Washington."

Jack beckoned him with a finger and the kid joined their circle.

"Show him the route we're taking, Dennis."

When Paull made no move, Alli traced the route on the map.

Thatë shook his head. "There are at least two good reasons why this route will get you into trouble. The first is here." His forefinger stabbed out. "This village, Dolna Zhelino, belongs to Xhafa. If we go anywhere near it, he'll know within an hour that you're coming."

Paull rolled his eyes.

Jack said, "What else?"

"The route takes you along this ridge above the Vardar River." His fingertip traced a line. "Here."

"It's the most direct route," Paull said. "Otherwise, we'll waste time going miles out of our way."

"It will be a waste of time," Thatë said, "once you're buried in a rockslide."

Paull made a noise in the back of his throat. "Alli, take the kid back inside the plane."

When the two had mounted the folding stairs and vanished into the jet's interior, Jack said, "What's your problem, Dennis?"

"My problem is this kid."

"Really? He's already proven useful."

"Why the fuck should I believe anything he says?" Paull's eyes engaged Jack's. They had dark circles under them. Lines of tension scored his face. "My sense is he's working for Xhafa, and if he is, he'll lead us right into a mortal trap."

"What if he's telling the truth?"

"Jack, he has no incentive to tell the truth and every reason to make sure we wind up dead."

INSIDE THE plane, Alli sat down in the seat nearest the door. After a moment's hesitation, Thatë sat beside her.

"Dennis Paull." She shook her head. "What a dickwad."

He laughed. "You're not afraid of anything, are you?"

"Shit," she said. "I'm afraid of everything."

"You're lying."

She laughed softly, mocking him.

"Then you hide your terror well."

"I've had a lot of practice, believe me." As if realizing she had possibly revealed too much, she launched into another topic before he could respond. "What were you doing up in the Tetovo area?"

Thatë stared straight ahead. "I was sent by the people who trained me. Russians. *Grupperovka.*" His eyes cut to her briefly. When she gave no visible reaction, he said, "You know that word?"

Alli nodded. "Yeah. Mobsters, whole families of 'em."

He appeared somewhat surprised. His eyes reflected the dim lighting of the jet's interior, turning them as glassy as marbles.

"I've been to Moscow," she said. "Why did the *grupperovka* send you here?"

"To train with Xhafa's freedom fighters."

Alli was aware of the slight hesitation; she didn't need to see his face to know that he was lying.

PAULL SHOOK his head. "What gives me pause is why you and I aren't on the same page."

"I have a feeling about him, Dennis."

"Jack, he's the fucking enemy."

"If you believe that, then kill him. Right here. Shoot him in the back of the head like the Russians do. If he's the enemy surely he deserves nothing less."

The two men stood toe to toe, their eyes locked, their wills silently battling. The spangled sword was gone. In its place was a sky compressed into layers of low cloud. A chill wind whipped through the trees, causing a great rustling, as if an armada of insects was moving through them. Paull had flicked off the pen flash. There was almost no light. The thick air made it seem as if they were on the ocean floor. Somewhere, not far off, an owl hooted.

"I'm not giving in, Jack. And I'm not going to kill him," Paull said. "We'll let him go when we get back here. Until then, the pilot and crew are more than qualified to keep him under wraps."

Jack took a step closer, his voice lowered. "You said you trust me. Well, I have a feeling about him, Dennis. I think he can help us get to Xhafa."

"That's why we have a geotech department."

"Has any one of them been to Macedonia, let alone anywhere near Tetovo?"

"Not necessary," Paull snapped. "They have computers—"

Jack leaned in. "Dennis, don't you get it? Computers don't mean shit out here. This is the wilderness, this is a zone that's redder than red. Don't you think the SKOPES unit relied on computer-compiled data?"

Paull's mouth was a stubborn line. "I can't hear you."

"You haven't been in the field for years, so don't be a fool, Dennis. Fate has given us an edge the SKOPES unit never even dreamed of, and you want to ignore it?"

Paull's mouth opened to reply, then he shut it with a snap. He let out his breath slowly and deliberately, as if he were mentally counting to ten to calm himself down.

"This is so fucked, Jack."

"Maybe it is, maybe it isn't."

Paull looked as if he wanted to hit Jack. "We follow my route. Period."

"You're not thinking straight, Dennis."

"He stays right here with the plane."

Jack read the stubbornness on Paull's face and

understood that his boss needed to feel in charge. This was his first field mission in a number of years; he was understandably nervous. He'd worked hard on the details of his chosen plan; deviating from it now would seem rash and dangerous to him. He couldn't win this fight. Pushing Paull further now would only damage their relationship.

"Whatever you say."

Paull's finger pressed against Jack's chest. "This is on you. If he steps out of line, my men have orders to subdue him but not to harm him, because you're the one who's going to put a bullet in the back of his head." He glared into Jack's face. "Are we clear?"

"Absolutely, but Alli is coming with us."

Paull hooked his thumb over his shoulder. "Do you really think I'd risk the life of my friend's daughter?"

"She'll be a help to us," Jack said. "She brings unique—"

"No."

"She can take care of herself."

"So we've seen."

Jack thought a moment. "How about this. If she can take you off your feet, she comes with us. If you put her down, she stays."

Paull snorted. "You can't be serious. She's only a wisp of a thing."

"You're not afraid, are you?"

"Fuck, no. But—"

"But nothing."

Jack went to the foot of the stairs and called to her. A moment later, Alli came down to them. He told her what he had proposed.

She stared up at him. "Are you insane?" she whispered.

"Do you want to come with us or don't you?"

He took her over to where Paull stood. She didn't waste a second, but strode inside Paull's defenses, extended her left leg, hooked her boot behind his ankle, and yanked him off his feet.

He sprang up and went after her. Alli calmly stood her ground and, when he reached out for her, grabbed his arm with her left hand and drew him forward. Using his own momentum against him, she drew him around and, as he stumbled, she kicked out. He went down on his face.

He lay there for a moment, one hand beneath him. When he rolled over, he had a Sig Sauer pointed at her.

Alli kicked to the side, the sole of her boot pinioning his gun wrist to the ground.

From his position flat on his back, Paull stared up at Jack. "You fucker," he said.

STAKEOUTS WERE the worst, Naomi thought, as she shifted her position behind the wheel of her car. First, your filled bladder caused your head to throb, then the cramps started behind your knees, then your ankles started to swell from a combination of the inactivity and the salty snacks you consumed out of sheer boredom.

Sitting several car lengths down the block from the entrance to McKinsey's building, she had cause to think of the blood spatter she'd found at the Stem. Was it Arjeta Kraja's blood? Was Jack right, was she dead?

She was Secret Service, not a homicide detective. She'd had no experience with murder investigations—with murder at all, for that matter. She'd been trained to preserve life, to forfeit her own in order to protect the POTUS and the FLOTUS. Heinous crimes were beyond her ken, and as she sat shivering in the night, waiting for something—anything!—to happen, she was haunted not only by the murders of Arjeta Kraja, Billy Warren, and the two men in Twilight, but by the specter of the person or persons capable of such extreme cruelty, such contempt for life. Who were these people and what were they doing infecting her country? She was gripped by both fear and a sense of outrage. She harbored fantasies of doing to them what they had done to their victims. *Christ,* she thought, *the world is a terrible place.* And she was in a position where it chose to reveal that side of itself over and over. Not so for her sister, Rachel, happily married to a divorce attorney who made seven figures a year. She lived in a huge house in Maryland, had two beautiful children, an Airedale named Digger, and a seven-series BMW. For Rachel, the world was a dream come true, filled with roses and candy canes. Naomi might be jealous, except for the fact that she'd suffocate in the banality of that life. She was quite certain she was not cut out to be a wife with two children. When she'd been younger, she had envied Rachel, but now her sister's life terrified her.

Shifting in her seat again, she stifled a moan. Her butt was killing her and she was dying to get out of the car and stretch her legs, but she couldn't take the chance of being spotted. So here she sat like a spider in the center of her web, waiting for a fly to entangle itself in the sticky strands.

Her thoughts returned to the Stem and its slavery auctions. Dardan had been part of it, certainly, but in his phone call Jack had mentioned someone named Mbreti, Albanian for "king." Who the hell was Mbreti? She had so little to go on—just the name—it was like trying to find a needle in a warehouse full of haystacks.

And then there was McKinsey. It was no coincidence that she had seen Pete coming out of the Fortress Securities building. Connected with Fortress, he had to know more about the three guards than she did, yet he'd failed to mention it over dinner. He was hiding something from her, maybe a great many things. The thought chilled her to the bone. The one person she needed to trust now seemed to be entirely untrustworthy. Minute by minute, she felt the ground slipping out from beneath her.

Several times she had tried calling Jack back, but either he wasn't answering or he wasn't in range of a cell tower. He hadn't said what he was doing with Dennis Paull and she knew better than to ask. Still, she wished she could talk with him, wished even harder that he was here with her, because she knew that he was the one person who could unravel the mysteries that confronted her. In order not to think about Jack—about how she really felt about him— she flooded her mind with anger toward Pete McKinsey. Armored in her anger, she felt safe from emotions that would otherwise swamp her, emotions she'd rather not examine too closely.

But then she heard Rachel's voice in her head: *"You make a fetish of not feeling anything for anyone. You think you're incapable of feeling deeply, but it's not true. You're just terrified; you think you'll be crushed."* She had shaken her head. *"You're too strong for that, Nomi. You're a tank."*

To her horror, Naomi discovered that she had begun to weep. *Oh, God, no,* she thought. But she knew that the heart wanted what the heart wanted. It was simply that what her heart wanted was unattainable.

Wiping her eyes, she shook her head. *Grow up,* she berated herself. *Just grow the fuck up.*

Was that her voice, or her brother's? The oldest of the three siblings, Damon had had an iron personality, a volatile temper, and a great love for his sisters. But his idea of love was to be even tougher on them than he knew the world would be.

"Girls get shafted," he'd tell them, *"and here's why: Girls are weak, they knuckle under to men all the time, they can't take the hard knocks of life. Bottom line: They're not tough enough."* Rachel had told him to go to hell, but, entirely without knowing it, Naomi had swallowed his philosophy whole.

"That's why you get into trouble," Rachel had told her once. *"That's why you're alone."*

By that time, Damon was dead, the body shipped home from Afghanistan. Their mother had collapsed in grief and had never recovered, dying thirteen months later. The doctor said it was a stroke, but Naomi knew it was a broken heart.

Naomi thought of her brother often, and when she did, he increased in stature, until he was larger than life. Every month she went to Arlington Cemetery to lay a wreath at his grave and to talk to him. She missed him in the way a child misses her father. Her sorrow was bitter and unending.

The night was growing thin. The gray sky, as fragile-looking as an eggshell, wavered as it tilted toward dawn. Cathedral Avenue, where McKinsey's huge Art Deco apartment building rose like the prow of the *Titanic,* was coming alive with traffic. A light rain fell and then, as abruptly as it started, ceased, leaving the road and sidewalks as slick as the surface of a skating rink. McKinsey's Ford was still parked down the block, cold and deserted, mocking her.

A gust of wind swept trash up into the air, sudden movement on a lonely, deserted street, and she shivered again. She was deathly tired; even her bones ached with exhaustion. She had been working non-stop for the last two days without even an hour of sleep. Unconsciously, her head tilted back, her eyelids closed, and she slid from awareness, only to snap herself awake. She glanced at herself in the rearview mirror, which reflected a face as pale and sunken as a corpse's.

Damn, she thought, *I need a vacation.*

At that precise moment, her gaze was drawn to a metallic flash as the door to McKinsey's building opened. A young woman in a broad-brimmed hat, stiletto-heeled boots, and stylish reflective raincoat stepped out. In one arm, she cradled one of those tiny teacup poodles with a rhinestone-studded collar. She put the dog down on the sidewalk and attached the leash. As she and the poodle trotted down the broad stone steps, McKinsey emerged and scanned the immediate vicinity. Naomi froze, scarcely daring to breathe.

Apparently satisfied, he went down the steps and headed for his car. She leaned forward, her hand on the ignition key, her right foot on the brake. The idea was to start her car when he did, so he wouldn't hear it. Her eyes followed McKinsey as he got into his car and slid behind the wheel. The instant he leaned forward to slot the key, she fired her ignition. A moment later, he pulled out. She counted silently to ten, then followed him into the traffic of Cathedral Avenue.

He took her south and then west into Georgetown. Turning left off M Street, he drove down to the water and parked. For some time, he sat in the car with the driver's side window down, smoking. In no hurry, he appeared to be staring out at the water.

At precisely 6:14, he got out of the Ford and strolled down to the water. Elbows on the railing, he leaned out over the water and stared down. Naomi stepped out onto the sidewalk and followed his path to the east side of the Sequoia Center. As she did so, McKinsey did a strange thing. He straddled the railing, then dropped over the water side.

Naomi broke into a run. A motor coughed to life. She arrived at the railing just in time to see McKinsey standing beside a man driving a small motorboat. They were heading out to Theodore Roosevelt Island. Naomi caught a glimpse of the man McKinsey had gone to meet. He was in his mid to late thirties, athletic in build, with thick, dark hair, curling at his neck. He sported a full beard. There was a flash of dark predator's eyes, set deep in his skull, before the boat swept away in a white spray of wake.

Naomi slammed her fists into the top rail and wondered what the hell her partner was up to.

THEY WERE already high in the foothills of the Korab mountains by the time the talons of dawn scraped the eastern horizon. At first, there was just a thin line of red, then, in the space of a heartbeat, the terrain was flooded with a golden light so dazzling they were forced to don sunglasses.

Alli walked between Paull on point and Jack at the rear. The trio wore climbing boots, jeans, and camouflage microfiber windbreakers. They carried ArmaLite AR 25 assault rifles, featherweight backpacks stuffed with food, water, and the DARPA weapons Paull had procured.

The ground's pitch steepened, the dips more shallow and, at the same time, the way became more rugged. The switchback path was strewn with larger and larger rocks, and clots of loose earth that skittered and slid out from under their boot soles, tumbling backward down the slope. Trees were bent as old men, twisted by the high winds of storms, and the scrub took on the lackluster color of clay, looking more dead than alive. High above them, hawks circled and dipped on the thermals, searching for prey.

With daylight full blown, Paull called a halt and they made temporary camp in the shadow of an enormous boulder, leaning like a giant's tooth knocked off true. They drank and ate a little, then took turns at lookout while the others dozed. When it was Alli's turn to stand guard, Jack rose and picked his way to stand beside her.

"Did you find anything interesting on Uncle Hank's cell?"

Her voice was soft and hushed, her eyes moving across the terrain, searching for any movement, anything out of place.

"Yes and no," Jack said. "There are only two numbers on that phone, odd enough in and of itself, but to make matters more mysterious both are assigned a single letter—A and D—rather than a name. The designations could be the first letter of names, or some code of your uncle's devising." He gestured. "Out here, there's no way of connecting with these numbers, so I'll have to wait to check them out."

Alli gave him a swift glance. "You think this means he knows about the Stem? About Dardan?"

"This cell, these coded numbers, may concern something altogether different, Alli. It's too soon to tell." Discussing Henry Holt Carson brought home to Jack a duty he had been reluctant to perform. There was no time like the present, he thought. Still, the trauma Alli had so recently sustained made this difficult task even more so.

"Alli, there's something I need to tell you. I know your uncle neglected to tell you." He took a breath, let it out. "The night Billy was murdered . . . your mother passed away."

Alli said nothing. She stared out at the unfamiliar terrain, blindingly outlined against a sky so blue that without sunglasses it made your eyes hurt. Hardwood, pines, miles of granite, split and jagged. Not a hint of human habitation anywhere.

Jack could hear her breathing. "I'm so sorry. I'll miss her."

"Uncle Hank knew?"

"Of course. He was called to the hospital, as were Dennis and I. They tried to contact you, but by then Fearington was in lockdown."

Alli's breathing seemed to shorten, to quicken. "Why didn't he tell me?" She turned to Jack, tears glittering in the corners of her eyes. "When I was at his house, when he locked me into his study, why didn't Uncle Hank tell me?"

"I can't answer that," Jack said softly. "But it's possible that being angry at him isn't the way to go at this moment."

She didn't respond.

"Alli?"

She shook her head fiercely. "I can't think about them—either of them."

"You will, sometime." His voice was both soft and gentle. "The longer you wait—"

"Shit," she said, and walked away.

Jack watched her for a time, a tiny, lone sentinel. Her back was ramrod straight, her stance as fiercely battle-ready as any soldier.

A stirring at his side alerted him.

"She's an enigma, isn't she, Dad?"

"That she is, Emma."

"Even to herself."

NAOMI SPENT a very frustrating day with Pete, collating all the information they had amassed, including the forensics on the knife found behind Alli's room in Fearington, which indicated that it was, indeed, Billy's blood on the blade. However, the handle had been wiped clean, which was consistent with both a premeditated murder and a conspiracy to set up Alli.

"The bloody knife is such a clumsy attempt to frame Alli," she said. They sat at facing desks, close enough for easy conversation. "I don't get it."

He picked his head up from his paperwork. He looked neat and tidy. He was freshly shaved. It looked as if his nails had been waxed. "What do you mean?"

"First the vial of roofies with Alli's fingerprints is found under her bed. Pretty damning, no? But then this bloody knife. Who in their right mind would dump a murder weapon behind where they live?"

"You forget, Naomi. She's not in her right mind. Hasn't been, apparently, since she was abducted."

She stared at him in disbelief. "You're missing the point."

"Which is?"

He seemed peculiarly disinterested, she thought, or unusually distracted. Maybe that amounted to the same thing.

"It's as if she was set up, then given this loophole."

"I don't agree." He shook out a cigarette, then, remembering he couldn't smoke in the office, shoved it back into the pack. "Why should she care about us finding the murder weapon if her prints aren't on it?"

She ran a hand distractedly through her hair. She was suddenly sick of him.

"What have you found out about Qershi Holdings, the company that rented out the space where the Stem was transacting their business?"

"Exactly zippo." Naomi was aware of how flat her voice sounded. She bitterly hated failure. Whoever said that you can't handle success until you've failed was full of shit. "It's a shell corporation, doing business out of the Cayman Islands."

"Which local bank does it use? The Cayman banks are more helpful to us nowadays."

Naomi sighed. "If only. No, all I could pick up was a PO box."

"So," he said, "another dead end."

She nodded. "For the moment, at least."

They burned the rest of the afternoon writing their first report for Henry Holt Carson, not an easy assignment, considering both the lack of hard information and the one bit of news sure to bring out their ad hoc employer's ire.

The more they worked on the draft, the more anxious Naomi became. "Let's emphasize the increasingly cloudy picture the evidence is providing," she said. "That's sure to please him." After a grunt from McKinsey, she plowed on. "And maybe we should omit the part about Alli being with Jack."

"What?" McKinsey's head snapped up. "Are you nuts? That's about the only solid news we have for him. She isn't lost and she isn't on her own."

"She's with Jack; just what he doesn't want. He'll have a shit fit."

McKinsey brushed away her words. "Not our concern. It goes in the report. End of story."

Naomi brought her eyes back down to the draft. He was right—of course he was. But she couldn't help thinking that the news would put Jack at the top of Henry Holt Carson's enemy list. She tried to continue typing on her computer keyboard, but found that her fingers wouldn't work. She sat brooding for a moment, aware that McKinsey was eyeing her. Then she pushed her chair back and went and got some coffee from the office machine. Its bitterness matched her mood. She said to hell with it, dumped in some half-and-half instead of two-percent milk, added three teaspoons of real sugar instead of Splenda, and knocked back half a cup before she got back to her desk. God forbid it should be hot, rather than lukewarm.

· After she sat down, she stared morosely at the text on her screen. She realized that she hated working for Carson. Hell, she hated Carson himself. He was so unlike his brother, whose sudden and shocking death still haunted her.

McKinsey looked up suddenly. "You're still thinking about him, aren't you?"

She said nothing, but could not meet his gaze.

"You're getting yourself into trouble, you know that."

Her eyes flicked up. "What the hell does that mean?"

He leaned forward, elbow on his desk. "Naomi, your feelings for McClure are one thing, but when they start to cloud your professional judgment—"

"Message received," she said shortly. "Let's just drop it, okay?"

He kept his eyes on her for a moment, then got back to work.

Naomi forced her fingers to start typing again. Inwardly, she was seething. What right had Pete to admonish her when he was working his own private agenda? But she could say nothing. She needed to find out what he was involved in, and why, before she confronted him.

After a cheap, heartburn dinner, they drove over to Twilight. There was no talk between them. Naomi's mood had continued to sour during the long, tedious day.

At the club, they interviewed patrons until after midnight. Many of them remembered Arjeta Kraja, but no one claimed to be her friend or to know any of her friends. As to her family, no one had a clue. It looked as if Schiltz had been right about her: an illegal immigrant, and, judging by her lack of friends, not very long in the U.S., either. Just after midnight, they called it quits, and Naomi had gone home, feeling frustrated and helpless.

After failing to sleep, she dressed, got back in her car, and drove to Cathedral Avenue. Parking across from Pete's apartment building, she sat with her arms folded, her mind full of anger and tangled emotions.

After what seemed like an endless time, sleepy gray light stole into the street. The facade of the massive building was sheened, as if it were weeping. Naomi stared at the entrance. The glass in the door shimmered with reflections from the occasional passing car or truck.

Then, as she watched, there was a brief flare of light, as if from a match or a lighter, and Naomi sat up straighter in her seat. She thought she caught a glimpse of Pete standing just behind the door, smoking. Had he made her? A film of sweat broke out on her upper lip.

A moment later, the door swung open and the

young woman, led by her toy poodle, came down the steps. They walked several feet, until the poodle pulled her to the curb. She waited patiently, smoking while the dog peed in the gutter. She wore the same reflective raincoat and stiletto-heeled boots, but this morning she was without a hat. Her blond hair looked like liquid gold. Naomi frowned. There was something decidedly familiar about the face, the eyes especially, which were neither hazel nor gray, but some color she could not define. Then her heart started to beat so fast and hard she felt as if it was in her throat. The woman looked in her direction. The poodle had finished its business. She stepped off the curb and walked diagonally across the avenue, heading directly toward where Naomi sat, trapped behind the wheel of her car.

Her strides were long, almost like a man's, her strong thighs working like pistons. Her high-heeled boots left imprints on the wet macadam. Naomi could not help envying the perfection of her legs. Then she was on the sidewalk, abreast of Naomi's car. Naomi engaged the automatic door locks. Leaning down, the young woman tapped with a fingernail on the window.

"Open the door," she mouthed. "Let me in."

Naomi stared at her, unmoving. A moment later, a silver-plated .25 appeared in the woman's hand. When she tapped on the glass again it was with the muzzle of the handgun.

Naomi calculated the time it would take to draw her gun, or start the car and peel out. The odds were stacked heavily against her. She opened the car doors and the woman slid inside. She gave a little tug on the leash and the toy poodle leaped into her lap. She had square-cut nails, like a man; she wore no jewelry of any kind.

"Are you going to tell McKinsey?" Naomi said.

"Why would I do that?"

She had a voice that hinted at exotic places. Naomi suspected that English was not her native language. Up close, her eyes were an astonishing mineral color, carnelian maybe. She had the kind of wide, sensual mouth Naomi would have killed for. There was a strength about her that caused a warning bell inside Naomi to sound.

"You two work together."

The woman cocked her head. "Where did you get that idea?"

"Yesterday, you came out of Pete's building at almost the same moment as him, at a very early hour."

"Well, it seems as if we're all up early."

Naomi stared at her. She tried to ignore the muzzle of the .25 that was pointed at her chest. "Are you claiming you and McKinsey don't know each other?"

"No, not at all," the woman said. "But we don't work together."

Naomi tipped her head slightly. "How did you know I was here?"

"Peter was foolish to let himself be seen leaving Fortress."

"So you've been following me? Who are you?"

A small smile curved the woman's lips. "You mean you don't recognize me?"

"I admit you look familiar."

"But you don't know from where."

Naomi nodded uncertainly. The answer seemed tantalizingly close. "I don't think we've met."

"No." The poodle made a small sound and the woman rubbed it behind its ears. Its tiny pink tongue came out and licked her fingers. "We haven't."

"Then where—?"

"But you *have* seen me before, Naomi." The smile spread. "Where, where, where, you're wondering? I can see it in your face." She took a moment to slide the window down and toss her butt into the gutter. "In Moscow. Fourteen months ago. Just before the last snow of winter."

"Good God!" Memories shifted in Naomi's head, gears clicked, and all at once her brain seemed to implode. She had been standing behind and just to the left of the FLOTUS in the enormous hall of the Kremlin during the reception that followed the signing of the security pact between the United States and Russia. The atmosphere had been festive, the air thick with hard, cryptic Russian. Jack had walked in with her, and later, after the POTUS was dead and the FLOTUS was in a coma, after they had returned home aboard Air Force One, demoralized and in mourning, Jack had told her . . . "It can't be."

The woman seemed delighted. "But it is."

"You're Annika Dementieva."

FIFTEEN

H<small>E STANDS</small> in the darkness. Alli can't see him, but she can feel him, which is much worse. He is like a nightmare given life; she has a sense that her life is over. And even though she's smart enough to know this is precisely what he wants her to feel, she cannot help herself. The situation is beyond her control.

As she feels him approaching, she struggles against the restraints, but she's held fast by wrists and ankles to the metal chair bolted to the floor. She wears what she had on when he abducted her out of her bed at school—panties and a men's T-shirt. Whatever semblance of dignity she had when he brought her here is now gone. He has seen every square inch of her body—not merely seen, but *observed,* as a surgeon will examine his patient, as a thing to be slit open. But this man has no intention of healing her—though that is, of course, his claim. This is early in her incarceration. Later on, she will agree with him. She will renounce her parents, her life up until this moment. She will be eager to do as he says.

She feels the burst of frigid Moscow air as she sees

the limo her father is in skid off the airport highway and slam into the electrical pole. She sees her mother gasping for air, her father white and dead, laid out on a makeshift bier inside Air Force One as they take off on their way back to D.C. She hears the frantic calls of the physicians who are trying to save her mother's life, and in the cracks between the soft sobbing of someone crying. Jack is with her, as is Naomi. But she feels nothing. She's withdrawn into the familiar icy shell. There are too many things she feels about her parents, conflicting currents that buffet her as if she's a sailboat in an Atlantic storm. At every moment, she's in danger of capsizing, and then there's nowhere to go but down into darkness.

She knows her parents love her, but it's the way they love her that hurts and disappoints her. Hellbent on micromanaging her childhood and adolescence, they have lost sight of her individuality. Instead, she has become an extension of the Edward Carson brand.

She resigns herself to being raped; had, in fact, prepared herself for whatever forms of sexual perversions he undoubtedly harbored. The thought of what is surely coming terrifies her, but she knows she can lock at least part of her mind away, keep it safe from whatever he might do to her. Emma had taught her how to do that; Emma was a master at locking herself away.

But she is wholly unprepared for how deeply and intimately he has invaded her life. And from the outset, he uses his knowledge to worm his way inside her brain and take up residence there.

His heat permeates the air and she smells him as

he leans over her, his rough, scaly hands covering hers, his lips in the fringe of hair over her forehead.

"I've seen you walking across campus with Emma McClure," he says. "I know you two were roommates." He laughs softly, unpleasantly, and a sudden whiff of rotting meat comes to her, almost makes her gag. "Well, but everyone at Langley Fields knows that you two were roommates, that you were best friends. But I know something more."

She closes her eyes against the assault of his voice, but it pushes farther inside her. She has no defenses against what he says next.

"I know that you and Emma were lovers. How do I know this? I've heard your squeals and moans of delight. I've heard you call her name just before it ends, I've heard her cursing softly when you did those things to her she liked best."

She doesn't want to respond, but she can't help herself—the first time of many during that week of darkness and disorientation. And the words are wrenched out of her throat, almost as a sob. "How? How?"

He breathes on her again, almost as a sigh of pleasure, but it might only be satisfaction. "She was a good teacher, wasn't she, Alli? A gentle and loving teacher, yes?"

Alli starts to sob, hot tears sliding down her cheeks, and she thinks, *Oh, my God, Emma. Emma!*

"Just as I am a gentle and loving teacher, Alli. In the coming days, I propose to show you what a lie your previous life has been, how you have been betrayed by those who profess to love you the most. Your parents don't love you, Alli—they never did.

They used you to further their ambitions, their political agenda. You've always hated them, you simply need to be made aware of it. They have debased you, stolen your identity, your very humanity. I will return these precious things to you. I'm the only one who can. You may not understand that now, but in time you will, I promise you. And the first step is to renounce them. This is the only way to gain back what they have taken from you. You will do this, I know you will. I have absolute confidence in you, Alli.

"A new day has dawned. From this moment forward, your life has changed. Isn't that what Emma told you that night she held you in her arms, one warm thigh slipped between yours, and rocked you to sleep?"

ALLI, SURROUNDED by the high crags of the Korab mountains, the wheeling hawks and black kites, her cheeks scrubbed by the harsh wind and grit of the increasingly steep trail, felt that week rush back at her like a tidal wave of rot. She began to retch, and almost vomited up whatever was in her stomach. But all she could expel was acid and bile. She felt abruptly dizzy and so ill she wanted nothing more than to lie down on her side with her knees drawn up to her chest. She wanted to go back in time. She wanted to take a pair of pliers and pull her destroyer's tongue out by its roots; she wanted to press her thumbs into his eyes until they turned to bloody jelly; she wanted to willfully ignore his pitiful pleas for mercy.

She wanted to go back to her parents seeing them as she does now, in the fullness of time. Did she ever tell them she loved them? She couldn't remember, and this, in itself, frightened her. She missed them now, but in a way that was unfamiliar and inexplicable to her. *Can you love people only after they're gone?* she asked herself. The possibility sickened her and she doubled over again on a boulder, though there was nothing left to vomit up.

She cried now for them, for herself, for the normal childhood she desperately wanted and never had. She hated them, forgave them, and loved them all at the same time. Dizzy and confused, she labored on, out of sight of the others. She couldn't bear anyone to see her like this, even Jack. She wished she could talk to Annika, because Annika could understand how you could love and hate a parent at the same time. And if she could understand it, maybe she could explain it to her.

So she wept for the loss of her parents, for herself, but also for Emma. Because, most of all, she wanted to change the moment Emma had asked her for help—asked Alli to come with her in the car that crashed, a crash that had taken her life. She wanted Emma back. Billy had been an experiment. It had been nice—he'd really cared for her, and he was gentle. But the relationship had only underscored how much she missed Emma.

She wanted Emma back. *My best friend, my only love.*

Then Jack was there.

"I'm fine," she managed to get out. "Please . . ."

But his strong arm holding her close undid her, and, sobbing, she buried her face in his chest.

"I don't . . ."

Her words were muffled; Jack felt them more than he heard them.

"Alli." He bent his head. "It's all right."

Her tears were bitter in her mouth.

"I don't deserve to live."

"I DIDN'T think you'd ever come back here," Naomi said.

Annika gave her a sharp look.

"I saw the e-mail you sent Jack. I know you killed Senator Berns."

A shadow passed across Annika's face and vanished.

They were still in Naomi's car. Across Cathedral Avenue, the entrance to McKinsey's apartment building had come alive with residents on their way to work. The dampness was all but gone from the concrete and macadam.

Annika laughed. "Someone sent an e-mail accusing me of murdering this senator—what did you say his name was?"

"Amusing," Naomi said, though she thought it anything but.

"You have no proof." Annika stroked the poodle's fragile back. "That e-mail can't be traced."

That seemed like an opening, and Naomi jumped on it. "How do you know that?"

Annika shrugged. "Only an idiot would make herself vulnerable to an electronic trace."

At last Naomi dropped her gaze to the muzzle of the .25. "What do you want, Annika?"

"Where's Jack?"

For an instant, Naomi's mind went numb. When her vision cleared, she said, "Jack doesn't want to see you."

"What are you, his mommy?"

In an instant, the flash of anger was gone, but it had existed long enough for Naomi to realize that there was something powerful enough to crack Annika's armor.

"I know where he is." Though she suspected it was both foolish and dangerous to lie to this woman, she'd had enough of feeling helpless.

"Then you'd better tell me."

"What is that, a threat?"

"Listen, Naomi, it's already out that Jack killed Arian Xhafa's brother."

"I don't know what you're talking about."

"Come on, Naomi, I lie for a living. Jack's in serious trouble."

Naomi's heart began a trip-hammer beat. "I'm telling you I don't know who Arian Xhafa is."

Annika stared at her for a long time, apparently trying to make up her mind. At last, she sighed. "I can only assume that he chose to keep you in the dark in order to protect you."

Naomi could hear the blood rushing in her ears. Her chest hurt with the desire for Annika to continue. The irony of her source being a professional liar wasn't lost on her. In fact, it pained her.

"Did he tell you he killed a man at the Stem?"

How do you know all this? Naomi asked herself, but she was canny enough to intuit that Annika would never tell her. She supposed she shouldn't be surprised, given what Jack had told her about Annika

Dementieva, but she couldn't help herself. This woman had a preternatural intelligence. A shiver of foreboding passed through her. She had the distinct sense Annika was three steps ahead of everyone else on the game board.

She nodded. "A man named Dardan."

"Dardan is—was—Arian Xhafa's brother." Annika took out another cigarette, stared at its unlit tip. "Arian Xhafa is one of the most feared warlords in Eastern Europe. His power and influence are growing exponentially every day."

"Is he the head of the sex slave trade ring that ran its auction at the Stem?"

"Ah, at least you know something." Annika cut her eyes sideways. "Yes, Arian Xhafa is running young girls from Russia, the Baltics, Macedonia, Albania, all over Eastern Europe, in fact. He imports them into Italy, Scandinavia, and, of course, here in America. It's a multimillion-dollar business, one that's made easy by international law enforcement's indifference. The girls are runaways, whores, girls sold into slavery to buy their family food and shelter. Whether they live in slavery or die of beatings, multiple rapes, AIDS, or a drug overdose, it's of no concern to the police of any nation."

"But there are laws, some very new, specifically put in place to—"

"Laws are only legislative pieces of paper, Naomi. They aren't effective if they're not enforced. These laws are not. In poor countries, they're often ignored, even in the larger cities and particularly outside urban centers. In the more developed countries, there is a network of corruption among officials in law enforcement and government, fed by both greed and blackmail, that ensures the sex trade continues to flourish across borders."

Naomi sat back. She had read articles about the widening international traffic in girls and the growing worldwide alarm it was causing. But she'd also assumed—idealistically, perhaps—that the new laws enacted in many countries were having an effect. Frankly, it came as a shock to her that they might be largely ignored.

"But this sex trafficking—"

"Both those terms are misnomers," Annika said. "What we're talking about is slavery." She slipped the cigarette back into its pack and her amber eyes lifted to engage Naomi's. "Let me ask you a question. Have you any idea of the worldwide number of enslaved girls and women at this moment?"

Naomi considered. "Hundreds of thousands, I would guess. Maybe a million?"

"Twenty-seven million."

"My God!" The sheer size of the figure took Naomi's breath away and made her feel sick to her stomach.

"To put the figure in perspective, that's the population of New York City and Los Angeles with nine million people to spare."

"That figure has to be an exaggeration."

"Really? One million children are forced into prostitution every year," Annika went on. "And that's only prostitution. To be enslaved can mean many things, not only in a sexual sense." She flicked her lighter open, the reflection of the flame burning in her eyes. "But in all cases enslavement entails the breaking down of the individual through humiliation, deprivation, torture, and, yes, many times, multiple rapes. It relies, in any event, on the total dependence on the enslaver. This can only come about through the annihilation of hope."

Naomi realized that she had been holding her breath. Letting it out now seemed like only a temporary relief. "And this is Arian Xhafa's business."

"Yes."

"What's your interest in this?"

"I'm a woman."

Naomi shook her head. "Please don't mistake me for an idiot."

Annika smiled coolly. "My interest is in Jack."

"You betrayed him."

"Whether I did or not is no concern of yours."

"Jack is my friend."

Annika's smile turned icy. "Oh, I can see that quite clearly."

Naomi looked away, stared at her hands on the steering wheel. "I don't see how I can trust you."

Annika wiped the corners of the poodle's eyes. "I imagine that depends on how badly you want to find Mbreti."

Naomi tried to make sense of the buzzing in her mind. "I want Mbreti." She lifted her gaze, but found it difficult to stare into those extraordinary eyes without feeling intimidated, worse, somehow diminished. "What do you know about him?"

Annika appeared to consider this for some time. Then she nodded. She waggled the barrel of the .25. "I'll tell you as you drive."

Naomi fired the ignition and turned the wheel,

checking traffic. When she pulled out onto the avenue, she said, "I drive better without a gun in my face."

Annika smiled and put the gun down beside the poodle. "What did Jack tell you about me?"

"Enough to know that you can't be trusted."

"No one can be trusted, Naomi. Not in our world." She kept the enigmatic smile on her face. "Turn right here, then make the next left, then left again."

"The directions make no sense."

"I want to make certain we're not being followed."

Naomi glanced in the rearview mirror. "Who would be following us?"

"Peter McKinsey, for one."

Naomi took some time digesting this comment. Ever since she had recognized Annika Dementieva she had felt like Alice down the rabbit hole. *"And if you go chasing rabbits, And you know you're going to fall . . ."* Grace Slick sang in her mind. And then the dormouse's final warning, like the ominous tolling of a bell: Keep your head.

Without missing a beat, Annika said, "How is Alli?"

"You know Alli?" Stupid. Of course, Annika had met Jack in Moscow, had traveled with him and Alli to the Ukraine.

Annika's smile spread like melting butter. "Better than you do, my dear."

A shiver went through the pit of Naomi's stomach. Annika might be lying—in fact, she probably was—but the thought that she might, indeed, know Alli so well gave Naomi the willies. *That poor girl,* she thought. *All she has is Jack now, and that overbearing and thoroughly repugnant uncle. How awful if this lying murderer gets added to the mix.*

"Alli is with Jack," Naomi said, more defensively than she had intended, "where she belongs."

"I couldn't agree more." Annika was staring straight ahead. "And where would that be?"

Naomi made no response.

"Now that we're in Georgetown," Annika said, "you should know where to go."

Naomi glanced at her for a moment, then headed down toward the water.

"You saw me follow Pete yesterday."

"I'm sure you saw him get into the boat."

"Roosevelt Island?"

"It's wilderness out there." Annika pointed to the parking area of a building beside Tidewater Lock. "An excellent place for a rendezvous." That smile again as Naomi pulled into a slot. "And secrets."

FOR SOME time, Thatë watched the crew members playing poker in the rear lounge, but his mind was elsewhere. He was remembering in perfect detail Alli defeating Dennis Paull not once, but three times. He liked the way she moved, like a ghost or a drift of smoke. He'd never seen anyone fight like that—the sudden whirlwind moves fascinated him. Or maybe it was Alli herself who fascinated him.

He cleared his throat, got up, and asked for a pillow and a blanket. One of the crew members put down his cards and opened an overhead compartment. The entire crew watched him while he pulled down what he wanted. He lay down across a row of seats some distance from them, pulled the blanket over him, and set his head on the pillow.

He drifted on and off for perhaps an hour or so.

When he opened his eyes, he saw a crewman sitting across the aisle, watching him. A handgun lay in his lap. He gripped it as Thatë sat up.

"I need to pee."

"Go ahead," the crewman said.

Wrapping himself in the blanket, Thatë went forward up the aisle, the crewman following in his wake.

So that's how it is, he thought.

The forward toilet was located almost directly across from the stairs leading down to the ground. He pulled open the toilet door. As the crewman stepped forward, Thatë threw the blanket over him, slammed his forehead into the crewman's nose, and dragged him into the toilet. The entire maneuver had taken no more than a second or two. Thatë risked a glance to the back. The rest of the crew kept up their game of poker, oblivious to what had just happened.

Ducking back into the toilet, he took the unconscious crewman's handgun, set him on the toilet, and emerged into the aisle, closing the door behind him. He stepped across the aisle, went down the stairs, and was free.

ANNIKA BOLTED out of the car, and, cursing under her breath, Naomi hurried after her. Annika carried the poodle in one arm. There was no sign of the .25, but Naomi was certain she had it on her somewhere. Oddly, and rather terrifyingly, she seemed oblivious to the fact that Naomi was armed. Her absolute confidence exploded a depth charge into Naomi's psyche.

Striding out onto the dock, Annika set the poodle free. It immediately scampered to a section of the

dock and jumped. Unconcerned, Annika walked after it. At the edge, she unzipped her boots and tossed
them after the dog. Then she stepped down into a
sleek, blue-and-white powerboat. Pulling out a key
on a float ring, she started the engine, then cast off
the bow line.

"Cast off the stern line when I give the signal," she
said without looking at Naomi.

Naomi stood at the stern of the boat. There was no
point, at least at this stage, in pitting herself against
the other woman, she told herself. Better to go along
with whatever she had in mind, always remembering
her service weapon, a 9mm Glock that, at this distance, could put a sizable hole in Annika's head. She
decided that would be a most satisfying outcome.

"Now," Annika said.

Naomi slipped the nylon line from the metal cleat,
then stepped on board. The moment she did so, Annika pushed the throttle and the boat nosed its way
out of the slip, angling toward the thick greenery of
the island. Naomi picked her way forward and stood
beside Annika, in much the same position Peter had
stood beside the unknown man yesterday morning.

The trip took no more than five minutes. The sun
was a hazy ellipse, partially obscured by a low-lying
cloudbank. As was the case the morning before, there
was no other boat traffic. The water lay serenely
blank, an opaque sheet intent on keeping its secrets
safe.

Annika tied up the poodle, who obediently lay
down, sighed, and went to sleep. They disembarked
onto the island, Naomi in her sensible shoes, Annika
in bare feet. The sun was fully up now and the day

was growing warmer. Naomi noticed that Annika did not take off her raincoat. Possibly this was where she'd stashed her .25.

Annika struck out to their left and Naomi followed. They skirted the shoreline, heading toward the eastern point of the island, but, almost immediately, Annika turned inland. Naomi tried to focus her mind on the island's shape. There were no buildings, only a memorial to Teddy Roosevelt near the opposite shore. Otherwise, all was wilderness. They picked their way through the underbrush, beneath heavy branches. The smell of damp earth and decaying leaves was everywhere. The sky vanished; they were enclosed in deep, cool shade, as if in the shadow of a monstrous edifice.

At length, they broke out onto a boardwalk of whitish planks, walking due south until Annika turned onto a right-hand branch. This took them on a short walk to a platform that overlooked a finger of muddy water and, beyond, a thick swath of uninterrupted forest that composed the bulk of the island. There was not a soul to be seen anywhere, no movement save for the twittering birds flitting from tree to tree.

Looking around, Naomi could see nothing she would not expect to find on such an expedition. "This is where Pete went yesterday?"

"Possibly." Annika stared off to their right.

Naomi followed her gaze, but could find no anomaly. "Who took him here, Annika? Who was driving that boat?"

"I hope you're not averse to getting your feet wet," Annika said as she stepped off the platform onto a protruding root, and from there down into the water. The hem of her raincoat caused ripples to expand out from where she stood, knee-deep.

Kicking off her shoes, Naomi grabbed on to the bole of the tree and swung down from the root, which was slippery, skinned now from Annika's weight, to the water herself. As soon as she was down, Annika picked her way north, up the narrow channel. The bottom was soft and mucky, and mud squelched between Naomi's toes. The water was surprisingly warm, thick as chowder. What was she stirring up with each footfall? she wondered. Tiny whirlpools of little fish and decayed leaves wove around her ankles, turning the brackish water ruddy. A sudden shadow overhead caused her to duck, and she heard a bird call, as if mocking her.

"Come on!" Annika called from up ahead. "Don't get lost!" Her voice was oddly flat, echoless, as if they had entered a strange and unknowable place where the natural laws of science didn't apply.

Naomi moved on, picking up her pace as best she could, but the footing had become unstable, the muck under her feet shifting and sliding as it deepened. Several times she stumbled and had to grab an overhanging branch to keep herself from pitching headlong into the water. She realized that the water was neither cold nor warm, but seemed to be the same temperature as her body.

Up ahead, she could see a flicker of Annika's raincoat, like the scales of a reptile moving slowly and inexorably toward its goal. Now she used the branches to drag herself forward, relying on her arms rather than her legs for locomotion, as if she were a chimpanzee.

Maneuvering around a small bend to the right, she stopped. Annika was standing with one foot on the low bank. One leg was raised. The raincoat had parted, sliding off the knee, revealing a section of naked thigh. What did or didn't Annika have under that raincoat? Naomi wondered briefly.

"Closer," Annika said, beckoning Naomi forward.

When Naomi came up behind her, she saw that Annika had been digging in the muck. She had uncovered something. Stooping down, she cupped her hands and threw water on it. A pale and shining patch shone through as the mud and leaf detritus slid off.

It was part of a hand.

Heart in her throat, Naomi saw again the splatter of blood on the old wooden boards deep beneath the streets of Chinatown, and tears shattered on her cheeks. Annika moved out of the way as she crouched down, unmindful of the water and the mud. Using her bare hands she swept away more of the earth. The body had been buried in the V-shaped gap between two massive tree roots, a hammocky space.

The hand was small, the fingers delicate, so Naomi knew this was a young girl. She dug almost frantically now, tearing a nail, then another, not caring. All she could think of was uncovering the girl's face, as if she were still alive and, unburied, could be made to breathe again, to live, instead of being yet another victim of these slave traders.

A brow came first, then the heartbreakingly beautiful swell of a cheekbone. She gasped to see the nose fractured, bruised and swollen to almost twice its size. At this point, the lack of decomposition brought home to her that the girl had been killed very recently, possibly within the last forty-eight hours, though only a coroner could tell for certain.

This was all on the right side of the face. As she brushed clean the left side, her fingertips felt for the telltale fracture, this one of the left eye socket. And there it was, just as it had been with Billy and the two men in Twilight.

"Same MO, same perp," she murmured to herself.

"That's right," Annika said from right behind her.

Then an arm encircled her throat, the pad of a thumb pressed against the bone just below her left eye.

And she heard Annika's voice so intimate in her ear as the pressure increased.

"This is how it's done."

Sixteen

"Someone is feeding her information," McKinsey said in a hushed voice.

"Naomi is a smart girl," Henry Carson said. "I told you that from the get-go."

"Shit, she's not that smart."

"It's a mistake to underestimate her."

They fell silent as the huge door to the National Cathedral opened and someone entered. An older woman walked down the central aisle, crossed herself before sliding into a pew halfway down. Her hands clasped and she bowed her head.

"Don't be an idiot." Carson's whisper was nevertheless a harsh rebuke. "Find out what she knows."

"That won't be easy," McKinsey said.

"If your assignment was easy," Carson replied, "I'd have given it to a monkey."

They kept still now as a priest appeared, crossed himself, then mounted the small dais to prepare the altar for the coming mass. They were seated on a pew in the last row; soon they would have to leave, but for the moment they were safe from prying eyes and ears.

"Listen, Peter, there's another player in the field."

McKinsey glanced at Carson for the first time. "Who?"

"If I knew that I wouldn't need you. Go forth and find out who it is."

"And when I do?"

"Neutralize it," Carson said.

The door behind them opened and they bowed their heads as another penitent made his way down the aisle. When he had found a pew, McKinsey said, "I'm sorry about your niece."

Carson stared at the priest, arranging his fetishistic symbols on the altar. "There will be consequences."

McKinsey bit his lip. He was dying for a cigarette. "It doesn't alter our plans?"

"Not in the least." Carson took a breath and let it out. "Time for you to go, Peter."

"Yessir."

Carson stayed some time after McKinsey left. He stared at the symbols of privilege and power affixed to the walls. The Catholic Church was on a slow and painful march to irrelevance, strangling on its own misdeeds. Before he left, he determined not to follow that path.

"You see how it works?" Annika said. "You see how easy it is from this position to fracture the occipital bone?" She kept up the pressure just beneath Naomi's left eye. "Both the zygomatic bone and, here, the foramen—the hole in the bone through which nerves and blood vessels pass—are vulnerable. Two deaths in one, one might say."

She removed her arm and thumb, but Naomi's

heart could not stop racing. She had to hold down the reactive nausea that had risen up through her gut into her throat when Annika had come up behind her and locked her in the death grip the murderer had employed four times in the last thirty-six hours. An insane thought was still ricocheting like a pinball around her brain: Was Annika the murderer? She had killed Senator Berns; how many before him had she murdered?

Naomi swallowed heavily. Her eyes were tearing and her nose was running. Ignoring her own distress, she stared down at the head and hand of the young girl buried between the roots of the massive tree.

"Who is this?" Her voice was thick and her tongue seemed too large for her mouth. "Do you know her name?"

"Does it matter?"

Naomi whipped around. "Damn straight it matters."

"Arjeta." Annika was looking at Naomi, not the dead girl. "In Albanian, it means 'golden life.'"

Naomi stood up. She felt light-headed. Her heart would not slow down. She tried to take deep breaths.

"You look pale," Annika said. "Are you all right?"

What the hell do you care? Naomi wanted to say, but she just nodded.

"Did you kill her?"

Now Annika's eyes sought the corpse. "It's so sad, isn't it? Such a waste of life."

Naomi's hands curled into fists. "I asked you a question."

"I have been trying to protect Arjeta." Her gaze swung back to Naomi's face. "I know her two sisters,

Edon and Liridona. They're younger than Arjeta. Edon has been taken, but so far Liridona, the youngest, has been spared."

"Spared what?"

"Arjeta's parents sold her to Xhafa's people. All three sisters are both beautiful and desirable. Unless something drastic is done, I fear Liridona and Edon will suffer the same fate as their older sister."

"The fate of so many," Naomi said sadly.

"Yes, but these girls are special. Their beauty makes them tremendously valuable to people like the Xhafa brothers. But their value is now exponentially greater. They possess important knowledge regarding, I'm assuming, Arian Xhafa. But that's just a stab in the dark. Liridona was interrupted in her last call to me and I haven't been able to reach her since."

"Where are they now?" Naomi asked.

"Liridona called me from Albania. Vlorë, where the family lives. She doesn't know where Edon was taken, though I strongly suspect that it's out of the country."

Naomi pressed her hand against the bole of the tree to steady herself. "It's a sickness, a disease."

"What is?"

"Greed."

"Greed and despair," Annika said. "They're epidemic."

Naomi pulled out her cell phone.

"What are you doing?"

"What do you think? I'm calling this in."

"Don't."

"Excuse me?" Naomi shook her head. "That sounded like an order."

"Just a suggestion," Annika said. "If you call it in, it will become public, and Mbreti will vanish into the shadows."

Naomi put the cell up to her ear. "I have to do what I have to do."

"Then you'll never find him. This I can guarantee."

Naomi looked off into the distance. The odor of Arjeta's death clotted in her nostrils. Her pale, bony face haunted her. The line connected and she heard a querying voice in her ear, thin and electronic.

"These deaths will go on and on," Annika said softly. "Is this what you want?"

Duty and desire, the two weights the cosmic scale held in balance, if not equilibrium, vied with each other for dominance.

At last, she took the phone away from her ear and killed the connection.

"All right," she said to Annika. "Was it Mbreti who killed Arjeta? Was it Mbreti who tortured and killed Billy Warren, and the two men at Twilight?"

"No, not him, though he may have ordered it," Annika said.

"Do you know the perp's name?"

"I beg your pardon?"

"The murderer."

"Yes. A man named Blunt. I believe you've met him under the legend name of Willowicz."

DOLNA ZHELINO was a tiny mountain village nestled in a finger of a valley dipping between two wooded hillsides high in the Korab mountains. At one end was a small watercourse, fed by the Vardar River; at the other was a wide, undulating, mostly cultivated valley, the gateway to Tetovo, Arian Xhafa's stronghold fifteen miles to the northwest.

About an hour ago, they had forded the river at a fairly shallow spot. But the rocks on the riverbed were slippery and Alli had stumbled, hitting the water with a splash. Before Jack could get to her, her head was under the water. An instant later, she surfaced, drenched from head to toe, but otherwise unharmed.

Now, hunkered down in the midst of a dense forest, Dennis Paull checked his folding map against his GPS coordinates. Jack looked over his shoulder. From their elevation, they had an excellent view down the length of the finger. The red-tile roofs of the whitewashed houses looked like a jumble of dice, except for the soaring minarets of the mosque. This area of the country was predominantly Muslim, so a mosque in every town or village was to be expected.

Twilight was still at least an hour away. Alli leaned against a tree and gazed out at the town. She seemed lost in thought, and Jack wondered what was on her mind.

"We're right on track," Paull said.

Assuming this is *the right track,* Jack thought, but he kept his opinion to himself. Paull already knew where he stood on the subject.

Paull checked his watch. "The best time to make it through the valley without being spotted is at twilight. We'll be able to see our way without lights, but for everyone else visibility will be poor. Looking at us will be like looking at clouds."

He glanced around. "We have time to grab something to eat." He jutted his chin. "Go tell Alli."

Jack rose and went over to Alli. "Eat while we have the time," he said.

She made no move.

"Alli, it's liable to be a long night."

She nodded, shrugged off her pack, and, squatting down, rummaged through it. Jack knelt beside her. When she offered him a protein bar, he took it. They ate in silence. Jack leaned back, then closed his eyes. He saw his Rubik's Cube, the icon of puzzle solving. Then came a flood of images from the past couple of days, which he sorted, intuitively placing some on the cube, while discarding others. This mental task might have taken most people the better part of an hour, but Jack's dyslexic brain accomplished it in a matter of minutes—as fast as he had solved the vexing riddle of the Rubik's Cube when he was young.

What stood out for him was a kind of equation his mind had etched into the cube:

$$GRASI = THAT\ddot{E} \; MBRETI = ?$$

He considered the equation, which was no real equation at all, and wondered what it meant. His subconscious knew, or was working on it, otherwise it would not have presented itself to him. Mbreti—king, in Albanian—was either a code name or a position rank of a major player in Arian Xhafa's American operation. Mathis, the manager of Twilight, was bringing Mbreti's money to the Stem. It must have been to deliver it to Dardan, which meant Mbreti was one of Arian Xhafa's crew, perhaps Dardan himself. In any event, Mathis worked for Mbreti—the king.

Jack realized that if he solved that riddle, it still

wouldn't help him solve the riddle of the equation. Thatë's nickname was Grasi—fat. But his real name— Thatë—meant skinny. The kid was neither fat nor skinny, so how did he come by the nickname? When things calmed down, Jack determined to ask him.

He opened his eyes. "How are you doing?" he said to Alli.

She looked at him and smiled thinly. "Better."

The silence stretched on. He knew better than to start probing; she was sure to take it as an interrogation and he knew how negatively she'd react to that, even if it was only her perception.

"I miss music," she said around a bite of food.

He took out Emma's iPod and his earphones. "Can we listen to something together?"

"How about My Bloody Valentine's 'When You Sleep'?"

Jack scrolled through the listings. "One of Emma's favorites. So it's one of yours, as well."

Alli swallowed and looked away for the moment.

Jack offered the iPod. "Do you want to do this yourself?"

She shook her head, and he plugged in the earbuds, then handed her one end. He pressed Play and they both listened to half the music. Jack disliked this form of listening so beloved of teenagers. He found it both ridiculous and useless, like listening to music on a cell phone at sixty-four kbps, so compressed the music might as well be spoken word. But, now, with MBV's iconic wall of fuzzed-out electronics and buried vocals in his ear, knowing that Alli was enjoying the other half, he felt peculiarly close to her. Or perhaps it was because they were both sharing a vital part of Emma—sharing it and loving it.

He was interrupted by a tap on his shoulder.

"Time to saddle up," Paull said.

The light was falling out of the sky like a sudden downpour. What was left of the sun was obscured by clouds. A few first-magnitude stars were just becoming visible, their remote glimmering foretelling a misty night.

Jack removed his earbud and Alli did the same. He rose, tucking the electronics securely away. Then he took out a pair of field glasses and went to a gap in the trees. After a moment, he sensed Paull approach.

"See anything?"

Jack shook his head. "But according to Thatë, Xhafa's men are out there."

Paull grunted.

"What's our route through the valley?"

When Paull told him, Jack said, "I hope the geotechs know what they're doing, because it seems to me that there's no good way across." He pointed through a gap in the trees. "See how the valley narrows down toward the far end? It's like a huge funnel. I can see why Xhafa would position his men here and why Thatë didn't want us to come this way."

"I didn't fall for one word that lying kid said." Paull settled his backpack. "C'mon. We're moving out."

"IT'S JUST like threading a needle," Paull whispered as they made their way to the edge of the forest. "The geotechs have plotted the path that gives us the lowest chance of being seen."

"I feel better already," Jack said.

Paull forged on, ignoring Jack's remark. Farther ahead and below them lay the soft lights of Dolna Zhelino, nestled in its funnel, so inviting to its residents, so dangerous for their little group.

At the very edge of the trees, Paull stopped them for a moment. He pointed at two spots. "There and there are the two high points, the best place to station lookouts. The geotech boys saw that in their 3-D renderings so they plotted our course accordingly."

"Better and better," Jack said.

"Button it," Paull snapped. "We have superior resources and capabilities, and I plan on using all of them to get us inside Tetovo's perimeter and blow Xhafa's tin-pot empire to smithereens before he knows what hit him."

They took up their ArmaLite assault rifles and struck out single file. Paull took the lead with Alli just behind him. Jack, as ever, was on rear guard.

The wastrel light had taken on the element peculiar to the dwindling of the day, when the sun has slipped below the horizon but night has not yet risen from its grave. There were no shadows; instead, there were, as Paull had pointed out, layers of illusion, within which they could safely make their way into the hammock and through it to the far end, where the watercourse tumbled down between enormous boulders.

They moved through the dense foliage of the western slope in a winding path that several times seemed to fold back on itself, though that couldn't possibly be right. As they progressed, Jack had to admit to himself that the course was a good one, complicated enough to keep potential sight lines to them constantly changing.

They trekked up a steep rise, then down into a shallow dell dotted with saplings and vigorous understory growth, as if a fire had torn through here in years past, burning off the older, established trees. Paull used hand signals to keep them crouched low to the ground as they passed through this relatively open patch.

Jack breathed a sigh of relief when they reached the far side and slipped in among the tall trees again. Shadows moved with them through the forest. For a time, they lost sight of both the valley and the village as the path took them higher onto the western slope, into denser, first-growth trees, which towered over them like titans.

Keeping one eye out for movement behind them and the other on Alli, Jack felt Paull step up the pace. It was at that moment that they began to take fire from the left. As one, they dropped to their bellies and, following Paull's hand signals, began to creep down the slope where it fell off on their right. Then more firing targeted them from the right. Jack crabbed his way over to Alli but she had already sought shelter in a thicket of underbrush. He stuck his head up, searching for Paull, but the withering fire almost took off the top of his skull.

They were trapped in a merciless cross fire.

SEVENTEEN

THE PRESIDENT met with Carson in the Rose Garden. It was well known that they were friends. Friends met in open, pleasant places, not behind closed doors, places where tongues could wag and create problems for both of them.

"I don't think giving Dennis Paull permission to take Alli away was a smart move," Carson said.

"That remains to be seen." The president, walking without an overcoat, hunched his shoulders against the wind. "But I had no choice. I couldn't give him any reason to think I was micromanaging his assignment or undermining his authority."

"I understand that, but—"

"No buts, Hank, we can't have him looking our way."

"You mean McClure."

"Of course I mean McClure," the president said. "But it would be the height of folly to underestimate Dennis."

They came to the end of a row and turned into the adjacent one. Across the lawn, the daffodils were up, and tulips had already opened their colored bells.

Carson sniffed the warmth of spring in the air. "I can take care of him, if it comes to that."

Crawford glanced at his security detail. "Damnit, what have I told you about that kind of talk?"

"My arrogance has gotten me where I am today."

The POTUS shook his head. "Can't dispute that." He clasped his hands behind his back. "I am concerned about Gunn."

"He's the best in the private security business, Arlen. The Pentagon uses him all the time."

"In Iraq," Crawford pointed out. "Gunn is the kind of guy who thinks the whole world is Iraq and acts accordingly."

"I can't get any clarity on what happened at my house," Carson said. "Gunn claims that Alli became increasingly agitated and then attacked one of his men when he went into the study to check up on her."

"She looks like she's sixteen years old, for the love of Mike!"

Carson nodded. "Her physical expertise was a surprise, I must admit."

"But not her emotional state. Hank, it must have occurred to you that Gunn might be right, that after her incarceration and brainwashing that she . . . that she'll never be the same."

Carson looked like he'd bitten into a rancid peanut. "I don't want to hear that."

"Still, Gunn might be right about what happened."

"And if he's not?"

The president turned toward his companion and leaned in. "Am I hearing you right?" When Carson made no reply, he said, "Jesus, Hank, you're as much of a cowboy as Gunn is. Forget him. Keep the plan in sight, would you? Forget about personal vendettas and concentrate. We're on schedule. I did my part. I sailed your takeover of Middle Bay Bancorp through the SEC and antitrust briar patch without a hitch. Now focus on the integration. Without Middle Bay we're dead in the water."

Carson kept his mouth shut. He despised being spoken to like that by anyone, including the president of the United States. Carson was from Texas, he was a self-made man, and now, with immense wealth and power, he considered himself a force of nature, an island-state unto himself. Not for him the laws of the common man—he was beyond all that.

"Don't worry about Middle Bay," he said, when he'd regained control over his emotions. "I've hired the best forensic accountants in the business. That work is getting done. But, understand, it's extremely delicate in nature. It can't be rushed."

"Agreed." The president sighed and put a hand on his friend's shoulder. "Hank, I sometimes worry about you."

Carson forced a smile. "I'm fine, Arlen. Just a little unnerved by my niece's recent activity."

Crawford nodded judicially. "I understand." He loved playing the father figure. "Completely." His hand squeezed his friend's shoulder.

You understand nothing, Carson thought as he took his leave of the president and the Rose Garden. It was Caroline, pure and simple—if anything in life could be deemed pure or simple. This difficult-to-control rage—the urge to personal vendetta—hadn't always been with him. It had manifested itself directly after Caroline's disappearance. Sometimes he felt possessed by the rage, as if he'd turned into some mysterious person with whom he had only a passing acquaintance. At those times, he went down to the soundproof basement of his town house and spent an hour with his handguns—a Glock .38, a Mauser 9mm, and a .357 Magnum—squeezing off round after round, blowing holes in the center of the target. The growing stench of cordite helped, but not as much as the shooting, which cooled the boiling of his blood, but not his need to know.

If he squeezed his eyes shut he could see Caro, as if she were the subject of a photo from some lost time he'd found in a dusty trunk in his attic. Over the years, she had ceased to be a real person. Rather, she had become an icon, a symbol of his rage and frustration, because in this one instance all his power and all his money had availed him nothing. She was as lost to him as if he were a beggar on the street who had turned his back to scrounge a bite to eat, only to find his daughter had walked off or been taken from him.

In the dead of night, when he screamed in his sleep, it was because in his dream he knew that she had simply walked away, evidence of her rejection of him, a possibility he could neither condone nor tolerate. So, a man drowning in his own guilt, he clung to the theory that she had been taken, because then he could find her, he could bring her home. She would *want* to come home.

IN THE face of the constant peppering fire, Jack calmed himself, closed his eyes, and imagined the terrain as a three-dimensional puzzle. The steep fall-off to the right meant that Xhafa's soldiers must be up in the trees in order to fire on them. They had the advantage of elevation, but it also meant that they were essentially immobile, unlike the men on the left, who seemed to be moving closer.

Then he understood: The trap wasn't a classic pincers maneuver, but a herd-and-kill mission. The object for the contingent on their left was to force the enemy to retreat down the slope where they could be picked off by the snipers in the trees.

The firing from the left was louder now, proof that his theory was correct. Jack knew he had little time to act. But before he could do anything, he heard an infernal whooshing and, to his right, the shock wave from an explosion rolling him across the ground away from where Alli was hiding. A fireball rose into the night sky as the fired rocket detonated, and Jack, cursing under his breath, thought, *Dennis has given Xhafa advance warning of the weaponry we're carrying.*

Then the night was lit up by another explosion, this one smaller, but much closer. Xhafa's men must have tossed a grenade in counterattack.

Crawling on his stomach, Jack snaked his way to the clump of underbrush and told Alli to hold her ground.

"What? I can't hear you."

He read her lips because the ringing in his ears made voice communication impossible.

He gestured and pointed emphatically. "Stay put. I'm going to find Paull," he mouthed.

Alli began to crawl out. "I'm going with you." When he began to protest, she put her lips against his ear. "What if you get lost or, worse, pinned down and can't get back here?"

After a moment's hesitation, he gestured, and together they eeled their way along the rocky ground. The volleying gunfire assaulted them as their hearing came back. Xhafa's men were trying their best to mow down the man who had fired the rocket at them.

Jack stopped them in the lee of a large boulder. He had caught a glimpse of movement just ahead and suspected they were near Paull's position.

"Dennis is less than ten yards from here," he said into Alli's ear. "Stay put and I'll be right back with him." He gave her a tight smile. "From this distance I can't get lost." He handed her his assault rifle and took out a Sig Sauer. "Whatever you do, don't fire your weapon. I don't want them to know we're here."

She nodded, and, rounding the boulder, he slithered off. He found himself on a slight incline, which made the going tougher. On the other hand, there was plenty of cover to conceal his movement. Halfway there, a break in the firing caused him to freeze. For a moment, he wondered whether Paull had been killed. Then the firing began again and he pressed on.

Just ahead of him was the ridge beyond which, from his previous vantage point, he'd spotted Paull. Now, however, he could not see over the ridge; he was effectively blind to what was happening, a particularly dangerous position to be in. He scrambled up to the lip of the ridge and cautiously peered over. This was met with a volley of fire that almost took the top of his head off.

Ducking back down, he took a look around. To his left, the topography rose steeply, to his right, it fell off. He needed to go left in order to surmount the ridge, but a problem presented itself. There was far less cover in that direction. In fact, there were several spots made bald by small rock slides. They weren't large. Nevertheless, they presented danger zones; crossing them would leave him totally unprotected.

Moving off to his left, he picked up a couple of rocks the size of his fist. As he came upon the first rockfall, he launched the first rock at a boulder off to his right. As it struck, he dived across the rocky ground, hearing a short volley of semiautomatic fire spang off the boulder.

He continued his climb past the far side of the rockfall. He could see the second. It was larger than the first, and flatter, which made it more dangerous still, like traversing a frozen lake with snipers in the surrounding trees.

This time, he threw the rock to his left, into the tops of the trees. As they shook and swayed, and more fire sprayed in that direction, he dashed across the open space. Just as he dived into the underbrush at the far side, a shot whizzed over his back. He rolled up onto the ridge and slid down the other side, all in one motion.

Silence now. Xhafa's men knew where he had been a moment ago; it would not take them long to vector in new coordinates. His best option now was to move and keep moving. On elbows and knees, he snaked through the understory, grateful for the web of tree branches over his head. Once he got to Paull, he'd have to find another way back to where Alli waited; he'd been lucky, but the two of them couldn't afford to expose themselves via the same path.

It was very quiet. No firing from either side, but there were also no bird sounds, which meant that

Xhafa's men were on the move, presumably heading toward where he had last been spotted; to assume otherwise was foolhardy. The silence made any movement more perilous. All he needed to do was crack a branch underfoot to bring the guerillas on the run.

A fitful breeze stirred the treetops, but the sky was entirely occluded by the branches. Darkness hung in the air like eternal twilight. There were no shadows. Jack brought his head up to get his bearings. From where he lay he could see where he'd spotted Dennis. It was possible that Paull had moved from there, but it was just as likely he'd hunkered down, waiting to make his break. Jack strongly suspected this was what Xhafa's men were waiting for—the moment he showed himself their gunfire would tear him to ribbons. He had to get to his friend first.

Rolling across the ground in deep shade, he inched his way forward until he could get a better look at where Paull might be holed up. Just ahead was a trio of huge trees.

Jack moved slightly, and now he saw Paull, crouched in the center of the space between the trees. He'd hacked down some of the surrounding underbrush, building himself a makeshift camouflaged hidey-hole. Jack could see him because of his angle and ground-level perspective.

As he stole closer, Paull stirred.

"Dennis, it's me," Jack whispered.

Paull froze. "Jack?"

"I've come to get you out of here."

There was a small silence. "I fucked up, Jack."

"Don't expect me to say I told you so."

"Ha-ha," Paull said without a hint of mirth.

Jack extended his left arm. "Let's go. On your belly. I'll cover you."

As Paull began to creep out from his rough, trembling shelter Jack gave him a smile. "We'll get out of this."

At that moment, a hail of semiautomatic fire ripped through the silence. Paull shoved his face into the ground, but it wasn't aimed at them. The firing was coming from behind them, where Alli was hidden.

GUNN EXITED his apartment building dressed in a navy blue chalk stripe high-end bespoke suit, John Lobb shoes, blue chambray shirt, and scarlet tie. He unlocked his BMW 5-series with the wireless opener, slid behind the wheel, and, after waiting for a break in the traffic, pulled out into the street. The break wasn't quite large enough and he had to peel out with a squeal of tire rubber and an angry blast of the horn from a car behind him.

Several moments later, a tan Chevy sedan pulled out, tailing him. Gunn stopped at a gas station, fueled up, then drove until pulling into a 7-Eleven. He walked briskly inside as the tan Chevy pulled up across the street, its motor running.

Five or so minutes later, the Chevy's driver noted him coming out, ducking into the car, and taking off. The driver put the Chevy in gear and dutifully followed.

Gunn stood at the back of the 7-Eleven in a spot out of sight of the rear wall-mounted convex security mirrors. After checking that his double's identical scarlet tie was tied with a Windsor knot like his own and assuring himself that every other detail of the man's haberdashery conformed to his profile, he had placed the keys to the BMW in the man's hand.

"You know what to do."

The man had nodded and, mimicking Gunn's stride, departed.

Now Gunn looked at his watch and started counting off the seconds to himself. By the time he had reached thirty, a man emerged from the toilets and came and stood beside him.

"It's a fuckup," Gunn said. "A total cluster-fuck."

"Calm down," his companion said. "We've gone through shit before, we'll get through this, too."

"I have been calm," Gunn said, "through all of this." He threw up his arms. "I sat back and let you do the planning. And guess what? One of my men is dead, and the two others wish they were."

"I'll take care of their rehab," his companion said. "Put the money out of your mind."

Gunn took a deep breath and leaned back against the cold-drink case. As always, it was impossible to get a read on John Pawnhill. He was in his late thirties, good-looking in an anonymous kind of way. He had thick, dark hair that covered the top half of his ears. His eyes were hooded and inscrutable. Gunn was acutely uncomfortable around him. It was as if Pawnhill generated a current that made those who stood near him jittery.

"It's not just the money."

"Oh?" Pawnhill said. "What, then?"

"It's the way this came apart."

Pawnhill seemed as relaxed as ever. "How did it come apart?"

"All at once and all over the place—like a terrier

with a rag doll." Gunn felt his anger building—anger at events that were out of his control, anger that he had been put squarely in Henry Holt Carson's gun sight, just where he didn't want to be. "I made a mistake by ignoring my own dictum: If you want it done right, do it yourself."

Pawnhill nodded, as if agreeing. An instant later, Gunn felt the tip of a switchblade at his throat. Pawnhill had stepped in front of him, pinning him back against the glass and stainless-steel case.

"Listen, motherfucker, you came to me, remember? And do you remember that I lost a half million when the Stem was infiltrated last night? Was I to blame for that? Was I to blame for Arjeta Kraja opening her big mouth to that little shitbird Billy Warren? And, by the way, how the *fuck* did she find out about Middle Bay in the first place? Think it was from me?"

"Not you, no, that's absurd." Gunn tried to swallow, but his mouth was dry, and, anyway, his heart seemed to be beating at the back of his throat. "It must've been Dardan. He's the only other person who knew about the bank."

Pawnhill drew the blade lightly across Gunn's throat, inking a line of red. "Dardan liked to fuck, not talk."

"Fuck and kill." Gunn stared into the other's pitiless eyes. "Listen, I have no doubt if you'd done the job Alli Carson would be dead now."

"Too dangerous. It wasn't possible." Pawnhill's black ardor appeared to have cooled somewhat. "We both needed an extra layer of protection. Your men provided that."

"The Secret Service agent—the girl—came snooping around."

"And what will she find out about those three?"

"Nothing," Gunn said. "They're squeaky clean. I told you that."

Pawnhill removed the knife and, after cleaning the blade on Gunn's crimson tie, folded it away. "You made a big fucking mistake accusing me—"

"I didn't accuse you."

"Don't fucking say you didn't do something when you fucking well did." Pawnhill held up an admonishing finger. "And neither Willowicz nor O'Banion are squeaky clean."

"Those two are professional ghosts. No one can connect them with Fortress or me personally."

"They're loose ends," Pawnhill said. "Tie them up and throw them away."

"Jesus, these guys are valuable."

Pawnhill leaned in. "Their liability outweighs whatever value you put on them. I want it done and done now. Understood?"

Gunn would just as soon kill this fucker where he stood, but he knew that would be disastrous for business, not to mention for himself. He had too many black deals going to risk the spotlight being turned on him more than it already was. Naomi Wilde was a smart and tenacious agent—McKinsey had told him so. He also knew that the three men she was investigating were a dead end; he'd seen to that himself. Soon enough, she'd have no other recourse but to turn her investigative spotlight elsewhere.

On the other hand, Pawnhill was daily becoming

more of a danger. This incident was merely the last straw. Gunn knew now that sooner rather than later he'd have to do something about Pawnhill, because everyone else involved lacked the guts to go after him. He wasn't afraid of the man's physical prowess or his connections, but he had to find a way to take him out without being hit by the inevitable shitstorm.

He felt a trickle of blood run down inside his collar and he smiled. He wouldn't forget Pawnhill's assault on his person. On the contrary, it would color the method of his demise.

"I apologize if I've offended you in any way, John. That was not my intention." He shrugged. "I don't like failure, that's all."

"Neither of us does." Pawnhill reached around Gunn and, opening the glass door, took out a couple of Coca-Colas. He handed one to Gunn and they popped the tops, clinked bottles, and took good, long swigs. "Who murdered our people at Twilight? Have you gotten anywhere with that?"

"It's too soon to—"

"It's clear they were killed for the badge that got Dardan's murderer into the Stem. That never should have happened, Gunn. You were in charge."

"I can't have my people everywhere, John. That kind of visibility in the midst of Billy Warren's murder would have been lethal."

"That fucking murder," Pawnhill said. "That fucking murder started it all." He tapped the neck of the bottle against his forehead. "Who's mucking around in our patch?" He downed more Coke. "Shit, we'll all suffer for Dardan's death."

Now Gunn understood the real reason why Pawn-hill was on edge. "What will the reaction be?"

Pawnhill grunted. "One thing I know, the man who murdered Dardan is a dead man. No matter where he is or where he goes, Arian will hunt him down and kill him like a rabid dog."

"And what of us?"

"What, indeed?" Pawnhill took another swig of Coke and swallowed noisily. "Someone will be coming, Gunn." He glanced around the store as if the individual might already be there. "Someone who won't be as easy to handle as Dardan was. Someone who will make us all pay the price for Dardan's death."

EIGHTEEN

NAOMI AND MCKINSEY were out canvassing the area around Twilight, still trying to find someone—anyone—who knew Arjeta Kraja. It seemed increasingly odd to them that she could be living in the neighborhood without anyone knowing her or even seeing her, save at the club.

In addition to this frustration, Naomi felt increasingly uncomfortable in McKinsey's presence. How much he was keeping from her she had no idea, but the fact that he was keeping anything creeped her out.

And there was the matter of Willowicz. If she could believe Annika Dementieva—and having crossed paths with him she was inclined to believe her—he was responsible for the torture and murder of Billy Warren, plus the murders of the two Twilight employees. In the normal course of things, she would have told Pete immediately. But this was definitely not the normal course of things and she felt the need to keep her own counsel. Still, how could she be effective on this case if she couldn't rely on her partner?

Briefly, she had contemplated going to their superior at the Secret Service, but she had no real proof of any wrongdoing on his part. Plus, she couldn't mention Roosevelt Island without spooking the mysterious Mbreti. And the more she thought about it, the more convinced she became that "the King" was the key to Arian Xhafa's operations in Washington— for all she knew, the entire United States.

They were about to knock on yet another door when her cell buzzed. Having called Jack several times, leaving voice mails as detailed as she dared, she hoped it was him as she checked the caller ID. It was Rachel's home number. It was an odd occurrence for her sister to call during working hours. Signaling to McKinsey to continue, she stepped several paces away and answered the phone.

"Nomi?"

Her heart skipped a beat. She wondered how one word could carry such pain and heartache.

"Rachel, what is it?"

"It's Larry." Her husband.

"Is he okay? Has he been in an accident?"

"You could say that." Rachel gave a shuddering laugh that collapsed into a fit of sobbing.

"Rachey, for God's sake, is he okay?"

"You know, for once in my life I don't give a shit."

Uh-oh.

"Hang on. I'll be right over."

Closing the phone, she beckoned to McKinsey, who was already coming away from the door, shaking his head.

"What's up?"

"It's Rachel. There's an emergency."

"Is she hurt?"

"Yes, but not in the way you mean. I've got to get to her house."

McKinsey took one look at her pinched, white face and said, "I'll drive you."

"I can—"

"The fuck you can," he said. "I haven't seen your hands shake like that since the night we spent doing Jell-O shots."

JACK REACHED out, grabbed Paull, and hauled him to his hands and knees.

"Those shots came from where Alli's hiding," he said as they crabbed their way toward the brow of the ridge.

But Paull pulled at him. "This way," he said, moving off to their left.

In this direction, the ridge was high, wilder, rockier. From the moment they slid over the top they were exposed, but they tumbled over without having their heads blown off, scrambled down the other side, a steep drop off that pitched them off their feet. It was impossible to keep their equilibrium as they tumbled head over heels. Jack tried to roll, but they had gained too much momentum. All he could do was relax his body in order to decrease the risk of breaking an elbow or a rib.

The bottom was even rockier than the ridgeback itself, and for a moment the two men lay stunned, their breathing ragged and irregular. Then Jack coughed heavily and rolled over. Paull was on his knees, head wagging slowly back and forth while he tried to focus his eyes.

"Come on!" Jack said.

Paull whipped his semiautomatic off his back and fingered the trigger. He nodded and they struck out through the dense brush and stands of trees to where the boulder marked the spot where Alli was hiding. Jack signaled and they split up, approaching the boulder from either side. Jack wondered why all the firing had stopped and was now acutely wary of a trap. But the thought of Alli spurred him on.

Both men came around the boulder's blocky sides at once. Alli stood up when they appeared. She wasn't alone. Beside her was Thatë, grinning like a lunatic. He was armed with a handgun and an AK-47.

"Welcome, gentlemen," he said with a jocularity Jack found eerie. "It took you long enough to get here."

"Alli, are you okay?" Jack said.

"She's fine, Jack." Thatë raised an arm and six heavily armed men appeared from out of the forest.

Paull was apoplectic. "I told you. Godammit to hell, I told you."

"HE'S LEFT me, Nomi. Left me and the kids."

"What? Just like that?"

"He's got a girl—a *girl*, Nomi! Maybe twenty-two or -three. Jesus!" Rachel ran a hand through her hair. She was, as usual, dressed impeccably, in a Michael Kors black-and-white polka-dot dress. Gold rings on her fingers, diamond studs in her ears, and a string of black pearls around her neck. She wore a pair of suede Christian Louboutin high heels. "You read about these things happening all the time—even to women you know—but, God, you never think it'll happen to you." Tears squeezed out of her eyes. "It's like getting a terminal diagnosis."

Naomi led Rachel into the living room and sat her down on one of the severe Italian sofas. McKinsey was outside, waiting in the car.

"No, it's not, Rachey." She put her arm around her sister's shoulders. "And how do you know how old she is?"

"Because the fucker showed me photos of her! Can you fucking believe it? He's proud of her, wanted to show her off."

"A twinkie? I wouldn't have thought it of Larry."

Rachel groaned. "If only! She's in her twenties and has a law degree from Harvard, which means she's both younger *and* smarter than me." She buried her face in her hands.

Naomi looked around the huge living room, filled with everything money could buy—carved Lalique crystal, a Calder sculpture, paintings by De Kooning, Basquiat, and Richter that would grace the walls of any museum of contemporary art. And then there was the explosion of photos of the family at graduations, parties, parasailing in Cancun, hiking in the Himalayas, snorkeling off the coast of the Maldives. And, finally, set aside in a space all its own, was a gleaming Steinway baby grand piano Rachel had un-successfully pushed both children to play.

"What about the kids?"

"What about them?" Rachel's words were muffled by her fingers.

Naomi tossed her head. "Where are they?"

"Out. Anywhere. I don't know. I tried their cells, but they're not answering."

"We should find them."

"Good luck with that."

Naomi touched the point of her sister's reconstructed chin. "Rachey, look at me."

Reluctantly, Rachel lifted her head. Her eyes were red-rimmed, but the Botox protected her forehead from the folds of extreme emotion.

"I'm so sorry. I know how close the family is."

Rachel made no response. Instead, she took in the grand room.

"He's going to screw me."

"What?" For a moment, Naomi thought she hadn't heard right. "Don't worry about that. I'll ask around, we'll get you the best divorce lawyer on the East Coast."

"Are you shitting me?" There was fire in her sister's eyes. Apparently, the period of mourning was over. "My soon-to-be ex-husband *is* the best divorce lawyer on the East Coast." She wrung her hands. "Dear God, what d'you suppose my future is going to look like?"

Naomi was taken aback. "Rach, aren't you the least bit—"

"What? The least bit what?"

"Isn't there any chance to reconcile?"

"Don't be dense. Larry's been cheating on me for months—maybe years. This"—and here she used a four-letter expletive that made Naomi shudder—"is probably one of a long line of heifers."

"I know he's hurt you, but—"

Rachel shook her head. "Don't you get it, Nomi?

He's made up his mind, and now he's going to rape me. No decent attorney will stand up to him and he's tight with every judge on the bench."

"Surely you'll get the kids. And he'll have to pay child support as well as alimony."

"What he'll give me is a pittance." Her fingers balled into fists. "I want my money, my home, my security. I won't have shit when he's done with me." She began to sob again, and then she wailed, "I want my life back."

Naomi sat back, feeling lost and helpless. Is this what life came down to, money? Is that all there was after the golden glow was gone? For the first time since they had been adults, she looked clear-eyed at her sister. For years she had bought into Rachel's fairy-tale existence. But who was Rachel, except an adjunct of Larry, a possession not very different from the De Kooning or the Basquiat? She was cast off, like the Steinway, a presentation piece that had out-lived its usefulness.

She sighed and took Rachel's hands in hers. They were as cold as ice. "What can I do to help?"

The calculating look she knew so well had once again taken up residence in her sister's eyes. "There's this bank account Larry uses. I'm not supposed to know about it, but I do. God knows what he uses it for, but huge sums of money go in and out pretty regularly." Rachel's eyes sought hers. "Use your con-tacts at Treasury to have the funds frozen, maybe you can get them to start an investigation."

On what grounds? Naomi was about to say, but a warning bell had gone off in the back of her mind. She knew herself well enough to pay attention when that bell rang. *". . . there's this bank account . . . huge sums of money go in and out regularly."*

"Nomi, this is life and death. Are you listening to me?"

Life and death, yes. And then it hit her like a thunderbolt. *Jesus Christ, I've been looking for a break in this case in all the wrong places.*

PAULL BROUGHT his assault rifle to bear on Thatë. "You may have had Jack and the girl fooled, but not me. It was obvious you were Xhafa's man all along."

"Lower your weapon," Thatë said softly.

Jack noted the change in his demeanor. Out here in the wild he was more confident, if not more aggressive. The kid's appearance could explain the cease-fire, but something in this encounter didn't feel right.

"Fuck you, sonny," Paull said.

Jack put his hand on the barrel of the ArmaLite and pushed it down. "Do as he says, Dennis. Confrontation isn't going to get us anywhere."

When Paull had reluctantly lowered his weapon, Thatë said, "Follow me."

His men parted and he took them through the underbrush toward the area where they'd been fired upon en masse. There, they found seven men sprawled on the ground. Some had been shot, others had had their throats slit.

Thatë pointed. "Here are Arian Xhafa's men. The snipers in the trees are also dead."

Paull gaped. "I don't believe it."

"Examine for yourself," the kid said. "Xhafa's men are Muslim, my men are Russian."

Paull put up his weapon and, crouching, went from

corpse to corpse. Even he could deduce the truth from the full, curling beards, the fanatics' eyes.

"*Grupperovka,*" Alli said.

Thatë smiled at her. "Kazanskaya, yes." He turned to Jack. "This was why I was sent here: To find out who was backing Xhafa with money and arms."

Jack gave him a hard look. "And did you?"

"I was forced to escape before my assignment was complete." His grin returned. "But now, thanks to you, I have returned to finish what I started, and to wreak my revenge on Arian Xhafa."

NINETEEN

"How is she?" McKinsey said when Naomi slid into the passenger's seat. She was just finishing a call.

Through the windshield, she could see the Mercedes, BMWs, and Porsches, arrayed like trophies on the street. "When you lie down with a scorpion, you're bound to get stung."

"She's your sister. That's a bit harsh, don't you think?"

"Rachel didn't love Larry or her kids, she loved his money."

"Yeah, but still. Don't you want to stay with her?"

"I told her I couldn't stay."

McKinsey cleared his throat, then started the car. "I'll drive you home."

"We're going to the main branch of Middle Bay Bancorp on K and Twentieth."

"It's almost three," he observed.

"I called the president of Middle Bay. He's expecting us."

McKinsey wrapped his fingers around the wheel, but he didn't put the car in gear. "My opinion? I think you ought to be with Rachel. She needs you now. I mean, who else does she have?"

"Rachel is more self-sufficient than I am." Naomi gestured with her chin. "Drive."

McKinsey sighed, then turned off the engine. "Why the hell are we going to Middle Bay Bancorp?"

"Because that's where Billy Warren worked."

"So?"

"He was a loan analyst."

McKinsey shook his head. "I don't follow."

"What if Billy discovered something unusual was going on inside the bank?"

There was a skeptical look on McKinsey's face. "Like what?"

"Like large sums of money going in and out that weren't being reported."

"Naomi, Billy Warren was shtupping Dardan's main squeeze. This has already been established. He was killed by Dardan's people."

"But why was he tortured? The question has been bothering me from the beginning. No, Billy had discovered something someone badly didn't want uncovered. Now drive."

"Naomi, this isn't a good idea."

She looked at him, finally. "What isn't?"

"Middle Bay is the wrong direction for this investigation to go in."

"Is that a warning?"

"I'm just trying to protect you."

"Pete, I've been to Roosevelt Island."

"Come again?"

"I've seen the girl—Arjeta Kraja."

"Would you please start making sense?"

She had to give him this, there was not a flicker in his eye.

"I followed you yesterday morning. I saw you going out to the island on a motorboat. Who were you with and what were you doing there, Pete?"

"Naomi, trust me, you don't want to pursue this."

"No, actually I do."

He stared out the window; his fingers drummed anxiously on the wheel.

"Pete, either you take me to Middle Bay, or I'll call a cab."

"It's just that . . ." He turned to her. "Do you remember our first day on the job together? We were sent to pick up the FLOTUS. On the way there, we got sideswiped by a van driven by a drunken driver. Anyway, you were trapped on your side of the car. We couldn't use the Jaws of Life because you were jammed up against the door. It took me over an hour to get you out."

"I remember." Naomi was acutely aware of the wariness in her voice.

"I don't want to have to do that again, Naomi. Because this time I might fail."

She gave him a wan smile. "Forget it, Pete, it's D.C."

He didn't laugh.

"Pete, we're partners; I shouldn't have to ask this. Do you have my back?"

"Isn't that what partners are for?"

She nodded. "Now are you going to drive or am I going to leave you here?"

"DENNIS, ARE you okay with this?" Jack asked, as Thatë, at the head of his dirty half dozen, led them along the roundabout route he had first suggested, east, then north, then northwest toward Tetovo.

"Do I have a choice?" Paull grumbled. "I fucked up, Jack. I don't know what got into me. I should've listened to your instincts." He shook his head. "But to be led to Arian Xhafa by this kid." Paull glared at Thatë trekking easily and confidently up ahead. "I mean, this kid should still be sucking up his mother's milk, for Christ's sake."

"He didn't have a mother," Alli said.

They both looked at her.

"At least," she continued, "a mother he remembers."

"Boo hoo!" Paull parodied crying.

"You never even gave him a chance," Alli said hotly.

"And you gave him too much of one." Paull jerked his head. "Let's just hope he didn't kill any of my men when he escaped from the plane."

"He didn't," Alli said.

"He told you that, did he?"

"Bite me." She extended her middle finger at him and, picking up the pace, wound her way through the Russians to walk beside Thatë.

"Thanks for that," Jack said.

"A word of warning," Paull shot back. "The next thing you know they'll be making the two-backed beast and then you'll never be able to pry them apart."

Jack considered for a time as the forest slid past them. Off to their left, they could hear the water-course that marked the far end of the valley. Over the ridge beyond lay Tetovo.

"I remember hearing about a man who turned so

sour on life he wouldn't believe a boy who rang his doorbell was his long-lost son."

Paull scoffed. "I know how this ends: he turns the boy away only to find out later that he was, in fact, his son."

"No," Jack said. "Against his better judgment, he takes the boy in, feeds him, clothes him, gives him a soft bed to sleep in. The two spend a week together, then another and another. Gradually, the man's guard lowers as he comes to appreciate the boy, then to mentor him. He realizes that, in the end, it doesn't matter whether this boy is his blood son or not.

"One night, he's awakened by unfamiliar sounds. He goes down the hall to his son's room. The door is open, his son's clothes are laid out, the bed is made just as it had been before he arrived. Grabbing a gun, the man goes down to the first floor and turns on the lights.

"Someone is sitting in his easy chair. This shadowy figure calls the man by his Christian name, even though the man is certain he's never seen the stranger before in his life.

"'Don't you recognize me?' the stranger says. As he stands up, a pair of enormous black wings unfold from points on either shoulder.

"'Where's my son?' the man shouts. 'What have you done with him?'

"'I?' the devil says. 'I have done nothing with your son. He's dead—dead and buried years ago.'

"'You're lying,' the man says. He's shaking with anger.

"'You may think so,' the devil says. 'But the fact remains he's not here. He never was.'

"All at once, the man breaks, falling to his knees. 'Why? Why?' he cries out.

"'Because,' the devil says, 'life is hell.' "

Paull moved his assault rifle from one arm to another. "Does this piece of crap have a moral?"

"You know the moral, Dennis," Jack said. "Why do you think that life is hell?"

Paull made a sour face. "What, have you suddenly found God?"

"My only compact," Jack said, "is with my daughter."

Paull came up short and turned. "What are you talking about? Your daughter is dead."

"The dead never leave us, Dennis. At least, their spirits don't." Jack looked him in the eye. "I suspect that's what you're struggling against."

ANNIKA DEMENTIEVA sat in the first-class departure lounge drinking a vodka martini. Her flight was scheduled to depart in just over an hour. She could have left the city later, but she had decided that the airport was the safest place for her now. She didn't want Naomi Wilde coming to look for her.

The preliminary phase of the plan had been successfully concluded. She was pleased to know that Naomi had no idea where Jack was. That meant virtually no one else did, either. A good thing because his destination was one of the most dangerous places on earth. She had witnessed the American SKOPES unit annihilated by Arian Xhafa's battle-hardened guerillas. She had had no interest in the guerillas themselves, but in the weaponry they employed.

Watching the massacre had proved the wisdom of her being sent to Tetovo. The array of Xhafa's cutting-edge war matériel was astonishing. No wonder warning alarms had been set off in her part of the world. The Macedonian situation was already on the verge of being out of control.

If the problem was simply Xhafa she could have handled it herself, but it stretched across borders, spanned oceans, was infused with incalculable amounts of money, fueled by a hatred and fanaticism beyond even Xhafa himself. She knew she needed help, she knew who she needed to help her. And he was the one person guaranteed not to comply.

She drank her vodka martini as if it were a beer, and ordered another, chewing thoughtfully on the liquor-soaked olive until the refill arrived. Through the thick, shatterproof glass, the world looked unnaturally dark, drained of color, unreal. She listened to the muted clatter of laptop keyboards, the clink of glasses, snatches of cell phone conversations. Within thirty seconds of entering, she had observed and catalogued every person in the lounge. She was like a jungle cat, interested only in danger and prey—everything else fell to gray ash.

But then gray was the color of her life; everything in it had turned to ash. The kidnapping and extended sexual and physical abuse by her father, Oriel Jovovich Batchuk, had set fire to her heart, reduced it to a blackened cinder of antimatter. In its place a void had opened up inside her that could never be filled. She had thought that her revenge on her father in the Ukraine last year would save her, or at least stop the void from widening, but the reverse had happened—she had fallen farther into the void, and now she suspected nothing could get her out.

This had not always been so. There was a time when she had childishly believed that Jack and Alli would be her saviors. But at the time she had met them, she had already betrayed Jack, and so their relationship was doomed before it began. As for Alli, she had been the one surprise in Annika's life. The short time she had spent with Alli and Jack had given her a false sense of security—for those weeks she had deluded herself into thinking that the three of them were a family. How could she not? It had felt so good, so right. And she was so certain that the void inside her had started to shrink back to a manageable level. But then she'd been forced to choose between Jack and Dyadya Gourdjiev. It had been her grandfather who had finally saved her from her father, so it was no choice at all. After he'd told her she could have no more contact with Jack, she had wept bitter tears through a long and lonely night. And then, defying her grandfather, she had broken protocol and contacted Jack, confessing her sin. Why she had omitted the real reason she had murdered Senator Berns she'd never be fully able to understand. Perhaps she needed to put herself on the rack, to flay herself open for Jack to see, as no one else—not even Dyadya Gourdjiev—had before or ever would again.

The truth was she loved him, but now she had ensured that he would never love her. Agonizing as that was, it was preferable to continuing to lie to him. Enmeshed as she was in concentric webs of lies, it nevertheless felt intolerable to lie to him.

Now Dyadya Gourdjiev was in the hospital following a serious heart attack. He faded in and out of consciousness. None of the doctors she had spoken to would venture a definitive prognosis. Instead, they spoke in the kind of circular logic peculiar to their profession. After such a long time, she was completely on her own.

She crossed her long, beautiful legs and stared at herself in the mirror. Everything about her was beautiful, and it was that incandescent beauty that from an early age had been a terrible curse. It was her beauty that had impaled her father with jealousy, rage, and, finally, unstoppable lust. It was her beauty that had allowed her to slip through her adolescence with a minimum of fuss so that she could use her brain for what she wanted most: revenge. With her grandfather's help, she had trained herself in all forms of weaponry and espionage. From one of his closest friends she had learned the intricate byways of the con game. Lying came naturally to her; she had lied to her father from the time she was four years old. Lies had been her only protection against him, therefore she had become expert at it. As an adult, she had come to view lying in the same way actors viewed a role: It allowed her to be someone she was not, allowed her to express opinions that were not hers. It allowed her, in other words, to hide in plain sight.

Her flight was being called, but it was not yet time for her to board. She had one more task to perform. While she took out her cell phone, she thought about Alli, about how the girl had touched her so unexpectedly and deeply. The two of them shared similar histories of kidnap, imprisonment, and abuse. From the few intimate stories Alli had shared, it was clear that she and Annika were kindred spirits. And, despite Annika's steely reserve, her fierce armor, she had fallen in love with Alli, the way, Dyadya Gourdjiev had told her, her mother had fallen in love with her the first time she had rested her tiny head on her mother's breast.

Now both Jack and Alli were lost to her. *Christ, emotion tears your guts out,* she thought, as she stared at the blank face of her phone. For the first time in her life she was aware of two forces battling for possession of her soul. The knowledge set her mind to thrumming.

Then she thought, *Fuck it!* and dialed a local number.

"Henry," she said, when Carson answered, "I'm leaving."

"Everything is in place on this end."

She could hear the relief in his voice. "This is far from over," she warned. "You still need to exercise caution."

"I'm covered."

She rose and, grabbing the handle of her rolling carry-on, said, "Naomi Wilde is on a collision course with Mbreti."

"Do you think that wise?"

"We'll find out shortly." She walked out of the lounge, riding the escalator down to the gates. "Henry, remember what I told you at the very beginning."

"'Trust eats its own children.'" His laugh was metallic. "Jesus, Annika, how could I forget such a dire fucking warning?"

TWENTY

NIGHT HAD passed its zenith. More stars appeared as the highest peaks of the Korab mountains shredded the clouds to ribbons. Dolna Zhelino was far behind. So were Arian Xhafa's dead guerillas. Thatë's men had found a satellite phone on one of the corpses, but it was unclear whether the man had communicated with his headquarters during the firefight.

"We have to make the assumption that Xhafa knows a force is on its way to attack him," Thatë said.

They all agreed. They were camped on the narrow rolling plateau of the final ridge beyond which lay the outskirts of Tetovo, its lights flickering indistinctly through the black mesh of trees.

Paull looked at the kid. "Do you know what happened to the American unit sent to eliminate Arian Xhafa?"

"They were annihilated," Thatë said. "I was in D.C. at the time, but these men told me. The American soldiers were killed within minutes. They didn't get within ten miles of Xhafa's headquarters."

"Fuck me. So they're dead, every one of them."

Paull gave Jack a sharp look. "How the hell could these guerillas destroy a heavily armed SKOPES unit in a matter of minutes? Christ, this situation gets worse by the second."

Jack felt it imperative to move on. "Have you been to Xhafa's stronghold?"

Thatë nodded. "All too briefly. I was made. I had to get the fuck out of there."

"Tail between your legs." Paull nodded. "No wonder you're so hot to go back there."

"How many men?" Jack asked, to ease the tension.

"Twenty to twenty-five." Thatë shrugged. "His is a decentralized system, like the Muslim terrorists. The bulk of his men are deployed, some in other countries arranging deals, receiving payments, or overseeing smuggling shipments. The cadre in and around the stronghold are personal bodyguards, the fiercest fighters."

"The Praetorian Guard," Paull muttered.

An owl hooted and there was a flurry of wings overhead, a soft cry, and then a small spray of blood as the owl carried off its prey.

"A fantastic hunter, the owl," Thatë said. "Its wings make no sound. That's how we will be." He indicated Paull with his chin. "Did your people give you a way in?"

Paull nodded, spread out the plastic-covered map, and lit it up with a penlight. The beam was powerful but didn't spread. He traced the path with his finger. Xhafa's stronghold was in the northeastern section of Tetovo, at the summit of a small rise.

"Do you have a problem with this section of the route?" Paull's voice was a challenge.

Thatë shook his head.

"The stronghold itself," Jack began.

"It's a stone structure of approximately fifty-two-hundred square feet," Paull said before the kid could answer. Once again, he was showing off the expertise of the American clandestine services. "No basement because in that area the bedrock is so hard it's apparently not worth the effort. There are two entrances, front and rear, and, here, on the west side, is what appears to be a soccer field, presumably to help keep the men in shape when they aren't on a killing spree."

"The intel comes from satellite imaging." Jack looked at Thatë. "Accurate?"

"Oh, it's accurate," the kid said, and Paull looked smug. "As far as it goes."

Paull scowled. "Meaning?"

"Xhafa's stronghold is actually a school. The soccer field is for the students."

"Sonuvabitch."

"It gets worse," Thatë said. "The students are orphans. They live there."

Another silence settled over the group. They stared through the trees at the lights of Tetovo. Somewhere out there Xhafa and his men were waiting for them.

"Well, that neutralizes our rockets and other middle-range weaponry," Paull said sourly.

"Not necessarily," Alli interjected.

They all turned to stare at her.

"We've got to get the children out of the school," she said.

"One of us needs to come up with a real plan," Paull said, pointedly ignoring her.

Jack held up a hand. "Wait a minute, Alli may be on to something."

"Have you lost your mind?"

Jack busied himself clearing away debris and drawing a map for himself in the dirt. Because he himself was drawing it, he could better visualize the terrain and how to navigate it. He stared at what he had created for some minutes.

"What if we split up into two groups? Dennis, you and I and Alli will form a traditional frontal assault."

"But Xhafa will be expecting that," Thatë said.

"Precisely," Jack said. "But what we'll put up won't be an assault at all. It will be a diversion under cover of which, Thatë, you and your men will silently take out the rear guard, infiltrate the schoolhouse, round up the kids, and herd them out of there. Once the building's clear, we can move in on both fronts."

Paull rubbed his chin. "It sounds good."

"Yeah, except it won't work." Thatë looked at them. "The kids are taught to be scared shitless of anyone who isn't in Xhafa's cadre. They'll never willingly come with us."

"They might," Alli said, "if they see me."

Jack reacted immediately. "Now just a minute—!"

"No." Thatë was nodding vigorously. "Alli's got it locked in. She doesn't look all that much older than the students, who range more or less from eight to seventeen. When they see her with us, they're likely not to bolt, especially if she talks to them."

"I don't speak Macedonian," Alli said.

"No problem. The older students speak English. They'll translate for the younger ones." Thatë saw the look on Jack's face. "This is by far our best shot to get Xhafa, trust me."

Jack glared at him. "I'm not exposing Alli to such a risk."

Thatë shrugged. "Then there will be collateral damage."

"There will be no collateral damage," Jack said slowly and deliberately.

"Then Xhafa's cleverness has stymied us," Paull said. "Our mission—"

"I know what our mission is," Jack said tightly, "and it doesn't include subjecting Alli to this level of extreme risk. She needs to be where I can keep an eye on her."

"Fine," Thatë said. "But with you or without you I'm leading my men in."

"Not if I kill you first."

It seemed, then, that all the weapons came to bear at once.

"Men," Alli said disgustedly. She stood up. "Did any of you testosterone machines think about asking me? It was my idea, I like it." She turned to Jack. "It's a good plan, or as good as we're going to get. I'm going in with Thatë." She held out a hand. "Now give me the iPod and earphones."

The kid looked into Jack's surprised face and laughed. "Fucking piece of work, ain't she?"

THE TWO groups decided to take different routes, so Thatë and his men, with Alli in tow, headed out before Jack and Paull, who would take the route outlined by the satellite intel. Each group had a sat phone for coordinating their assault—one Thatë's men had, the other that had been confiscated in the firefight at Dolna Zhelino.

Before he left, Thatë went over the topography Jack and Paull would encounter, seemingly leaving out no detail. Jack was grateful to him, but he was also terribly apprehensive as he watched Alli, amid Thatë's band of Kazanskaya thugs, vanish all too quickly into the dark.

"Another insane scheme that's dependent on whether or not we can trust that kid," Paull said as he hefted his assault rifle. He checked to make sure the magazine was fully loaded. "Talk about a delicate balance."

Jack stood brooding. Then they set off, following the path laid out for them by the geotechs at the DoD.

ALLI WAS aware of the tension in the men as one is aware of the electricity in the air during a lightning storm. The stars were very clear above them, winking in and out as gaps in the trees presented themselves and then closed. No one spoke, for which she was grateful. After last year, one of the things she had done to help her overcome her grief was to learn Russian from the Rosetta Stone program. She was astonished at how effortlessly she picked up the language, and she suspected that she'd be able to learn most any language with similar ease. She recognized root words almost instantly, and making sense of the grammar allowed large chunks of phrases to slot into her rapidly expanding understanding.

Oddly, she felt comfortable among these thugs.

They didn't resent her or think she was a freak. On the contrary, they understood her function in the plan—a function none of them could fill, and which might very well lead to victory. She felt like their little sister; she felt as if she belonged, as if she had been born to the wrong parents in the wrong country. Now and again, her nostrils flared. She smelled Russia on them; she liked that smell.

For one hundred minutes, they moved silently without incident. By that time, the forest had given way to plowed fields with the occasional stone barn, then the farms were stamped out by a jumble of houses. Then the paved streets began and, along with them, the gridlike order imposed by all gatherings of human habitation, whether they be villages, towns, or cities.

The men grew more cautious and, for a time, their progress was slowed as they took more and more frequent detours to avoid the citizens of Tetovo. Skirting the town proper, they moved northwest with the intention of looping around and coming upon the stronghold from the north.

Of course, there were obstacles to that route—knots of Xhafa's guerillas strategically placed along the perimeter of Tetovo. But guard duty was inherently boring. Night after night, peering into the flickering darkness could cause the attention of even the staunchest fanatic to occasionally waver. There was no antidote for this boredom, Thatë had explained to her when they had begun their trek, and it was this inattention he proposed to exploit.

The first to present themselves to Thatë's men were three guerillas. He kept Alli beside him as he used hand signals. Three of his men nodded and melted into the darkness. They returned soon enough with trophies: AK-47s, daggers, and a satellite phone. Not a sound had been uttered. The band moved on. Alli saw the three guerillas sprawled on the ground, their throats slit. Their blood glittered black in the starlight.

"THERE HE is."

Paull's whisper came to Jack along with the other night noises.

"We could go around him," Jack pointed out.

"We can't go around them all."

They were crouched in the protection of a clump of underbrush. The guerilla was outlined against the starlight. To his right was a ridge, black as a pit. To his left were lights at the outskirts of Tetovo.

Paull scrambled off and Jack put down his assault rifle, shrugged off his backpack and camouflage jacket. Then he ducked out into the starlight, came around a bend and, seeing the guerilla, continued on.

The guerilla, for his part, came immediately alert and brought his AK-47 down to the ready position.

Jack stopped several feet in front of the guerilla and said, "*Më falni, unë jam I humbur.*" Excuse me, I'm lost.

"*Ju jeni shqiptare?*" the guerilla asked with a good deal of suspicion. You're Albanian?

"*Lindur dhe rritur atje, por e biznesit tim është këtu.*" Born and raised there, but my business is here.

The guerilla nodded. "*Ku jeni drejtuar?*" Where are you headed?

"Ozomiste."

The guerilla laughed. "*Ju mori një kthesë shumë të*

gabuar, shoku im." You took a very wrong turn, my friend.

He pointed to the east, a direction behind Jack. As he did so, Paull, stealing up behind him, jerked his chin up, exposing the neck, which he slit. The guerilla's eyes rolled up in his head and he slid to the ground.

Ten minutes later, after spotting and skirting two groups of guerillas, they came within sight of the schoolhouse and began to set up shop.

"You'll have to watch out for those groups," Paull said. "Once we start firing, they're bound to be drawn to this spot."

"I'll be ready." Jack pulled out the shoulder rocket launcher and loaded it.

When Paull was set up, he called Thatë to give him the signal to go ahead. Then he manned the machine gun he'd set on its tripod and waited for Thatë's call.

THE MOMENT Thatë got off the sat phone, he signaled his men forward. They spread out in a rough semicircle as they slipped through the trees. Keeping to the shadows, they approached the rear of the schoolhouse. Along the way, five of Xhafa's men were overpowered and killed without them opening their mouths. There were more in the woods, of this Thatë had no doubt, which was why he now widened the cordon of his men. He had only six men, plus Alli, but he was ready to pit any one of them against two or even three of the guerillas.

There was another knot of guerillas lounging around the back door, talking and telling jokes. Two of them were dozing. Thatë signaled his men, then unhooked Alli's backpack and took her assault rifle from her. She unbuttoned her shirt and pushed the waistband of her trousers lower around her narrow hips, exposing her midriff.

"How's this?"

He fluttered his hand back and forth. "It will have to do." Then, in response to her scowl, he gave her a big grin.

"You'll do fine. Don't worry, okay?" he whispered. "We have your back."

She nodded.

"Are you frightened?"

"I think so." In fact, her heart seemed about to explode through her chest.

He laughed soundlessly. "That's the right answer. So am I." He gave her a quick kiss on the cheek. "Time."

Alli appeared in the light, weaving slightly. The guerillas saw her and she began to sing "Gimme Shelter." She was close to them, under their scrutiny and their guns when she got to the chorus.

"'War, children, it's just a shot away, shot away . . .'"

Just as Thatë predicted, their eyes were on her opened blouse, not her face, and certainly not on the *grupperovka* soldiers creeping up on either side of them. Alli was completely terrified, her tongue cleaving to the roof of her mouth so that the sound broke off abruptly. Not that the guerillas cared. Young girls were their thing and she fit the bill of fare to a T.

Alli knew what she had to do; she and Thatë had gone over it during a short break in the trek while his men had surveilled the area just ahead. She now had to do it. She recalled with perfect clarity the

Ukranian mistress Milla Tamirova and her dungeon
with its restraint chair that had brought back with a
sickening rush her week at the mercy of Morgan
Herr. Something inside her quailed and tried to
shrivel up. But she wouldn't let it; she was stronger
than that now. The guerillas' eyes burned into her
pale flesh. The inner halves of her breasts were exposed, moving as she approached them. She walked
as Milla Tamirova walked, putting one boot directly
in front of the other so that her hips and buttocks
swayed gently back and forth.

She was close enough to them now to smile, her
white, even teeth shining in the light of the bare bulb
above the door. She kept her lips slightly open. She
had moistened them just before she had stepped into
the light.

And then something odd—and thrilling—happened. Their very stares, which had terrified her a
moment before, buoyed her. Their eyes caressed her,
moving over one body part after another. They
weren't repulsed; on the contrary, naked lust suffused
their faces, warming her, fueling her. Emma had made
her feel beautiful. But now, for the first time, she realized that her childlike body was not connected to the
womanly power inside her. This was the moment of
her final flowering into womanhood, the moment
when all childhood things were left behind, when she
saw who and what she could become.

Finding her voice, she began to sing again. The
guerillas licked their lips seconds before they died.
She watched them with a curious dispassion as the
light went out of their eyes, and she shivered, suddenly cold.

"Fucking beautiful," Thatë said. He called Paull and gave him the all clear.

As soon as the chatter of machine-gun fire bit into the night, he led his men into the school.

Alli followed him, feeling like a shell sucked up in a powerful undertow.

THREE OF Thatë's men had been killed by the time the kid brought her face-to-face with the orphans. Until that moment, he had kept her safe in the rear guard, guarded by two of his *grupperovka* foot soldiers. But she had heard the sounds of fierce fighting, cries, and grunts as the forces met head on. She recognized all three of the dead men as she was led past them, and felt a slight tugging at her heart, shocked by how young they were.

The orphans were huddled in one darkened classroom. Before she stepped into the doorway, she handed Thatë her assault rifle.

He offered a handgun. "Don't go in there unarmed."

She looked at him and shook her head. "They need to trust me."

As she stepped into the room, she sensed the orphans shrinking back, and knew she had been right to come in without a weapon. Then, as they saw her, expressions of surprise and perhaps curiosity bloomed on their faces.

"I don't speak Macedonian," she said. "Which of you speak English?"

There was a rustling of bodies. Then a voice from the rear said, "English?"

A young girl pushed her way to the front of the

group. She was delicate, her porcelain beauty all the more potent for it. But there was a tigerish look to her eyes and this made Alli wary.

"You are English?"

"American," Alli said. And then, because there was no time and, really, no other way to state it: "There is danger here. These people are bad."

"I know," the porcelain girl said.

One of the other girls behind her said, "They are our teachers."

Alli, hearing the fear in the girl's voice, thought about Morgan Herr, who had claimed to be her teacher. "Yes, but they're teaching you only what they want you to know. They're making sure that when you grow up you'll be just like them—terrorists, smugglers, and murderers. I'll take you to a better place, where you'll be free to make up your own minds about what you want and don't want."

There was a brief silence, and Alli decided to concentrate on the porcelain girl.

"My name is Alli Carson."

"Edon." The porcelain girl looked into her eyes. "Edon Kraja."

Arieta's sister! A thrill of elation and foreboding ran down Alli's spine.

The rest of the children remained stone-faced. Assessing their continuing hesitation, Alli held up Emma's iPod. "Michael Jackson. 'Thriller.'"

A smile split Edon's face. "Michael Jackson. Really?"

Alli nodded.

"We're not allowed to listen to Michael Jackson," Edon said. "No American music."

"Where I'm going to take you, you can listen to any kind of music you want."

Fitting the earbuds to the iPod, Alli scrolled down to the track she wanted and pressed Play. She offered the earbuds to the girl, who cringed back until Alli put one of the earbuds in her own ear. When she offered the other one, the girl took it and hesitantly put it into her ear.

Her grin returned. "Michael Jackson," she said. "'Thriller.'"

Alli began to mimic the dance in Jackson's video and, as Edon hesitantly joined her, the other orphans crowded around. Alli passed the earbuds to a couple of the closest kids.

"Okay, Edon, we have to go. Now. You must tell everyone."

She did as Alli asked. Alli took back the iPod and earbuds as, like an inverted version of the Pied Piper, she led the orphans out of their personal rat-infested Hamelin.

When they were safely away, hidden in shadows of the trees, Edon turned to Alli.

"Thank you," she said, "from all of us, even the ones too young to yet understand." She burst into tears.

Alli put her arm around Edon's shoulders. "That's all right. You're free now."

"Yes, I," Edon said through her tears. "But my sister Liridona is not."

JACK WAS forced to begin his rear-guard action sooner than he had expected. No matter, he had plenty of ammo and convenient cover. He took out three of Xhafa's guerillas before they fell back, re-grouped, and came at him from both sides. Behind him, he could hear the continuous roar of the machine gun. The sound calmed him. Paull had his back.

As the two groups of guerillas began to converge on him, guided by his shots, he crab-walked straight ahead, into a dense copse of trees. Turning around, he fired into their flank, mowing down half of them before they could adjust and return fire. By that time, he had climbed up into one of the trees. Lying out on a thick branch, he brought them into his gun sight, picking them off as they scrambled futilely for cover.

Dropping down, he went from man to man, checking them for breath or pulse. Finding none, he turned back to where Paull was continuing his fusillade. It was then that he felt the cool breath on his cheek.

"Dad."

He felt death coming from behind him and darted to his right. The knife blade slashed through cloth and skin just above his hip bone. If he hadn't moved, the thrust would have punctured his liver. Stepping into the attack, he whirled and, cocking his elbow, slammed it into his assailant's throat. The guerilla staggered back, gasping, and Jack drove the butt of his assault rifle into the man's nose. Blood and cartilage whipped through the air, and the butt whacked the side of the guerilla's head so hard his neck snapped.

Leaping over the corpse, he joined Paull just in time to pick up the phone. He listened to Thatë's voice, cut the connection, and said, "The kids are out."

Paull did not let up the volleying for even an instant. "You know what to do," he said.

Jack picked up the shoulder rocket launcher he

had previously loaded, took aim at the school through the launcher's telescopic sight, and yelled, "Fire in the hole!" just before he pressed the trigger.

The night exploded into white light and a tremendous thunderclap that resounded throughout all of Tetovo.

TWENTY-ONE

MIDDLE BAY Bancorp was one of those newly minted powerhouse regional banks that came through the recent CDO and mortgage-backed securities meltdown relatively unscathed. In fact, at the depths of the recession, its prescient CEO, M. Bob Evrette, snapped up three failing regionals for ten cents on the dollar, more or less, in the process making himself both rich and a local hero for saving so many jobs.

There was a price to pay, as there always was: Like many great leaders, M. Bob Evrette was afflicted with hubris. In short, within the space of twenty months, Middle Bay became a victim of its own success. It grew too fast, outstripping not its resources but the expertise of its managers. Evrette had thrust it into the heady arena where the really big boys played, and even he wasn't up to navigating it.

At that point, perhaps six months ago, Henry Holt Carson had stepped in and made Evrette an offer he couldn't in all conscience refuse. For one reason or another, Middle Bay had been on Carson's radar screen for some time. Carson had built his fortune on knowing the right time to make an acquisition and when to sell it. Six months ago Middle Bay was ripe for the plucking. He set up one meeting with Evrette, where the merger with InterPublic Bancorp was proposed, then a dinner, where the deal was struck, and, finally, a weekend at the hunting lodge, where, over a brace of buckshot-riddled ducks, the deal was finalized.

Middle Bay boasted over twenty branches in D.C., Virginia, and Maryland, but its main branch resided at Twentieth and K Streets NW, in a florid building of white granite blocks so massive they'd give even Hercules palpitations.

"I spoke to M. Bob Evrette himself," Naomi said as they got out of the car and trotted up the steps that rose between two rows of immense Corinthian columns.

"What do *you* call him, Pete? He's a friend of yours, right?"

McKinsey laughed and shook his head. "Jesus, give it a rest, would you?"

Beyond the high revolving doors was a massive space clad in marble with wood and brass accents. The ceiling rose to a height of a cathedral's, and, at this late hour, there was a hush unnatural even for a bank. A bank of tellers' stations lined the right wall; a phalanx of gleaming ATMs was to their left.

A young man bustled out from behind a waist-high wooden partition. He wore a wasp-waisted suit, a solid-color tie, and a tight smile. His gleaming hair had an old-fashioned part in it. He looked as if he'd just come from the barber's.

He held out his hand, which was firm and dry. They introduced themselves and he led them back through the gate, past the cubicles where the investment and customer-relations officers normally plied their trade. Pausing at a door just long enough to punch in a six-digit code, he opened it and ushered them down a cool, low-lit hallway, its gleaming mahogany panels speaking of both money and discretion.

"Mr. Evrette is expecting you," the flunky said unnecessarily.

At the end of the hallway was a wide wooden door upon which the flunky rapped his knuckles.

"Come," a muffled voice said from within.

M. Bob Evrette was a hefty, florid-faced man in his midfifties, balding and running to fat, but there was no mistaking the youthful fire in his eyes.

"Come on in," he said with a friendly wave as he stood up behind his desk. "No good will come of standing on ceremony with me."

He had a good ol' boy accent and an aw-shucks attitude that belied his business acumen. Naomi disliked him on sight. She distrusted friendliness before there was a reason for it. He bounced out from behind his desk and indicated a grouping of chairs near the window a stone's throw from the Exxon Mobil Corporation offices.

"So," he said, as they took their seats, "how can I be of service?"

Naomi looked at him with gimlet eyes. He reminded her of a department store Santa who got his secret jollies snuggling little kids on his lap.

There was a small silence. She became aware that

McKinsey was watching her with the wariness of a hawk.

"We're investigating a triple homicide," she began.

"Excuse me, Agent Wilde, but I'm curious why the Secret Service—"

"It's a matter of national security," she said stiffly.

"Of course." He nodded. "I understand." His tone indicated that the matter was as clear as mud. He spread his hands. "Please continue."

"One of the victims in this case is William Warren."

An expression of sorrow dampened Evrette's face. "One of my best analysts." He shook his head. "Shocking, truly shocking. And, of course, sad. Incomprehensible."

"We're trying to make sense of it." Naomi cleared her throat. "Toward that end, we'd like to take a look at Mr. Warren's computer. Have the Metro police been here?"

"Not yet," Evrette said. "But a Detective Heroe will be over first thing tomorrow morning. She said not to let anyone in Mr. Warren's office."

"We've taken over the case; Detective Heroe simply hasn't gotten the memo yet," McKinsey said.

Naomi added: "We'd also like to examine the files on the loans Billy Warren was working on."

"Of course." He rose and, returning to his desk, punched a button on his intercom. "We have visitors from the federal government. After they're through in Mr. Warren's office, I'll bring them directly to you."

He rubbed his hands together as he returned to where Naomi and McKinsey sat. Naomi watched him and, when she could, McKinsey, to see if there was any hint of a prior meeting or relationship, but neither seemed particularly interested in the other. Evrette seemed entirely focused on her.

"As you may or may not know," he said, "we're in the midst of being engulfed and devoured by Inter-Public."

He laughed good-naturedly, and again Naomi was reminded of that dirty-minded department store Santa.

"As part of the transition, InterPublic hired a forensic accounting team to examine our books for the past five years." He waved them toward the door with a little puff of breath. "You wouldn't be wrong in counting that a damned daunting job. In fact, that's precisely what went through my mind. But then this gentleman showed up and started directing his team, and, let me tell you, he's something of a genius."

He led them down another corridor to an office appropriate in size and furnishings to a midlevel executive. Blinds were down over the window. Peeking through them, Naomi saw the window grid of the building across K Street.

"Okay," she said.

Looking at Billy's workspace, she said, "I think we'd better get Forensics over here."

"Consider it done." McKinsey drew out his cell phone and made a call. As he began to speak, he walked out of the room. A moment later, he returned. "All set."

Naomi nodded. Snapping on latex gloves, she first went through all the desk drawers. Then she fired up the computer.

"Has anyone been in here since Billy's death?"

"Not since I got the call from Detective Heroe."

Evrette shrugged. "Before that, I suppose the cleaning people the night he was . . . killed. If anyone else was, I'm afraid I can't say."

"Please find out who among the cleaning staff was in here," she said, fingers flying over the keyboard. "I'd like to interview them."

Evrette nodded. "Just give me a moment," he said, and went out.

Out of the corner of her eye, Naomi saw McKinsey standing with his arms crossed. He seemed to want to look everywhere at once.

She spoke to him while she checked the folder tree of Billy's hard drive. "Peter, are you nervous?"

"I told you I'd have your back."

"You also told me not to come here. How well do you know Evrette?"

"I've never met him before today."

She glanced up and sensed that he was telling the truth. "Did you tell anyone we were coming here?"

"No."

For a long moment, they held each other's gaze. Then Naomi nodded and went back to her work. When she found the folders she wanted, she went through the desk drawers until she found a package of blank DVDs. Placing one in the plastic tray, she copied all the folders and files that looked relevant.

"If there was anything untoward going on," McKinsey said, "I very much doubt Warren would be stupid enough to keep the files on his hard drive."

"Sadly, I agree." She pulled out the loaded DVD and pocketed it. "But it would be foolish to assume anything."

She methodically went through the drawers, looking for locked sections or false backs, but found nothing of interest. At that point, Evrette returned and handed her a slip of paper with the name, address, and contact number of the cleaning person who was on duty the night Billy was murdered. Naomi thanked him and pocketed the paper.

"Okay," she said, standing up.

As she headed toward the bank of filing cabinets, Evrette said, "They're all empty. The files were taken to the vault by the forensic accounting team."

"Then lead the way," she said. "But first I need to make a pit stop at the ladies'."

"Certainly." Evrette gave her directions.

She wanted to try one more time to speak to Jack. Failing that, she wanted to update him again. But once she got into a stall and rummaged around in her handbag for her cell, she recalled that it was still in its charger in the center console of her car. She'd run it down to zero. Cursing her own stupidity, she returned to Billy Warren's office and Evrette led them down the hall.

"The forensic team insisted on working on-site. We chose the vault because it's quiet and out of the way of both our staff and our clients," Evrette explained as they proceeded down one hallway, then another.

The vault was at the end of a long corridor, the last third of which offered blank walls rather than the usual office doors. The huge round opening beckoned. With its massive hinges and seven-foot-thick hardened steel-and-titanium door opened inward, the entrance looked like a modern-day equivalent to Aladdin's cave.

As they stepped inside, a cool breeze from the internal air venting system stroked their faces. A table and chairs had been set up in the middle of the vault, but at the moment only one man sat, poring over masses of files and folders.

As Evrette announced them, he put down his pen, stood up, and turned around to face them. A good-looking man in his late thirties, he was impeccably dressed in an expensive, European-cut suit of midnight blue silk, a starched white shirt, and a modish paisley tie. He had thick, dark hair left longer than most people in his trade. His eyes were hooded, dark, and intelligent. He smiled and Naomi felt a curious sensation along her skin when he approached, as if he were giving off some kind of powerful energy.

M. Bob Evrette made the introductions. "Agents Wilde and McKinsey, this is John Pawnhill, the head of the forensic accounting team InterPublic hired."

"SO WHAT do you do, if you don't mind me asking?" the man sitting next to Annika said. When she hesitated, he said hastily, "That's all right. If you'd rather read, I understand completely."

She laughed softly. "No, I was getting bored anyway."

They were wearing their seat belts. The plane, slicing through the night on its way to Rome, had encountered a powerful storm, and they had experienced some unpleasant turbulence before the pilot had taken them up to 43,000 feet. Below them, vicious streaks of lightning flashed in the remote blackness of their time-annihilating flight.

"May I see what you're reading?"

She handed him the book. He had the face of a Roman senator, aggressive without being arrogant. His tan almost camouflaged the pockmarks on his cheek. The backs of his hands were scarred; they were work hands, which she liked. His gray eyes scanned the book jacket.

"*The Copenhagen Interpretation: the Orthodoxy of Quantum Mechanics, or The Wavefunction Collapse*." He glanced at her as he handed back the book. "That's quite a title. Are you a scientist?"

"A detective, of sorts," she said with a mischievous smile. "A very *specific* sort. I'm looking for the Higgs boson."

"The what?"

"A particle so small it's virtually beyond human comprehension." She waved a hand. "It's complicated and, for a layperson, probably boring."

"Not to me." He settled in, apparently content to listen to her as long as she wanted to talk.

"I work for CERN at the LHC," she said. "Also known as the Large Hadron Collider."

He tapped a finger against his lip. "I've heard about . . . didn't your team just break a record once held by Fermilabs?"

"That's right." She appeared delighted. "The LHC is in a massive tunnel on the border between France and Switzerland, in a space that's the coldest in the known universe."

In time, she could see him becoming infatuated. Not with her, precisely. He was in love with the lie she had spun, the image she had projected on the screen of his mind. It was an art, really, this ability to understand the power of lies, the way a lie—even a small one—had the power to bore its way through anyone's defenses. Her genius was in making this lie, no matter how small, into a truth that someone could believe in, because believing was the same as falling in love. Someone in the throes of infatuation had no defenses.

This is what she had done with Jack because it was the only way she knew how to live life. But then somewhere in the midst of the Ukraine something had changed. That lie had become a bitter pill, poisoning their relationship. She began to hate herself, and then to hate him for believing her lie. She had wanted, more than anything, for him to pull aside the curtain of her lies, to reveal her as Dorothy revealed the Wizard of Oz.

It was only afterward that she understood why she had defied her grandfather and confessed to Jack. She wanted him to hate her, she wanted to push him as far away from her as possible, and then to see if he would come back. Because if he did she would know that for the first time in her life she had met a man for whom the lies didn't matter. She would know that he loved her, not the persona she had presented.

The man in the seat beside her—Tim or Tom or Phil—was laughing at something she said. She could read his lust for her in every expression, every gesture he made. He was a wealthy businessman. He owned his own firm, which he was about to take public. The IPO would net him over a billion dollars. He was under the mistaken impression that she would be impressed, but her current persona had no interest in wealth or status. He readily admitted that he'd never met anyone like her.

"If you'll excuse me." She unbuckled her seat belt.

A tentative smile played across his lips. "Would you find it offensive if I accompanied you?"

As a gift, she presented him with her softest laugh. "Not at all. What a perfect gentleman you are."

He unbuckled his seat belt and followed her up the aisle to the toilet. It was nearly 5 A.M. Eastern Daylight Time and everyone in first class was either asleep or absorbed by the electronic flicker of their personal video screens. One of the attendants appeared from the galley and asked if they'd like some fresh-baked sugar cookies. They declined and she vanished the way she had come.

Opening the toilet door, Annika was aware that she didn't really want to do this, but her body was so conditioned that it was working on its own momentum. She did not stop Tim or Tom or Phil when he stepped into the toilet after her and awkwardly closed the door. Nor did she stop him when his hand groped beneath her skirt, the hem rising up his forearm as he found what he was grasping for.

Through it all, she clung to him. She felt unmoored, as if she weren't here on this plane, or over dark and troubled water, deeper even than the void in her chest. She was wherever Jack was at this moment. Her mind was filled with him.

She was oblivious to Tim or Tom or Phil's grunts, his bull-like lunges, the pain cutting across her buttocks as they rhythmically struck the sink edge.

She barely heard herself moaning she was weeping so copiously.

———

"HE'S NOT here. The fucker's not here!"

Thatë was in a state. They were inside what was left of Xhafa's stronghold. Burned bodies lay everywhere. The stench of roasted flesh was nauseating. Here and there in the corners of what had once been rooms, flames still flickered and danced. Otherwise, all was black ash, but that didn't stop the kid from kicking every corpse he came across, turning the ones on their stomachs over so he could examine the faces.

"What the fuck? What the fuck?" His equilibrium had shattered at the bitter taste of Pyrrhic victory. They had won everything, but had lost the only prize any of them cared about: Arian Xhafa.

Jack and Alli were examining a laptop computer, twisted out of shape by the explosion and resultant fire, when Thatë began screaming.

"Tell me! Tell me!"

Jack ran over and pulled him away from a badly wounded guerilla. There was spittle on Thatë's face; he was virtually frothing at the mouth. For his part, the guerilla slid to the floor. His body was a mass of deep burns and his face was bloody and distorted out of all proportion.

Paull tried to hold the kid back, but he just shook the older man away. Jack looked at Alli and she went over and took Thatë by the arm. It was a restraint, the only one he would tolerate at the moment. He gave the guerilla a venomous glare over her shoulder.

Jack squatted beside the guerilla. He could see at a glance that his wounds were mortal. "What's your name?"

One bloodshot eye stared back at him. "Bek . . .

Bekir." The other eye was swollen closed, so heavily bruised it looked like a fist.

"Where is Arian Xhafa?"

"He isn't here."

Jack sat back on his haunches. He gave Thatë a querying look, but the kid was still livid with rage.

"Give me five minutes with him," Thatë said.

"The poor bastard doesn't have five minutes," Jack told him. "Besides, what can you do to him that hasn't already been done?" Turning back to Bekir, he said, "Where is Xhafa? Where did he go?"

"In . . . into the wind." Bekir's mouth was red and black, the lips so distorted it was unclear whether even his mother would recognize him. "He left a little while ago."

"How little?" Jack pressed.

"Twenty minutes, maybe fifteen."

"Christ, we just missed the fuck," Paull said.

Bekir started coughing. His condition was clearly declining rapidly.

With time running out, Jack tried another tack. If Bekir couldn't solve the mystery of where Arian Xhafa went, maybe he could solve another mystery. "Bekir, were you here when the American unit tried its assault?"

Bekir nodded. His eye could not stop rolling in its socket. He must be in terrible pain, Jack thought. But it was too late to do anything to save him.

"For God's sake help him," Alli said from over Jack's shoulder. "Give him water, at least."

"His lungs are filling," Jack told her. "He'll drown in even a tablespoon of water."

He returned his attention to Bekir. "How did Xhafa defeat the American unit?"

"Fast." Bekir's voice was thick with phlegm and blood. "Very fast."

"Not like with us."

The one eye stared at him.

"See, this is what I don't understand." Jack edged closer. "I know you had sophisticated weaponry, but so did the American unit."

Bekir's eye stared at Jack for what seemed a long time. Then his lips moved, as if of their own volition, and the voice came out, hollow as a drum. "The weaponry helped. How could it not? But Xhafa had an edge that meant the Americans' certain death."

Jack's insides went cold. Then he felt Paull leaning closely in.

"And what was that?" Paull said.

Bekir's lips curled up into a smile, which began another coughing fit that produced a prodigious flow of blood from his mouth. When he calmed somewhat, he spoke. "He knew they were coming. He's got an American informant."

"That's a fucking lie," Paull said dismissively.

Jack rocked back on his heels. "Bekir, my friend, here's my problem with what you claim. Even with his newfound money and links to international arms dealers, Xhafa is unlikely to have that kind of political or military connection. Very, very few people do."

There was a peculiar light in Bekir's good eye, and Jack knew he was preparing himself to die. During the interview, his breathing had become shallow. Now it was irregular. Blood drooled out of one ruined ear. And yet he was determined to persevere for at least one more moment, at least long enough for him to deliver his farewell message.

"Then whoever is funneling money and arms his way is one of those elite people."

JOHN PAWNHILL smiled a magnetic smile that momentarily caused Naomi's knees to feel as if they'd turned to jelly.

"How may I be of assistance?"

"Agent McKinsey and I are investigating the murder of Billy Warren, a loan analyst at the bank." For any number of reasons, the torture aspect of Billy's murder had not yet been made public.

"Yes, I've been through some of his work." Pawnhill gestured. "Very talented young man. Pity he's no longer with us."

"We need to see the files that were taken from his office."

"By all means." Pawnhill went to the table and, counting out stacks, slid one to a spot in front of an empty chair. "Knock yourself out, Agent Wilde." He nodded as she sat down. "If you need any deciphering, don't hesitate to ask."

"Believe me, I won't." She pulled the first folder off the top of the pile and opened it. "Are these in alphabetical order?"

"No," Pawnhill said. "They're in chronological order with the latest loan on top."

The others hung back, but there was no conversation from behind her. She scanned the documents inside the folder, then set it aside and picked up the next on the pile. This process went on for perhaps forty minutes.

Pawnhill pointed. "That particular loan was never consummated. Mr. Warren discovered a problem with the applicant's financials."

Naomi ran her finger down the sheet. "Did he often find such problems?"

"No, he didn't." This from Evrette. "When it comes to its loan applicants, the bank employs a rigorous vetting process."

Naomi turned a page. "But sometimes—like here—something slips through the cracks."

"Well, no system is foolproof," Evrette admitted. "That's one of the talents that made Mr. Warren so valuable. He could sniff out even the faintest whiff of an applicant's shaky finances."

"What about off-the-books loans?"

"I beg your pardon?"

Evrette came around into her line of vision and she could feel McKinsey take a protective step close behind her.

Naomi gave him a steady look. "I think you heard me, Mr. Evrette. Did Billy Warren discover any off-the-books loans that hadn't been reported?"

"This is preposterous. Of course he didn't."

Pawnhill intervened. "Agent Wilde, if I may, had there been any such machinations I and my team would have found them."

"But—and correct me if I'm wrong—you're not finished with your forensic audit."

"Almost," he said. "But not quite."

"Hmmm." She tapped her fingertip against a line on the page. "Then perhaps you can explain to me why this company—Gemini Holdings—showed up in one of Mr. Warren's case files on his computer."

"That's hardly surprising," Evrette said. "He was just doing his due diligence. The loan was denied."

"I see." Naomi nodded. "But what's curious was that Mr. Warren continued to follow the activities of Gemini Holdings after he recommended that their loan application be turned down."

"I don't know what you're getting at," Evrette said.

Naomi's finger swept down the page. "According to the information in Mr. Warren's electronic file, Gemini never went to another bank." Her eyes were fixed on Evrette. Sensing that she had struck a nerve, she pressed on. "Not only that, but it seems that Gemini Holdings got their loan money not ten days after they were turned down here."

Evrette shrugged. "That's none of my concern."

"Really?" Her lips pursed in admonishment. "I think Billy Warren discovered that it was very much your concern. I think that's why he was keeping an eye on Gemini long after their loan was turned down."

That was when she heard the soft metallic click. As she began to rise from her chair, McKinsey's firm hand pushed her back down hard. Then the cold metallic press of a gun at the base of her neck.

Behind her, McKinsey pulled the trigger, and she was slammed forward. Immediately, blood spurted, warm and cherry red.

PART THREE

CHERRY BOMB

Two Days Ago

Don't fall in love, don't fall in love, she
seemed to be trying to say to me.

—*The Skating Rink*, ROBERTO BOLAÑO

Twenty-two

A RIAN XHAFA stepped off the military air transport at Vlorë Air Base in southwest Albania into a driving rain. The dark, fulminating sky seemed as low as the treetops, and a filthy wind battered him.

An armored car pulled up and he got in. He was carrying no luggage; none had been needed. At once, the armored car pulled away, exiting the base without going through either immigration or customs.

"Good to be home?" the Syrian said.

Arian Xhafa nodded. "Always." He was a man of swarthy skin, dark curling hair, which merged with his full beard. His face seemed chiseled by wind and sun, the deep-set eyes, the high cheekbones, the hawk's-bill nose. He might be Albanian by birth, but his aggressively Middle Eastern blood had forged his physiognomy.

The Syrian sighed. "I have no home."

"A long-held dream, soon to be realized, my friend."

Even next to Xhafa, the Syrian was a big man, tall, his shoulders and arms knotted with muscle, as if he had been a hod carrier or a bricklayer all his life. His hands were big and square, calloused, their backs ropy, dark as coffee. But his eyes had in them the talent of a sculptor. It was, of course, his eyes that were most remarked upon. One green, the other blue, each seemed to be buried in a different head or, more accurately, connected to a different brain.

People were terrified of the Syrian, and with good reason. You never knew what he was thinking or how he would react. He had a real name, of course, the one his parents had given him, but it had been so long since he had used it that it had been all but forgotten. Xhafa, for instance, had never known it.

"So," the Syrian said now, "how was Washington?"

"I despise that city," Xhafa said, "and it despises me. Dardan has been killed."

"Is that such a tragedy?" The Syrian was not one to mince words or care who he defamed. "I warned you about him. He was weak."

"He was family," Xhafa said stiffly.

The Syrian grunted. "Sentiment is itself a weakness."

Xhafa fought to swallow the rebuke. He feared the Syrian as much as everyone else, he simply refused to show it. It would do no good, he knew, to remind his companion that he had lost all his family to war. The Syrian never invoked their names; it was as if they had never existed. While in Washington, Xhafa had read of a recent DNA study that proved, genetically, at least, there wasn't much difference between the Arabs and the Jews. Something else he dare not mention to his dour companion. On the other hand, losses were much on his mind.

"It's not only Dardan," he said now, "but my men in Tetovo. The entire fortress was destroyed."

"That was, of course, always a possibility," the Syrian's face darkened, "but I cannot understand how the enemy escaped the ambush you laid for them in Dolna Zhelino." His tone made it sound like the error was somehow Xhafa's.

"They killed all my men."

"Yes, but how?"

"My men—"

"Were no doubt happy to die for the cause," the Syrian said with a dismissive sweep of his hand.

"My men are not yours," Xhafa said. "They're not ignorant mountain fanatics who die without a thought."

The Syrian was not offended. In fact, he laughed. "This is true, Xhafa. The men of the mountains of Afghanistan and Western Pakistan are the defeated, the disenfranchised who were chased into their mountain lairs by stronger tribal forces. The mountains' lawless state attracts the fanatics, the extremists, the outcasts of society. But, listen to me, Xhafa, they are my most valuable resource. Their ignorance breeds fanaticism and that is my stock in trade. They are my creatures because I tell them what they want to hear. In return, they do what I tell them to do."

He puffed out his cheeks, his eyes alight. His ideas made him restless. "What they want is simple: They want to blow up the society that cast them out. This is the opportunity I give them and they are grateful."

"They have proved to be the best weapon we have against the West," Xhafa said.

The Syrian snorted. "The West believes that it is their fanaticism that makes them cruel, but, no, this is incorrect. What makes them cruel is their monumental ignorance. They have no conception of the world. Good for me. Even better, they don't care, so I don't even need to lie to them. They'll never get what they want, of course, but in the meantime they are useful as agents of chaos. And because they wish to martyr themselves for their doomed cause, they keep coming. They die and they rise endlessly."

The Syrian stroked his beard. "But never mistake me for one of them, Xhafa. As you know, I come from the lowlands, from a wealthy family. I'm well educated, a graduate of universities in both the East and the West—under different names, of course. You might say that I'm a man of the world. A prerequisite to understanding the enemy."

A certain tension informed his body. "What must be understood is the cause of the enemy's success." Being a master tactician, he was understandably focused on battlefield failures. In contrast, the loss of human life was of importance to him only inasmuch as it affected his plans. "The failure in Dolna Zhelino might be explained away by happenstance, but not the complete destruction of your fortress in Tetovo." He tapped his forefinger on his knee. "No, there is another factor here of which we're ignorant."

Xhafa shook his head. "I still don't understand the need for such complexity."

"That's because you haven't studied this Jack Mc-Clure. His mind works best within complicated situations. To him, that's the way the world works, and he's not far off the mark. Give him something simple to solve and he'll become immediately suspicious.

Frankly, he's a con artist's worst nightmare. To my knowledge only one person was able to con him, and then not for long."

"Annika Dementieva."

"Correct." The Syrian sighed. "You know, Xhafa, I tried to do this the simple way, but, try as I might, I couldn't get to Gourdjiev. I lost half a dozen of my best men in the process. Even at his age, that wily old fucker is still formidable."

The Syrian stretched in his seat and cracked his knuckles. "So I had to tackle the problem from another angle entirely. I decided to go after Annika. But I knew I couldn't do it directly. I had to move softly and take a roundabout route."

"Which is where McClure comes in."

"There is something between Annika and McClure, of that there can be no doubt." The Syrian smiled his crooked smile. "As I said, sentiment is itself a weakness."

"Maybe she's continuing to play him."

The Syrian scratched at the thicket of his beard, which was shot through with white. "That possibility has occurred to me." His smile widened. "But the beauty of my plan is that it doesn't matter. She is so heavily defended and almost as wily as her grandfather that McClure is the best way—probably the *only* way—to get to her. And she, my dear Xhafa, is the only way to get to Gourdjiev and all the secrets locked up in that brilliant mind of his."

He sighed again. "The truth is, I cannot go forward without those secrets."

Xhafa pricked up his ears. This was the first time

the Syrian had come close to defining the goal of his plan—a plan he had been forced to go along with if he wanted to continue the very profitable arrangement he had with the Syrian. A powerful incentive, since this arrangement had provided him with capital and influence in exchange for a third of his smuggling operation. Now Xhafa's small fleet of new and larger planes were filled with the Syrian's mysterious cargo as well as Xhafa's stolen girls.

"Just what are those secrets?"

"Enough criminal dirt and serious indiscretions to take control of his worldwide constellation of politicians and security officers."

Xhafa would have staked his life on the fact that the Syrian was not telling the truth or, at least, not the whole truth, but he let it go because, humiliatingly, there was nothing he could do. The hard truth was that he felt like a child beside this man, this monument to power.

The rain beat down hard against the reinforced metal top and the landscape outside was gray and hazy, like a painting whose colors had run together. They had been joined by a phalanx of motorcycle police fore and aft, the caravan cutting a swath through the streets with the seething din of war.

The Syrian shifted again, the aura of his power rippling outward, filling the entire vehicle so completely that Xhafa could scarcely draw breath.

"And as to the other part of your mission . . . ?" The Syrian let his last words hang between them like an implied threat.

"Arjeta Kraja is dead," Xhafa said. "I killed her with my own hands."

"THE LAST time I saw Naomi Wilde?"

"That's what I asked."

Peter McKinsey shifted in his chair. It was a stiff chair with one of those minimalist backs guaranteed to make you more uncomfortable the longer you sat in it. He was downtown at Metro Police HQ, in a separate suite of offices reserved for the Violent Crimes Unit.

"Yesterday, at about a quarter to five in the afternoon. We'd been using my car. I dropped her back at the office. She got into her car and drove off."

"Did she say where she was going?"

McKinsey nodded. "She told me she was going home."

"Directly home?"

"'I'm going home, Pete. I've had it.' This is word for word what she said to me." He spoke neither quickly nor slowly, but his voice was appropriately tight. After all, his partner of six years was missing.

Chief Detective Nona Heroe's head came up. She had been scribbling in a small spiral-bound pad. "Agent Wilde said, 'I've had it'?"

McKinsey nodded. "Yes."

Heroe tapped her pen on her notebook. "What did you take that to mean?"

He shrugged. "That she was beat. We both were. We'd been up and working for more than two days."

"In that time you two never went home?"

"Just to shower and change clothes."

Heroe marked this down as if it would someday be used as evidence against him. He hated her even more.

She looked up. "Where were you before you arrived at the office?"

"We were following up several leads concerning the trafficking network that brought Arjeta Kraja into the States illegally."

"And?"

"Unfortunately, they led nowhere."

"Why were you so interested in Ms. Kraja?"

"That was Naomi's idea. According to Alli Carson, the Kraja girl was seen with Billy Warren the night he was tortured and killed."

Heroe processed his tone. "And you didn't believe Ms. Carson."

"Let's put it this way. I'd have liked the opportunity to question the Carson girl more closely."

"What stopped you?"

McKinsey shrugged. "You know as well as I do. She's a protected entity."

Heroe made more notes. "And you never found Ms. Kraja's body."

McKinsey sighed heavily and pressed his thumbs into his eye sockets. "She vanished into thin air."

"Just like Agent Wilde."

"I hadn't thought about it that way, but I suppose you could say so, yes."

Heroe scribbled industriously. She was good at it. Engaging his eyes again, she said, "Agent McKinsey, I'm afraid I have some bad news. We found Agent Wilde's car. It had gone off the road in rural Maryland. We had the devil's own time pulling it out of a concrete abutment at the base of the embankment."

"Did you find her?" Suitably anxious tone. "Did you find Naomi?"

"No."

He frowned. He was good at it. "What about her handbag, her cell? I've been trying to call her for hours."

"There was nothing in the car," Heroe said. "The driver's side door was open and the seat belt hadn't been engaged when the airbags deployed."

McKinsey shook his head. "I don't understand."

"That makes two of us, Agent McKinsey."

Heroe flipped closed her notebook and stood. McKinsey admired her while she stretched. She was an imposing woman, with a good figure, fine features, and skin the color of bitter sweet chocolate. She seemed to be on the good side of forty, young to be the head of Violent Crimes. Either she had offered herself to all the right people, he thought, or she was very, very smart.

"Why don't we take a break." It was not a question. She gestured to a sideboard on which stood some kind of stainless-steel-and-glass apparatus that looked like it belonged in a Starbucks. "Would you like some coffee?"

"As long as it's not swill."

Her laugh seemed to him corrosive.

"I make my own. Stumptown."

That meant nothing to him. While she busied herself, he looked at his hands. Steady as a rock. But he sorely wanted to get the hell out of there. He wasn't used to being interrogated, and now he regretted his rash action at the bank. But he had had no choice. Naomi had discovered the connection between Middle Bay and Gemini Holdings. He was now in the middle of a shitstorm and he knew that bastard

Pawnhill blamed him. He'd tried to warn Naomi away from Middle Bay but, as always, she had been like a dog with a bone. He'd admired that in her. Truth be told, shooting her dead had frazzled his nerves. That was a surprise. Before coming to the Secret Service he'd killed before, more times than he'd like to count, but this kill was different. It was Naomi. Christ, it was like a marriage—in many ways, more intimate. They'd had each other's back. Until yesterday. Truth be told, he was still in shock. He continued to stare at his hands, wondering when they would begin to shake.

He looked up as Heroe returned with two tiny cups, setting one down in front of him.

"What the hell is this?"

She resumed her seat opposite him. "Haven't you ever had an espresso?"

"I drink coffee," he said.

"Espresso *is* coffee." She took a sip. "Only better."

He downed his in one gulp.

"About Agent Wilde's car," Heroe said. "I don't think she was in it when it crashed."

McKinsey almost choked. "I don't . . . I don't follow."

"Forensics. No blood, bits of skin, the kind of evidence you'd expect to find somewhere in the interior—the front seat, the headrest, the steering wheel. There was nothing at all."

Shit, he thought, *I was so freaked out I forgot to plant the forensics.*

At that moment, when he needed a reprieve the most, he got it. The door opened and Heroe's boss,

Alan Fraine, stuck his head in and signaled. Excusing herself, Heroe rose and went out of the room with him. He had counted off a hundred seconds when she returned, a scowl on her face.

She put her back against the open door. "You're free to go."

McKinsey grinned at her as he went out, and couldn't help saying, "See you around the block."

AFTER MCKINSEY had left the building, Heroe and Alan Fraine had a sit-down in his office. Unlike most offices, it was fanatically, almost obsessively, neat. Fraine himself was the same way. A man on the downward slope of middle age, balding, with a high, freckled forehead, he had small hands and feet, delicate fingers. His usual outfit was a neatly pressed long-sleeved shirt and suspenders, rather than a belt to keep his pants up over his narrow hips. He sat behind his desk while Heroe pulled over an armchair.

"I still wonder whether my leaking McKinsey's whereabouts was a good idea," Fraine said. "I was listening and it seemed to me that you were actually getting somewhere with him."

Heroe sighed. "It was more important to find out who his rabbi is. So give."

"You were right, it wasn't his boss at the Secret Service," Fraine said. "It was Andrew Gunn of Fortress."

"Damn, isn't that something!" Heroe punched the air. "Okay, now we're getting somewhere."

"You think McKinsey's dirty?"

"I know it," Heroe said. "Furthermore, I think Naomi Wilde is dead—not missing, not abducted. I think she was killed because of what she knew or maybe discovered. And Peter McKinsey's my prime suspect."

"One federal agent murdering another? Jesus, Heroe, even for you that's a lot to swallow in one gulp, especially with nothing tangible to back it up."

"Take as many gulps as you want. The fact is Naomi Wilde's car went off the road without her in it. Someone else dead-manned it to go off the road precisely where it did. I'm going to go over his alibi with a fine-tooth comb."

Fraine swung his chair around and looked out the window with his thousand-mile stare. "If she's dead why wasn't she in the car?"

"My best guess? Her murder was a spur-of-the-moment thing, and it was messy. Also, if I had to go further, it's possible that the manner of her death might have led us to suspect McKinsey."

Fraine was used to Heroe's speculations. The reason he didn't shoot them down was that more often than not they proved correct. He spread his hands. "Okay, say you're right on all counts—"

"I know I am." She produced a cell phone and placed it on the desk between them.

Fraine glanced at it. "Is that supposed to mean something to me?"

"This is Naomi Wilde's cell. We found it in the center console of her car, where it was protected during the crash."

"So?"

"Don't you think if she were heading off to a dangerous place she'd have it with her?" She shook her head emphatically. "No, she was with someone she trusted when she was killed."

"Someone like Peter McKinsey." Fraine rubbed his forehead. "If you're right—and that's a big *if*—this isn't going to go down well with the brass, not well at all."

"Not my problem."

"It will be if you can't find the body. Not a word of this can be breathed to anyone until it's found."

"And if it's not?"

"Then your theory never leaves this office."

"I can't let that happen."

"Where is she, Nona? Where is Naomi Wilde?"

"Fuck if I know." She made her voice into a hoarse rasp. "But wherever she is, she's sleeping with the fishes, just like Luca Brasi. And like a Corleone I'm going to track down whoever murdered her and get my revenge."

Fraine turned back and leaned forward with his elbows on his desk. "Revenge is a mighty disturbing word coming from a law enforcement officer."

Heroe rose. She was like a Valkyrie—fierce, dark, determined. "Yeah, well, murdering a Secret Service agent is a mighty disturbing business."

"WHAT DID she say just before she died?"

Arian Xhafa turned, but the Syrian appeared quite serious.

"She said, 'Why?'"

The Syrian's eyes went briefly out of focus. They were like pits, merciless and brutal. "That's what they all say. You'd think someone would be more creative."

Perhaps you will be, when you die, Xhafa thought.

"Arjeta Kraja possessed knowledge, Xhafa, and knowledge is like a virus—it can so easily spread exponentially." The Syrian raked his fingers through his beard, a sign that he was lost in thought. "Did she say anything else?"

"Yes." Xhafa shivered. He had hoped the Syrian wouldn't ask. "She said, 'Where I'm going, there are no more secrets.'"

The Syrian started as if he'd been stuck with a hypodermic. "I knew the moment she ran," he said, "and now here's the proof of it. You see, you fool. She *did* know."

Once again Xhafa felt like a child being reprimanded for his ignorance. Suddenly, he was possessed by a murderous rage, and he spent the next thirty seconds consciously uncurling his fingers, keeping them from becoming fists. Ever since the Syrian had brought up Arjeta Kraja, Xhafa had felt a cold lump forming in the pit of his stomach. The orphan student body at the Tetovo school was larded with girls—recruits to slavery his agents had stolen or bought from their desperate or unscrupulous families. One of those was Arjeta's sister, Edon. Did she know what her sister knew, had her sister spoken to her before Xhafa had had a chance to silence Arjeta? He didn't know. Come to that, he didn't know whether Edon Kraja had survived the attack on the school. He prayed to Allah that she hadn't. In either case, he dared not say a word about Edon to the Syrian. If he did, he knew it would be the end for him.

Oblivious to Xhafa's mounting tension, the Syrian gazed out the smoked window, deeply immersed in his own thoughts. The caravan pulled into a huge estate, passed through an electronically controlled gate in a high fence topped with rolls of electrified razor wire, and now rolled along a drive of crushed marble so white that even in the gloom it sparkled. Men holding huge attack dogs on leashes appeared on either side of the house. The dogs strained at their leashes, their eyes golden and greedy.

The Syrian ignored them. "She saw and she must have heard someone mention the name."

"But who would mention the name?" Xhafa said.

The armored vehicle came to rest precisely in front of an immense oak door, snatched from a looted medieval cathedral, that rose, as if on a plinth, at the top of six wide white stone steps.

The two men emerged from the vehicle. The attack dogs' flanks quivered but they remained stationary; the scents of the two men were known to them.

The door was opened by Taroq, the compound's chief guard. They exchanged greetings as he ushered them into a space as large as a football field and as spare as a monk's cell. There was no furniture to speak of, only a number of silk prayer rugs, large cushions, and one low wooden table on which sat a tall teapot with a long S-shaped spout, six small glasses in brass frames, and an antique hookah. The two men removed their shoes on the doorstep and stepped into soft leather slippers with turned-up toes.

Light flooded the space from a series of windows on either side wall. Against the rear wall, a good distance away, was a simple desk and chair. On the desk were three computers—two desktops and a powerful but thin laptop. All were hooked into a high-speed modem with which the house had been specially provided, according to the specifications of the person sitting at the desk, peering from one screen to another.

"Hello, boys," the figure said in a darkly sweet contralto. She spoke in English. "Back already?"

The chair swiveled around as the whisper of the men's slippers approached. A young woman sat in the chair. She was thin as a reed with a pale, ascetic face whose main feature was a broad, high forehead. Her blond hair was pulled back in a neat ponytail that came to rest between her knife-thin shoulder blades. She wore a pair of black jeans and a man-tailored shirt of the same color with the sleeves rolled up to the elbow, revealing silken hair that was almost white. She wore no makeup or jewelry, but her deep-set emerald eyes glittered with a fierce and almost feral intelligence.

Then she stood and came toward them in long, athletic strides. She was tall, but not nearly as tall as the Syrian. She had to arch upward, standing on tiptoe, to kiss him on the lips, a long, lingering kiss whose naked passion forced Xhafa to look away.

The Syrian's face broke into a smile of what might, for him, be termed bliss.

"Caroline, my *habibi*," he said. "What terrible mischief have you been up to while I've been absent?"

TWENTY-THREE

THREE SIGNIFICANT things happened in the aftermath of the destruction of Arian Xhafa's stronghold in Tetovo. First, Alli discovered that not all the students were orphans. Most of the young girls, in fact, either had been kidnapped or sold into slavery. Second, there was cell phone service in the area. As Jack's cell buzzed to life, locking onto the signal, he saw Paull listening intently as Alli spoke with the children's spokesperson, a beautiful girl with the most perfect skin he'd ever seen, whom Alli seemed to have bonded with immediately.

There were three messages from Naomi Wilde. Figuring that she had been trying to get in touch with him in order to update him on her progress, he listened with a sense of both shock and mounting alarm to the brief but succinct reports on her theories.

In the first, she spoke of her mounting suspicions concerning her partner, Peter McKinsey, and his possible connection with Fortress Securities. She also told him about the conflicting evidence against Alli, as if two opposing forces were at work countering each other, an occurrence that, frankly, had her baffled.

In the second message, she described her tailing McKinsey into Georgetown and the marina there along the Sequoia boardwalk. McKinsey had met an unknown man who, by Naomi's detailed description, seemed most certainly an Arab of some sort. The Arab had driven McKinsey out to Theodore Roosevelt Island, where they had disembarked and vanished into the foliage. Naomi didn't say how long they were on the island. Possibly, she hadn't stuck around to find out.

The third and final message was a total bombshell that rattled Jack to his core. Naomi detailed her meeting with a woman who had taken her out to Roosevelt Island. There, the woman had shown Naomi the newly buried corpse of Arjeta Kraja. The implication was that the two men had buried her. Had the Arab killed her or had McKinsey? Impossible to tell. Naomi said the woman had mentioned Arjeta's sisters, Edon and Liridona, both of whom, it appeared, she knew, and who seemed somehow important. The sisters knew a secret, most probably concerning Arian Xhafa or his network. The woman said the Krajas lived in the Albanian coastal city of Vlorë. Liridona was presumably still there, but Edon had run away, probably from Xhafa's men.

Possibly to better allow him to absorb her news, Naomi left the identity of her mysterious benefactor until the end, but when Jack heard Annika's name his blood ran cold. He sat down on a tree stump. His heart was racing; he felt icy hot, a sensation that threatened to annihilate his thought processes.

Annika had resurfaced, and, of all places, in Washington. Then he heard Naomi in her last line: "*I think she's behind everything, and she knows where you are."*

Jack, realizing that he'd been holding his breath, struggled to get oxygen into his lungs. He felt as if he were trapped underwater. He tried to calm himself, to figure out what the hell was going on, but it was as if his brain had shut down. Annika, the rogue Russian FSB agent whose life he had saved, only to find out that she was not FSB and the man he thought he'd saved her from was a confederate of hers. She had been working for her grandfather, Dyadya Gourdjiev, all along. He'd accepted that because for a brief time, at least, he and Gourdjiev were on the same side. He'd been powerfully attracted to Annika from the moment they'd first met in the bar of his Moscow hotel last year. And that attraction had turned into a love he'd believed was mutual until on his last day in Moscow he'd received an e-mail from her telling him that she had killed Senator Berns, a murder that had created a political firestorm and had been the starting point of Jack's investigation into political corruption at the highest level in both the American and the Russian governments.

I neither regret what I did nor feel pride in it, she had written. In peace as in war sacrifices must be made, soldiers must fall in order for battles to be won—even, or perhaps especially, those that are waged sub rosa, in the shadows of a daylight only people like us notice.

So you hate me now, which is understandable and inevitable, but you know me, what I can't stand is indifference, and now, no matter what, you'll never be indifferent to me.

God damn her, he thought now. He put his head in his hands. Over the intervening months he had tried to put her out of his mind.

My grandfather warned me not to tell you, but I'm breaking protocol because there's something you have to know; it's the reason I haven't come, why I won't come no matter how long you wait, why I'm not being melodramatic when I say that we must never see each other again.

Her involvement all but paralyzed him. It threw the entire scenario into another arena entirely, and all at once, pieces, tiny and disparate, began to fall into place. Another murder that set an entire group of people into motion, most notably him—and Alli. Could this be another elaborately staged setup choreographed by Annika? It had her hallmarks, certainly, but there were marked differences, not the least of which was the brutal torture of Billy Warren. That wasn't Annika at all. Her rage at her father had exploded quickly and definitively. Annika had been the victim of physical abuse; there was no circumstance under which Jack could imagine her torturing someone, unless the person had done grievous bodily harm to her or to someone she loved. This was not Billy Warren's profile.

All at once, he became aware that Paull had broken away from Alli and the girl, and was standing beside him.

"Everything all right?"

"Fine," Jack muttered.

"You look as if someone just walked over your grave."

All Jack could manage was a wan smile.

Paull cleared his throat. "Listen, I'm useless here," he said. "If I'm being perfectly honest with myself, worse than useless. I almost got us all killed."

"Could have happened to anyone," Jack said.

Paull smiled and clapped Jack on the shoulder. "You're a good friend. I appreciate the support, but you'll have to continue on without me." His eyes cut away for a moment. "The truth is my field days are behind me. I've lost the feel. Wet work takes a different kind of person than I've become. My years behind a desk have changed me, Jack. Like it or not, my expertise is now in lending my people tactical support and protecting the missions against political meddling. Believe me when I tell you that I can be of more help to you in D.C."

Jack nodded. It was difficult to argue against his friend's assessment.

Paull indicated the girl with the porcelain skin. "I think you'd best take a listen to what Edon has to say."

Instantly, Jack pricked up his ears. "What did you say her name was?"

"Edon." Paull looked perplexed. "Edon Kraja."

THE BEST way to lead a man unwittingly to his death is with a beautiful girl. This was a motto Gunn had lived by during the time he'd toiled in the spook shadows. It was a method old as time, but that was what made it virtually infallible. Occasionally, he'd had to substitute a beautiful boy for a beautiful girl, but the mechanism remained the same.

Vera Bard was still a day away from returning to Fearington from her weeklong medical leave, and he called her. Of course she said yes, this venture was right up Vera's twisted little alley. He gave her her instructions.

"How long will it take you?" he said.

"I'm not far away," Vera said. "Forty minutes max."

Forty minutes later, he took the stairs down from the official Fortress offices to the auxiliary office used by Blunt between assignments. Try as he might, he could never get used to Blunt's new legend name, Willowicz.

Blunt was making coffee, or what passed for it in this stinking hole.

"I've got a job for you and O'Banion."

"It had better pay well," Blunt said, "I've got gambling debts up the wazoo."

"As a matter of fact, it does," Gunn said. "It's a rush job—gotta be done today."

"I don't like rush jobs—they have a nasty habit of turning out messy."

Gunn was anticipating his answer. "How's triple your fee grab you?"

"Right in the nuts. Who, where, and when?"

Gunn gave him the particulars and left. He couldn't get out of there fast enough, but he didn't go back to his office. He had another destination. He had pondered his plan in agonizing detail ever since his thoroughly unpleasant meeting with Pawnhill. He was dealing with ghosts—very dangerous ghosts who between them had been responsible for twenty kills,

possibly more. He wondered fleetingly whether Pawnhill had any idea of what a difficult assignment he'd
given him. Knowing the bastard, he didn't give a shit.
Pawnhill wanted what he wanted; Pawnhill knew he
was in no position to defy him.

Someday, he thought, he was going to get out from
under Pawnhill's thumb. But, sadly, that day was not
today.

"THE SCHOOL was nothing more than a front,"
Edon said. "There are six orphans here—enough to
keep the illusion going. The rest of us are like me—
girls sold into slavery by their parents, or snatched
off the streets. Either way, no one is looking for us."

They had taken the children down from the burning, ruined school, out of Tetovo, and into the deep-
est part of the first-growth woods to the northwest,
where, safely far enough from civilization, they made
temporary camp in a small clearing. Thatë sent his
remaining men out to gather wood for a fire. Restless, he put himself on guard duty, walking the perimeter.

Edon's eyes searched Jack's. "This is how it is, no
danger to Xhafa or his people."

"How about when he moves the girls around?"

Edon gave a bitter laugh. "He uses bribes and pay-
offs to local officials. You have to admire the machine
Xhafa has put together. And he's got something on
everyone. The officials are taped taking their bribes—
money, or sex from the little girls. I've seen some of
the tapes because Xhafa would play them for his men
while they drank and laughed. They were awful,
disgusting—impossible to describe. Animals behave

better. Afterward, Xhafa's men would rape us, over and over.

"For the girls, this was nothing new. The idea is to break their spirit. They're treated like trash, used and beaten. They're starved if they resist, and God help them if they rebel. They're tied up in a lightless room, beaten, drugged, and gang-raped. The real hard cases are shot up with heroin. Once hooked, they become instantly compliant; they'll do anything for their next fix."

She recited this litany of horror with an eerily detached voice, as if she were talking about a movie she had seen. But Alli was white-faced with rage. Jack could feel her trembling beside him.

"This happened to you?" Alli said in a hoarse voice.

"I was smarter than them," Edon said. "I did what was asked of me, I ingratiated myself with them, just as Arjeta had done. I became a favorite, they fell in love with my face instead of my body. Oh, occasionally one of them would try to rape me, but Arian always stopped them. Once, he beat his own man to a bloody pulp and no one came near me again."

Alli let out a long-held breath, but her fists were still tightly clenched and her eyes seemed to throw out sparks.

"Speaking of Xhafa," Jack said, "when did you last see him?"

"Days ago," Edon replied, "a week or more."

"But one of his men said he'd left the school only a half hour or so before the attack."

"He's lying," Edon said. "I saw him leave."

There was no mistaking her certainty. Jack admired her core of inner strength. He wondered whether that was a trait all three sisters possessed. And that thought brought him to the question of whether or not this was the right moment to tell Edon that one of her sisters had been murdered. Deciding that there was no good time for that kind of news, he determined to tell her. But first he needed to ask her a question.

"Alli and I are friends of Annika's." He sensed Alli's instant consternation, but she had the good sense to keep her mouth shut. "She's mentioned your name."

Edon's face lit up. "You know Annika? That's fantastic. My sisters and I love her."

"How do you know her?"

Edon frowned. "Arjeta met her first, I think. Father has a terrible sickness—he can't stop gambling. We were always in debt, sometimes horribly so. One time a representative of Xhafa's came to him. He paid off his debt by selling Arjeta. Then it was my turn. By that time, Arjeta had become Dardan Xhafa's favorite, and when Dardan was sent to America, Arjeta went with him."

That explained a lot, Jack thought. More pieces of the puzzle falling into place, bringing with them a new and expanded view of the picture. Annika had been in Washington recently. A coincidence? He didn't think so.

"Why did Annika contact Arjeta?"

"She wanted her to spy on Xhafa. If she did, Annika said, she'd make sure Arjeta would be free of Xhafa forever."

And now Arjeta was, Jack thought, though not in the way Annika must have meant. And all at once, another possible piece slipped into place and he excused himself, went off alone, took out the cell phone

Alli had taken from the locked drawer in Henry Holt Carson's desk, and fired it up. Only two numbers in the directory, one marked A, the other D. Neither were U.S. numbers.

Could it be? he wondered. He pressed the key to dial the number attributed to A. After what seemed like an eternity, the connection went through and he heard it ring three, four, five times. No voice mail was engaged.

He was about to hang up when he heard her voice, and with his heart in his throat, said, "Hello, Annika."

THE MOMENT Gunn left, Willowicz contacted O'Banion. He had finished brewing the coffee. It looked like sludge, but with six teaspoons of sugar, it tasted fine.

"What are you doing?"

"Getting laid," O'Banion barked. "What the fuck d'you want?"

"Gunn." He gulped down the coffee, savoring the intense sweetness along with the acid bite. "We have a job."

"I told you." O'Banion let out a series of rhythmic grunts. "I'm busy."

Willowicz put the mug in the stainless-steel sink. The incriminating substances that had gone down its drain, he thought. "Triple our usual fee."

"That should've been your lead." O'Banion was breathing hard. "I'm in."

"And now you need to get out."

O'Banion wheezed a laugh, then let out a long, drawn-out groan. Willowicz heard a loud noise, then nothing.

"O'Banion?"

After a moment: "Yeah, yeah, yeah. I dropped the fucking phone."

"That good, huh?"

"Meet?"

Willowicz gave him his instructions. "One hour," he concluded. "Don't be late."

"When am I ever?"

Willowicz cut the connection, grabbed the paraphernalia he'd need, jammed it into the voluminous inside pockets of his custom-made overcoat, and went out into the hallway. As he pressed the call button for the elevator he thought about his partnership with O'Banion. It went back many years. Sometimes it seemed as if they had plowed through every shithole backwater of the Middle East, had climbed every dust-strewn mountain, stuck their necks out in every cave, and blown up half the Taliban. And still they came, like cockroaches overrunning an open box of sugar. He and O'Banion shared everything, there were no secrets in the mountains of Afghanistan and Western Pakistan where they had plied their bloody trade. They were closer than brothers; there wasn't anything they wouldn't do for each other.

But all bloody things come to an abrupt end. At some point, he and O'Banion had said fuck it. They had salted away enough money and they were tired of offing ignorant fanatics. Time for a change of scene. Which was when they'd come home, and almost immediately had hooked up with Gunn. He had shit for brains, just like all the ex-Marines who were now milking the government for millions. What they were doing wasn't exactly rocket science. All you needed to do was produce torture and death, no questions asked, and the money showered down like manna. Oh, yeah, you needed the one thing he and O'Banion didn't have—political connections. Gunn had them in spades, example in point: Henry Holt Carson's patronage. On the other hand, as shit-for-brains bosses went, they could've done a lot worse than Gunn. At least he paid them top dollar, and he'd always been straight with them.

The elevator was still on the top floor. Cursing under his breath, he turned to the stairs door, pulled it open, and started down. Swinging around the landing, he saw a woman on the floor below. She was bending over, after having cracked off a heel of her lace-up boots. She was wearing a breathtakingly short skirt under which he could see that she was wearing nothing at all. Immediately, his second brain—the tiny, reptilian thing low down in his body—was activated. He felt a stirring in his trousers and, licking his lips, he strolled down the stairs.

She heard him coming and whipped upright. As she turned around to face him, he saw that her cheeks were flaming. She was hot—dark and exotic-looking. He thought she might be Eurasian.

"Good Lord," she said, "how long have you been there?"

"Don't worry." He grinned. "Your secrets are safe with me."

At which her cheeks continued to redden, which inflamed him all the more.

"Can I help you?" he asked before she could reply.

"Damn five-inch heels." She held out the one that had broken off.

"I think you'd better take off your boots," he said. And then with a wry smile, "Or I could carry you down."

"That's all right," she said hastily. And, unlacing the boots, she handed them to him. "Would you be a gentleman?"

The moment he took them from her, the door to the hallway opened, Gunn came silently through, armed with a handgun fitted with a noise suppressor. Maybe Willowicz saw something in Vera's eyes, but he was too besotted with her, and his reflexes failed him. He was in the process of turning when Gunn shot him twice; once in the back, once in the head.

Vera's fuck-me boots clattered to the raw concrete. Stepping over the corpse, she picked them up. As she brushed past Gunn, she said, "You owe me a new pair of Louboutins."

SOMETHING, PERHAPS his reptilian brain, remained alive after the girl and his murderer had left. His heart was barely beating and he lacked any sense of where he was. Nevertheless, the organism knew it was dying. This is, in the end, what separates man from beast. The foreknowledge of death.

Blunt or Willowicz or whatever his name really was became dimly aware of his cell phone lying against his cheek. It must have dropped out of his pocket when he fell. The shot to his back had severed major nerves. His legs felt paralyzed. He could scarcely move a muscle, yet he had just enough life left in him to move one finger. Trembling, it struck the side of the phone. As if on its own, it moved a fraction to the left and hit the autodial key.

The call went through and O'Banion's voice echoed in the staircase.

"Willowicz? Hello? Willowicz?"

Blunt's lips moved, forming pink bubbles that looked like membranes. Three times he tried to speak and failed. Then, at last, as the light began to fade, as even he lost his desperate hold on life, he managed two agonized words.

"He's coming."

Twenty-four

"WHAT ARE you doing with this phone, Jack?"

"Calling you, apparently. I assume the other number on it will connect me with Dyadya Gourdjiev."

Annika sighed in his ear. "It would have, yes. Unfortunately, my grandfather is in the hospital."

"Don't worry," Jack said, "the old boy's too tough to die."

There was a small silence, during which Jack saw Alli watching him like a hawk. He tried to smile, but it came out a grimace, which only amped her obvious anxiety.

As if divining the direction of his thoughts, Annika said, "How is Alli?"

"I think you know as well as I do."

"I miss her."

"I doubt that."

"Now you're being peevish. I've never made a secret how I feel about her."

"Annika, you're keeping one secret after another."

Her laugh sounded forced, a small explosion of mixed emotions. "It's true."

Jack felt tongue-tied. He had been certain he'd never see or speak to Annika again, and here he was on the phone with her.

"Don't come after me, you wrote me," he said, "don't try to find me."

"And now I've found you. That's what you're thinking, isn't it, Jack?"

He wasn't able to reply.

"Did Emma warn you I would come back into your life?"

Jack's heart turned over. He recalled his conversation with Emma, her telling him that she wasn't a seer. And yet, she had spoken of his continuing connection with Annika.

"Something like that."

"She's a smart girl."

He was gripped by a sudden selfish impulse to sever the connection, but instead squeezed his eyes shut.

"What do you want, Annika?"

"What I've always wanted, Jack. To win."

"I don't understand."

"Oh, but you do. I need you, Jack. I need you and Alli."

His eyes snapped open and he looked at Alli, who was standing not twenty feet away. She was staring at him, her head cocked to one side. At that moment, she looked so small, infinitely fragile. Damaged. Just like Annika was damaged. And for the first time, the thought hit him: Was Alli on her way to becoming another Annika? God forgive him, if that were true.

"Jack, I've said this before, but it bears repeating now. We're all soldiers in the night, and because of this, like it or not, we're pawns. No matter how strong we are, no matter how powerful our mentors and friends, there are always forces that wield more power. The more powerful they are, the deeper their cover. So on the surface this shadow war we wage seems impossible to win. We'll always be defeated by those deeply hidden forces, no? But you and I know there is a path to beating them, because we know that the deeper these forces are buried the more secrets they hold. We only need one of those secrets to defeat them, yes?"

Jack, still staring at Alli, said, "That's right, Annika."

"You didn't answer my question," she said at length.

"What question?"

"How did you get this phone?"

"You mean Henry Holt Carson's phone?"

Silence.

"What do you and Carson have going?" Jack said.

"It seems we both have questions that need answers."

"Yes, we do."

"So, then, we are agreed," Annika said. "It's time we met."

"How CAN you rely on a . . ."

"On a woman?" the Syrian said to Arian Xhafa.

"And look at how she's dressed!"

The Syrian chuckled. "Indecent, isn't it?"

They were sitting in the garden at the rear of the walled compound. It was large, planted with citrus and fig trees that were burlaped in the winter in order to protect them from frost. There was also an enormous oak whose sturdy branches spread cooling shade. Benches were strewn around at strategic locations to capture the sunlight and shade, depending on the season. The two men sat on one, a bowl of fresh fruit between them. The rain had ceased and one of the guards had dutifully wiped down the bench, making it ready for them. Other guards armed with AK-47s were stationed at each corner, backs against the concrete walls, but they were too far away to overhear the conversation, which was, in any event, conducted in hushed tones.

"You are a good Muslim, I myself have seen examples of this more than once," Xhafa said. "And yet you allow a woman—a Western infidel at that!—such license and power. It is, frankly, a mystery I cannot comprehend."

Overhead, the low clouds were being stripped away by a westerly wind, revealing tatters of pearlescent blue sky.

"Caroline is a closely held secret, that much is true." The Syrian picked out a fig, popped it into his mouth, and chewed reflectively. "Listen to me, Xhafa, because I will only say this once. At first blush, it may sound like heresy, so if you repeat it to anyone I'll deny it." He paused, allowing the small silence to indicate the other consequence for Xhafa. "There is a fundamental flaw in Islam and it is this: Unlike the other major religions of the world, Islam can find no place for itself in the modern world. It is hidebound, Xhafa, bent on turning back a clock that cannot be tampered with. No matter how many infidels we kill, no matter how many terrorist attacks we launch, we cannot return the world to the way it was centuries ago. We cannot destroy modern culture any more than we can destroy time. To continue to do so is to become Don Quixote, tilting at Western windmills. Defeat and madness are the only possible results."

Xhafa was silent. Not daring to meet the Syrian's eyes, he stared fixedly at the bowl of fruit, which now seemed to him to be seeping a dark, viscous poison. He watched, almost paralyzed, as the Syrian's hand dipped into the bowl.

"Here is a blood orange," the Syrian said, holding the fruit on his fingertips. "Shall we bite into it now? Of course not. The bitter skin will spoil the sweet meat inside. However—" Here he began to peel the skin off. "—if we are insightful enough to pare away the bitter coat, see what delight awaits us." He broke off two sections, offered one to Xhafa, then took the other between his lips, chewed, and swallowed.

"Now think of Caroline Carson as this blood orange. If I had insisted she cover herself up in the strict Islamic tradition, I would never have found the delightful skills awaiting me." He peeled off another segment and ate it. "And just as this orange is a metaphor for Caro, so, too, is Caro a metaphor for modern Western culture. It isn't evil, it does not want to destroy us. This is the argument used by the fanatics among us—and believe me, Xhafa, when I tell you that fanatics are the same the world over. They cannot cope with reality, so they retreat to their mountain lairs and strike out at everyone and everything that had cast them out."

Another segment disappeared into his mouth, while Xhafa still held his as if it might come alive and bite him.

"But there is evil in the world—plenty of it. Correctly identifying it is the real trick. There are *individuals* who are evil, *individuals* who want to destroy us, and it is here that we can make our mark, it is here where we can do some good, it is here we will find success."

His eyes lowered to the piece of blood orange Xhafa still held. "So here's what I say to you, Xhafa. Either you believe me, or you don't. Either you eat that, or I will."

Xhafa did not move, did not utter a sound. But when the Syrian tried to pluck the blood orange from his fingers, he resisted.

The Syrian's frightening gaze was insistent, pitiless. "Now is the time, Xhafa. There will be no other."

BEFORE MAJOR General Peter Conover Hains designed the Tidal Basin, and it was installed, Washington's drainage problems were so monumental that on certain dog days, when the air was still and leaden, the stench from the marshes on which the city was built was overwhelming. The major general died in 1921, but his name lives on in Hains Point, a spit of land at the confluence of the Potomac River and the Washington Channel. The point is actually at the southern tip of East Potomac Park. Quite fittingly, it overlooks both Fort McNair and the National War College, which are across the channel on the eastern shore.

It was to Hains Point that Gunn had directed Willowicz and O'Banion.

Who has more fun than I do? Vera Bard thought as she drove into East Potomac Park. Gunn was curled inside the trunk of the Saab. He'd very cleverly rigged a cord that would keep the trunk from popping open yet afford him enough fresh air.

She drove slowly and carefully while her mind turned over the sequence of events and her part in them as Gunn had outlined them to her. She only had to be told once; she was an instant study. This ability would have vaulted her to the top of her class at Fearington were it not for Alli Carson. No matter what she tried her hand at, Alli always did her one better. Though they were roommates and Vera made certain that they became friends, she deeply and irrevocably envied Alli. And, with Vera's psyche, it didn't take long for envy to curdle into hate. Of course, she told all this to Gunn, and, at some point—she could not now recall precisely when—he had taken more than a passing interest in her roommate. Then, a week ago, he'd asked her if she'd like an assignment. Intrigued, she'd said yes. That was how Alli's fingerprints had gotten onto the vial of roofies, the contents of which Vera had taken herself.

Not a problem. She was used to self-abuse, having spent her prepubescent years cutting herself on her inner thighs so as not to be caught. She had had constant weight problems, and self-image discrepancies. When she looked at herself in the mirror she saw a fat clown, or worse, a misshapen reflection in a funhouse mirror. She used to have nightmares about the awkwardness of her physicality. Her sleeping mind constructed a haunted house so vast it became an entire world. It was festooned with staircases that went sideways as well as up and down, contained rooms that changed shape and content each time she entered them, foiled her at every turn. She came back time after time. Sometimes it was a school, at other times a hotel, an office, or apartment building, though from the outside it always looked like Norman Bates's Victorian house in *Psycho*.

When she was seven, she had spied on her father fucking his protégé in the master bedroom, though neither of them ever knew. All she could think of that night was the woman leaving her intimate spoor on the sheets for Vera's mother to lie in. She got sick twice. Once she made it to the toilet in time, once she didn't.

Understandably, then, she cleaved to her mother. When her father complained to his wife of his daughter's coldness, she replied that it was only natural for daughters to bond with their mothers. To which he'd replied, I wish we'd had a son.

Time passed, but Vera's nausea at life did not. On the contrary, it grew like an infestation, infecting her with its poison until she had only her mother in whom she could find comfort. Understandably, she hated boys, and she found the girls at school shallow. Friendships with them were, in her opinion, senseless.

Inevitably, she got into trouble, mostly fistfights with girls in her class who teased her, but occasionally boys, too. After her first bloody nose, she befriended a Thai girl who was a kickboxer. Her mother was surprised when Vera brought home the Thai girl, even more so when her daughter asked to take kickboxing lessons. She happily gave her money and her blessing. Six months later, Vera sought out the boy who'd bloodied her nose. She let him pick a fight with her, then nearly stove in the side of his head with her first kick.

That little stunt got her suspended for thirty days and a visit to the school shrink, but it was worth it. No one ever bothered her again. Better still, she got an insight into how to turn her loathing of males to her advantage. She now evoked in them fear and awe, vulnerabilities she quickly learned to exploit. As she began to manipulate the boys in her class—and, increasingly, older ones—her self-image reversed itself. Now she could look at herself in the mirror and instead of cringing see what she was really made of. She was a beautiful girl, but not in that icky girl-next-door way. She exuded sex appeal; it oozed through her pores like attar. And the boys were drawn to her like bees to a just-opened flower.

And then, one day, the ultimate betrayal: Her mother suffered an aneurism and died instantly. She had been making breakfast for Vera, had just set down a plate of blueberry pancakes. She kissed her daughter on the top of her head, said, Eat up or you'll be late for school, turned around, and simply collapsed onto the kitchen floor. No blood, no pulse. Emptiness.

Vera went into shock and was still sedated in the hospital when her mother was buried. Afterward, she was so infuriated that she never went to her mother's grave. She never spoke about her again to her father, or to anyone. Outwardly, it was as if she had never existed, but inside, the grieving never ceased, the wound festered, never healed; it continued to bleed into her own life, altering it forever.

All this flashed through her mind as she drove through East Potomac Park, where her mother had often taken her on sunny Saturdays and Sundays, while her father worked or was out of town. It had always been a special place to her, the place where her dream house was situated, where it still abided somewhere in the recesses of her subconscious.

She passed the place where her hands had become sticky while slurping down a chocolate ice-cream cone, and there was the spot she had fallen while running and skinned her right knee and elbow, and over there, where the weird sculpture of *The Awakening* used to be coming out of the ground was where she had been stung by a wasp. The pain had been intense but she hadn't cried. She never cried. Crying was for people without backbones, people who hadn't screwed up their courage and found their way through her Norman Bates haunted house.

Seeing the man who fit Gunn's description of O'Banion, she slowed. He turned as he became aware of the car approaching.

"He's expecting his partner, so he'll be surprised to see you," Gunn had told her. *"He's sure to be on edge. In order to allay any suspicion, make sure you stop well before you get close to him. At that point, you can go to work."*

Under O'Banion's stern and unflinching gaze, she stopped the car, turned off the ignition, and got out. As she did so, he produced a Glock 17, fitted with a AAC Evolution 9mm suppressor.

Vera held up her hands, palms outward. "Gunn sent me."

"Wrong answer." O'Banion gestured with the Glock. "Get your ass over here."

She did as he ordered; her heart rate accelerated. *Something's wrong here,* she thought. *He's reacting negatively to Gunn's name. That can't be good.*

When she was close enough, O'Banion grabbed her and pressed the working end of the suppressor against her temple. Then he expertly patted her down with his free hand. He spent an inordinate time checking between her thighs.

"I'm not carrying." She was thinking as fast as she could. "I'm Andy's girlfriend, that's all." When playing for time, tell the truth.

"So why are you here?"

"Your friend, Willowicz"—she looked at him with a doe's expression—"that's his name, right?"

"What about him?"

"He's had an accident. Andy's with him in the ER at George Washington. He sent me to get you."

A crack had appeared in O'Banion's suspicion. "What the hell happened?"

"Apparently, the elevator was out. He took the stairs and fell. I don't know, maybe he tripped or something."

"But our assignment."

"Canceled or postponed or something."

"Why didn't Gunn call me?"

"No cells allowed in the ER."

O'Banion watched her, clouds of indecision forming on his brow.

Vera put all the urgency at her disposal into her voice. "I think your friend is hurt bad. Andy said you should come right now."

O'Banion studied her face for several more seconds. Then he put away the Glock. "Okay," he said. "Let's go."

Vera turned and walked as steadily as she could back to the car where Gunn waited, curled like a serpent in the trunk.

"What happened to your shoes?" O'Banion said.

"When I was a kid, my mother took me here on weekends. The first thing I did when I got here was to take off my shoes."

O'Banion shook his head. "Fucking women."

CAROLINE TOOK a tiny gold key from around her neck, inserted it into the lock on the bottom left-hand drawer of her desk. Inside was a large book with a moss-green cover on which was affixed an illustration of a tumbledown shop on a tumbledown block. It was an old book, much worn, thumbed-through, and read. Its title was *The Little Curiosity Shop,* a heavily illustrated children's book, full of stories of fayries and magick. Caroline pressed her palm against the cover, caressing it, as she often did when she was absolutely certain that she was alone. She had read it so often she could still recite whole sections from memory.

Locking the book away, she got up from her computer workstation and stretched. Ever since the Syrian had returned with Arian Xhafa in tow she'd found it difficult to concentrate. Walking into the kitchen, she opened the refrigerator and took out a bottle of beer. She was the only one in the compound allowed to drink; she was the only one who wasn't Muslim. She enjoyed drinking in front of them, just as she got a kick out of dressing as she wanted. The Syrian was lenient, even Western in his views, but she knew not to push him past a certain point. She was valuable to him—more valuable than a platoon of suicide bombers—but that didn't mean she could do whatever she pleased. Everyone had boundaries here, even him.

Popping the top of her beer she went and leaned against the sink, her ankles crossed as she stared out the window at the two men sitting side by side in the garden. She did not need to hear their conversation to know its subject. Xhafa, like all his kind, hated women. He disguised the hatred by wrapping it in religious text, but his prejudice was plain to her all the same. She'd had a great deal of experience with men's hatred of women—their abuse, both psychological and physical, their contempt, their complete and utter dismissal. To Xhafa and men like him women were an inferior form of human being, a second-class citizen meant for breeding or, far worse, receptacles for the release of men's pleasure.

She watched the pantomime for a while, providing the words she could not hear. When Arian Xhafa placed the segment of blood orange in his mouth, she laughed silently.

IN THE firelight, the blood looked black. Jack ached all over, but otherwise he felt okay. He sat on a tree stump near the fire Thatë's men had started. The heat felt good on his back. Alli, kneeling beside him, rummaged in her backpack for the first-aid kit.

When she opened it, she said, "Shit, the gauze is sopping wet."

"Those kits are supposed to be waterproof," Paull said, peering over her shoulder.

Her fingers ran around the rim. "One of the hinges is broken," she said. "That's how the water seeped in when I slipped in the river." She plucked out a small tube. "The Krazy Glue's fine, but we still need something to bind Jack's wound."

The bullet had torn a more or less horizontal strip out of Jack's side. The wound wasn't deep, but if it wasn't treated there was the danger of infection. Alli cleaned the wound with alcohol and waited for it to dry. Then she handed the tube to Jack.

Jack looked at Paul. "We have to get these children to a place of safety."

"There isn't one anywhere near here," Alli said.

Paull nodded. "We'll take them on the plane."

Jack's face clouded. "If you take them back to the States they're going to run afoul of INS, which, these days, is nothing more than a pack of jackals on the hunt for aliens they can imprison or deport so it can look good with Homeland Security."

Paull grinned. "Then I'll just have to circumvent INS, won't I?"

"And how do you propose to do that?"

"These days INS has its nose stuck up Homeland Security's ass," Paull said. "I put up Hank Dickerson to replace me. He'll do what I ask him to do."

Alli called Jack's attention back to the wound. While she held the two sides of the wound together, Jack applied a thin line of glue. She kept the pressure on while Jack capped the tube.

"Hurt much?" she said.

Jack smiled at her.

"We still need to protect it or it might open and start bleeding all over again."

"I can help with that." Edon turned her back to them, slipped her shirt over her head, and, using her teeth, began to tear it into long strips.

Jack's head came up, his eyes fixed on the burnished skin of her back. "Wait a minute." He stood up and went over to her. Covering her breasts, she began to turn around, but he said, "No, stay right where you are."

He turned her slightly so that her back was more in the light cast by the flames. He touched her tenderly.

"Where did you get these scars?"

"I was punished. Once."

"Who did this?" Though the scars were fresh, their length, the pattern was identical to those on Annika's back. "Who punished you?"

"Arian Xhafa himself," Edon said. "This is his mark, his punishment."

Jack felt all the breath go out of him as everything fell into place. No wonder Annika was so interested in coming after Arian Xhafa—it was he who had marked her, just as he had marked this girl. Jack put his hand to his head. Every time he thought he had come to the core of Annika, another layer of secrets and lies was revealed.

God help Arian Xhafa, he thought.

TWENTY-FIVE

THE SYRIAN tilted his face up toward the sun. "Pity about Oriel Jovovich Batchuk," he said. "We had a lucrative deal with him, and once he became Russia's deputy prime minister he was our best single customer."

Xhafa shot him a glance. "That was months ago. We've replaced him ten times over."

"Ah, but Batchuk was also the father of Annika Dementieva, and she is so very special."

Xhafa shifted uncomfortably on the hardwood bench.

The Syrian knew better than anyone the relationship between Dementieva and Xhafa, though "relationship" was an inadequate term to describe what had happened between them. The knowledge sickened him; it was no surprise that their hatred for one another knew no bounds; Xhafa was obsessed with her. This enmity would prove dangerous for him if he allowed Xhafa to go after her. Xhafa wasn't exactly rational when it came to the subject of Annika Dementieva. He and Xhafa were tied together through Gemini Holdings, the shell corporation that

Caroline, in her genius, had set up for them to make their international deals legitimate. He was at risk as long as Annika remained alive. Though Caro had assured him that no one could trace either of them back to Gemini, he was not at all certain that included Annika and her devil of a grandfather.

Caro was incredibly smart and incredibly proficient at whatever she set her hand to; he had seen that for himself many times over. She was an autodidact—she had taught herself pretty much everything she knew about business, computer programming, and the Internet. He was stunned at what she could accomplish at her workstation.

"You must let it go, Arian. This is business. You must leave Dementieva to me," the Syrian said now. "You need to keep your eyes on the prize—and on Jack McClure. The magnitude of his interference is an unexpected complication."

Xhafa sighed. "I suppose I needn't remind you it was through McClure that you lured Dementieva out of hiding."

For a moment, the Syrian went dead still, and was aware of the blood draining from Xhafa's face. Yet that wasn't enough for him.

"When I need reminding, I'll ask Caro." His words were delivered with an acid bite. He realized, belatedly, that he had confided too much of his plan to his man. He bit his tongue at the mistake; he'd not make it again. No one understood his mind, save perhaps Caro. This was her true value to him, one he'd rather die with than divulge to anyone.

"Apologies," Xhafa managed to get out, after an oppressive silence.

These were two proud men, preeminent within their own spheres. But both were acutely aware that the Syrian's sphere was vastly larger than Xhafa's, and sometimes this discrepancy caused friction. But managing friction was one of Xhafa's strong suits, even if, in this case, it meant putting his tail between his legs.

"Apologies," Xhafa said again. "The loss of my longtime base was something I never imagined."

The sun was gone now, the shadows lengthening, the air growing cooler.

The Syrian sighed. "Sometimes it seems to me that life is constructed only of unexpected losses." This was as far as he was prepared to go to mollify Xhafa.

"HABIBI."

The whispered voice from behind Caroline stopped her from returning to her work. She turned slowly, her lips turned up in a mysterious smile.

Taroq was standing in shadow, in a place where he couldn't be seen by the two men in the garden. Like his master, he was Syrian, a distant nephew, in fact. Tall and bronzed with wide shoulders and a slender waist, he exuded a certain solidity. His full beard was light brown, almost copper-colored in sunlight, and his long eyes were gray. Still as rock, he watched her with an avidity she could feel though twelve feet separated them.

Caroline hated men, but she didn't hate Taroq. She had cultivated him almost from the moment the Syrian had brought her to the compound. Caroline was one of those people who felt no remorse, no guilt, no sense of loyalty. She defined herself as amoral; a psychiatrist would no doubt render a diagnosis of anti-social personality disorder, because her major traits fit like a glove: patterns of deceitfulness, a failure to conform to societal norms, blatant disregard for the rights and safety of others. An ignorant person might call her a psycho, but that would be a misnomer; Caroline's disorder was far more complex.

The best thing about Taroq—besides his strength, that is—was that he was drawn to her, rather than being repulsed as the other guards clearly were. Taroq was smart enough, and close enough to his master to be curious about Western civilization—not the TV shows or films or designer clothes, but the concept of having choices. For him, Caroline presented a doorway into a new world, in more ways than one.

"We're quite alone." His voice was already thick with lust. He held out a hand, his need shining like a beacon in a storm. "Let's go—"

"No." She beckoned. "I want to look at him while we do it."

This was apparently too much for Taroq. He stood very still and shook his head.

Caroline stared into his eyes as she began to slowly unbutton her shirt. She was wearing nothing underneath and by the fourth button the inner halves of her breasts were visible. She kept opening buttons without parting the shirt. When she was finished, she unbuttoned her jeans and slowly pulled down the zipper.

Taroq's eyes grew wide; she was naked underneath.

Her arms hung at her sides. Some mysterious inner working rolled the tiny swell of her belly.

"Come," she said, and Taroq was compelled to do as she commanded.

GUNN, CURLED in the trunk of Vera's car, heard the doors open, then felt the weight of two people getting into the car. This indicated that Vera had been successful in luring O'Banion. He turned and, pulling open the Saab's pass-through from the trunk to the backseat, he crawled through, only to find O'Banion on the backseat, pointing a suppressed Glock at his face.

"Howdy-do, Gunn." O'Banion's grin was chilling. "You proved yourself to be a snake just like all the rest of your kind. I don't think snakes live very long, but in any case longer than you."

Gunn wanted to say something—anything—but, frankly, he was speechless. How had the bastard known? Willowicz was dead, so that left Vera. Where the hell was she? Probably cut and run. That fucking bitch!

O'Banion took possession of Gunn's Sig Sauer and stuck it in his waistband without taking his eyes off his adversary. "Believe me, it's going to be a pleasure watching your head fly apart."

At that moment, Vera's head popped up above the front seat back. She had something stretched between her hands—the long lace from one of her boots. Before O'Banion could pull the trigger, she whipped the lace over his head and across his throat. Then she pulled mightily.

O'Banion's body lurched up with his head and the shot he squeezed off reflexively buried itself in the seat back ten inches from Gunn's left shoulder. Gunn grabbed the suppressor despite how hot it was in an attempt to wrest it from O'Banion's grip.

In the front seat, Vera had her feet braced against the seat back and was pulling with all her strength. O'Banion's face was dangerously engorged as blood pooled with nowhere to go. His free hand was clawing at the lace, but it was one of those new ones that were round and waxed, so his fingers couldn't get a decent purchase.

Gunn pried one of O'Banion's fingers off the grip, then bent it backward until it cracked like a rifle shot. O'Banion grunted, but would not cede control of the 9mm.

"Fuck you, Gunn," he said in a strangled voice. "Fuck you and your little bitch."

Abandoning his futile attempt to free himself, he chopped down onto Gunn's wrist with the edge of his free hand, and Gunn's arm went numb. From behind him, Vera uttered a guttural noise in the back of her throat. Lunging forward, she bit off the top half of O'Banion's right ear. He howled in shock and pain, and in that instant, Gunn was able to gain control of the 9mm. He turned it and shot without bothering to aim.

The bullet slammed into O'Banion's left shoulder. Blood was now streaming down the side of his face and along his arm.

"That all you got, shithole?" O'Banion could scarcely speak, but his eyes seemed alight with an unearthly glow. "You and the bitch'll have to do better than that."

The next shot took off the side of his head. He jerked backward, and Gunn shot him again, this time through the right eye. Blood spurted in torrents, covering him from head to toe. Bits of pink tissue and brain matter littered Vera's cheeks.

"Jesus," she said, as what was left of O'Banion's head arched back at her. "Jesus Christ."

TAROQ'S HEAT threatened to scald her, or so it seemed to Caroline. He took her at the sink. As she turned her back on him, he pulled down her jeans. Bracing her elbows on the sink top, she wrapped her long fingers around the spigot. He entered her, roughly and without prelude. The first time, when he had begun to caress and fondle her, she told him to stop. Now she lifted her head to stare at the Syrian.

The rhythmic battering commenced. As usual, she felt neither pleasure nor pain. Sex was for manipulation, not ecstasy. Besides, from an early age she had been unable to lose herself in sex. She had never experienced a climax, or even anything approaching it. Sex for her was like fixing a car's engine. Satisfaction came when the engine started up and the car began to move in the direction she desired.

Men, women, she had experimented with both— and multiple combinations—but the result was always the same. How ironic to possess a body made for sex and to feel nothing from it. That was just one of the tricks life had played on her. No remorse or guilt. For her, "cruelty" was a word without meaning. When she was a child, she had read the definitions of these words in a dictionary, but she could not get her mind around the concepts. She might as well have been reading Martian.

When she grew older, trolling through the libraries

in D.C., she had read through various psychiatric texts and learned about herself, or, more accurately, learned how the world would view her if it ever got to know her. She knew then and there that job number one was to ensure that it never did. This work began with her parents. No biggie there. Her father was so preoccupied with his Machiavellian designs, not to mention his serial mistresses, he paid her scant attention. As for her mother, she was addicted to all manner of psychotropic pills, which she compounded with the precision of a bartender mixing cocktails. Each one of her powdered elixirs was dependent on the time of day and where she was in her menstrual cycle. As a result, she was uninterested in anything other than herself, though when the occasion called for it she could give a convincing performance as a good wife and mother. She had a personality as fragile as porcelain. Her father—a force of nature—had married her because of her family's Philadelphia Main Line pedigree and connections inside the Beltway, which, in the early days, he used to brilliant advantage. That he soon crushed her with the brute force of his personality was of little matter to him. He'd gotten what he needed from her and, in all but name, had moved on.

Caroline's teachers were more difficult to hide from. They sent her to psychologists who wanted to probe the inner workings of her mind. She spit in their faces and left school. There was no scandal, no possibility of consequence, her father saw to that. Not out of love or concern; it was a knee-jerk response.

Finally, her parents, or what passed for them, woke from their self-inflicted torpor and insisted that she "get help." After six months of planning, while remaining unresponsive to the shrinks' various techniques, she vanished—completely, utterly, irrevocably. It had taken her that long to ensure that when her father sent his hired minions after her, they'd never be able to find her. She used computers to help her, erasing not only her tracks, but all trace of Caroline Lynette Carson.

Taroq had the endurance of a Tantric practitioner, but she knew how to bring him to his limit. The pounding was now so intense tears rolled down her cheeks. She'd had enough of this particular scenario, so she squeezed her inner muscles with such force that Taroq emitted a deep groan, despite his innate caution. She smiled at her pale reflection in the window, superimposed over the Syrian, all unknowing, as he sat, deep in the discussion of men, to which she was excluded.

She was still a teenager when she had found the Syrian. Or perhaps he had found her, it was difficult to say. The point was that they had discovered a common ground, a place where the chaos of life made sense to both of them. On the same wavelength, they began to work together—tentatively at first, each wary of the other. But, at length, there sprang up between them a working relationship of sorts. It was, by necessity, clandestine. Each for their own reasons, neither of them wanted the relationship known, and so it became their most closely guarded secret.

Then, either by accident or by design, someone found out about it and all hell had broken loose.

Behind her, Taroq spent himself, and with a flick

of her hips and shoulders she shook him off her. His legs folded up beneath him and he slid down onto his haunches, leaning against her legs. Without either thought or emotion, she ran her fingers through the moist warmth of his thick hair.

"*Habibi,*" he said, still panting, "one of these days you will surely be the death of me."

CHIEF DETECTIVE Heroe sat in her office, for the fifteenth time poring over report after report on the three murders and the disappearance of Agent Naomi Wilde, which she believed to be the fourth murder. Her gut told her that all four were connected, and yet, she could find no tangible evidence to link them. She'd sent her people out to interview all of Warren's friends and associates. She herself had run down his public history on government databases and had scrutinized every file on his hard drive at work. A more squeaky-clean individual would be hard to find.

This same crew was now in the process of running down all of Naomi Wilde's friends and associates. Grabbing her coat and pocketbook, Heroe left the office, went down to her car, and took off. She was due to interview Wilde's sister in less than an hour from now, but she doubted that would lead anywhere. The woman's husband had just left her and she was a basket case.

She weighed the merits of making another unannounced visit to M. Bob Evrette at Middle Bay Bancorp before or after she hauled Andrew Gunn's ass in for questioning. The forensics detail she had sent

over to Middle Bay had spent hours spraying, pow-
dering, irradiating every last goddamn thing in Billy
Warren's office. They'd found nothing, except what
you'd expect to find: Warren's own fingerprints. She
looked over the list of bank personnel one more
time, though what she expected to find there she
couldn't say.

This was the most damnable case she'd ever run
across in her decade in the department. Heroe was
something of a wunderkind at Metro. She was the
youngest detective to make highest grade in the department's history. She was such a legend that head-
hunters from virtually every branch of the federal
clandestine services had made a play for her. She'd
turned them all down, not because she wasn't intrigued, but because she was incredibly loyal. As a
female in a male-dominated universe it was of para-
mount importance to her to have a boss who both
understood her and wasn't intimidated by her. Alan
Fraine had plucked her as a new recruit, mentored
her, made sure she took all the right exams, and had
protected her from the good-old-boy cabal at work
in every police department that had, at first, sought
to impede her progress.

She was smart enough to understand that no matter her talent and expertise, she never would have
risen so high so fast were it not for Fraine's efforts.
In fact, without him, she might not have risen at all.
She was what might be called a three-strike woman.
Besides her gender and her mixed race, she had her
physical appearance going against her. She was beautiful and built like a brick shithouse, as her granny
used to say. She was part African-American, part

Cherokee. She'd been born and raised in New Orleans, mostly by her granny. When she was six, her father had died in an oil rig accident—a fire on an offshore station that had left no trace of him. Her mother had tried to carry on, but Heroe's father had been the love of her life, and she'd never recovered, spiraling down into a drunkard's purgatory, despite her mother-in-law's efforts. Granny, a full-blooded Cherokee, was not someone to be trifled with. She was revered in New Orleans, had often, in her younger days, been Queen of the Mardi Gras. At ninety, she still turned heads when she walked down the streets of Tremé, where she had lived all her life. Heroe got most of her looks from her granny.

When she was a kid, Granny used to tell her stories before she went to bed. Tales of Cherokee warriors and maidens, of course. But the stories Heroe loved best were the ones concerning Aladdin. She was sure Granny had made up most of them, because she was an inveterate storyteller. The story Heroe liked best concerned the genie who lights the way. This was not the famous genie in the lamp, but another one, who taught Aladdin how to see in the dark when everyone else was blind.

Fraine was her genie who lights the way.

She was no more than five minutes from Rachel Cowan's house when her cell phone emitted a peculiar ring. She unclipped it, then saw her phone was unengaged. The ringtone continued. Rummaging in her handbag, she drew out Naomi Wilde's cell. For a moment she stared at it, as if it had grown a head. The screen read UNIDENTIFIED CALLER. She pressed the green button and heard a man's voice.

"Naomi?"

"No. This is Chief Detective Nona Heroe, head of the Violent Crimes Unit at Metro. Who's calling, please?"

There was silence for so long, Heroe felt compelled to say, "Hello. Are you there?"

"This is Jack McClure. Where is Naomi and why are you answering her cell?"

JACK, SITTING in the 737 waiting for all the children to get settled, felt the bottom drop out of his stomach. A chief detective answering Naomi's phone could not be good news.

". . . why are you answering her cell?"

"Mr. McClure, I've heard of you."

"You didn't answer my questions." His anxiety lent him impatience.

"Agent Wilde is missing."

"Missing?" Given her communiques while he was out of touch, that was ominous.

"We found her car. It had gone off the road, down an embankment in rural Maryland. But we didn't find her body, nor did we find any trace that she'd been in the car when it went off the road."

Now Jack was truly worried. "What does her partner say?"

"Frankly, Agent McKinsey hasn't been much help, and now, thanks to the intervention of Andrew Gunn, I can't talk to him."

"Fortress Securities," Jack said, "that Andrew Gunn?"

"None other."

Gunn had ties to Henry Holt Carson. "Why wasn't it McKinsey's boss who extracted him?"

"A question that needs to be answered." There was a small pause. "Listen, Mr. McClure—"

"Jack. Please."

"Fine. I know from talking to Naomi's associates that you and she were friends, so I'm thinking maybe I can trust you."

"You can, Chief."

"Cut that out. It's Nona."

Jack laughed. He liked this woman.

"I'm very sorry to say this, but my gut is telling me that Naomi is dead."

Jack struggled to accept this. "What gives you that feeling?"

Heroe told him about her suspicions concerning Peter McKinsey.

"It might very well be that you're right," Jack said. "I'm in Macedonia. While I was out of cell range, Naomi left three voice mails and now I'm very sorry I didn't get them until a short time ago."

Then he told Heroe about Naomi's suspicions regarding her partner, following him out to Teddy Roosevelt Island. He did not tell her about Annika's possible involvement, telling himself that bringing her into it would muddy the investigation unnecessarily. Not that that wasn't true, but for his own reasons he was determined to protect Annika until he could determine exactly what her part in all this was.

"Christ," Heroe said, "I think I'd better haul my ass out to the island tout de suite and have a look-see." There was a short pause. "The man who was with McKinsey, could he be this Mbreti you told me about?"

"It's possible, but I have a feeling not. Judging from Naomi's description this man is an Arab of some sort. The way these people work, it makes more sense that Mbreti is a Caucasian American."

The moment the words were out of his mouth, Jack knew he'd hit upon something important, but for the life of him he couldn't figure out what.

He was silent so long that Heroe said, "What is it? Have you thought of something else?"

"I'm not sure. But, listen, since it seems clear that neither Naomi nor you trust McKinsey, is there any way to track her movements in the hours before she went missing?"

Heroe sighed heavily. "Without trusting him, I don't know how. He claimed they were following leads on how Arjeta Kraja was brought into the country. He also said the leads were dead ends. According to his account, they then went back to the office. They were exhausted, which I can believe. He said Agent Wilde said she was going home. That, I'm afraid, is the sum and substance of his account."

"Doesn't sound like much."

"No," she said, "indeed it doesn't."

Jack considered. "So you can't get to him."

"He's become a protected entity," she said. "Just like your friend, Alli Carson."

Jack heard the slight rebuke in her voice. "Alli was framed. Believe me, she's got nothing to do with this."

"You can't deny that her frame was the trigger for three, maybe four homicides."

Now they were skirting too close to Annika for his

comfort. "All I'm saying is that pursuing her is going in the wrong direction."

"Agent McKinsey doesn't think so," Heroe said.

"Can you think of a better reason to look elsewhere?"

THREE MINUTES after exchanging cell numbers with McClure, Heroe pulled up outside Rachel Cowan's house. She figured she'd have to work ten lifetimes to afford that kind of mansion. Plus, the only black people around here were probably housekeepers and gardeners. The nannies were all young girls from Ireland or the Baltics.

She opened Naomi Wilde's file, which she had obtained from Naomi's superior, and read it again. Thirty-six years old, born in Wheeling, West Virginia, moved to D.C. when she was four. One living sibling, Rachel, two years her senior. Graduated with honors from Georgetown University, majoring in criminology, minoring in psychology. Tried her hand at forensic pathology before applying to the Secret Service. Partnered with Peter McKinsey for six years. Assigned to protect the FLOTUS following the election of Edward Carson a year and a half ago. Commendations, highest marks, et cetera, et cetera. Heroe decided that she was looking at the jacket of an exemplary agent, and she felt a particular pang of sorrow, of loss, as if Naomi Wilde were her own sister.

She got out of the car and, checking out the sprinkling of A-list cars, went up the steps and rang the bell. She had a flash of a uniformed maid opening the door, but it was Rachel Cowan, ragged as a battlefield pennant, who greeted her and ushered her inside.

The interior did not disappoint. It was a breath-taking display of egregious consumerism run rampant. They stood in the vast living room. Rachel was either too aggrieved or too rude to ask her to sit down. Glancing around, Heroe didn't know whether she would want to. This level of consumerism gave her hives.

"I apologize for disturbing you at what must be a difficult time," Heroe said.

"And yet you did."

Not a promising beginning.

Rachel, perhaps appropriately dressed in the color of dried blood, stood with her hands clasped in front of her. There were deep circles under her eyes, which were red and raw-looking. She looked exhausted, as if she hadn't slept in days, and her eyes kept darting here and there. Heroe wondered whether she was on some medication, or ought to be.

"No matter," Rachel continued as if there had been no pause. "What is it you want?"

Heroe took out her pad, giving her a bit more time to assess her subject. She strongly suspected that she needed to strike the right tone to get Rachel to open up.

"I understand your sister was here to see you yesterday."

"That's right." There was a wary note in her voice.

"Can you tell me about it?" Heroe said as casually as she could.

Rachel turned gimlet-eyed and she crossed her arms over her breasts. "Why? Are you investigating her or something?"

Heroe gestured. "It's nothing like that, I assure you."

"Because if you are, there isn't a better or more dedicated agent in the Secret Service."

"Your loyalty is admirable, Mrs. Cowan, and I appreciate your opinion. But not to worry, we're interested in Naomi's partner."

Rachel seemed to relax somewhat. "I doubt I can help you, then. Peter stayed in the car while Naomi and I were together."

Heroe made a notation. "You mean he drove her here?"

Rachel nodded. "That's right."

"So you didn't see her car?"

"They came in one car, that much I saw, and it wasn't hers."

Interesting, Heroe thought. *So it stands to reason that Wilde and McKinsey went from here directly to the place where she was killed, otherwise she would have retrieved her cell from her car.*

"Do you know McKinsey well?"

Rachel made a sound, as if releasing a puff of air. "I don't know him at all, beyond meeting him a couple of times."

"Your sister never spoke to you about him?"

"Naomi never spoke to me—or anyone, for that matter—about anything pertaining to her work. She made that clear to every person she knew, including me."

Heroe wrote that down, but she needed to be certain, so she said, "Did your sister mention Peter McKinsey yesterday in any context whatsoever?"

"No, she didn't."

"Okay, I guess that's it, then." Heroe thought a minute. "By the way, Mrs. Cowan, did Naomi mention where she was going after she left you?"

"Work, she said." Rachel shrugged. "That's typical of her; work is where her head always is." She said this without rancor.

Heroe looked up, her inner radar suddenly on high alert. "So she wasn't going home."

"No, I told you. Work, work, work." Rachel bit her thumbnail, her eyes turned inward. "Something I'm quite certain I'm going to have to look into now."

Heroe nodded and moved toward the entryway. "Okay, thank you, Mrs. Cowan. You've been very helpful."

The compliment appeared to stir Rachel out of her dark ruminations, and she turned toward the chief detective. "Really?"

Heroe knew when to turn on her smile, whose wattage was considerable. "Really." She paused. "By the way, did Naomi by any chance tell you where she was going, specifically?"

Rachel wrinkled her brow. "She did, actually. Now what was it?"

"You mean *where* she was going, specifically."

"I *said* what and I *meant* what." Rachel clicked her fingernails on the crown of her diamond-studded gold watch. "Let me see. What were she and I discussing? Oh, yes. The secret bank account my husband keeps. The moment I mentioned that her face lit up." She laughed, and for a moment the years, and with them the care and worry, seemed to slip off her face. "I knew that look. I knew it would be useless to ask her to stick around." Then she pointed. "Now you're doing it."

"What?"

"Lighting up like a beacon."

With good reason.

"A bank, you say." And Heroe thought, *Middle Bay Bancorp. Bingo!*

TWENTY-SIX

"JACK, I need to talk to you."

Alli came and sat next to him. The 737 had been in the air for forty minutes. It would be less than twenty until they set down at a secured airstrip outside Vlorë. Since speaking with Chief Detective Heroe he had been sunk deep in thought. His mind wanted to go to his upcoming reunion with Annika, but it kept slipping back to Naomi. He felt her loss acutely. She had been of great help to both the FLOTUS and Alli after the accident in Moscow that had killed Edward Carson, proving herself quick-witted and unflustered by even the most grievous of events. Afterward, she had kept in touch with him. She always asked about Alli's emotional state. He could still remember how genuinely happy she'd been by the news that Alli had decided to go to Fearington. *"Finally,"* she'd said, *"she's on a path that will serve her well."*

In addition, he was concerned by the widening gyre of the conspiracy he found himself investigating. The mission given Dennis Paull and, by extension, him, was on the surface a simple one: Track down and terminate Arian Xhafa. And yet, now, only days later, it wasn't simple at all. If Naomi was dead, it was at the hands of her partner. McKinsey had been extracted from the Metro police by Andrew Gunn, not McKinsey's boss, who had somehow been neutralized. McKinsey and Naomi had been pulled out of Secret Service and seconded to Henry Holt Carson. Why them? Was McKinsey secretly working for Carson, as Gunn seemed to be? The odds seemed to favor that theory. But how did these people tie in to Arian Xhafa and his American representative Mbreti? And then there was Annika's involvement.

Every investigation had a trajectory, but Jack's mind worked in three dimensions. He saw the layers at work here: Carson, Xhafa, Annika. He now knew Annika's connection with Xhafa, but not what she had been doing in D.C. For the life of him he couldn't see the connection between Carson, Gunn, McKinsey, and Xhafa. Was it the Stem? The sex trade? And who the hell set out to frame Alli? The puzzle, complex as it seemed, had nevertheless taken on dimension and feel. It was the context that was missing. He was too close to the trees to see the forest. He needed to pull his perspective back and look at the disparate pieces as a whole.

At the same time, another part of his mind was busy working on the name equation he suspected would lead to Mbreti's real name. Grasi=Thatë; Mbreti=X. Despite his best efforts, it remained unsolved. And yet, he couldn't help believing that the solution was right in front of his face. If only he could see it.

Turning his mind away from these conundrums,

he smiled at Alli, grateful for the distraction. Let another part of his brain unravel them, he thought, while she engaged him in conversation.

"You've done extremely well with Edon," he said. "I'm proud of you."

She seemed stunned, and sat back in the seat. "Huh! No one's ever said that to me before."

"I'm sorry I'm the first," he said with a wry smile, "but I'll have to do."

Impulsively, she left her seat to give him a kiss on the cheek. "Thanks for believing in me."

"Always."

Alli returned his smile, but almost immediately she became serious. "Are you going to tell me about Annika?"

"She's in Albania, that's where we're going now. The plane will drop us off, refuel, then take Paull and the children back to the States."

"You said you'd never see her again."

"No, honey, *she* said that." He made a vague gesture. "She says she's involved in this situation with Xhafa."

Alli's eyes rose to engage his. "Do you believe her?"

"I wasn't sure—until I saw the scars on Edon's back."

"Yeah, they're just like the ones on Annika's back." Alli licked her lips. "She's after Arian Xhafa, isn't she?"

He nodded. "I wouldn't bet against it."

"But you weren't thinking about her when I sat down here."

Jack sighed. "Alli, Naomi Wilde is missing. I spoke to a chief detective who thinks she's been murdered."

Alli's gaze dropped to her hands, which fidgeted in her lap. "I liked Naomi," she said after a time.

"Me, too."

"D'you really think she's dead?"

"No way to say at this point."

She picked at her nails, which were already bitten short. "What's gonna happen to Thatë?"

Jack shrugged. "That will be largely up to him."

"You don't have a plan for him? You have a plan for everyone."

"I think you're giving me too much credit."

"Do you have a plan for Annika?"

He remained silent for some time. "It's not just me who has a connection with her."

When she gave him a startled look, he said, "What, did you think I wouldn't notice?"

Alli was back to staring at her hands.

"Alli, talk to me."

She heaved a sigh and shook her head as if to clear it. "Last year, when we were in the Ukraine, it was almost like . . ." Her words grew fainter and fainter until they faded out altogether.

Jack waited a moment, then leaned forward. "Like what?"

Tears grew in Alli's eyes, glittering and fragile-seeming. "There were moments—at that awful restaurant, at the apartment—when we were like . . . like a family." She almost winced when she said the last word. "Is that a horrible thing to say?"

He took her slim hands in his. "Why would it be horrible?"

She gave a tiny sound that was as much a sob as a bitter laugh. "Because, Jack. Because of so many things." Her voice was a whisper. "Because she lied to both of us, because she murdered an American senator, because . . ." Her nails dug into his palms. ". . . oh, Christ, don't make me go on."

"Alli, look at me, we're all of us angels and demons. We choose our paths, but there are forces, vast and hidden, that compel us into situations, sometimes against our will—"

"Are you excusing what she did?" It was less accusation than plea.

"I'm saying that when it comes to Annika the truth is always hidden, and when it does come to light—if it ever does—it's far more complex, and conflicted, than we can imagine."

She nodded. "That I can understand."

He smiled. "I know."

She withdrew her hands from his. He knew from experience that there was only a certain amount of physical contact she could tolerate.

"Where are we meeting her?" she asked.

"In Vlorë."

Alli risked a glance over her shoulder. "There's something I want to ask you. It's about Edon. Her sister, Liridona, is in Vlorë. Edon doesn't know what's happened to her, but she's deathly afraid that Xhafa's people will get ahold of her; maybe they already have."

"Alli, much as I feel for Edon and her sister, we can't spare the time to—"

"You can't," Alli said. "But I can."

THERE WAS a police boat waiting to take Heroe to Roosevelt Island when she pulled up at the dock in

Georgetown. During the short trip over, she thought about Naomi Wilde and her sister Rachel. She herself had three brothers, scattered all over the world. One was a trauma surgeon in Oregon, another a lawyer at The Hague, the third an intel officer in Afghanistan. She had always wanted a sister, someone to help counter the testosterone barrage. She wondered how Rachel would take the loss of her sister. Coming after the betrayal of her husband it wouldn't be good—by the looks of her she was already unraveling. She made a mental note to keep an eye on her in the coming weeks.

The patrol boat nosed into the island and Heroe hopped off. She turned on the GPS function of her phone.

"Give me a half hour," she said, "before you come looking for me."

The officer adjusted the boat's GPS to home in on her signal. "What are you expecting?"

Heroe grimaced. "I wish I knew."

"Good luck, Chief."

Nodding, she pushed into the dense greenery until she found the boardwalk. She walked to her right. Finding nothing, she retraced her steps and continued on. Not long after, she discovered a branching to her right, and took it.

This boardwalk was shorter, ending at a small inlet that meandered off to her right. She took a look around and saw nothing but trees and underbrush. A bird sang in a branch above her head and water spiders skimmed across the surface of the shallow finger of water.

She was about to turn around and go back to the

boat when something stuck in the periphery of her vision. Squatting down, she looked more closely. Off to her right there appeared to be a footprint in the black mud beside the water. It was a partial, but still. Slipping off her shoes, she stepped cautiously into the opaque water. It came up to her calves, but the mud was so thick she sunk in another couple of inches. Drawing her service revolver, she headed straight up the inlet. She was surprised that the water wasn't cold. It was, instead, the temperature of blood. This thought sent a shiver down her spine.

Heroe was not prone to superstition, but from the time of puberty she had been visited by premonitions. They did not come often, but when they did they always proved correct. At first, she hadn't told anyone about her visitations for fear of being ostracized, but a year after they manifested she could bear the burden no longer and, one night, she confessed to Granny. For a long time after she was finished speaking, Granny said nothing. Her eyes had gone opaque as they sometimes did when she sat in her rocking chair in the evenings or on dark afternoons when rain clouds burst open and lightning forked through the sky.

"You have inherited the gift from me," Granny said after a time. "I inherited it from my grandmother. That's how the gift works; it skips generations." Granny's eyes cleared and she smiled as she touched Heroe's cheek. "Don't be frightened, child."

"I'm not," Heroe had said, sounding braver than she felt. "But I don't understand."

Granny's smile broadened. "The world we experience with our five senses is only a sliver of what exists. Remember this, child, as you go through life. You and I have glimmers of what really exists beyond the limits. We are the fortunate ones."

"But the premonitions—"

"Whispers from the other side of things, whispers from souls whose bodies have already turned to dust. Where they are, time doesn't exist. Time is, after all, constructed by humans to make sense out of chaos. But in the vastness, past, present, and future coexist, as they must. It's only that we lack the . . . tools to experience it the way it really is."

Now, wading through the swampy water, Heroe was visited by a premonition. She "saw" the water as blood and knew that somewhere up ahead death awaited. And then into her mind swam Naomi Wilde's face. It was covered in mud, distorted by caked blood. So vivid was the image that Heroe was forced to stop in her tracks. She held on to the branch of a tree, much as Naomi had done days before when Annika had led her to the buried body of Arjeta Kraja. For a moment the world seemed to spin wildly around her and she heard the familiar roaring in her ears. *Someone else's blood,* Granny had said when she had described the sensation.

"Who are you?" Heroe whispered. "What are you trying to tell me?"

Slowly, she regained her sense of equilibrium. The world, and, with it, her breathing, returned to normal. She stared at her fist, the knuckles white where she held on to the branch as if for dear life. Letting go, she pushed forward through the muck until she came to a large tree with spreading roots. More footprints here—fresh footprints, in fact. And between two of the largest roots the earth had been recently turned over.

The footprints went off into the foliage. She was looking in that direction when a powerful arm snaked around her throat and she felt a terrible pressure on the delicate bone just below her left eye.

"No," Jack said. "I forbid it. For you to go after Liridona alone would be the height of madness."

"I suspected you would say that," Alli replied. "That's why I've asked Thatë to go with me."

At once, he saw the trap she had sprung on him, and while he admired her cleverness, he also knew that what she proposed was out of the question.

"I'm sorry, Alli. Your heart is in the right place, but under no circumstances are you going off on this wild-goose chase." Even as the words came out of his mouth, he recognized them as what Edward Carson had told him when he assigned Jack to investigate Senator Berns's death.

Alli's eyes were blazing. "You have no right to order me—"

"This isn't a democracy, young lady. In case you have conveniently forgotten, the moment we step off the plane we're back in enemy territory. An enemy, I might remind you, whose principal business is the enslavement and trafficking of girls and young women."

She lifted her head. "I'm not frightened of Arian Xhafa."

"That's just what I'm afraid of, Alli, because you should be."

"Well, shit, of course I am, Jack. I'd be an idiot not

to be frightened of him. On the other hand, I'm not going to let that fright paralyze me. I mean, who does Edon have except us? Who can save her and Liridona from Xhafa, if not us? Her parents? Her father is the one who sold her and Arjeta to Xhafa's people to pay off his gambling debts. Do you think he's going to stop gambling and losing?"

Now it was she who took his hands. "Jack, Edon's already lost one sister. I can't stand by and watch her lose another."

THE PRESSURE in Heroe's head exploded behind her eyes like a mortar blast. She gasped as the shock wave drove through her, but her brain was far from paralyzed. She raised her service revolver until the muzzle pointed directly behind her. She pulled the trigger.

The percussion effectively deafened her in her right ear, but the agonizing pressure beneath her left eye vanished. She was released, and she staggered to her knees.

She was staring down, half-dazed by shock, the point-blank percussion, and the violent surge of adrenaline that had surely saved her life. Her knees had not sunk into the muck. They were resting on something hard. Dropping the service revolver, she dug her fingers in the muddy earth, scraped it away, and saw two faces appearing. One was of a young girl, very beautiful despite the disfigurement of her nose. Heroe had never seen her before. Feverish with dread, she uncovered more of the second girl and saw that it was Naomi Wilde's face precisely as she had experienced it in her visitation.

She began to cry. But that release of emotion and tension brought her back to herself, and, bracing herself against the tree, she rose to her feet.

Turning, she saw Peter McKinsey sitting against the bole of a tree. The left side of his head was running red. Where the ear had been was a scorch mark, ragged and bloody.

He looked up at her and snapped his teeth together. In utter shock, she watched him lurch to his feet and come after her. She wanted to run, she wanted to defend herself, but her service revolver was at her feet.

And then he was upon her, and her nostrils dilated with the stench of death. His fists beat her down to the muck, until she was lying with Naomi Wilde and the unknown victim. And in that moment, she understood the nature of her visitation. The water turned to blood—her blood, her death. Nothing to be done, then. The future was already written. Today she would die.

McKinsey was on top of her, pounding her, and then he had her service revolver. He pointed it at her, grinning now, victory in sight. And then the world turned inside out, colors coalesced and collided. She no longer felt pain. There was no sound save the rushing of blood in her ears. *Someone else's blood.*

And at that precise instant, she saw the specter of Naomi Wilde rising up behind McKinsey like a twist of smoke, drawing her gaze to the ruined side of his head. No time to weigh a decision, or even for thought.

Lashing out with her left hand, she struck squarely on the gunshot wound. McKinsey howled in pain, rearing up, hands to his head. She struck him a two-handed blow that knocked him sideways. His cheek struck Naomi's face and he howled again.

Struggling out from under him, she smashed her fist into his right eye. The blow drove the left side of his head into the ground and his eyes rolled up in their sockets. She grabbed her service revolver out of his hand and aimed it at him as she staggered to her feet.

"Get up," she ordered. "Get up now!"

Instead, he lunged at her. She pulled the trigger.

IMMEDIATELY FOLLOWING his speech to the NAACP at the Kennedy Center, President Crawford headed for the men's room. This had already been vetted by a member of his Secret Service detail, and was staked out, ensuring no one could enter while the POTUS was doing whatever it was he needed to do in there.

Everyone, that is, except Henry Holt Carson. The president was not happy when Carson strode into the men's room.

Crawford gave him a jaundiced look. "A Secret Service agent. Hank, for the love of God!"

"Calm down, sir."

The president stared at him in the mirror that ran along the wall above the sinks. "I will not fucking calm down. Where in all our planning did we ever contemplate murdering a Secret Service agent?"

It was a rhetorical question. Carson was quite certain it required no answer, so he kept his mouth shut.

"And Naomi Wilde, of all people. Damn it, Hank, she was one of our best and brightest. I read the reports of how she handled the crisis in Moscow, how she took charge of your sister-in-law. I've spoken with her several times—I *knew* her."

Time for rebuttal, Carson thought. "You and I both know it never would have come up, let alone been on the table. It was a spur-of-the-moment decision. Wilde had gotten too close. If McKinsey hadn't acted, she would have blown us out of the water—"

"Murder of a federal agent. That's a capital offense."

"—and then where would we be?"

Crawford ran his hand distractedly through his hair. He seemed incapable of looking directly at Carson, but continued to engage his image in the mirror.

"This has gotten out of hand, Hank."

"As far as anyone is concerned, Naomi Wilde is missing. We've neutralized her boss, there is no body. Calm down. We're almost there."

"The hell we are!" The president stopped, suddenly aware that he had raised his voice. "This has got to stop, right here, right now."

"You know that's impossible. We've come too far; we've crossed the line of no return."

"I'm telling you, Hank—"

"Cheer up, Arlen, the Middle Bay audit is almost complete. When it is, we'll have what we want."

For the moment, the president's eyes had turned inward, and when he spoke it was as if he was addressing himself. "There's a line you promise yourself you'll never cross, because once you do, all is lost."

For the first time, Carson spoke sharply. "It pains me to have to remind you that we're both implicated in the Middle Bay merger. If we don't complete what we started—if we *fail*—well, it will be a pretty bleak future for both of us."

Crawford's eyes refocused. Leaning forward, he put his hands on either side of the sink. The skin on his face was pale and slack. Suddenly he looked ten years older. "God in heaven, what this job takes out of you."

"There are a lot of people who wonder why anyone would want the burden."

"Well, right now, Hank, I'm beginning to think they're right." The president sighed. "Okay, so what do we do now?"

"Clean up the mess McKinsey made."

"Don't speak that name to me ever again!"

Carson nodded. "As you wish, of course."

"When you lie down with fuckers, you're sure to get fucked," Crawford said bleakly.

Carson offered a thin smile. "Leave it to me."

"What the hell does that mean?"

"You don't want to know, sir."

"Tell me anyway."

Carson crossed behind the POTUS to the line of urinals, unzipped, and began to pee. "I'm going to cauterize the wound."

Crawford opened his mouth, possibly to ask what that specifically meant, then changed his mind. Instead, he turned on the taps, pumped foaming soap from the dispenser, and commenced to wash his hands.

Carson watched him. *Like Lady Macbeth*, he thought. *But the stink of guilt will never wash off, trust me on that.* Finished, he zipped up and joined the POTUS at the sinks, washing and drying his hands.

"She's going to be buried with full military honors."

Carson coughed. "May I remind you, sir. There is no body."

"And you better make sure there won't be one." The POTUS shook his head. "Damnit to hell, Hank, what's gone right today?"

Patting the POTUS on the back, Carson said, "Buck up, Arlen, you just delivered one helluva speech that'll put the African-American vote in the bag."

TWENTY-SEVEN

"Is he dead?"

"As a doorpost."

Heroe closed her eyes. "Shit, shit, *shit*!"

"He got a name?"

"Agent Peter McKinsey, United States Secret Service."

"You're kidding, right?"

Heroe looked up at him. The pain in her head was distracting her from what she needed to do. "Do I fucking look like I'm kidding?"

"Okay, okay. But forget about him, Chief, and just lie back," the officer said. "I've called for an EMS evac chopper. I don't want to chance taking you back to the mainland in the boat."

"Officer, I'm on a grave with two bodies. One of them is McKinsey's partner. I'm not lying back."

"My God," the officer said, "what the hell is this place?"

THE MOMENT the 737 hit the tarmac and taxied to a stop, Edon Kraja come up to Jack and said, "I want to get off here with you. I need to find my sister. I'm afraid something terrible has happened to her."

"I'm sorry, that's not possible," Jack said as gently as he could.

Edon's eyes welled up with tears. "You don't understand. The chances are my father is going to sell her to Arian Xhafa." The girl looked desperate. "Liridona is not like Arjeta and me, she's the youngest, she doesn't have the toughness. She's vulnerable. She'll crack wide open."

"Come with me," Jack said. He led her to the front of the plane, where they could be alone, and sat her down facing him. "Edon, I have something difficult to tell you."

Right away she started to tremble.

"Arjeta has been found. She's dead."

"Oh, my God, oh, my God . . ." She was shaking, and her head started to whip back and forth, as if she could somehow negate what had happened.

Jack took her by the shoulders. "Look at me. Edon, look right here, into my eyes."

Slowly, the girl did as he asked.

"It's all right," he said softly. "It's going to be all right."

"How?" she wailed. "How can it possibly be all right?"

The commotion brought Alli at the run. Jack looked up at her. "I told her."

Alli sat down next to Edon and put her arms around her. At once, Edon buried her face in the crook of Alli's shoulder. She was sobbing inconsolably. Alli stared at Jack.

"Don't do this," she whispered. "You have to let me go."

"Alli, I have you to think about."

"And I have Liridona." She stroked Edon's head. "Okay, I have a solution. Let's let Annika decide."

"What?" Jack was truly alarmed. "No."

"Why not?

"Because it's nuts to trust her judgment."

"You've done it before," Alli rightly pointed out. "Besides, when has she ever, ever tried to hurt us?"

He said nothing.

"You know she'd never let anything happen to either of us."

In peace as in war sacrifices must be made, soldiers must fall in order for battles to be won. "In fact, I don't know that."

She cocked her head. "I don't believe you."

"That's unfair. I've never lied to you."

"Let's not talk about unfair, okay? I'll have Thatë to protect me." She looked at him steadily, and all of a sudden she seemed terribly grown-up. "Jack, you can't protect me every second of my life."

"I know that, but I can still make decisions—"

"From now on I'll make my own decisions."

HEROE RESISTED going to the ER, but she'd had no choice. They strapped her to a gurney and choppered her to Walter Reed, but not before she called the ME and gave him orders to get out to Roosevelt Island stat.

At some point, she must have passed out, because the next thing she knew she was in a hospital bed and Alan Fraine was sitting in a chair beside her. He smiled when he saw she was awake.

"You took quite a beating."

"I gave as good as I got."

"Better, I'd say. Much better. You'll be ready to roll in a couple of hours. Just a few more tests—"

"Fuck the tests, I don't need tests. How long have I been out?"

"A couple of hours, more or less."

"Jesus. Any word yet on the cause of Naomi Wilde's death?"

His smile quickly faded. "On that score, I'm afraid I have some bad news. The bodies of Wilde, McKinsey, and the unknown vic have been taken from us."

"What the fuck does that mean?"

Fraine sighed. "Nona, I think you know."

"The Feds."

He nodded. "A whole platoon of them appeared at the island and commandeered the crime scene. Our people were summarily dismissed."

"So we have nothing?"

"Less than nothing." Fraine couldn't meet her fiery gaze. "I've been given orders to forget the incident ever happened."

"Forget? How can I forget—?"

"Nona, I'm very sorry." Fraine shook his head. "As of now, you're on leave."

"What? You mean I'm relieved of duty?"

"I mean you haven't taken a vacation in, what?"

"How about never."

"Okay, then." He brightened. "No time like the present."

"This is total bullshit," she said.

"This is my decision, and it stands."

She sat up straighter. "How could you?"

"Nona, I want you out of harm's way. Now. Before something really bad happens." His eyes met hers at last. "I chose column A. Was I wrong?"

She was so angry sparks should have been shooting out of her eyes. "Alan, this blows."

"I hear you."

"Scylla and Charybdis."

He cocked his head. "This is what comes of being so well read in a dumbed-down world."

"Trapped between two monsters. There is no good choice."

He shrugged. "Life works that way sometimes."

"Tell that to Naomi Wilde." Her voice had turned savage. "Who's going to be her advocate? Who's going to speak up for what was done to her now that it's going to be swept under the carpet?"

Fraine leaned forward, elbows on his knees. "Nona, listen to me. I understand what you're feeling—"

"How can you?" She looked away for a moment. "Sorry. It's unfair to snap at you."

"Nothing about this situation is fair." He lowered his voice. "There are some very big fish involved in this mess. The best thing for you now is to disappear, at least until it blows over."

"Yeah, I could go to Sicily like Michael Corleone."

"I'm deadly serious. Nona, you've got to forget about Naomi Wilde. You got the guy that killed her. Leave it at that."

She looked at him for a long time. She hated the sickly sweet medicinal smell of hospitals. She couldn't wait to get out of here. At last, she nodded. "Okay,

okay. You've gotten through to me. I'll take that long-delayed vacation."

"Thank God."

She lay back and closed her eyes. "Maybe I'll head down to New Orleans, see some old friends."

"Sounds good."

At that moment, two federal suits entered the room. One was Midwestern blond, the other dark-haired, old-school Ivy League.

"Chief Detective Nona Heroe?" Ivy League said.

She opened her eyes. "Who wants to know?"

They both revealed their IDs. They were DoD, not to be trifled with. Fraine rose and immediately realized the gravity of the situation.

"This can wait until Chief Heroe has fully recovered."

Blondie nailed him with a glare. "For our purposes, Chief Heroe is fully recovered."

Ivy League brushed past Fraine. "Chief Detective Heroe, you are formally charged with the capital offense of the willful murder of a federal agent. You are hereby directed to come with us immediately."

"But—" Fraine began.

Blondie swung on him. "One more word and you go, too."

"No buts," Ivy League said to Heroe. "No ifs, no ands. Get up now or I do it for you."

Heroe rolled out of the bed, gathered up her clothes, and went into the bathroom. As she dressed, she fished out her cell and sent the following text message to Jack: MIDDLE BAY BANCORP. Hurriedly, she continued drawing on her clothes. She was just about to step into her shoes when a rude knocking rattled the door.

"Let's go." She heard Ivy League's voice. He sounded irritated.

She opened the door and stepped out. As she brushed past Fraine, she handed off her cell. He gave her a quick look and she gave him a tentative smile back.

"Don't worry, Nona," he said.

Blondie smirked as he took her into custody. "Those are the last words the condemned always hears."

"NOT TONIGHT." Vera wrapped her raincoat around herself.

Gunn stirred on the bed. "Why is tonight different from any other night?"

"My medical leave is over." Vera stepped into the new Louboutins he had bought her. Actually, he'd bought her two pairs. He could be generous like that. "I have to get back onto campus before midnight."

Rolling over, Gunn checked the alarm clock on the bedside table. "There's still an hour and a half." He wore underpants and nothing else. That's how he slept.

"Andy, I don't want to get into trouble my first night back." She picked up the shopping bag with the second pair of Louboutins. "Besides, I'm dead tired. Even you've got to admit it's been a long fucking day."

He took her hand and began kissing it, rising up her arm. "Tish," he said with a fake Spanish accent, "you know how your words inflame me."

"Poor Gomez," she said with Morticia's cool, regal voice. "You'll just have to take care of yourself tonight."

OUTSIDE, THE night air refreshed her and she began to walk. The stink of blood and brains remained in her nose, and she snorted like a bridling horse. At a brisk pace, she walked three blocks west, then one block south, where she paused to look around, as if getting her bearings. As she did so, a black Lincoln Town Car appeared around a corner and cruised slowly toward her. She ignored it until it began to slow, then watched as it stopped abreast of her. It had smoked windows, so it was impossible to see inside. The front passenger's window slid down and the driver, leaning her way, said, "Would a hundred dollars do it, doll?"

She leaned down. "You've got to be kidding."

The driver shrugged. "Five, then. How about that?"

"Yeah, how the fuck about it?"

She pulled on the handle of the rear door, it swung open, and she climbed in. The moment she plunked herself down on the backseat, the Lincoln took off. She noticed that the partition between the front and back was up. It, too, was opaque.

"How'd it go today?" Henry Holt Carson said from the other side of the seat.

Vera gave him a vulpine smile. "You know, Daddy, you really are a sonuvabitch."

JACK WAS briefing Paull on the situation back in D.C.—minus Annika's involvement—when he received the text message from Heroe. Reading it, the hairs on his forearms stirred. Middle Bay Bancorp. Could this be the nexus point that linked all the disparate elements together?

Wondering why Heroe had texted him instead of calling and explaining herself, he punched in her number. The phone rang four or five times before a man's voice answered.

"Who's this?" Jack said.

"I'd ask the same of you," the voice said.

Something was very wrong. "Jack McClure. Where's Chief Heroe?"

"This is Alan Fraine, Chief of Police. I'm Chief Heroe's boss. Unfortunately, Nona has been taken into custody by the Feds. She's been charged with the murder of Secret Service Agent Peter McKinsey."

"What the hell happened?"

Fraine told him about Heroe's trip to Roosevelt Island and the discovery of two bodies, one being that of Agent Naomi Wilde.

Jack's heart sank. He took a deep breath, steadying himself. "That second body is without doubt Arjeta Kraja, an illegal alien and part of the white slave trade business that Heroe and I and Naomi were investigating. McKinsey was involved in the ring in some way none of us yet understand. But it's clear that he murdered Naomi Wilde because she got too close to identifying certain individuals connected with the ring."

"Your enemies are exceptionally powerful and well connected, Mr. McClure. Nona's in serious trouble. When it comes to the Feds these days . . . well, I don't have to tell you how difficult it will be even getting to talk to her let alone finding her top-flight representation."

"Hopefully it won't come to that. My boss, Dennis Paull, is on his way back to D.C. I want you to hook up with him the moment he steps off the plane and brief him completely. Then I'd like you to compile a list of Middle Bay Bancorp personnel—"

"Funny you should say that," Fraine said, "Nona had compiled just such a list. Hold on a moment. Ah, yes, here it is."

"Would you read off the names, please?"

Fraine did. Seventeen names, but none of them rang a bell. Jack wondered what he was missing. "Is there anyone else?"

"Well, you said bank personnel. As you may know, Middle Bay is in the process of being acquired by InterPublic Bancorp."

Henry Holt Carson's bank. Jack stood still as a statue while his brain, working at the speed of light, placed Carson and InterPublic alongside Middle Bay at the nexus of the conspiracy universe and began to follow the tentacles reaching outward. He was riding this wave of thought so completely that he almost missed what Fraine said next.

"So, of course, Nona had added the members of the forensic accounting team auditing Middle Bay's books to the list of the bank's personnel."

Jack was dizzy with the sudden swirl of calculations. "Let's have them all, Chief Fraine."

"There are five individuals on the team." He named them. Nothing. "And then there's the team leader. His name is, let me see, ah yes, John Pawnhill."

Annika had said, *"We're all soldiers in the night,*

and because of this, like it or not, we're pawns." And
at that moment, two disparate things collided in
Jack's head, and the unknown part of the name equation he'd been trying to solve at last swam into focus.
Thatë's nickname was Grasi—fat. But his real name—
Thatë—meant skinny. The kid was neither fat nor
skinny, so how was he given the nickname? Jack had
been looking at the equation through the wrong end
of a telescope. Mbreti wasn't the unknown in the
equation, it was the key. Mbreti meant king. And
what was the opposite of king on a chessboard?
Pawn.

John Pawnhill was Mbreti!

TWENTY-EIGHT

"Vera, you're a chip off the old block."

"A heart like black ice." Vera crossed one leg over the other. "Like my new shoes?"

Carson didn't bother looking; he knew his daughter's tastes all too well. "Tell me about today."

Vera's smirk widened. "Let's see, what happened? Oh, yes, my lover, Andy Gunn, recruited me to help him terminate two lowlifes."

"Names, Vera, names."

"Willowicz—though Gunn referred to him as Blunt—and O'Banion."

Carson wet his lips. "They're both dead? You're sure?"

"Could not be deader." Vera watched his profile, which was vexingly noncommittal. "Why?"

"I'm wondering why he killed them and why now."

"He was very focused, I can tell you that. Like he'd been given a deadline."

"Odds are he had been. He's taking orders from someone other than me."

"But you knew that already."

"Yes, but not who he's playing both sides with." Carson seemed to be staring at nothing and everything at once. "I had him followed, but he slipped the tail. He must have gone to meet with the person who gave him today's marching orders."

"Any ideas who it might be?"

"That's something you're going to find out for me."

Vera closed her eyes for a moment. "Listen, you fixed me up at Fearington so I'd become Alli Carson's roommate. Alli knew Caroline. You thought Alli might know where she is; she doesn't. No one knows where that bitch has got to."

"Don't call your half sister that," Carson said sharply. "You haven't earned the right."

"She left, just like that. We shared so many things, and then *poof* she was gone. And after that she never contacted me."

"She never contacted anyone."

Vera clenched her fists. "This is all your fault, you shithead."

"Down, girl. You should see a doctor about that overabundance of testosterone."

"Ha ha." There was little mirth in Vera's voice. "Only if you come with me to see about your satyriasis."

"Now who's the bitch."

"Neither of us can help it, that's the way you made us."

Carson made a derisive sound. "Oh, yes, blame it all on Daddy."

She turned to him, draped one leg over his lap, snuggled up to him, and said in a little-girl-porn voice,

"Oh, Daddy, I'm just worried about you, is all. I don't want you to go into cardiac arrest while you're plowing away."

"Vera." His tone held an unmistakable note of warning.

"So many furrows, so little time." Her fingers traced the whorls of his ear. "I know, Daddy, time is running out, soon enough you won't be able to get it up at all."

"Godammit, Vera!" He pushed her roughly away from him. "What the hell is the matter with you?"

"Nothing a little parental love wouldn't cure." She gave him a mock-pout from her corner of the seat.

"Bullshit. You wouldn't know what to do with parental love."

"Good thing," she said, "because you don't know how to show it."

This exchange was followed by an oppressive silence.

Finally, she said, "You asked me to get close to Andy. We both knew what that meant, so when you think about it, you've been pimping me out."

"I'm doing what any good spymaster would do, keeping an eye on my people."

"If you give yourself any more credit I'll throw up."

"Don't get superior. I'm not the whore in this scenario."

"That's really how you see me, isn't it?"

He turned away, but remained silent.

Vera spent several minutes fantasizing about punching him in the face. "Why are you expending so much energy on trying to find Caro, anyway?"

"Why do you think? She's my daughter."

"Now who's bullshitting, Daddy? Caro's a thing. She ran away from you, so you couldn't have her."

"Oh, please!"

"As opposed to me, who ran right back into your arms." The vulpine smirk returned to Vera's face. "Caro is someone neither your wealth nor your influence can affect. That's something you simply can't tolerate, Daddy."

"Not true."

"Of course it's true. You think I don't know you. You're so fucking defended a fucking termite couldn't get in, that's what you think, isn't it? You don't fool me, you old bastard. You stand naked in front of me, I see you for what you are."

He continued to stare ahead. "I made myself what I am today; I didn't have anyone's help. Not that I didn't take favors when they were offered or exchanged for others. Only an idiot would have refused. But I'm my own man, Vera, always have been. That's the one thing I'm most proud of. So when you . . . I'm not interested in anyone's opinions of me—especially yours."

"Why would you? You're the center of the world."

"That's the spirit, honey!"

She chuckled. "Oh, Daddy, you're so transparent, and d'you know why? Because you're such a shitty parent. Having kids was never your thing. Your wanting Caro back has nothing whatsoever to do with her being your daughter."

"Your attempts at psychoanalyzing me are laughable."

She ignored his jibe. "It's about you, Daddy. Everything's all about you. Caro ran away from you and that's what you can't tolerate."

"That's nonsense and you know it."

She shook her head, moving out from her corner to close with him again. "You keep trying to undercut me, but I'm the *only* one whose opinion matters to you."

Carson stared out the window at the blur of the passing cityscape. "Eddy's opinion mattered to me."

"But your brother is dead, Daddy." She slid farther toward him. "And that's the crux of it. You never got over your brother. He was younger than you and yet he was elected president of the United States."

"Not without my help!"

In the small silence, Vera said, "You see? It's all laid out like the grid of a landing strip. If only you could see it."

Carson's voice was bleak. He seemed suddenly lost in time. "See what?"

"How much Edward meant to you, how much you loved him." She stared at her father for a moment, and when she spoke again her voice had softened considerably. "Did he love you back, Daddy?"

"I . . . I don't know."

"Sure you know. You must know."

"He accepted my help. He was grateful. He—"

"Fuck it, Daddy! Would you for once tell the truth?"

"It would be easier if he hadn't thanked me."

"But he did."

"Oh, yes. Thanking people was always one of Eddy's strong suits."

"You say that like it's a congenital defect."

"It made him less sincere," Carson said, "in my opinion."

"Uh-huh, too nice for you, was he?" She nodded. "I can see how you'd view that as a defect."

Carson's lips moved without him saying a word out loud. Then he pinched the bridge of his patrician nose. "The trouble was, I never knew where I stood with Eddy."

Vera threw back her head and laughed, causing him to whip around as he glared at her.

"What's so damn funny?"

"Your brother made you insecure. God, I didn't think anyone could do that to you."

"You never knew Eddy."

"And whose fault is that?"

"Well . . ." Carson stared at his hands. "There was no way I could let you meet him. You understand that."

"I understand that you had to keep your Main Line connections intact until you acquired enough power on your own."

He shot her a sharp look. "That's a pretty cynical way of looking at it."

"Ours is a cynical world, Daddy."

He nodded, almost, she thought, ruefully.

"Damn if it isn't."

THEY MET Annika in an open field near the airstrip. The wind was blowing, dragging her hair sideways across her face. Her hands were dug deep in the pockets of her trench coat, a stance like Humphrey Bogart's in *Casablanca*.

Jack came halfway toward her, then abruptly stopped. Alli, at his side, broke away and ran pell mell toward her. Just before she reached her, Annika took her hands out of her pockets. Jack automatically tensed. This was a weird moment. He was half expecting her to have a Sig Sauer in one hand.

Instead, Annika threw her arms wide and enfolded Alli, hugging her tight.

"I can't believe it," Alli said. "I've missed you so much."

Annika kissed the top of her head. "Honey, honey, honey," she crooned.

Then she looked past Alli to where Jack stood. The most peculiar smile broke out across her face, part solemn, part impish, but altogether tentative.

All this time, Thatë, present under Jack's sufferance, stayed back at the periphery of the field. It was difficult to know what he was looking at, impossible to know what he was thinking.

Alli, though reluctant, knew it was time to walk away. That left Jack and Annika. They were standing twenty feet from each other.

"I was too late with Arjeta and with Billy." With one hand, she drew her hair off her face. "I found him before the cops did, but there was nothing I could do."

"You could have called me."

Her smile changed shape slightly. "And how far would that have gotten me?"

She was right, of course. At that point, he never would have listened to her. He came toward her, aware that his heart was beating painfully hard. He felt a roaring in his ears.

"I've seen Edon's back."

"Yes, well, where you were, I imagined that might happen. Thank you for saving her and all the rest of them."

"Why are these three girls so important?"

"They know a secret."

"Edon doesn't."

"No. But Arjeta told Liridona. I went to Washington to find Arjeta, to save her, but I was too late."

"You want to know the secret."

"I care about these girls. Deeply."

"But the secret—"

"Jack, please recall what I told you. Secrets are our only weapon against the forces that seek to manipulate us."

Jack believed her. No matter that he wanted to believe her, that, like Alli, he needed to believe her. He kept walking until he was just a handsbreadth away from her. He could smell her then, and his heart melted a little bit more.

"Before we go any further . . ."

"Yes, Jack?"

"I need to know about Senator Berns. I need the whole truth."

"And nothing but the truth, so help me God?" Her tone was mocking.

He didn't laugh. "You don't believe in God."

"Not after what's happened to me."

The sun was shining in her eyes, and he knew that he had dreamed about them. He'd only known that he'd woken in the morning drenched in sweat, sad beyond bearing. He'd put every emotion he possessed on hold, throwing himself into tending to Alli and to his job, which kept changing shape like a chimera. Now he understood his sorrow, and his paralysis. Somewhere inside him, he'd been waiting for this moment; somewhere inside him, he knew it would happen.

"Senator Berns wasn't one of the good guys, Jack."

"Meaning?"

"He was dealing with a very nasty element here in Eastern Europe."

"Enemies of your grandfather."

"Enemies of mine," she said. "And now enemies of yours."

Jack was shocked. "Arian Xhafa?"

"Berns was facilitating the arms deals with Xhafa. Cutting-edge stuff, just off the DARPA assembly line." She cocked her head. "Evil comes in all flavors and guises, Jack. It's a sad fact of life." Her smile turned rueful. "You don't believe me. Berns was chairman of the Senate Military Appropriations Committee, which includes DARPA. Check for yourself."

Jack didn't have to; he'd already discovered this fact for himself. And now he was angry. "Why the hell didn't you tell me this last year?"

"You weren't ready to hear it."

"Damnit, Annika, how could you know that?"

"I made a reasonable assumption. Was I wrong?"

"Stop, for pity's sake, making decisions for me!"

Her extraordinary eyes watched him closely. "This is what you do with Alli, no?"

Yes, it certainly was, but he wasn't about to give her the satisfaction of admitting it. "That's different."

"I disagree. You and Alli are both adults."

"The analogy is spurious. I have far more experience."

"And that means you know what's best for her."

"Yes."

"At all times."

He clamped his mouth shut.

"Jack, consider how you bridled when I told you you weren't ready to hear the whole truth about Senator Berns."

She was as maddening as ever. Somewhere inside him was a burst of laughter because this maddening trait was one of the things that caused him to fall in love with her with a passion that turned him inside out.

Taking a deep breath to center himself, he said, "What happened after you killed Berns? Xhafa's still getting armaments—even faster and in more bulk."

"It's the devil-you-know theory. The person who stepped into the vacuum is worse than Berns. Far worse."

"Who is it?"

In the last failing glimmers of sunlight, Annika's carnelian eyes seemed so lucid it was possible to believe he could see clear through them into her soul. This was one of the unique assets with which God and her mother had blessed her.

"Tell me, Jack, have you ever heard of the Syrian?"

"ANNIKA DEMENTIEVA has entered Albania."

The Syrian, listening to this news, found that his knuckles had gone white where they gripped his satellite phone. Involuntarily, he moved farther away from Arian Xhafa, who was embroiled with Caroline in another of their religio-political-postfeminist debates. The Syrian found them amusing, but Xhafa, true to his nature, took them as deadly serious.

"Where in Albania?" he said, when he'd gone outside.

"Vlorë."

Then she must know, the Syrian said to himself. He heard the snuffling of the dogs as they scented him, saw the deep bowl of the sky, indigo at its apex. A gaudy sunset began to show itself. Tree frogs and crickets started up.

To the man on the other end of the line, he said, "Do you have a specific fix on her?"

"She's been shadowed from the moment she flew in."

The Syrian made an instant decision. "Then take care of the situation at once. I don't want Xhafa getting wind that she's nearby. Take her to the safehouse. You know which one."

There was an instant's hesitation. "She isn't alone."

The Syrian closed his eyes. "How many?"

"Three. A man, a girl, and a boy."

Not so many, he thought. "I want her alive. Terminate the rest of them."

"Your will, my hand."

The Syrian put away the sat phone. He spent about fifteen seconds wondering what Annika was doing with a girl and a boy, but soon a landslide of business matters dismissed the thought from his mind, and it did not resurface until much later.

"I THINK we ought to move to a more secure location," Annika said. She gestured. "I have a car waiting."

"I promised Alli I'd let her talk to you about Liridona."

Annika looked around. "In the car."

"Why did you want to meet in such an open space?"

"Trust," Annika said. "I wanted you to feel perfectly comfortable."

He nodded, but said nothing. Gesturing to Alli and Thatë, he walked with Annika into the deep shadow of a thin line of trees within which an enormous car was waiting, its engine thrumming in a deep register.

"I should introduce the kid," he said, as Alli and Thatë came up to them.

"No need." Annika grinned at Thatë. "He works for me."

Thatë and Alli got in the front seat with the driver, leaving Jack and Annika standing beside the open rear door.

"One of these days," Jack said, "you're going to give me a heart attack with your surprises."

"God forbid!"

She placed a hand on his arm. It was a spontaneous gesture and yet it set off a fireworks display inside him. She must have somehow felt the ripple because she smiled.

"Oh, Jack, I never want to hurt you again."

"But you will."

"Not deliberately, this I swear to you."

She leaned in and the kiss she gave him was as tentative as that first enigmatic smile. She drew back, but he caught her behind her neck, pulled her to him, and kissed her as he'd dreamed of kissing her in a reality he'd never thought could exist again.

He felt the world drop away from him. All that existed was the two of them, locked together, falling through space and time, back to when they had been together in the Ukraine last year, before the betrayal that was still a betrayal, but on another, slighter order of magnitude. A betrayal that could be forgiven without damages being assessed.

The pines above them shook and shivered, clouds passed by overhead, and the velvet evening seemed to wrap them in its cool embrace.

How quickly hate returns to love, he thought.

As they were about to get into the car, he said, "Annika, about you and Xhafa."

"Later, my love. I'll tell you everything."

BALTASAR CLOSED his phone and went back to his surveillance of the Dementieva woman.

"Everything all right?" he said to Asu.

"They went into the line of pines." Asu, the driver, put his field glasses down and pointed.

They were in an armored vehicle similar to the one that had brought Arian Xhafa and the Syrian from the air base to the compound. It was still light enough to see the stand of trees. The pines looked delicate in the gathering twilight, like a Japanese watercolor.

"What are our orders?" Yassin said from behind them.

"The woman is to be taken to the safehouse in the western district of Vlorë. The other three are to be killed."

Baltasar could feel Yassin's excitement coming off him in waves.

"Now," he said. "As soon as we determine—"

At that moment, the huge car slid out from behind the trees and headed off to the east.

"Go," Baltasar said. "Go!"

Asu started up the vehicle and put it into gear. The advantages of the vehicle were many, including its inch-and-a-half-thick armor plate and its two .30 caliber machine guns, mounted fore and aft, its maneuverability over any sort of terrain, and its storehouse of other weaponry, including tear-gas grenades, a handheld rocket launcher, and a flamethrower. On the other hand, it was noisy, relatively slow, and not as maneuverable as a car on normal surfaces. Even so, Baltasar favored it over the other forms of ground transport at the Syrian's disposal.

The large car ahead had its head- and taillights on, but Baltasar instructed Asu to keep theirs off. They were phenomenally lucky that the 737 had landed at sunset. Now, in the twilight's uncertain illumination, they could follow without fear of being detected.

The car bumped down country lanes into larger streets and then took the ramp onto the ring road that circumnavigated Vlorë. There was no telling where it was headed, and Baltasar was anxious not to lose sight of it.

Yassin leaned forward, body as tense as a drawn bow. "We should drive them off the road," he said.

"Wait," Baltasar said without turning around.

"And then, as they come out of the car, use the flamethrower to incinerate them one by one."

Now Baltasar turned to him. "And what do you

think the others will do while the first one is roasting, sit on their thumbs and wait to be set afire?"

Yassin grinned. "There's always the thirty caliber. *Poum, poum, poum!*"

"All good things come to those who wait, Yassin." He handed Yassin the specially reconfigured U.S. Army M24 SWS sniper rifle. "Check the magazine and get ready."

FOR THE first forty-five minutes after the 737 took off from Vlorë, Dennis Paull reviewed what he himself knew about the multiple murders in D.C., beginning with the torture-killing of Billy Warren. He married that with the new information Jack had given him, including the damning evidence against Peter McKinsey from testimony from both Naomi and Chief Detective Heroe. The news that Naomi had been murdered by her partner had shaken him to the core. The very idea of such a thing was so alien he'd had to spend several minutes trying to get his mind around it. He'd been in the intelligence services long enough to have experienced or heard about various kinds of betrayals. All were heinous by their very nature, but this was in a category by itself. If there were, indeed, levels of hell, he hoped to God that McKinsey was inhabiting the lowest.

He took out a pad and pen and began jotting down notes. He also tried to make a perp tree, as they called it at Metro, of all the principals involved in the multiple-murder case. After some long and hard contemplation, plus some overseas calls, he had to admit that Jack's instinct was right. Middle Bay Bancorp was the nexus point for everything. Henry

Holt Carson's bank, InterPublic, was in the process of buying Middle Bay—its books were even now being vetted by a team of forensic accountants led by John Pawnhill. If Jack was correct, Pawnhill was Mbreti, the American kingpin of Arian Xhafa's sex trade empire. He thought a moment, then jotted down the name "Dardan Xhafa" with a question mark after it. If Pawnhill was the kingpin, what had Arian's brother been? Or had he been there to keep an eye on Mbreti? Blood was thicker than water to these people, he knew.

But how did Middle Bay figure into the equation and what was Carson's involvement? Alli's discovery of the take-out menu from First Won Ton, the restaurant below which Xhafa's slave market auctioned off its cherries, as they were called in slang, meant that her uncle was somehow involved in all this. But how? And, most baffling and frightening of all, why had President Crawford himself fast-tracked the buyout through the federal regulatory process?

Thinking of Alli put him in a depressed mood. He rose and went into the toilet to splash water on his face. He'd acted abysmally toward her all during the mission. He'd made himself believe that it was because her presence on a clandestine wet-work mission was highly inappropriate. He'd made himself believe that he was pissed that a tiny slip of a girl could best him in hand-to-hand combat. And those reasons might have been legit until he'd seen her in action. Both her courage and her prowess under extreme conditions were exemplary. He'd actually been proud of her, but he'd quickly tamped down on the feeling, preferring instead to keep needling her.

Now, staring at himself in the mirror, he was forced to admit his intense jealousy. The close relationship Jack had with her was what he'd always dreamed he'd have with his own daughter. Instead, he had driven her away and the fact that she'd returned, his grandson in tow, only underscored what he hadn't had with her.

The truth was, Paull didn't like what he saw in the mirror. He had come to a point in his life when, inevitably, he had begun to look back and rue his mistakes, failings, and failures. It was a bitter time for him, made all the worse by his inability to readapt to field work. The only saving grace was that he'd yanked himself out of the field before Jack could suggest it.

Back in his seat, he lost himself in work and, an hour later, he had the skeleton of a plan he thought would work. He called Chief of Police Alan Fraine, and together they went over iterations of the plan until both of them were satisfied that, though far from perfect, it had the best chance of success. Both of them knew that they were up against powerful enemies bent on keeping the reasons for the murders secret. The murder of Naomi Wilde and subsequent arrest of Chief Heroe was proof of their enemies' utter ruthlessness.

When at last all his work was, for the moment, done, Paull closed his eyes and slept for an hour. When he awoke, he was ravenously hungry. He rose and went directly to the galley to fix himself a sandwich. On the way, he took the time to confirm that the children were okay.

That was when he realized that Edon Kraja was missing.

EDON HAD chosen her moment carefully. She had slipped out of the 737 while Paull was deep in conversation with Jack, while Alli was talking with Thatë. With everyone engaged in their own private dramas, she had grabbed her opportunity to slither away, unnoticed.

Turning her back on the plane, she had jogged through the woods. She knew precisely where she was, knew intimately the cluster of small houses a half mile away. From the backyard of one of them she stole a bicycle, and, bending low over the handlebars, began her journey into Vlorë, to search for her sister Liridona.

Her first stop would be her parents' house. She had no way of knowing whether Liridona was still at home or whether she had also been sold to feed their father's insatiable gambling lust. Cycling as fast as she could, she prayed to Jesus and the Madonna that her sister was still free, that she'd be able to extricate her from home and take her far away from both their father and Arian Xhafa's people.

The thought of what had happened to her happening to Liridona was a goad that drove her to pedal faster and faster. Xhafa was a brilliant organizer, she had learned. But he was also a ruthless killer and, even worse in her experience, a world-class sadist. For him, pain and suffering were the aphrodisiacs he needed to satisfy his sexual needs; without them, he was impotent.

From the moment he'd become aware of her, he'd taken an unhealthy interest in her. Weeding her out of the latest bowl of cherries, he had begun her "training," as he called it. She called it torture. It wasn't on the order of what the other cherries who'd come in with her suffered through—the gang rapes, the beatings, starvings, and then more gang rapes. He hadn't wanted to strip her of her individuality, her humanity, as was being done in a coldly methodical way to the other cherries all around her. Culled out of the herd, she had been isolated. She had seen only him. He'd trained her to crawl on her knees to him, to lick his dirty feet clean, to grovel when she wanted food. Oddly enough, it was he who washed her every day, as tenderly as a parent bathes his infant, caressing her as he cleaned every gentle mound and shadowed dell of her body.

When she had completed the first stage of her training, he had begun to hurt her, first in small, subtle ways. Then the bruising began. He seemed to love looking at the bruises even more than causing them, as if she were a canvas and he, the artist, periodically standing back to admire—or, sometimes, adjust—his art. Pain as art, that defined the Arian Xhafa she knew. He had spent hours on end with her, as if she were to be his masterpiece.

And then he had marked her—branded her, more like it. He used a stiletto reserved for the occasion, whose tip he heated in the flame from a bronze brazier surmounted with strange bas-relief sculptures until it glowed cherry red. He had her lie flat on her stomach on the thin pallet he provided for her to sleep on. She wasn't strapped down or bound in any way; he had trained her too well. Straddling her, he'd applied the glowing tip of the blade. One long wound a night for five nights. Five parallel lines, running red, to prove that she belonged to him.

Very few girls received this privilege, he'd told her. Less than a handful. She was among the elite of his empire, a concubine. She would never be sold; she was his forever.

"Count yourself lucky, Edon," he had said the night it was over. *"You're one of the few. You're my special little cherry."*

TWENTY-NINE

"**B**EHIND US," Annika's driver said. "And the exit's coming up."

"Right." Annika smiled. "Let's go."

Jack turned around and stared out the blacked-out rear window, but he could see nothing. "Who's following us?"

"Xhafa's death squad."

The car veered into the right lane and, a quarter mile later, took the exit ramp off the highway. The driver turned left, went beneath the highway's overpass, and a half mile later turned right. Almost immediately, they were in a densely forested area.

"One mile to the bend," the driver said.

"Slow down," Annika said. "We don't want them to lose us."

Alli shivered. "And you *want* them to follow us?"

Annika turned to her, her expression wolfish. "How d'you think we're going to find Xhafa?"

"WHERE THE hell are they going?" Asu said to no one in particular. "This is dead vacant wilderness."

"Don't be dense," Yassin said. "Where better to have a safehouse?"

Baltasar fitted a tear-gas grenade to the adapter at the end of his rifle. "It doesn't matter; we're thirty seconds from taking them."

Asu was using the car's headlights to see where they were headed. "There's a bend in the road coming up," he announced. "The road dips down and then it's straight as an arrow."

"Perfect." Baltasar popped the hatch over his head. "As soon as it straightens out come up behind the car to within fifteen feet. Keep a steady pace while I deliver the payload. Yassin, you'll pick them off as they exit the car. The darts will put them to sleep so get all of them, including Annika Dementieva. Then, when they're down, you can put a bullet in the back of the heads of the other three."

The car ahead entered the bend in the road. As it dipped into the swale, Asu momentarily lost sight of it. Baltasar stood up so that his head and upper torso were above the vehicle's roofline. Fitting night goggles over his eyes, he looked out at the landscape ahead. He saw no sign of lights, front or rear, and he adjusted the goggles. Several moments later, he saw the headlights, then the car. Immediately thereafter, Asu accelerated, and the vehicle shot ahead.

Baltasar counted the seconds as Asu closed the gap. He was an excellent driver; Baltasar had absolute confidence in his abilities. Nevertheless, something was bothering him. From his elevated position, he should have been able to pick up the headlights even while the car was at the bottom of the swale.

Now they were on the straightaway. The acceleration leveled out, steadied, and, bracing his elbows against the rooftop, he took aim at the rear window of the car. He counted slowly to three, exhaled, and squeezed the trigger.

The tear-gas grenade smashed through the glass and detonated. Now it was only a matter of waiting until the driver lost consciousness. The car would begin to weave, then veer off the road as the driver lost control. Perhaps it would come to rest in a ditch or sideswipe a tree. In any event, Yassin's turn would come. It was a beautiful thing, Baltasar thought, when everything proceeded according to plan.

He waited, but the car did not weave. It slowed. Asu put on the brakes and the military vehicle paced the car. Baltasar frowned. He wondered whether the driver, in his semiconscious state, had the presence of mind to step on the brake. But the moments of losing the headlights still bothered him, and he couldn't rid himself of the nagging notion that something was wrong.

The next moment, the car stopped. Baltasar unscrewed the grenade launcher and changed magazines to regular rounds. All the time he kept his eyes glued to the car.

"Let's go! What are we waiting for?"

He heard Yassin's whisper from just inside the hatch. Yassin was right; they should be on the ground now, approaching the car. But something stayed Baltasar's hand.

He ducked back down and said to Yassin, "Change in plan. Take one of the AK-50s and go over to the car. Asu will cover you with the thirty caliber."

Asu popped his head out of the open hatch. He flipped the safety off the forward machine gun, then signaled that he was ready.

Yassin climbed out of the hatch and dropped to the ground. He circled the car warily, crouched down, the AK-50 at the ready. It was loaded with heavy, maximum-grain ammunition. Except for the chirruping of insects, there was absolute silence. No traffic, and whatever wind there had been had died.

Yassin had made half a circuit around the car without seeing any sign of life. Then, a single shot caused him to spin around. Asu lay sprawled across the roof, his head a bloody pulp.

Yassin, instantly calculating the direction of the shot from the way Asu's body lay, opened fire with the assault rifle while darting behind the protection of the car.

A second shot, coming from directly behind him, pitched him forward. He struck the rear fender of the car, then slid off onto the ground. He did not move. His blood became a black pool around him.

At once, the military vehicle rumbled into life, swinging around to face the spot where the second shot had come from. A thin whine was followed by a long gout of flame that penetrated the first line of pine trees with a blast of searing heat. First, the flames set the carpet of fallen needles alight, but soon enough the trees themselves were engulfed in flame and dense, black, chemical smoke.

FOR WHAT seemed like several moments after that, nothing happened. Then a figure, black and peeling beneath a hellish coat of flames, rushed from the smoking trees. Halfway to the military vehicle, it jerked upright, as if on a leash. Then it collapsed onto its knees, slowly folding over onto itself, forming at length a pyramid of crisped flesh and cracking bones.

The vehicle came to a halt, the rear battle slits snapped open, and a hail of machine gun fire bit into the trees on the other side of the road. In that moment, Annika ran from cover near the smoldering trees, primed a grenade, and slammed it between the front wheels. She was almost back inside the tree line when the blast blew the near-side wheels off and a hole appeared in the vehicle's armor plate, into which the stinking smoke from the blast was drawn as if down an open flue.

Seeing this, Jack broke cover, sprinted across the road, and leapt into the back of the vehicle, which was stalled and hotter than an oven. As the top hatch popped open and Baltasar emerged, eyes streaming, Jack grabbed him and hauled him bodily out of the vehicle, throwing him down onto the road, where Annika was standing.

Baltasar grunted as he hit the pavement on his left shoulder. Annika kicked him in the stomach, and he flopped over. By this time, Jack had checked to make sure the vehicle was empty. Now he dropped down beside Baltasar. Together, they dragged him over to the pile of bones within which tiny flames still flickered and danced. Mostly, though, the superheated chemical fire had turned everything to brittle ash. But the nauseating stench of roasted meat was still in the air.

"Vasily!" Annika called.

Jack looked up to see Vasily, the remaining *grup-*

perovka member, striding over. Right behind him were Thatë and Alli. Jack could see how protective of Alli the kid was, and he was grateful.

Annika signed to Vasily.

The big Russian gripped Baltasar by the back of his head and slammed it down and ground it into the smoking pile of bones. Flames leaped into Baltasar's beard and thick, curling sideburns and he began to yell. No one paid him the slightest attention. Then Annika delivered a vicious kick to his kidney and he fell onto his side. She rolled him onto his back so that he was looking directly up at her.

"Where is Arian Xhafa?"

He stared at her, his lips clamped firmly together.

"You *will* tell me what I want to know."

He smiled up at her. His beard continued to smolder.

"Vasily, please stay with our friends," Annika said.

She signaled to Thatë, who left Alli's side. He grabbed Baltasar by the back of his collar, and together they dragged him into the woods.

Jack and Alli stood together, with Vasily's tattooed hulk.

"I'm sorry for your loss," Jack said in Russian.

Vasily grunted, but Jack could see that he was grateful. The big man turned and went to scavenge weapons from inside the military vehicle.

As soon as the car had entered the swale, the driver had doused the lights and, at Annika's direction, they had exited, sprinting for the safety of the first line of pines. All except the driver, who had switched the lights back on and had set the car in motion with a homemade mechanism that had gradually released the gas pedal, so that the car would slow several thousand yards farther down the straightaway.

"What will Thatë do to him?" Alli said.

As if in answer, an unearthly howl pierced the night. It came again. There was nothing human about it, nothing familiar. The third howl made Alli shiver. It was impossible to imagine what kind of creature could make that sound, or what could be causing it.

Alli made a motion to go into the woods after Annika and Thatë, but Jack put a gentle hand on her forearm.

"I wouldn't," he said.

She looked at him. "She'll get what she wants, won't she?"

"I believe she always gets what she wants."

Alli nodded. "Did you suspect that Thatë was hers?"

Jack sighed. "I should have."

"In retrospect, it all makes so much sense: his position inside Xhafa's network, his being sent to Tetovo to spy on Xhafa, his commanding an elite group of Russians in Western Macedonia."

They saw Annika walking toward them. Thatë appeared out of the pine shadows a moment later. He was cleaning something on a wad of fallen pine needles; they couldn't see what and Jack refused to speculate on what it might be.

"I know where Xhafa is," she told them when she came abreast of them. "I also know where he's holding Liridona. Unfortunately they're on opposite sides of the city."

Thatë now joined them. There was no sign of whatever he'd been cleaning off, no sign on either of them that they had been interrogating a member of the enemy.

"These were not Xhafa's people," she said to Jack. "They were the Syrian's."

"I don't understand," Jack said.

"I didn't, either, until Thatë and I convinced this man—Baltasar—to confess. As I told you, the Syrian has stepped into Berns's shoes and become Xhafa's arms connection. This has been beneficial for Xhafa because, believe it or not, the Syrian's access to cutting-edge weaponry is better than Senator Berns's was. But the situation is now far more explosive. In return for the weapons, Xhafa allows the Syrian to export his particular brand of terrorism all over the world via Xhafa's private fleet of planes. The Syrian has connections with the Colombian and Mexican cartels, who are moving massive amounts of drugs from Afghanistan and the Golden Triangle in Southeast Asia for perhaps a half-dozen Muslim extremist organizations who are using the drug money to pay the Syrian for arms. It's a toxic global network with the Syrian at the center."

Jack had to stop himself from calling Paull immediately to tell him how much more dire the situation had become. Arian Xhafa was merely a symptom; the Syrian was the disease. He needed some answers first.

"What does all this have to do with the Syrian sending a death squad after us?"

"Let's get back in the car," Annika said.

When they were on their way back to the highway, she said, "For the past four months, the Syrian has been trying to get to my grandfather. Having failed in those attempts, I fear he's now coming after me as the only other way he can think of to get to Dyadya Gourdjiev."

"What does he want with your grandfather?" Alli asked.

"Dyadya Gourdjiev's brain. It's a storehouse of secrets," Annika said.

"That sounds pretty vague," Jack interjected.

All he got in response was one of Annika's enigmatic smiles. "Here's our problem. We need to get to Xhafa and the Syrian as quickly as possible, but the same holds true for Liridona. She's being held in a safehouse in the western part of Vlorë. The Syrian's compound is in the northeast."

"Which means we need to split up," Alli said. "Thatë and I will get Liridona."

"And I said no."

"You haven't," Alli said hotly. "Not explicitly."

He was about to once again expound on the subject of letting her loose in hostile territory when he caught Annika's expression, and he remembered their discussion about knowing what was best for Alli. He recalled how he'd bridled when she'd told him that she'd made the decision about what was best for him to know. He tried to tell himself that this was different, but the argument wasn't holding water.

He steeled himself for one of the most difficult things he had to say. Difficult because he suspected he knew what Annika's answer would be. "I promised Alli that she could ask you your opinion."

"I think she's right, Jack. We have two objectives that need to be addressed immediately." She searched his face. "If you agree with me, I'll send Vasily with her and Thatë, while you and I go on to the Syrian's compound."

Jack looked from her face to Alli's. This was an important moment for all of them, there was no question of it. But beyond the operational imperatives, he recognized this as an emotional crossroads in Alli's development. Despite her defiance and Annika's arguments, he knew the decision was on his shoulders. No matter her own feelings. Alli wouldn't go unless he gave her his blessing. In an odd way, he recognized this as the moment when a father gives his daughter to the man she is about to marry. In a very real way, she was passing out of his protection into a world filled with peril, heartache, and exultation. He also knew that she would never forgive him if he forbade her this mission. The intimate bond that had been forged between them would be ruptured and nothing he would ever do or say would restore it.

He thought of all the mistakes he'd made with Emma and, perhaps inevitably, he felt the cool wind as she settled in beside him.

—Emma?

"This is what must happen, Dad."

—Do you know? he said. Do you know if she'll be all right?

"I'm not a seer, Dad."

She had told him that already.

"But I'll be with her. I promise."

Jack took a deep breath. His gaze on both the women, he said, "What are we waiting for? Let's roll."

MORNING IN Washington found John Pawnhill eating eggs Benny at an old-school dive west of Dupont Circle. It was the kind of place where the same people came to have breakfast or lunch every day of the week, the kind of place tourists never heard about.

In the booth with him was his laptop, which he had hooked into the Middle Bay Bancorp secure server. It amused him no end that InterPublic Bancorp had hired his firm to perform the due diligence on Middle Bay's books. Of course, he had envisioned an endgame when, following Caroline Carson's detailed plan, he had set up the Syrian's cash flow business, via Gemini Holdings and a host of subsidiaries, through Middle Bay. It was just the kind of bank the Syrian needed in order to keep from being a PEP (a Politically Exposed Person) like Liberia's Charles Taylor, high-profile targets like deposed heads of states, paramilitary leaders, heads of drug cartels, and arms dealers like Viktor Bout, all powerful and clever individuals who, nevertheless, had eventually been caught. Caroline deemed Middle Bay a perfect target: large enough to have international connections, but small enough to pass under the radar of the various federal task forces involved in ferreting out terrorist and money laundering operations.

Pawnhill, Caroline Carson's eyes and hands on the ground, hadn't found the actual work all that difficult—she was the genie who lit his way. The American government's fractured intelligence structure allowed so much illicit international activity to fall between the cracks that you had to make an egregious mistake to come to its attention.

It was the private sector that gave him the most

fits, primarily Safe Banking Systems, a small Long Island company with proprietary software that was incredibly efficient at weeding out international banking transactions like the ones that provided the lifeblood of the Syrian's organization. God forbid the Feds should start using Safe Banking's software—he and the Syrian would have to fold their tents and find some other sucker nation through which to siphon illicit transactions.

Popping a bite of eggs Benny into his mouth, he pressed a key on his laptop and the last of the incriminating data on Middle Bay's servers was deleted. Next, he remotely ran a program Caroline had created that electronically shredded the deleted files, scrambled them, then overwrote the data again and again until there was, literally, nothing left. Finally, returning to the files from the last five years, he satisfied himself that it was as if the accounts he had opened and used had never existed. There was no gap, no scrap of data, not even a single kilobyte out of place. Satisfied at last, he closed all his programs, put the laptop in sleep mode, and slipped it into its case. He snagged the waitress and ordered fresh coffee, then settled himself to finish his breakfast.

His mind was hardly relaxed, however. He was haunted by the possibility that Billy Warren, having discovered the Gemini Holdings accounts, might have hit upon their significance. If he had, Pawnhill thought, surely he'd be smart enough to make electronic copies of the files. And he wouldn't keep them in his office at Middle Bay. The cops, and then Warren's family, had all been sifting through his apartment. Nothing had been found, which was a tremendous relief, because with all the activity, Pawnhill had been unable to send a team in to do his own snooping.

He hated loose ends. He also feared them. It was loose ends that invariably tripped you up. He couldn't afford to be tripped up. He couldn't afford to allow the Syrian's dealings to be exposed.

Ever since the Syrian had started preparations for the assassination of President Edward Carson, Pawnhill had been making contingency plans for the day when they might need to pull up stakes and disappear off the American intelligence radar. When the Syrian had seen which way the last U.S. election was going, he had vowed to have the incoming president killed. The last thing he wanted was a moderate president in power. The previous incumbent, surrounded by his bunkered neocons, had exported American aggression into the Islamic world with such a high degree of religious zealousness that his administration had done much of the Syrian's work for him. He had never had so many recruits clamoring to strap on packets of C4 and blow themselves up in the name of Islam. "A hated America is a weakened America" was a mantra the Syrian often used in his speeches to the new inductees.

It had been a dark day when Edward Carson had been killed in a car accident in Moscow. A random event for which the Syrian's people could not credibly claim authorship without coming into conflict with the Russian government. So, though the Syrian got what he wanted, he didn't get it in the way he wanted. There could be no propaganda value attached to President Carson's death, no righteous revenge that could be claimed, and so a once-in-a-lifetime opportunity had slipped through his fingers. Not one to dwell on missed chances, the Syrian had set his sights on other ways of bringing misfortune and disaster to the United States. He had sifted through many schemes, finally selecting one that had a particular appeal to him.

Pawnhill had received an MBA in international accounting from a major American university and then had gained an advanced international finance degree from Oxford. It was at Oxford that he had met the Syrian. Both had been using different names. They had had a brief but intense weeklong affair, after which they had amused themselves by exchanging girlfriends, much as, long ago, kids traded baseball cards.

Through a series of Gemini Holdings' subsidiaries set up by Caro, Pawnhill had begun to buy up residential mortgages, package them, and sell them to brokerages and other banks, with the promise of ultrahigh yields. The Syrian had directed Pawnhill to accomplish this utilizing the accounts he had set up in Middle Bay Bancorp. The banks and brokerages, in turn, sold these collateralized debt obligations to their clients.

It was astonishing to Pawnhill how quickly these CDOs got snapped up. Everyone involved was so busy making obscene amounts of money that virtually none of the institutions bothered to look inside the CDOs to see that many of the individual mortgages had been obtained from first-time homeowners without even a down payment or a check on whether they would be able to afford the balloon payments five years down the road. The few that did bother to look told their clients that they were buying a basket of mortgages so that if one or two failed it wouldn't matter. The problem was, when the reckoning came, all the mortgages failed.

By that time, the Syrian and Pawnhill had long since banked their profits, laundering them through the accounts at Middle Bay, and moving them so many times, through Caroline's maze of offshore accounts and shell companies in various quarters of the world, that they were untraceable.

Even Pawnhill had had no idea of the scope of the calamity the CDO frenzy would cause. In the aftermath, when the American financial system was on the brink of collapse, when the knives had come out and culprits were being hunted, it had been Pawnhill's job to keep Gemini Holdings and its now non-existent subsidiaries from being discovered by Safe Banking Systems, a task far more difficult than dealing with the inept probing of the federal authorities. This was where Pawnhill had earned his money. He'd kept the Syrian off the PEP lists and he'd provided Gemini with an impregnable safe harbor. He was just beginning to accept the Syrian's congratulations on a job well done when he'd become aware of Annika Dementieva.

She was the joker in the deck, an element he could not have accounted for because he had known nothing about her toxic relationship with Xhafa. The partnership had troubled him from the first—adding another personality to the mix was always a risk, and especially one as volatile as Xhafa's—but the Syrian had brushed aside his objections. *"I need this man,"* the Syrian had told him. *"His ambition has made him into the visible one, the leader of a new international organization. And he's perfect because his terrorists are also revolutionaries fighting for the freedom of Albanians inside Macedonia. It's a beautiful setup. He's seen as a hero to others outside Islam, which makes him invaluable. And, if anything should go wrong, he'll take the heat, while you and I melt away into the shadows."*

Pawnhill was certain that Dementieva had become aware of the Syrian's activities through her investigation of Arian Xhafa. But it was only in the last week that he had come upon an ambiguous and seemingly innocuous bit of data. Following it had proved immensely difficult and it had taken him three days to crack. What he discovered had floored him. In some way he could not fathom, Dementieva and Henry Holt Carson were communicating with one another. Curious enough, but what had put the fear of God in him was that the substance of their communication was Middle Bay Bancorp. This intel was so new that he'd not yet had a chance to bring it to the Syrian's attention. He knew he needed to do so as quickly as possible, but he also knew his boss wouldn't take it well at all. Therefore, he needed a piece of good news to offset the bad.

He thought for a time while he sipped his coffee, which was black and strong, the way he liked it. The recovery of a copy of the account data from Billy Warren would both appease and please the Syrian. Pawnhill's discovery of Carson and Dementieva discussing Middle Bay was an extraordinary stroke of luck. But just the fact that they were discussing Middle Bay at all had set off deep-level warning bells inside his head. Though he had long ago used a number of tried-and-true methods to put M. Bob Evrette in his hip pocket, there were always forces outside the bank he might have to contend with one day. For this and many other reasons he had aggressively pursued the forensic accounting assignment with InterPublic. He had done business with them before—another one of his fail-safe measures should he have felt the need to move accounts to a larger bank.

When the waitress passed by, he asked for a slice of devil's food cake. It was now possible to take a step back and see the InterPublic buyout of Middle Bay in a different light. The possibility that Carson suspected both the existence of the accounts and their connection with the Syrian and Arian Xhafa sent chills down his spine. By nature, Pawnhill was not prone to panic, but this development had disaster written all over it. This was why he had attacked Middle Bay's books with such thoroughness, wiping clean not only the accounts themselves, but any electronic footprint their deletion might leave behind.

Pawnhill finished his cake. Asking for the check, he threw some bills down on the table, leaving his customary large tip, and went out. It was late morning, humid, the clouds yellowish with the threat of a storm coming up from the south. He walked for a couple of blocks until he spotted a cruising taxi and took it to within three blocks of Billy Warren's apartment. After the crime scene investigators were done with it, Billy's father had slept there for a couple of nights, further impeding Pawnhill's access. But now the people Pawnhill had surveilling the building reported that the father was gone. The apartment was empty; it hadn't been visited in more than forty-eight hours.

Time, Pawnhill thought, to go in.

WHEN THE Syrian didn't hear from Baltasar at the appointed time, he spent a fruitless thirty seconds trying to raise him on his sat phone. Then, with a grim expression, he went to where Caro sat hunched over her computer and whispered in her ear.

Her fleeting startled expression was quickly replaced by one of resignation. All her work was either on her laptop or on remote servers in Holland. Nothing was ever saved on the desktop here. Still, she shut it down, removed the hard drive, and destroyed it. Then she packed up her laptop. The Syrian had gone to talk to Xhafa. She unlocked the drawer, removed *The Little Curiosity Shop,* and lovingly nestled it into the case beside the laptop.

As she was walking to where her shoes sat beside the front door, Taroq appeared.

He eyed her laptop case. She hardly left the compound, and never at night. "Where are you going?"

"The Syrian and I have a meeting outside the compound."

"At this hour?" Taroq frowned. "I was told nothing about a meeting."

Her expression hardened. She had no time for Taroq's jealousy. "You're told what you need to know, nothing more."

He stood looking at her for a moment. He was hurt, of course, but something had stirred his inner alarm. The Syrian was exceedingly deliberate in all his appointments and meetings. The word "spontaneous" did not exist in the Syrian's world, therefore anything that smacked of it was suspect.

She was spared further discourse on the subject as the Syrian returned and joined her at the door.

"Taroq, we'll be gone for several hours," he said without a hint that anything might be wrong. "In the interim, keep Xhafa here."

Taroq blinked. "Here?"

The Syrian offered an encouraging smile. "He'll be safer inside the compound."

They took the big black Lincoln Navigator that had been imported as a gift by one of the entities he supplied. He had many cars; he'd paid for none of them.

"You didn't want to take Taroq or a driver with us?" Caroline asked.

"In this situation," he said tersely, "it's best to travel light, the better to ensure that we arrive at our destination."

He drove very fast and with the lights off. He knew these back roads well.

"What's happened?" she asked.

"The enemy has arrived." He made a sweeping turn, then stepped heavily on the accelerator. "The enemy is coming."

She sat cradling her laptop case as if it were an infant. She supposed she should feel concerned, but, as usual, she felt nothing at all. "And just where is our destination?"

The Syrian stared straight ahead and smiled.

PAWNHILL MADE three circuits of Billy Warren's building without seeing anything out of the ordinary.

Via his Bluetooth earpiece, he was in constant cell contact with his surveillance team, who reported no police activity anywhere in the vicinity. It appeared as if the neighborhood had returned to the sleepy state it had been in before Warren's torture-murder caused a media frenzy. Since no photos of the crime scene had been leaked, even the tabloids, both print and online, had moved on to fresh fodder. And in America in this day and age there were more than enough scandals in Hollywood and inside the Beltway to feed even their insatiable appetites.

Pawnhill set a slim attaché case on the ground and opened it. The case was considerably smaller inside than out, but there was still room for a number of items, including a one-inch-thick laptop, a small zipped leather case, and latex gloves, hood, and booties. These he put on, then he took out the leather case, and snapped the lid shut.

He possessed an aptitude for vocations other than finance. These had been taught to him by the Syrian during the crazy time they'd enjoyed at Oxford. Unzipping the leather case, he selected several professional picks from a set. In no time, he was through the rear door. Warren's apartment was on the third floor. Pawnhill took the stairs; since childhood he'd had a fear of being trapped in an elevator. The same could be said for revolving doors.

The building was old, the stairs bare wood. He removed his loafers, climbing in absolute silence. Reaching the third floor, he went along the hall. He could hear a radio playing, also a baby crying briefly. Then only the music, muffled to almost all percussion, rose up the stairwell. No one was in the hall.

For some time he stood in front of Billy Warren's door, simply breathing. The yellow crime-scene tape had been taken down; everything appeared normal. Then, leaning forward, he put his ear to the wood. When he was certain no one was moving inside, he picked the lock. Then slowly he turned the doorknob and pushed the door inward.

He let the door swing all the way open. Standing on the threshold, he stepped back into his loafers. From the attaché case, he produced a plastic hood with elastic around the opening for his face. He slipped it over his head and adjusted it. Now he was protected from inadvertently leaving a hair in the apartment. Then, softly and silently, he entered, closing the door behind him.

He found himself in a small three-room apartment, bright and relatively neat, considering all the recent activity. It was furnished in fairly upscale style, tasteful in a modern way, but without much flair. Placing his attaché case on the carpet beside the coffee table, he stood in the center of the room, turning slowly in a circle in order to take in everything that came in sight. He went methodically through the bedroom and bathroom without finding anything. Returning to the living room, he let his eye fall on one piece of furniture after another—the sofa, the pair of easy chairs, the rug, a Travertine marble–topped coffee table on which was a ceramic decorative vase, a green crystal sculpture of a frog, a stack of coasters, along with a single coaster marred by a water stain. Pawnhill looked more closely. It was logical to assume that the glass that had recently sat on the coaster had been taken by the forensic team, along with Warren's personal computer and cable modem.

Against one wall was a modern lacquer sideboard above which was a cabinet that held a bookshelf stereo, stacks of CDs, a flat-screen TV, a cable box, Blu-Ray DVD player, and a couple of popular commercial DVDs. The rest of the space was taken up by books—mostly texts, but also a handful of contemporary thrillers—and a couple of photo albums. Pawnhill leafed through one without interest. He wasn't interested in a visual chronicle of Billy Warren's early life. The second held Warren's doctorate paper, according to the title page. Pawnhill slid it back beside its twin. Then he opened every CD jewel case and DVD package. In this case, he was looking for a DVD onto which Warren might have burned the incriminating data. He'd already tried to hunt down a USB thumb drive that Warren might have used for the purpose.

The result was that after spending almost an hour carefully ransacking the apartment, he had found nothing. He was on his way out when his gaze happened to fall on the stack of coasters, which were discs that seemed to him larger than normal. He went through each one in the stack, but they were precisely what they purported to be.

Then he picked up the coaster with the water stain and turned it over. There, winking up at him with its rainbow glimmers, was the slick surface of a DVD.

THIRTY

THE SAFEHOUSE was a three-story building on the corner of a quiet residential street. An alley along one side revealed a wall almost completely covered with mature ivy vines. There was a streetlight at the rear, but it wasn't on. The other side of the house overlooked a narrow, heavily shaded street. The windows had been boarded up. At the rear was what looked and smelled like an open sewer. As they had crossed the city, they had observed periodic blackouts; many of the intersections were in chaos. Homemade banners announced student protests starting at dawn.

"There's only one way to do this," Alli said when she, Thatë, and Vasily had completed their surveillance circuit of Xhafa's safehouse. "You take me in."

"Impossible," Thatë said at once.

Vasily watched the two of them with complete impassivity.

"The place is a virtual fortress," Alli said. "There's only one way in or out. What's our other alternative, to let Vasily bull his way in?"

Thatë licked his lips nervously.

"As far as these people know you're part of Xhafa's American operation. You have the medallion, you know the code words. You'll bring me in as a new cherry."

Thatë grinned suddenly. "More like a cherry bomb."

Alli turned to Vasily. "Do you have a better idea?"

"Once you're inside, I can't help you," he said.

"But you can," Alli said. "Give us—what, Thatë?— fifteen minutes, then create a diversion."

"A big one," Thatë added.

Vasily flexed his muscles and hefted the flame-thrower he'd salvaged from the military vehicle. "No fucking problem."

"Okay, then." Thatë glanced from one to the other. "Let's synchronize watches."

WHEN ALAN Fraine was a decade younger, he was a successful hostage negotiator. Before that, he was the best sharpshooter Metro had seen for more than twenty years. People inside the department still talked about him and the string of astonishing hits he'd made without ever harming a civilian even though some of them were standing right next to or right in front of his target.

Stepping up off the street had been a mixed bless-ing. It had brought with it a higher salary, an entrée into the inner circle of Metro police, as well as an opportunity to come to the mayor's attention, never a bad thing in the highly politicized atmosphere of D.C. Occasionally, though, when he played poker with the mayor, or with his belly full with rich food, he felt a shadow of sadness pass through him, as memories of his salad days surfaced, and he turned briefly melancholy.

Following his electrifying phone conversation with Dennis Paull, he'd got to work, pulling together a team of experts from all divisions of Metro—a half-dozen men he knew personally and trusted implicitly.

They had no difficulty locating John Pawnhill. Almost immediately, they reported that he was traveling with a crew of three—an antisurveillance team. So he ordered his men up onto the rooftops. He himself and one of his team rode Harleys, dressed in Hell's Angels leathers they had borrowed from the impound room at HQ.

The moment Pawnhill pick-locked his way into Billy Warren's building, Fraine gave the order for his men to go to work. In short order, they had picked up all three of Pawnhill's men. He spent a fruitless thirty minutes interrogating them.

"This is useless, they won't give me anything," he said when he'd turned away from the third of the men. "Tony, take them down to HQ for arraignment."

"On what charge?" Tony said.

"Suspicion of terrorism," Fraine said. "A matter of national security, so no calls whatsoever."

"Got it." Tony passed them off to the patrol officers they'd called in.

"Go with them," Fraine said. "I don't want any fuckups."

"Yessir."

Fraine returned his attention to the rear of Billy Warren's building. Then a thought struck him and he turned back. "Tony, on second thought keep them here. I want them in a lineup."

Tony laughed.

THATË'S ABSOLUTE calmness served to keep Alli's mind clear as they approached the front of the safehouse. Apart from the two men lounging on the steps, it didn't look much different than the other residences on this fringe of the city.

The guards rose, their bodies tensing, as Thatë approached with Alli in tow. She was squirming, trying to get away from him. Her fear and anxiety, expertly feigned, had the expected effect on the guards. They smiled and engaged Thatë in a short exchange, during which Thatë produced his pendant. Another even terser conversation ensued, which Alli assumed was an exchange of code phrases.

She must have been right because one of the guards nodded and went up the stairs while Thatë dragged her along. The guard unlocked the door. As she passed alongside him, he gave her a hard pinch. Snarling, she lunged at him, and bit off the lobe of his ear.

He yelped, the other guard came running, and Thatë kicked him hard in the groin. He went to his knees without a sound, and Thatë drove the heel of his shoe into the side of his head. At the same time, Alli slammed the heel of her hand into the bleeding guard's mouth, then drove her knee into his solar plexus. As he went down, she took his head in her hands and smacked it against the side of the door frame.

They went inside, closing the door behind them.

PAWNHILL OPENED the attaché case and thumbed the laptop out of sleep mode, inserted the DVD, and had a look. Sure enough, the Gemini Holdings account data was there. Enormously relieved, he closed the attaché case and pressed the metal tabs home one at a time.

Exiting the apartment, he made sure the front door was locked before he closed it. In the stairwell, he took off his hood and booties, but kept the gloves on. The same radio was playing, the music louder now. The baby had returned to squalling. The stairwell smelled of cold pizza and the grease that's left in a bucket of KFC when the chicken is eaten.

Down on the first floor, he stood very still, listening for any anomalous noise. Hearing none, he pulled the locking lever down, opened the rear door, and stepped out. The moment he did so, a thin man in Hell's Angels leathers appeared.

"Mr. Pawnhill." He gestured. "Walk with me."

Pawnhill said, "Do I know you?"

"You will," Fraine said.

Pawnhill shook his head. "I don't think so."

Fraine pulled back the flap of leather jacket to show his service revolver.

Smiling with his teeth, Pawnhill revealed the Sig Sauer in its shoulder holster.

"You don't want a shoot-out," Fraine said.

Pawnhill moved his hand toward the butt of the Sig Sauer. "You ever see *Reservoir Dogs*?"

"Actually, it's a favorite of mine. But that won't happen today." Fraine called and two Metro officers paraded Pawnhill's team, hands behind their heads, into view.

"You're out of uniform," Pawnhill said.

"Surveillance work." Fraine grinned, then motioned with his chin. "Whatcha got in there? Something you picked up while you were ransacking Billy Warren's apartment?"

"Your people did too good a job. I didn't find anything."

"Uh-huh. Walk the attaché case halfway to where I'm standing, set it down on its side, lay your weapon next to it, then back up."

"I told you I didn't find—"

"I have men on the rooftops," Fraine said. "If you don't comply, you'll be dead inside of thirty seconds."

Pawnhill shrugged and followed Fraine's instructions. When he had backed up sufficiently, Fraine said, "Now raise your hands and don't move."

"I wouldn't think of it."

While his men kept a bead on Pawnhill, Fraine walked over to the attaché case. He pocketed the Sig Sauer, then put his hands on the snaps.

"Go ahead," Pawnhill said. "I've got nothing to hide."

The snaps popped open and Fraine lifted the lid. Instantly, there was a loud hiss, and a thick black cloud billowed into the air. Fraine leaped back, his eyes already on fire. The *pop-pop-pop* of rifle shots were heard, but when the smoke cleared Pawnhill was nowhere to be seen.

Fraine did not have to order his team to spread

out in a dragnet; they were already sprinting in every direction.

One of the officers came up to him, slipped an oxygen mask over his head, and made sure he was breathing okay. "Shifty fucking bastard," he said. "Cheer up, sir. At least we have the evidence."

Fraine's throat and nostrils felt as if they had been scrubbed raw with sandpaper. Coughing still, he returned to the open attaché case and crouched down. Then he tore off his oxygen mask. The acrid stink of acid stung his eyes.

"Godammit!"

Everything inside the case was melted. He could see the vague outline of a laptop computer and a curled section of what once must have been a DVD. All useless now.

Jack and Annika were crouched in the darkness of the trees surrounding Arian Xhafa's compound. They both wore lightweight backpacks into which Annika had placed various paraphernalia.

"According to Baltasar, there are seven guards and two attack dogs protecting the compound," she said.

"Do you believe him?"

She glanced at him. "Do you have a better idea?"

Jack pointed. "One thing your victim failed to mention is the electrified razor wire on top of the wall."

Annika rose. "Let's take a walk."

They picked their way slowly around the compound until they came to the rear. Then she pointed upward to the branches of an ancient oak tree, two of which arched over the wall and its lethal top.

"How are you at climbing?" she asked.

They moved as close to the wall as they dared. Jack wove his fingers together, Annika stepped onto them, and he launched her up toward the lowest branch. By stretching to her limit, she was just able to grab hold of it with one hand. Jack pushed her upward several inches and she swung one leg over the branch, rolling her torso until she lay horizontally on it. From her backpack, she uncoiled a length of rope, tied one end around the branch, and threw the other end to him.

A moment later, Jack had joined her on the branch. With his weight, it dipped down perilously close to the razor wire, and they began to wriggle their way toward the trunk, over the wire and wall.

They found themselves hanging above a courtyard garden that smelled strongly of citrus.

"Just a matter of time before the dogs scent us," Jack whispered. He looked around. "Get me a rock about fist size."

While Annika crawled across the branch and shimmied down the rope, Jack slipped off his backpack and jacket, unbuttoned his shirt, and, using a knife, slit out the entire back. Then he put it back on, and the jacket over it. As Annika was climbing up the rope, he unzipped his pants and relieved his bladder into the square of cloth until it was thoroughly saturated.

By this time, Annika had regained the branch, but now a wind had sprung up, one that bobbed the branch up and down. Again and again, it dipped dangerously close to the electrified wire. Annika froze, waiting for the wind to subside, but it didn't. In fact, it started to blow harder. Closer and closer she came, until Jack stretched out on the limb and slowly pulled her toward him and off the far end of the branch.

He took the rock from her, wrapped it in the soaked square of shirt, then tied it off with a piece of plastic cord ripped from one of the outside pockets of his backpack.

"Ready?" he whispered.

Annika nodded, and he threw the makeshift bundle into the far left corner of the garden. Almost at once, a howling commenced and two huge dogs came racing and skidding around the corner of the house, heading directly toward the unfamiliar spoor invading their territory. Jack and Annika shinnied down, keeping the tree trunk between themselves and the dogs. They reached the opposite corner of the villa and pressed themselves against the cool stucco wall as a pair of guards, AK-50s at the ready, sprinted into the garden to see what was driving the dogs into a frenzy.

They had very little time before the dogs scented them. Jack opened a side window and Annika climbed through. He was about to follow her when he heard a stirring in the shadows and another guard appeared. The moment he saw Jack he swung his assault rifle toward Jack's midsection. Stepping toward him, Jack shoved the barrel of the AK-50 to one side and delivered a sharp blow to the guard's throat. Then he grabbed the assault rifle out of the staggering man's hands and drove the butt into the bridge of his nose. The guard went down and stayed down. Slinging the AK-50 over his shoulder, Jack dragged the unconscious guard to the windowsill and tipped him inside. Then he followed him in.

He was in a darkened bedroom. Closing the window behind him, he looked around for Annika, but she was nowhere to be seen. Cursing under his breath, he stepped out into the hallway, looked both ways, then went to his right. He soon found himself in the large kitchen with its line of windows overlooking the garden. Two guards lay sprawled on the floor. Three down. Two were outside with the dogs. That meant one last guard left. He had to find Xhafa and the Syrian before the other two guards grew suspicious and decided to check the interior of the house. He unslung the AK-50.

Moving stealthily, he came upon the vast living room with its prayer rugs, modern task chair, and desk. He soon discovered that the computer was without its hard drive. He saw a connection for a high-speed modem but the modem itself was missing. He turned. Had Xhafa somehow known they were coming? Had he and the Syrian abandoned the house, leaving the guards as bait?

Then he heard the gunshot and he broke into a run.

THATË, HIS hand around Alli's arm, was met almost immediately by an Albanian thug who was clearly higher up the crooked ladder than the guards outside.

"A new cherry," Thatë said. "And a feisty one."

The thug grinned. "We have a cure for that." He ogled her openly. "We'll break her spirit soon enough." Laughing at her expression, he grabbed at one of her breasts.

Thatë pulled her away before she could receive more of a mauling. "Absolutely not. Now that Edon is gone, Arian wants this one for himself. Where are the special cherries housed?"

"Third floor in the rear." The Albanian frowned. "But I didn't hear anything about another special."

"What d'you mean?"

"We have Edon's sister up there. She belongs to Xhafa."

Thatë sighed. "I only do what he tells me. Call him, if you need to."

"That's just what I intend to do."

The Albanian pulled out his cell and Alli jammed her elbow into his kidney. Thatë used the barrel of his handgun on the Albanian's neck, cracking several vertebrae. The Albanian crumpled to the floor. Thatë nodded at Alli and, together, they raced down the corridor and up the central staircase.

Behind them, the Albanian's cell activated with an incoming call.

"Ilir, are you there? Ilir, check in."

ANNIKA FOUND Xhafa in a small room, perhaps a study, because there were piles of books on the floor. He was sitting in a chair, a Sig Sauer in one hand.

"I knew you'd come," he said. "Like a dog to its own stink." He lifted the handgun and pulled the trigger.

Annika, in shadow, was already moving. The bullet whizzed by her ear. Then she kicked out with her right boot, connecting with the point of Xhafa's chin. The chair tumbled over backward. Reaching out, she plucked the Sig Sauer from him and pulled the chair back onto its feet. Xhafa sat dazed, blood drooling from a corner of his mouth.

"Sure I came back," she said. "You're the dog, you're the stink."

That's when the barking of the dogs rang through the house.

Xhafa smiled through his pain. "Bang, bang," he said. "You're dead."

THIRTY-ONE

THEY WERE pounding up the safehouse stairs when Alli felt a breeze on her cheek, cold enough to make her shiver.

"They're coming."

It was Emma. Alli fought down a certain terror. Emma spoke to Jack only when he was near death or in dire straits. Was it the same with her?

"Prepare yourself, Alli."

"Company," Alli said to Thatë.

—Emma, stay with me.

Two men appeared on the second-floor landing. The moment they saw Alli and Thatë, they opened fire with AK-50s.

"I guess our cover's blown," Alli said as she scrambled out of the way.

Thatë opened fire with his assault rifle and the two men scattered. He advanced upward, Alli in his wake. She saw one of the men above them prone on the landing, aiming his weapon at Thatë, and she shot him. Her hands were firm, her mind unclouded. These were the lessons Jack had taught her, even before he'd brought her to the firing range for the first time. A firecracker could have gone off next to her and her concentration wouldn't have wavered. Jack was a zen master when it came to concentration. For him, it was a necessity. In order to function more or less normally in the world took enormous amounts of concentration on his part. Anything flat with letters on it looked like a pinwheel or the inside of a lava lamp.

They were almost at the landing. Where was the other Albanian? As they reached the second floor, Thatë indicated that she go left while he went right. To the left, the banister ran along the second floor for about fifteen feet before arching upward on the flight to the third floor. Just before she reached the landing, Alli swung onto the banister. Here her smallness and light weight were a distinct advantage. Hooking her ankles through the uprights, she inched her way along. Behind her, she heard a spray of bullets and, turning, saw Thatë coming toward her. He was pointing upward; he had nailed the other Albanian.

They launched themselves up the staircase. Alli checked her watch. Less than four minutes until Vasily started his diversion.

They were only partway up, when a commanding voice called from behind them. "Stop where you are! Lay down your weapons and kneel with your hands behind your head!"

JACK COULD see Annika in the shadows, heard her speaking, presumably to Xhafa, when the barking of the attack dogs announced their entry into the house. He turned and, in a half-crouch, prepared to defend their position.

The first of the dogs appeared, its claws skittering

on the wooden floor. Jack got off a shot just after it saw him. He hit a flank, but that hardly stopped the animal. It merely bared its teeth and came on. He shot it in the chest, but he was distracted by the sight in his peripheral vision of the second dog. The first dog was hardly slowed down by the two bullets and was barely two feet from Jack when he shot it in the head. It dropped in front of him, but now the second dog was upon him, its long claws extended, its jaws snapping as if it were rabid.

The sheer weight of it bowled him over. He jammed the barrel of the AK-50 between its jaws to keep it at bay, but its claws were tearing through his jacket as it if were made of tissue. He cracked his elbow into the side of the dog's head, but that only made it angrier. The dog had hold of the AK-50 and wasn't going to let go. He twisted it so hard, he heard the animal's neck vertebrae click. In that moment, he let go of the weapon and used his crooked arms to jerk the dog's neck even farther. The vertebrae cracked like a gunshot, the light went out of the animal's eyes, and its weight slumped on top of him.

He took a deep breath and was about to retrieve the assault rifle from the dog's clamped jaws when a voice said, "I'll take that."

He found himself staring up into the face of one of the guards.

ALLI TURNED to see the man with one green eye, the other blue; monstrous eyes, revealing a pitiless and relentless soul. She shivered and even Emma, beside her, seemed to quail.

"He'll kill you, Alli. Give him the chance and he'll kill you."

Thatë made the mistake of trying to reason with him. "I work for Arian Xhafa. We're here for Liridona. We have no quarrel with you."

"The blood you've spilled is quarrel enough." One eye seemed to speak while the other was deep in scheming. He was addressing Thatë but seemed to impale Alli with his implacable gaze. "No one leaves my safehouse."

"Yours?" Thatë shook his head. "This safehouse belongs to Arian Xhafa."

"Arian Xhafa belongs to me."

The Syrian lifted a pearl-handled M1911 but before anyone could react, a ferociously hot fireball raced up the stairs with a massive lightning crack. The Syrian turned. Thatë shot him in the shoulder, but the Syrian, seemingly unperturbed, fired the .45. The full-metal-jacket bullet buried itself in Thatë's chest, throwing him back against the stairs. From that semi-prone position, he fired again and again, forcing the Syrian back into a room on the second floor.

"Thatë!" Alli cried, bending down to see to his wound.

But he thrust her roughly away. "Upstairs. Find Liridona and get out of here. I'll keep this fucker out of your way."

"I'm not leaving you."

"Don't be stupid." He glanced up at her. "This is what I've trained for, this is my life. Now leave me to it."

He began to fire again.

"Thatë—"

He shoved her hard. "Go!"

"*Run, Alli.*"

Tears running down her face, she turned and bolted up the stairs.

ANNIKA IGNORED the shots and the animal growling that came from the room behind her. This appeared to surprise Xhafa, until he said, "You're not alone."

Without a word, she hauled him out of the chair and, spinning him around, slammed him down on the floor.

"You'll always be mine, you know," he said. "Whatever you do, until the day you die."

Annika straddled him. Taking a huge bowie knife out of her backpack, she proceeded to strip off his clothes, baring his back. The muscles rippled in anticipation.

Pressing the blade point to his skin, Annika proceeded to score seven concentric circles into his back, carving each circle deep into the muscles. Blood flowed, Xhafa screamed and kept on screaming.

CAROLINE WAS sitting in the passenger seat of the Syrian's car, cradling her laptop, when she heard the volleys of gunshots. The car was parked a block away from the safehouse but the cracks sounded much closer. She turned to look out the side window just as Taroq pulled the door open.

She got out and Taroq embraced her. For all the emotion inside her, she might have been embraced by a boxcar.

"You had no trouble following us?"

He shook his head. "None at all."

"All right. Let's go."

He pointed off to their left. "My car is this way."

At his side, she walked quickly away from the Syrian's car and never looked back.

THE FIRST screams caused the guard to look beyond where Jack lay, buried beneath the attack dog. In that moment, Jack located his Glock, brought it out, and shot the guard in the head. He was taking no chances. Grunting, he began to shrug off the dog's corpse, when it juddered back into him, struck by two bullets fired from the second guard's gun. He slumped to the floor as if shot.

Through slitted eyes, he saw the boots of the second guard coming hesitantly toward him. He was taking a calculated risk, he knew, but the dog was so big that it covered all of his torso and head. His hand with the Glock in it was beneath the attack dog's neck and so able to move.

When he saw the boots close enough, he edged the muzzle of the pistol forward, tilting it up. It was then that the left boot slammed down on the Glock, trapping it.

At once, Jack let it go and, slithering out from under the animal, fired at the guard with the handgun in his left hand. He missed, and the guard slammed the barrel of his pistol into Jack's cheek. Even as the pain jolted him, Jack stepped forward, inside the guard's defense, delivering a flurry of vicious blows to his adversary's head and neck.

Undeterred, the guard drove his fist into Jack's wounded side, and Jack crumpled in agony. Grinning, the guard stood over him, pointing his pistol at Jack's head. One instant his finger was about to pull the trigger, the next the blade of a bowie knife was buried hilt-deep in the left side of his chest.

He looked up, past Jack, but he was already arching backward and all his glazing eyes saw was the ceiling before his heart, sliced in two, ceased to beat.

Jack looked back over his shoulder and saw Annika standing in the doorway.

ALLI HAD just reached the third floor when she heard the pounding of boots. She had just enough time to duck into a room before six or seven armed men came charging down the hall, drawn by the gunfire and the smoke and flames from the ground floor. When they had passed, she darted out, running full-tilt down the hall. She flew by rooms with young girls in them, lying on mean pallets, or, more likely, deep in drug-induced slumber. She wanted to free them all but in their current state and under the circumstances that was impossible. She was here to find Liridona.

Liridona was in the back room, caged like an animal, on her hands and knees because there was no room to stand. Alli rattled the door, but it was padlocked.

"Edon sent me," she said to the terrified girl. "Where's the key?"

When Liridona failed to answer, Alli shouted, "Stand back!" Then she shot off the padlock, opened the door, and brought Liridona out.

"Do you speak English?"

When Liridona nodded, she said, "My name is Alli. Edon sent me."

"Edon is alive?"

"Alive and well," Alli assured her. "Now it's time to get you out of here."

"But how?"

A good question. Thatë said there was only one entrance. But Vasily was there and the guards would be clogging the entrance, putting out the fire. What to do?

"Where do the guards sleep?"

"We're not allowed to go—"

"Quickly, now!" Alli commanded her out of her terror-induced stupor. "Show me the way!"

Liridona stumbled down the hall, Alli at her back, guarding her like a lion with its cub.

JACK, COVERED in blood, heaved the attack dog's corpse off him and rose shakily to his feet.

"Are you all right?" Annika said.

"I should be asking you that." He brushed by her into the room. "Good God."

Arian Xhafa was on the floor, his naked back a mass of bleeding wounds. His fingers were curling and uncurling spastically and he was trying to get up on his hands and knees.

Jack walked toward him. "What the hell did you do to him?"

"What he did to me." Annika was right beside him.

He watched Xhafa crawling his way toward the chair.

"Only worse."

"Only worse," she affirmed.

Jack glanced at her. "Is it over now?"

Her carnelian eyes were hard and, also, he thought, a bit sad.

"You know better than that."

Behind her, Xhafa, hands on the chair's arms, pulled himself up.

"I only counted five guards," he said. "And where is the Syrian?"

Out of the corner of his eye, he saw Xhafa's right hand slide beneath the chair's cushion. In an instant, he had whipped around, a 9mm in his hand. Pushing Annika, Jack squeezed off two shots. One passed through Xhafa's neck, the second took off the back of his head.

Annika did not turn around. Instead, she stared into Jack's eyes. "All that work," she said, "for nothing."

Was she serious or being facetious? That was the thing about Annika. You could never be sure.

LIRIDONA LED Alli into a warren of well-furnished, almost opulent rooms. She crossed the floor and opened one of the windows. This was the side where the ivy grew thick against the wall.

Liridona, at her shoulder, looked wide-eyed. "What are you doing?"

"Getting out of here."

"I can't." Liridona shook her head wildly. "I'm afraid of heights."

"We have no choice. This is the only way out."

Liridona shrank back. "No."

"Look." Alli pointed to the streetlight that rose up at the rear corner of the house. "All we have to do is get over there and it will give us an easy way down."

"I can't. Please."

"I won't let you die here." Alli grabbed her. "Put your arms around me." She felt the girl's rail-thin body as she climbed onto her back. "Now when I swing out, wrap your legs around me, too."

Holding on to the window sash, Alli put one leg over the sill, and grabbed for the nearest vine before realizing that their combined weight was too much for her.

Then she felt Emma close beside her.

"Use your fingers and your toes."

Alli nodded. Quickly, she untied her boots, kicked them off, and dropped them out the window. Then she swung her leg out again, this time using her toes as well as her fingers to hold on to the ivy where the vines were thickest.

Behind her, Liridona sounded like she was praying. Across they went, moving laterally, hand over hand toward the streetlight. After three handholds, Alli could feel the weight trying to drag them off the vine. Then she heard a brief ripping, as one part of the vine pulled away from the wall, and her heart beat like a triphammer.

Liridona, her eyes squeezed shut, interrupted her prayers to whisper, "What was that?"

Alli was too busy to answer her, and Liridona did not ask again. A fist of ice had formed in the pit of her stomach and she fought down a wave of panic. She thought of Jack and took deep breaths to calm herself, but the streetlight still looked as if it was a football field away. For a long, gut-wrenching moment, they swung above the narrow concrete walkway between buildings. If they fell, there was nothing soft to break their landing. Gritting her teeth, she returned to crabbing her way across the network of vines. One step at a time, she told herself. One step at a time.

They were still several arms' lengths from the streetlamp when the vine gave way. Liridona shrieked as they began to fall.

Kicking out against the wall, Alli swung them back and forth like a pendulum. At the apex of the arc nearest the streetlight, she let go with fingers and toes. For a moment they flew through the air. Then the streetlight smacked her in the stomach and they slid down until she could get her arms and legs around it. She hung there for a moment with Liridona shivering on her back. Then she inched them down. When they reached the cement, Liridona continued to cling to Alli, sobbing with relief and shock. Alli rocked her for a moment, then pushed her gently against the side of the house.

"Stay here," she whispered.

Liridona's eyes went wide. "Where are you going?"

"I can't leave Thatë and Vasily behind."

She went quickly along the side of the safehouse until she reached the front corner. Peeking around, she saw Xhafa's men drag Thatë's body out the front door and pile it on Vasily's corpse.

PART FOUR

BLOOD TRUST

The Present

And so time turns a corner, or flows down a well, only to return to the place where it began.

THIRTY-TWO

ALLI WAS in the middle of the student riot in the city plaza. The fog, a metallic brown from gunpowder, garbage, and the grit of the streets, thrust itself like a living thing against her. She was buffeted by the currents of running people. Screams found her, as insistent as the tolling of bells from the cathedral, which seemed to watch indifferently with its elongated El Greco face.

In the melee, Alli lost sight of Liridona altogether, and her heart beat even faster in her chest as she plowed her way through the mob, nearer now to the mass of truncheons lifting and falling, to the sprays of blood and bone, to the tilted bodies, to the cries of pain and terror.

Then she spotted one of Arian Xhafa's men, his tall frame sinister as a bat, rising for a moment above the heads of the students. Her way lay directly in the path of the militia. She calculated that there was no time to circle around, so she plunged ahead until she was close to the line of truncheons, advancing en masse like a phalanx of Roman soldiers. On hands and knees, she made herself inconspicuous, crawling through the churning legs of the militia until she eeled her way to the other side.

Scrambling to her feet, she looked around and spotted the men pushing Liridona around a corner. On the fringe of the mob at last, she ran toward the corner. Running with her heart in her mouth, running toward the sudden roar of gunshots that spurted at her from around the corner.

"No!" she cried. "No!"

Hurtling around the corner, she was jerked off her feet. She stared into the monstrous eyes of the Syrian. The blue eye, the green eye. They regarded her a if each had a separate intelligence, both cold as permafrost.

From somewhere out of her sight, she heard Liridona weeping, and, like glass shattering against stone she began to struggle free. But the Syrian shoved the barrel of his pearl-gripped .45 into her mouth.

"Once again, quiet." His voice a constricting iron band. "Before the end."

The air shivered as Edon, appearing out of nowhere, swung a tire iron into the Syrian's back. His body arched forward and he let go of the .45 as he fell. Darting down, Alli picked it up.

"How—?" She aimed the pistol at the Syrian, but she heard Liridona's scream.

"There's no time!" Edon shouted, turning and running down a dank back alley.

Alli sprinted after her. "Stay back!" she called "Stay back, Edon!"

Catching up with the girl, Alli ran past her. She could see Liridona between the two men. On the run, she shot one of them in the shoulder. The other urned his handgun on her and she shot him dead. The first man grabbed his wounded shoulder, then, shaking himself like a dog coming in from the rain, ran straight at her. Liridona leaped, barreled into the back of his knees, and he stumbled down onto the filthy concrete. Liridona scooped up his handgun and, as he twisted his torso up and took a swing at her, shot him point-blank in the face.

THIRTY-THREE

"SHE'S REMARKABLE, you know."

Annika, sitting next to Jack on the ferry from Vlorë to Brindisi, on the eastern coast of Italy, looked over to where Alli was talking animatedly with Edon and Liridona. The first thing they needed to do when they reached Italy was to go clothes shopping.

Jack was dog-tired, and he ached all over. He wondered whether he had a fever. He'd lost his antibiotics somewhere during their strange and bloody odyssey. It would be good to get home.

"Is that what you meant to say?" His voice was soft.

Annika glanced at him for a moment. "I feel . . . I don't know, I feel close to her."

"She feels the same way toward you."

This brought the ghost of a smile to Annika's face. "I must get back to my grandfather."

"Surely he has people taking care of him."

She nodded. "Very good people."

"Then come back to D.C. with us."

Her eyes looked inward. "Maybe," she murmured, as if to herself, "if only for a little while."

Now it was Jack's turn to look at the three girls across the companionway. "I saw you talking with Liridona."

Annika was silent for a moment. The ferry rocked lightly from side to side. The great diesel engines vibrated through the decks.

"She told me the secret that cost Arjeta her life, and almost cost her hers. Arjeta had been in the compound in Vlorë. Apparently, it wasn't Arian Xhafa's compound. It belonged to the Syrian."

"The man Alli encountered at the safehouse and then again in the street."

Annika nodded. "The Syrian had a woman with him in the compound."

"A mistress?"

"Possibly, but from what I've heard about the Syrian I doubt it. No, this woman is a computer prodigy. She handles all of the Syrian's international transactions."

"A computer whiz."

"A first-class hacker."

Jack shook his head. "Okay, but why would the Syrian consider her a secret worth killing for?"

"Because," Annika said, "her name is Caroline Carson."

GUNN SAT in his car, smoking a cigarette. He was parked in the lot of a sleazy motel off a highway in suburban Maryland. From what he could see during the forty minutes he'd been parked, the motel was a trysting place for traveling salesmen and account executives getting their rocks off with someone else's secretary. Every once in a while a delivery would be made to one of the rooms. When that happened Gunn got out of the car and followed the delivery boy t see if he'd been summoned to room 261.

Gunn, following John Pawnhill like a bloodhound had seen him make his escape and was briefly im pressed. He'd seen him get picked up by a man Gunn didn't recognize. He had followed them out here t this motel with its blinking neon sign, buzzing fluo rescent lights, and a soda machine that didn't work The sound of passing traffic was a roar as relentles as the surf.

At 10:52, a white car with the logo of a nearb Chinese restaurant pulled into the parking lot. Onc again, Gunn removed himself from his car and stretching, strode after the young man. He delivere two large paper bags to room 261. Gunn saw glimpse of Pawnhill's driver as he took possession o the food and handed over some money. He screwe the suppressor back onto his Glock. The delivery ma went down the stairs, got into his car, and drove away

Gunn walked up to the door of room 261 an knocked.

"Who is it?" a voice came from the other side o the door.

"You didn't give me enough money," Gunn sai in a passable simulation of the delivery man's voice.

The door opened a crack, Gunn shoved his Glock through it, and shot the driver squarely in the fore head. As the driver's body arched backward, Gunn kicked in the door and strode inside. Pawnhill threw a white cardboard container of food at Gunn. Gunn dodged away, aimed, and shot Pawnhill twice in the

hest. Pawnhill crumpled. Gunn walked up to him
nd, for good measure, put two more bullets into
im. Then he turned and left.

THE NIGHT is a time for memories, Vera thought as
he lay on her bed in Fearington. She remembered her
hildhood, when she and Caro shared a room. Of
ourse, they each had sumptuously decorated bed-
ooms, but she and Caro had insisted on being to-
ether at night. She remembered how Caro used to
ead to her from her favorite book, *The Little Curiosity Shop,* stories about a fabulous old store in
London's World's End, crammed to the rafters with
nagical wonders. She sat up suddenly and, swinging
er legs over the side, stared at the bed across from
er. Alli Carson's bed. It was empty now, of course.
Who knew where Alli was, or if she was still alive?
Vera glanced over at the foot of the bed, and then,
because she couldn't help herself, she stared at the
neatly tucked-in sheet, she stared at the pillow with
ts black case imprinted with white skulls. Strange
ucking girl, but, oddly, she missed her. Maybe she
nissed hating her.

She lay back down, but knew right away that sleep
vas on some other continent. So she did what she
always did when she couldn't sleep—went to her
desk, turned on the task lamp, and fired up her lap-
op. She was going to open her Web browser when
she noticed a new folder on her desktop. It was titled
"curio_cabinet."

She felt a little thrill go through her. There had been
a curio cabinet in *The Little Curiosity Shop* where all

the most magical items were kept under lock and ke
She scanned the folder with her security softwar
but it was clean. Also, it was encrypted. Every tim
she tried to open it, she was asked for a passwor
She thought for a moment, then typed in "TLCS
That didn't work. Then she thought of the curio cal
inet itself. Of all the special items in it, the mos
magical to her was the book that opened a doorwa
to the Land of the Fayries. What was the name c
that book? She screwed up her face in concentratio
Ah, yes.

She typed in "Maeve's World."

Wham, she was inside the folder. Her heart bea
faster. Could this mean what it seemed to mean? The
her heart sank. The folder contained only one minus
cule file. But still . . . She opened the file and read:

HEY THERE, SIS. HOWZ TRICKS?

JACK COULD see the stars. They looked close enoug
to reach out and touch. The military jet Paull ha
had waiting for them in Brindisi was taking them a
home.

Alli came and sat next to him. "How do you feel?

"Like I've been hit by a train." He laughed softly
"Several trains, actually."

She hesitated only a moment. "I wanted to than
you."

He turned to her.

"You believed in me."

"Annika believed in you."

"You had faith in me, Jack. I never got that fron
my parents." She frowned. "I suppose you thin

here's something wrong with me because I haven't grieved for them."

"You grieved plenty for your father."

She looked thoughtful. "Maybe I did."

"And as for your mother." He shrugged. "Perhaps that will come in time."

"And if it doesn't?"

"Then it doesn't."

She was silent for some time. Then she took a deep breath and slowly let it out. "Every doctor who examines me tells me there's something wrong with me." Her eyes cut to his. "You know exactly what I mean."

Of course he did. He'd been told the same thing when he was young.

"But sometimes I feel . . ." She turned her head away. "I feel as if I'm numb inside, as if I'll never feel anything deeply again."

Jack took her hand. "You know that's not true."

Tears trembled at the corners of her eyes. "I wish to God I did."

Jack desperately wanted to help her, but in this instance he knew he needed to be patient, especially because right now she couldn't be.

At that moment, Annika came by.

"Am I interrupting anything?"

Jack glanced at Alli and shook his head.

Alli leaned over and kissed him on the cheek. "See you later." Then she stood up and walked with Annika to another set of seats, where they sat down together.

For a time, Jack tried to think about nothing at all, but his brain, working out the last of the conspiracy, wouldn't rest. Then his cell phone buzzed and h caught the call from Alan Fraine, the D.C. Metr Police chief.

"I'm afraid I have some bad news." Fraine's voic sounded thin and far away. "Pawnhill got away."

Jack stared into the blackness of the night. "Wha happened?"

"We tracked him to Billy Warren's apartmen He apparently found a DVD, but it was in a booby trapped attaché case. The DVD was almost entirel dissolved by acid. Nothing usable was left."

Jack thought a moment. "Billy must have stashe the incriminating data he'd found on Middle Bay' servers. That's why he was tortured and then killed.

"So it was Pawnhill, not Dardan Xhafa, who di it."

"Pawnhill hired McKinsey, who was nursing grudge against Billy," Jack said.

"Your boss, Dennis Paull, ordered all of Middl Bay's files, records, and computer data confiscate even before he landed, but so far he tells me there' no sign of incriminating evidence."

"And there won't be," Jack said. "Pawnhill ha had unlimited access to the bank's data for the pas week. He's sure to have deleted it all."

Fraine sighed. "Probably. But Paull claims he's go some first-rate techs in data recovery. They may finc something Pawnhill overlooked."

Jack saw no reason to say what was on his mind He didn't think Mbreti had left even a single kilo byte to find.

"Well, one good thing," Jack said. "You can ge Heroe out of custody."

"Really? How's that?"

"Now that the data's gone, there's no longer a need for a cover-up."

"I'm not so sure it will be that easy."

"Chief, she'll be sprung the moment you make the request, trust me."

There was a slight pause, then Fraine said, "Do you know who's behind the cover-up?"

"I have a good idea."

"Then you're going to need some help when you get home. These people play at the highest level."

"I appreciate the offer, Chief. But go take care of your own. I'm better off handling this myself."

"I owe you one, Jack. If ever you need me . . ."

"Yeah." Jack laughed. "I know where to find you."

"BREATHE," ANNIKA said. "Breathe, darling."

Alli shivered. "I . . . I don't know how I'm going to live like this."

"Like what?"

"Not feeling."

Annika shook her head. "I'm not at all sure I follow. If you don't feel anything why did you risk your life to save Liridona?"

"That's not the same."

"Why isn't it the same?"

Alli was trembling uncontrollably now, tears running down her cheeks. And then she sobbed. "I miss Emma so much."

Annika enfolded her, kissed both her cheeks. "I know."

"No, you don't know. I—"

"But I do know, Alli. If I were to lose Jack . . ."

She let her words trail off and Alli stiffened in he
arms.

"You love him," Alli whispered.

"Yes."

Alli collapsed against her. "Then you do know."

"I know your heart is broken."

Alli buried her face in the crook of Annika's shou
der. "You won't tell Jack."

"Of course not, darling. You will."

Alli pulled away from her. "But I can't."

Annika smiled. "But you must. Don't you see tha
the secret is a barrier between you. Telling him wi
bring the two of you closer. Besides, this is you
authentic self. Embrace it."

Alli wiped her eyes with her sleeve. "What if h
doesn't understand?"

"Jack?" Annika appeared deeply amused. "Dea
God, girl, you must be joking."

DENNIS PAULL met them when they landed in D.C
just shy of six hours later. While he was arrangin
for Edon and Liridona to enter the States, Henry
Holt Carson showed up. That was a surprise, bu
one that Jack welcomed. Carson was at the heart o
the conspiracy, Jack knew that much. It was the why
that needed confirmation.

He approached Alli, but when he tried to put hi
arm around her, she shrugged it off her.

He was looking at his niece, but he addressed
Jack. "You kept her safe from harm, I see."

"She kept herself safe from harm."

Now Carson did look at Jack. "I'll never forgive
you."

"For taking Alli away," Jack said.

"He didn't take me away." Alli's tone was indignant. "He saved me from being arrested."

"You wouldn't have been arrested," Carson said. "I would have seen to that."

"I'm not in your control," Alli said. "I'm an adult. I make my own decisions."

Carson shook his head. "This is what you did to her."

"Mr. Carson," Jack said slowly and deliberately, "you're hardly in a position to lecture anyone on parenting skills."

All the blood drained from Carson's face and his hands curled into fists. "You'll regret saying that, McClure."

Jack took a step toward him. "I've had it with your threats and your bullying. I know you're behind all of this."

"All of what?"

"Everything that's happened."

"You don't know what you're talking about."

"On the contrary," Annika said, appearing as if out of nowhere, "he knows precisely what he's talking about."

"You!" Carson goggled at her. "What the hell are you doing here?"

"You don't give a shit about your niece," Annika said. "What you can't forgive Jack for is meddling in your little scheme."

"And I would've gotten away with it," Carson snapped. He turned to Jack. "Your meddling cost me everything."

"You're the one who hired John Pawnhill," Jack

pointed out. "And Pawnhill was working with the Syrian, bringing over Xhafa's girls and selling them at the Stem."

This seemed to surprise Carson. He was silent for some time. He looked deflated. When he spoke again, his voice was quieter, all the belligerence drained from it. "I was just trying to do the right thing." He glanced away for a moment. "Just after Eddy was elected, I learned of a plot to assassinate him. The man behind the plot was the Syrian.

"In the absence of more information on the attempt itself, I decided that the best course of action was to go after the Syrian's infrastructure. Someone at my bank suggested we look at other, smaller banks, to see if the Syrian was using them to move money around. I knew that if we could intervene there, we could shut down his financial system.

"I was directed to a company called Safe Banking Systems, because their antiterrorist software is the best in the business. They identified Middle Bay, but couldn't get any farther because no one knows the Syrian's real name or his aliases, so he isn't on any PEP list. Then Eddy was killed and I was devastated. Directly after Arlen was sworn in, I went to him and told him about the plot. Together, we decided to go after the Syrian. I decided to buy Middle Bay. This way, I could find out just how the Syrian was using the bank, and once I knew that, I could control him."

"So Crawford intervened and fast-tracked the buyout through the regulatory process."

Carson nodded. "Time was of the essence." His shoulders slumped. "But somehow the Syrian got wind of what I was doing. Pawnhill has a rep for being the best international forensic accountant in the business, but he must be working for the Syrian. Pawnhill destroyed all the records of the Syrian's accounts and transactions."

"Maybe not all. Billy Warren stumbled across the transactions and made copies."

Paull frowned. "Pawnhill found his copy and destroyed it."

"I think our clever little Billy made more than one copy." Jack turned to Alli. "Remember when I asked you about Billy you said he was a closet neo-Luddite?"

Alli nodded. "Sure. He thought computer data was too insecure. He said, 'Give me a pen and a sheet of paper any day.'"

Jack nodded. "That's why I think he stashed a hard copy of the Syrian's account data."

JACK WENT through Billy Warren's apartment more or less as John Pawnhill had done earlier, except he knew what he was looking for. Alli, Annika, Carson, and Paull watched him, Carson still with a fair degree of skepticism.

At length, Jack returned to the living room and looked more closely at everything. Then he went to the lacquer cabinet that held the books, stereo, CDs, and the like, and took down the first of the two large albums. This one held photos of Billy's life. After paging through it to the end, Jack put it back and took out the second. Writing on a page.

Jack calmed his mind, gradually stopped the spinning of the whirlpool, reducing it to lines of text. Haltingly at first, then more easily, he read the title page of Billy's graduate school thesis. The first ten pages were more difficult because there were twenty two lines of type filling each page. Jack skimmed struggling.

Then he turned to the eleventh page. It was totally different, and so were the next fifty pages. Pages and pages of numbers, six columns to a page. These were the Syrian's account transactions from Middle Bay Bancorp.

Jack looked up and handed the album to Carson "I believe this belongs to you."

Epilogue

ALLI RETURNED to Fearington Academy after dinnertime. She had spent the afternoon and early evening being debriefed by Paull, Alan Fraine, and Nona Heroe. Then she had dinner with Jack and Annika at her favorite restaurant in D.C. Liridona and Edon were still with Dennis Paull, recounting in incriminating detail all they knew about Arian Xhafa's business. Paull had promised Alli that he would set the sisters up in an apartment and see they got jobs. Alli was determined to see them as often as she could.

She was sitting on her bed listening to Inbar Bakal's gorgeous, ululating vocals when Vera walked in. The moment Vera saw her, she stood stock still. Alli took her earbuds out.

"No one told me you were back."

Alli stared at her. "I know what you did."

"What are you talking about?"

"I know you dosed yourself with the roofies."

Vera looked over her shoulder as if she expected the police to be coming out of the shadows in the hallway. Then she stepped into the room.

"I should report you."

Vera seemed mesmerized by her as she sat down on her own bed. "Why haven't you?"

Alli shrugged, put her earbuds in, and lay down on her bed, her iPod between her breasts.

Vera stayed that way for a very long time. Then she came and sat on the edge of Alli's bed. After a moment, Alli stopped the music and freed her ears.

"I hated you from the moment we became roommates."

"You didn't hate me," Alli said, "you envied me."

"Isn't that the same thing?"

Alli laughed softly. "Maybe for you it is."

It seemed to Alli that Vera's ultrahard shell had begun to crack. She watched curiously as Vera stared down at her hands.

"The truth is . . ."

Vera wiped her palms down her thighs. Could she be nervous? Alli wondered. That would be a first. She concentrated all her energy on this woman.

"The truth is," Vera began again, "except for hate, or maybe, like you said, envy, I don't feel much of anything."

"Join the club."

Vera's head snapped up and she scrutinized Alli's face, possibly to see if Alli was making fun of her. But quite quickly she saw that Alli was serious.

Vera gave a little cry that was a half sob. "How I hate being numb!"

"Yeah, it sucks."

"But what can we do about it?"

Alli sat up. "The only thing we can do, I guess. Talk about it."

ANNIKA, NAKED, her long, heart-stopping legs dangling over the side, sat on the bed in Jack's old, rambling house at the end of Westmoreland Avenue. She was bent over while he traced his fingertips gently down the vertical scars on her back.

Jack thought about Edon's ordeal at Arian Xhafa's hands, and then immediately turned his mind away from gruesome matters.

"That's important only to you."

She sighed deeply and, turning around, slipped into his arms. "Do you think it will ever be possible for us to be a real family?"

"If we want it, Annika, then we'll have it."

The question he left unsaid was: Do both of us really want it?

"Until I met Alli, I never thought about having children," Annika said.

"You wish Alli was your daughter."

She pulled back a little to peer into his eyes. "Is that so terrible a desire?"

"Not at all." He ran a hand down her cheek. "On the other hand, I don't see you changing diapers."

She put her head down, resting her forehead on his shoulder. "That's not so terrible, either."

"What's wonderful is the love Alli has awakened in you."

"My mother loved very deeply—and you know what happened to her."

Jack did. She had taken her life after Annika's exceedingly powerful father had kidnapped Annika at the age of four.

"You're not your mother, Annika. She was weak; you are anything but."

She was silent for some time. He could feel her heart beating in her chest, could imagine her blood coursing through her veins and arteries.

"Annika," he said softly, "this isn't what you want to be talking about."

She remained silent, but connected to him in the most intimate, visceral way.

"What is it you want to ask me?"

She stirred at last, as if from a dream. "Nothing." She kissed him warmly on the lips. "Nothing at all."

AUTHOR'S NOTE

Safe Banking Systems does, in fact, exist. Located in Mineola, New York, SBS provides the financial services industry with software solutions that combat money laundering, fraud, terrorist financing, and other criminal activity. SBS has the unique capability to find the "bad guys" by uncovering hidden risk and identifying the "six degrees of separation" between disparate individuals and entities.

SBS's public service report, issued in June 2009, identified terrorists and drug kingpins with valid FAA licenses, including the infamous PanAm Lockerbie bombers. When this story broke in *The New York Times,* six FAA licenses were revoked within twenty-four hours, but not without some embarrassment in Washington, D.C. The story resonated in the halls of Congress and received national media attention. How this relatively small, privately owned company could find a serious threat to U.S. national security that went undetected by the government agencies mandated to do so generated much interest. David and Mark Schiffer, the principals of SBS, were invited to meet with the chief counsels and their investigative teams at both the U.S. Senate Commerce Committee and U.S. House Committee on Homeland Security. As a result, there was an official mandate for improvements to the vetting process and interagency cooperation between the FAA and TSA. The inspector general's office also contacted SBS during its investigation of the vetting process. The IG's report has not been made public yet.

In October 2010, *The Enterprise Report* published a three-part exclusive article on Viktor Bout, the alleged notorious worldwide arms dealer currently under arrest in Thailand. SBS's data mining and analysis determined that Bout may hold a private pilot's license issued to him by the FAA in 1993. SBS also identified seven key associates and participants in Bout's aviation cargo transportation businesses.

Turn the page for a preview of

FATHER NIGHT

Eric Van Lustbader

Available in September 2012 from
Tom Doherty Asssociates

A FORGE BOOK

ONE

Alli Carson's back slammed against the mat.

"I missed my opportunity."

"Patience is opportunity."

She stared up at the broad face with almond eyes and thick black eyebrows.

"I don't understand," she said, regaining her feet. "I missed my chance."

Sensei smiled his enigmatic Ent-like smile. "You mistake chance with advantage."

He squared to her, his bare feet set at shoulder-width. He was small and wiry, yet more powerful than a six-foot-six linebacker. "In hand-to-hand combat you must always seek the advantage. Advantage comes with patience." He cocked his head. "Please explain."

"I can't," Alli said.

"Yes," Sensei insisted, "you can."

Alli screwed up her face, but let her mind wander freely. "Everyone has a weakness."

Sensei's smile widened. "Everyone."

"Even you, Sensei?"

"Together, we shall find out." He lunged at her

and she backed away. "Stand your ground. Parry, move not an inch, cede nothing."

For the next five minutes she did as he ordered. She neither retreated nor advanced, no matter the method of his attack, and at the end of that time she saw the opening on his left side every time he advanced. She waited, patient, for his next attack, and when it came, she was ready, feinting left, then right, under his attack. She was just about to land her blow when his right arm whipped around, his hand gripped her shoulder, and he spun her off her feet.

He stood over her for a moment, a big grin on his face. As he leaned over her, he said, "One half learned, one half only." He held out his hand and, after a moment's hesitation, she took it. "You must make certain your opponent is not gulling you into a mistake."

As he pulled her up, she whipped her left leg up, planted her foot on his chest, and pushed from her lower abdomen, the force traveling through her thigh, snapping her bent knee straight, extending through the sole of her foot.

Sensei stumbled backward, but did not let go of her hand. She was yanked forward, a sharp pain in her extended leg. He sought to take advantage of the momentary weakness the pain caused her, wrapping his right arm around her neck as she was falling against him. But she used his own momentum against him, rolling onto her left shoulder, dragging his body up and over her, slamming his shoulder blades against the mat.

Up on one knee, she rested a moment, breathing deeply to allow the pain to flow through her and dissipate. She found that her heartbeat was accelerated; she could hear her pulse in her ears.

Sensei rose to his feet, bowed, and, turning, walked out of the practice room without so much as a backward glance. He said not a word; none was expected. Praise was something Sensei never extended, feeling it gave rise to ego, which had no place in his dojo.

She remained where she was and wiped her damp forehead on her sleeve. Then she collapsed, sitting on the mat in the center of the room, knees drawn up, arms locked around her shins, as she replayed the last two minutes with breathless wonder.

Some moments later, her roommate, Vera Bard, poked her head into the dojo. "Ah, you're finished. Good." Her expression troubled, she stepped into the room and tapped her iPad. "I've got to show you something. It's pretty weird."

As she was about to step onto the mats, Alli waved her back, rose, and came across to her. Plucking her coat off a wooden peg, she slipped into it, and they went outside into the chill December weather. A brilliant blue sky sparked overhead and frost danced on their exhalations. The campus of Fearington, one of the prime secret services training centers in the D.C. area, surrounded them, the Federal-style buildings interspersed with stands of tall pines and chestnut trees. Farther away, hidden in a series of natural swales, were the Pits: obstacle courses, firing ranges, and the like.

Alli breathed in the fresh air. Her body felt limitless, her mind drunk on her victory over Sensei. She took Vera's iPad and checked the screen. Vera took it from her and brought up an Internet site titled allicarsonbitch-slave.com.

Alli gave a little gasp. "What the hell?"

"The link to the site was e-mailed to me and to everyone else at Fearington."

"Who sent the e-mails?" Alli asked.

"They were sent by *you*."

"What? But I didn't—"

"Of course you didn't," Vera said.

There were a series of photos of nude girls bound and tied, arms extended over their heads or out to the sides as they sat in a heavy wooden chair. All had Alli's head or face Photoshopped onto them. Below each there was a price for photo sets and short films that could be ordered. Farther down were comments: filthy whore, pervert, hot bitch, and the like, but all of them ended with either a smiley face or LOL, cyber-shorthand for "laugh out loud."

"The good news is that this cyber-smear attack is being viewed as a practical joke inside Fearington. It's likely someone here is the culprit."

"Well, it's not funny." Alli kept reading. "Look here . . . here at the end, a date for my supposed death—December twentieth." She looked up at Vera, appalled. "That's two weeks from now."

"Hey, come on, you can't believe this death threat is real. It mean, someone's gaming you, sure, and we have to stop it, but . . ."

"After what I've been through I take everything seriously," Alli said.

"Okay, but . . . I mean, no one in their right mind would think that's really you in those photos. Look, here and here again, the lighting's off."

But Alli, who had felt a chill run down her spine the moment she saw the images of girls bound into that nightmarish heavy wooden chair, didn't think so. And her fear only increased when she saw the date of her supposed death.

"Forget it," Vera said. "The authorities will find out who it is, put him away, and that'll be the end of it."

Alli began to shiver uncontrollably.

At once, Vera put her arm around her roommate's shoulders, pulling her close. "You're cold as ice. What is it?"

Alli remained mute, but her mind was churning with terror. December twentieth was the fifth anniversary of the day she had been kidnapped by Morgan Herr.

Alan Fraine, captain of detectives of the Metro Police, was halfway through his strenuous thrice-weekly workout when he saw a man enter the cavernous second floor of Muscle Builders Unlimited, wrap a towel around his neck, and check out the rows of StairMasters. Something familiar about the man made the short hairs at the back of Fraine's neck stir. He continued with his second set of biceps reps, but his mind was no longer in it, and he set the dumbbells aside before he injured himself.

He watched with curiosity as the man strode over to his section. It was then that he recognized Dennis Paull, secretary of the Department of Homeland Security.

Paull straddled the bench next to Fraine and said, "Alan, how's it going?"

Fraine had had occasion to work with Paull and

Jack McClure several months ago in connection with Henry Holt Carson and Middle Bay Bancorp. Carson had been part of a conspiracy to frame Fraine's best detective, Nona Heroe. Paull had gotten her out from the Feds' custody.

"Sorry." Fraine tried to hide the depth of his surprise. "I didn't recognize you out of your suit, Mr. Secretary."

"Hardly anyone does," Paull said. "That's a gift sometimes."

"So I imagine."

"I had no idea you were a member," Fraine said.

Paull produced a complicit grin. "I joined this morning."

Fraine waited for the shoe to drop. The secretary wasn't here to break a sweat or to exchange pleasantries.

"Alan, I have a proposition for you."

Fraine's ears perked up. "I'm listening."

"I'm putting together a special group."

"What kind of group?"

Paull leaned forward. "A SITSPEC—"

"A what?"

Paull waited while a couple of gym rats passed by, talking reps and sets and punitive diets. "A black-ops group. Situation-specific, hence the acronym."

"Fed-speak."

"What?"

"Nothing. Go on."

Paull nodded, lowering his voice, forcing Fraine to lean toward him. "This one is very special. I'd like you and Nona to be part of it."

"Mr. Secretary, much as I appreciate the offer, but

Nona and I are local and I'm sure your SITSPEC is not. It's probably not even domestic."

"There you're wrong. It *is* domestic and, as of this moment, it's local to the D.C. area."

Fraine thought for a moment. "Why us?"

"I know I can trust you. You and Nona owe me; at the end of the day, I know you won't turn me down." He smiled. "Besides, before it's over, there's a good chance we'll be intersecting with Henry Holt Carson's interests." His smile turned sly. "I know you can't pass up that opportunity."

"There's a time and a place for everything," the General said.

"Even peace?"

"No." The General lit a cigar with a wooden match. He had a head like a helmet, with a fringe of prematurely white hair like a priest's tonsure. "Of course not peace."

The other man, small-boned, sharp-nosed, and gray as a rodent, shifted in his wing chair. He wore a pale-colored suit and a black tie. By his side was a carved hickory walking stick; one of his legs was shorter than the other. His name was Werner Waxman, though he also might be known as Smith or Jones, Reilly or Coen, depending on what country and what year he was in. In any case, Waxman was not his real name. "But you said—"

"For me, peace doesn't exist."

The two men were sunk into the dim, woody interior of a hunting lodge deep in the forests of Virginia. Far from the media spotlight glare inside the Beltway, they sat on either side of an enormous fireplace composed of stones as large as their heads. It was late, only a few scattered lamps left on, their pools of lights burnishing the wide polished floorboards. A tray with the remains of coffee and dessert sat unnoticed on a low table nearby.

The General lifted his cleft chin, blew smoke at the coffered ceiling. "I, personally, don't know what peace is, and, frankly, I don't want to know."

Waxman leaned forward, his muscles tense. A blue vein beat at the corner of his left eye. "Peace is death."

The General's gaze came down, fixed Waxman with the accuracy of a lawn dart. "Yes." He seemed as much impressed as he was surprised. "You've caught the essence precisely."

"Well." Waxman inclined his head, a formal Middle European gesture. "That's my job, isn't it?"

"I wouldn't want that." The General rounded the ash crown of his cigar on the lip of his plate. "I wouldn't want the responsibility of making sense of it all."

"We all have our roles to play." Waxman's eyes glinted as he turned his head. "You, General, are a man of action. You carry out a plan to perfection."

The General stirred, wondering now what Waxman wanted. "This enterprise of yours—it had better work."

"Trust me, General."

"The last individual who said that to me is six feet under."

Like a conjuror, Waxman produced a thin smile as if from nowhere. "As to that, I have no worries."

The General sucked on his cigar. "The stakes are astronomical."

"Such melodrama! This isn't Hollywood."

"You can't afford to be wrong." The General stared at the ash at the end of his cigar. "About anything." He glanced up. "Or anyone."

Waxman's thin smile seemed set in cement.

The General regarded Waxman with carefully concealed distaste. He seemed pale and weak, unfit for anything outside a well-ventilated room, but, as he had said, they all had their roles to play, all of them. Each brought a different expertise to the enterprise. They were bound not by friendship, but by need. Better, by far, than friendship, the General judged. It was unthinkable to betray someone you needed. And betrayal was the one thing they all feared. He knew that, because it was what he feared, the fear muscled way down in the depths of him, but always keeping a wary antenna out for red flags.

The members had made a covenant with each other a long time ago, on a dark and turbulent night filled with blood, death, and terror. They were determined to fill the power vacuum Waxman had foretold would come to pass in the Middle East. And, despite Acacia's first failure, he had been right, damnit, all the way down the line, right.

"I know you," Waxman said. "You like to give the people around you a hard time."

"That's *my* job."

Waxman nodded. "The reins of power. I understand."

"What reins? We're all in this together."

Waxman's eyes grew diamond-hard as he sat forward on the edge of his chair. Had it been anyone else, the General might have been alarmed. But Waxman was Waxman; he lived in his own head.

"There's bullshit and then there's bullshit, General. You may have fooled the others, but never for a minute believe that you've fooled me." Waxman inclined his narrow torso like an arrow aimed at the General. "History informs us that while rule by consensus may work for a short time, it breaks down." He spread his white hands. "We're all human, General, we all want what we want—and it's never the common good. You want what you want, General. I know it and you know it."

And what is it exactly that you want? the General asked himself.

He set aside the remains of his cigar. "You're really in love with that mind of yours, aren't you?"

"Mind games." One corner of Waxman's lips twitched. "You don't want to start with me."

"Is that a threat?" The General's voice was languid as he rose.

Waxman had no choice but to get to his feet. One shoulder was noticeably lower than the other, as if he were poised to make a fast getaway. The General towered over him; nevertheless, he appeared anything but intimidated.

"Sun Tzu wrote, 'All war is deception,' General," Waxman said as, leaning on his stick, he brushed past. "You would do well to keep that in the forefront of your mind."

The tick-tock of the walking stick was like the beating heart of a clock. The General watched Waxman disappear into the innards of the hunting lodge. At length, he turned and picked up his cigar, but it was already cold. The taste he loved was gone.